NO VIPERS IN THE VATICAN

This book is dedicated to the many good people
who worked voluntarily and professionally
for the Communications Centre and the Communications Institute
over the past thirty years

No Vipers in the Vatican
A Second Anthology of Sorts

by

Joseph Dunn

the colur

First published in 1996 by
the columba press
55A Spruce Avenue, Stillorgan Industrial Park,
Blackrock, Co Dublin

Cover by Bill Bolger
Origination by The Columba Press
Printed in Ireland by Colour Books Ltd, Dublin

ISBN 1 85607 167 7

Each chapter heading is the title of a Radharc/RTÉ television programme, with the date of first transmission.

Author's Explanation and Preface

This book, as it's title may suggest, is a companion volume to *No Lions in the Hierarchy*, published by Columba Press in 1994. As in the previous volume, the chapter headings recall the titles of a selection of programmes made for Irish Television by Radharc Films, an independent TV production unit which I helped to found, and now direct.

Each chapter is complete in itself, so one can dip in at any point – which is why it is called an anthology. With two exceptions, the chapters are in the order in which the programmes were made, which is a random order in so far as the themes are concerned. The main exception is that I have put some chapters related to the church and communications at the end, because of a certain relationship between their subject matters.

The whole is part travel book and part autobiography, but it is mostly about the issues raised by the experience of making the programme in question. For this reason the subheadings may sometimes give a better indication of what a chapter is about than the actual programme title itself.

Apart from a desire to keep to related titles – which began in 1986 with *No Tigers in Africa* – I have at least two reasons for choosing the present title.

No Lions in the Hierarchy referred on one level to a recent saintly and reforming pope, John XXIII, whose coat of arms featured the Lion of St Mark. *No Vipers in the Vatican* recalls another saintly reforming pope, Tebaldo Visconti, Blessed Gregory X (1271-1276). Popes in Gregory's time didn't go in much for heraldry, but the arms of the Milanese ruling family of Visconti was a viper swallowing a man, so medieval artists gave Pope Gregory the Visconti viper for his coat of arms, while the prophecies of Malachy called him '*Anguineus vir*' which means 'The snake-man'.

The historian Philip Hughes, who was by no means a sycophant when it came to writing about Popes, gives us this pen picture of Gregory:

> The new Pope, a man perhaps sixty years of age, was one of those figures whose unexpected entry into the historical scene seems as evident a sign of God's care for mankind as was ever the appearance of a prophet of old. He was large hearted, he was disinterested, a model of charity in his public life no less than in private, free from any taint of old political associations, simple, energetic, apostolic ... Nowhere, at any time, did Gregory X's action leave behind it resentment or bitterness.

Gregory might well be a suitable model for the next Pope. He summoned a general council within four days of taking up office. He didn't just talk about ecumenism, he brought about a reunion of the Greek and Roman Churches – an extraordinary feat after centuries of division. Unfortunately the union didn't last long after his pontificate, but that wasn't so much his fault as the fault of the reactionary policies under his immediate successors.

Gregory believed in collegiality and consultation. He asked bishops to send in statements before the Council setting out the main reasons for the spiritual decay in the contemporary world, and more importantly, he asked them to propose remedies.

After the reunion of the churches, reform of the clergy was the principal work of this Second Council of Lyons. Philip Hughes notes that Pope Gregory brought the Council to a close with a sermon about the state of the church 'in which he declared that bad bishops were the principal cause of all that was wrong!'

Gregory was also concerned with reform of the Roman Curia, and in particular with papal elections. With some modifications, the decree he enacted to govern the conclave still governs papal elections today.

If I am permitted a little joke at this stage, it is to say that the viper in Gregory's coat of arms appears to have been a medieval mistake. Tebaldo Visconti was not in fact related to the Milanese Visconti. So there *were* no vipers in the Vatican after all!

The title of a book, I like to think, can bear different layers of meaning, and so does this. The word 'Viper' for a Christian always recalls Christ's sevenfold indictment of the scribes and Pharisees, the religious authorities of his day. The gospel of Matthew, chapter 23, concludes his indictment with a fearsome phrase: *'Serpents, brood of vipers, how can you escape being condemned to hell?'*

There are a number of different themes and issues raised in this book, but the commonest thread relates to what many see as different failures of judgement on the part of the central religious authority in the Church of Rome. I think it is important therefore to point out at the outset that I, like other believing Catholics, not only support the concept of centralised authority in the church, but more than that, believe it is part of the divine plan. Furthermore, I recognise that the men and women – mostly men – who work in the Roman Curia are dedicated to promoting the kingdom of God on earth. So the title *No Vipers in the Vatican*, though a negative phrase has a positive meaning. While reminding us that Christ bitterly criticised the religious authorities of his day (which is an important point to make, because many good people are shocked by such criticism), it draws back from the force of his indictment. It seeks to avoid any suggestion that in criticising the Roman Curia one is somehow implying that there are people there plotting to grasp power for it's own sake, or to cause hurt or unhappiness to others. It seems fair to say that the Roman Church has as highly motivated, moral and decent a civil service as one could hope to find in an imperfect world. But it's still in essence a civil service, and therefore no less prone to the errors of judgements that civil servants tend to make: and just as much in need of criticism.

Like a mother hen, the church can gather her chickens under her wing to protect them, or – with the best of intentions – can sit on her brood and stifle them!

Another subject raised in several chapters of the book is church and media. I have been involved with communications media in different ways throughout my life. *No Tigers in Africa* gave me an opportunity to put down some of the history of the Radharc film unit. This third volume touches on the history of the Irish hierarchy's response to the Vatican Council's Decree on Communications in chapter 21 and succeeding chapters. I am not pretending it is an unbiased history, because I was too involved in it for that. But maybe a biased history is better than none at all.

Most of the quoted material in each chapter is from interviews associated with the programme under review, and where this is not so, the source is, I hope, usually indicated. However, some of the material quoted may not necessarily have appeared in the programme, because the interviews as filmed were of course more extensive than could ever be fitted into twenty-six minutes, the normal length of a Radharc documentary.

Film making is a group activity, and if I don't often mention friends or collaborators who were also involved, or give them credit, it is not for lack of appreciation, but for the same reasons that make me hope that if they write a book about their own experiences, they will keep me out of it! The record however demands that the names of those who undertook research, interviewing, or script writing for the programmes referred to in the book be at least mentioned. They were, in alphabetical order, James Caffrey, Eleanor Cunney, Desmond Forristal, Michael Kelly, Peter Kelly, Peter Lemass, John Murray, Ciaran O'Carroll, Tom Stack and Darach Turley. As film editor, Dáibhí Doran also made a very significant contribution to the form and structure of most of the programmes.

I am especially grateful to a number of people who read and commented on the text before publication. I don't like to mention the names of the living, but Fr Damien Byrne, former Master General of the Dominican Order has since gone to glory, so he will hardly mind. I mourne in him the loss of a wise, good man, and a friend.

1
KRISHNA AND CHRIST
*Building bridges between Oriental religions and Christianity
– and knocking them down again!*

The call of the East

Beginning in the 1960s, many young Europeans were drawn to the East, and particularly to Hindu philosophy and the Hindu sense of the sacred. I met one such young man in India. He had long dark brown hair, flowing beard and moustache, and was probably in his late twenties. His accent was British – middle/upper-class, his name John Sullivan. Clad only in a loincloth, he sat in the lotus position outside his home – a simple hut roofed with palm leaves beside the sacred Cauvery River – and there he told me some of his story:

> I always thought that complete renunciation would be the first step on the spiritual path, but I didn't want to do it as an oriental *Sanyassi* (holy man). However, St Francis came to me and said 'You can do it within your own Christian tradition'. So I took the vows which were relevant in St Francis's life – no money, a single robe, no shoes and no staff; not to stay in one place for more than three days. I wandered around North America like that for about nine months and at the end of that time, a Franciscan priest to whom I went to ask for a new robe gave me one of the Franciscan habits. With that I then travelled down to South America. It had always been my ambition to go down the Amazon river in a canoe, and after about six weeks of sitting in a canoe and letting the current take me where it willed, I came to a missionary station where there was an old Spanish Capuchin, and he said I was a disgrace to the Order and I was only using the robes to con people out of food and shelter and that I should surrender the robes to him. I said, 'No, I can't do that, I haven't got any other clothes'. I went off and stayed with one of the local villagers. And then I had a dream which said, 'If you are asked for your coat, you must give your shirt as well'. So at five o'clock the next morning I had the robe bundled up and, wearing a pair of pyjama pants that I had been given, I gave him the robe and he gave me a tee shirt in exchange, and I went off down the river for the other four or five

months of the journey, having just been defrocked, as it were, by
the Spanish Capuchin.

After South America, Brother John came to India and found what
he was looking for – a guru to lead him on his spiritual path. We
included John in the film not so much for his own story, which had
its own interest and fascination, but for his almost perfect evocation
of the concept of the guru. For his guru was at the centre of our
story.

> I came here after having been in the Himalayas, having actually
> been initiated as a *Sanyassi* by a Hindu holy man. And what hap-
> pened in the first four or five days that I spent here was that the
> whole jigsaw puzzle of my own life and my own aspirations sud-
> denly were put together. And that is, according to the Hindus,
> one of the functions of the guru, that he should take all the vari-
> ous aspects of one's own personal aspiration and fit them – make
> them somehow gel together. And truly he has done that for me.
> Then I see in his own example (if the Lord is gracious), the possibil-
> ity of what I myself would like to become. I see in him the actuality
> of a man whose whole life has been dedicated to spirituality, and
> who has a clarity in the light which comes from his body, a purity
> in his approach to all religions, and an ability to enter into the
> heart of every person who comes into this ashram – to really
> touch them with his love and with his vision. So he is the teacher,
> he is the incarnation, the real manifestation of an ideal which one
> intuits within oneself, and which becomes real when you see the
> reality.

The guru from Oxford

The guru that John Sullivan found in South India was not an Indian,
or even a Hindu, just another Englishman – by name, Bede Griffiths.
He wore the simple saffron robes of a Hindu holy man, and at the
time we made the film, had lived in India for twenty years. I can
picture him now, sitting on the ground, a group of disciples forming a circle around him, with the morning sun rimming with gold
his long white flowing hair. His face was eager, welcoming, his
nose aquiline his eyes deep and blue. He was everything one would
expect an Old Testament prophet to look like – and he must have
realised that himself. The image was good. And the reality?

Having studied literature at Oxford, the young Mr Griffiths
attempted to live a primitive, self-sufficient life with two friends in
a Cotswold cottage. The experiment ended for him with a spiritual

and psychological crisis, followed by conversion to Catholicism. A few months after conversion, he entered the Benedictine monastery at Prinknash Abbey. Twenty-two years later – in 1955 – he took the boat to India 'to find the other half of my soul'. In India he prayed and studied and taught, and found his true purpose in life – helping to build a bridge between Hinduism and Christianity. At Kurisumala in Kerala, and later at Shantivanam, near Trichinopoli, he created an ambience of study and prayer which brought together people of many races and creeds, anxious to explore those deep mystical roots that are so strong in the Indian tradition.

The dwelling place of peace

Shantivanam means the dwelling place of peace, and peace in one's spiritual quest is what many people seemed to find there. Sr Pascalina was prioress of a Benedictine community in Kansas city when she decided to come to India.

> I was novice mistress for many years in my community and I'd been deeply concerned for years to do something deeper for myself and for my sisters. I had attended things like 'Prayer of the Heart' workshops that were given by some of the Trappists in the United States, but nothing seemed to go deep enough, and I had heard of Fr Bede Griffiths and some of the things that were being done here in India. Then I heard that India's gift to the world is interiority. I wanted very much to come and experience it, to taste it and to try out some of the meditation techniques to see if these would in any way help all of us back in the West. I had to resign as prioress, and that was a difficult choice for me. My sisters wanted to know if I didn't love them, if God wasn't everywhere, and why did I have to come so far to find him. Something really pulled me here and I would like to believe it's the Holy Spirit – here in India there's a simplicity about the people in their way of life. And I have not been disappointed. In fact, I received far more here in these four months than I ever dreamed I would receive.

Picture Shantivanam as a lightly wooded area with some banana and coconut trees on the banks of what, in the monsoon season at least, must be a very large meandering river. When I saw it one had to cross a wide stretch of sand and pebbles to reach the shrunken stream. Visitors to the Ashram slept in a row of tiny cells with plain cement walls and palm-leaf roof. Their bed was a concrete ledge and the window had no glass – one shared the space with sand and flying insects. Cooking took place in the open air, and while there were plenty of vegetables, no meat was ever served. Even casual Westerners like ourselves were expected to eat our meals off banana leaves, sitting on the ground in Indian fashion. The strongest drink available was Indian tea. Meditation took place at dawn and dusk – people found their own favourite spots down by the river. During the day the guru would give conferences on theology or meet some of the many visitors who came to the Ashram. Some were local villagers asking for his prayers or blessing. Many came from overseas, old and young, rich and poor, believers and unbelievers. Shantivanam seemed to be open to anyone who wished to take part in the community life. The group we filmed included people from England, France, Germany, Spain, Switzerland, Italy, North America, South Africa, and Australia, as well as natives of India; not only Christians, but Hindus and Jews, and those still looking for a faith to follow.

Hinduism, the religion of India

At 2.4% of the population, Christians in India hardly count. Hinduism is the religion of the great majority of the people – something over 80%. It's a religion of many gods, who are worshipped in many temples and under many forms. One of the temples we photographed was the Meenakshi temple in Madurai, an enormous building, 282 x 264 yards external dimensions. Four great towers, one reaching to 160 feet, are covered in representations of the gods – each with his or her own name and legend and band of devoted followers. When the gods appear on earth, they can take various human or animal forms which are known as avatars, and it is under these forms that they are often depicted. Sometimes a number of different gods are shown in the one figure. Natraj is represented as the god of the dance. Shiva and his consort are depicted mounted on the sacred bull. Ganesh is the elephant god, a jovial and popular figure. Among the statues, live monkeys roam, sacred to Hanuman, the monkey god.

Inside the temples one finds a religion which clearly recognises the importance of ritual and symbolism and bodily gestures in its worship. Statues of the gods are venerated with fire and incense. Bells are rung, and a lamp is passed to and fro in front of the statue by the temple attendant. The worshippers join in with gestures like touching the flame with their hands and passing their hands over their heads.

Penitential rites

Hinduism also recognises the need to keep the body under control, an element in the religion which has attracted much attention in the West. While fasting and self-control are an essential part of the life of an Indian holy man, the extravagant penances of those who thrust knives through their flesh or sleep on beds of nails is a source of embarrassment to many Hindus. We didn't see a bed of nails but I did photograph a man walking slowly towards the main entrance of the Meenakshi temple, body covered with what seemed like white ash, coconuts hanging from pins through the flesh on his shoulder, and a large straight knife holding his teeth apart – driven through one cheek and out the other. I found that hard to take.

God in Hinduism

No one knows the names of all the Hindu gods, least of all the devout masses who throng the temples every day; but they have their own favourites to whom they pray, rather as Christians pray to their favourite saints. More sophisticated Hindus will say that the different gods are really one and the same god, who is worshipped under different names and forms. Hindu sacred writings include the *Upanishads*, written around the same time as the principal books of the Old Testament, and the *Bhagavad Gita*, which contains the teaching of Krishna, an incarnation of the god Vishnu. Krishna is sometimes compared to Christ.

A religion with a theology going back thousands of years and supported by many millions of people must have an important part to play in God's dispensation for mankind. Fr Bede's mission in life was to try to find where Hindu and Christian might meet.

Our real aim is to bring into our Christian life the Hindu experience of God. That is what we feel today. There is a unique experience of God in Hinduism which originated in the *Upanishads*, written about the sixth century before Christ. I say 'originated', although it really comes from the *Vedas*, which go back to the second millennium, but it flowered in the *Upanishads*. They are a wonderful expression of this mystical experience which really underlies the whole Hindu religion, and we feel as Christians that we ought to be able to enter into that experience and bring it into relation to our life in Christ. But deeper than that is the meeting in what is called the 'cave of the heart'. This Hindu experience is an experience of God in the depth of the heart. Beyond words and beyond images, you see, that is where you have to meet. You come up with great problems trying to meet on a doctrinal level; it's very difficult. But when you meet on this level of prayer, of meditation, of the experience of God, then the Hindu and the Christian begin to understand one another, and that I feel is the great hope. Mind you, of course, there is a danger in that because the Hindu tends to think that all differences are ultimately unreal and therefore he's rather too much inclined to say, 'Yes. We differ in our rituals, in our doctrines, but in essence all religions are the same,' and I think we have to maintain that there is a *real* difference, and that it does make a difference to one's whole experience of God.

The Church Universal – or European?

Whatever about other Christian churches, the Roman Catholic Church in the past seemed to want to mark itself out in India as European, not Indian. The Portuguese, who had responsibility for the Church in India in the beginnings of the colonial era, insisted that converts to Christianity give up Indian ways – even so far as to dress like Portuguese. Christians were therefore generally despised and dismissed by educated Indians who called them *Parangi* – despised particularly when they wore shoes because leather was considered impure. Conquest by the Raj brought in the British army – many of whose foot soldiers were Irish Catholics, who often helped build churches in garrison towns and cities. All the Catholic churches in India are similar to what one might expect to find in Europe. The institution which claims to be catholic and universal built its churches in India in French gothic, Italian romanesque or English neo-classical styles. Over the porch of one of them I photographed the Latin words *'Haec est Domus Domini'*.

What was true of architecture was also true of more important matters like prayer and the liturgy. Indian converts in the past went to Mass in Latin. Fr Bede however was in the line of a few other exceptional people who tried to break out of this tradition of European cultural imperialism in Asia. Two of them were Italian Jesuits.

Roberto De Nobili

Roberto De Nobili, a Jesuit missionary of Italian aristocratic background, came to Madurai, Tamil Nadu, in 1606. He set up in a simple dwelling of his own, and adopted the appearance and lifestyle of a member of the Rajah class. Once installed in his ashram, he steeped himself in the ancient wisdom of India, and began reformulating Christian teaching to bring it more in harmony with the religious thought-patterns of India. Needless to say he met a lot of opposition, particularly from Portuguese Christians in Goa. The case was referred to Rome. De Nobili came under a cloud for thirteen years, during which he was forbidden to carry on his mission. After much hesitation, Pope Gregory XV approved De Nobili's approach in 1623, although with certain cautions. However this approval was later withdrawn. Any concessions to De Nobili's approach finally ended with a bull of Benedict XIV in 1744 which ordered all missionaries to swear to a sixteen-point oath. Some of the sixteen points were as follows: In the course of the baptism ceremony, the missionary is obliged to touch the ear with his saliva, saying 'Ephata – be thou opened'. This use of saliva was regarded by the Hindus as abhorrent (and is no longer part of our baptism ceremony). The baptised must take the name of a saint in the Roman martyrology. Marking the brow with ashes or coloured paste in the Indian manner was forbidden. Reading the Hindu religious texts was forbidden under pain of excommunication. And so on and so forth. The oath was revoked by Rome in 1940, after two hundred years!

By presenting Christianity in harmony with Hindu wisdom, De Nobili and his successors in Madurai built up a Christian community of 150,000 before the mission was finally closed with the suppression of the Jesuits in Portugal in 1759. In retrospect, his approach was only ever tolerated by Rome – and then only for a brief period – it was never encouraged or supported. And unfortunately it remained a local phenomenon rather than a pattern to bring Christ to India.

Indianisation of the Indian Church

After the Second World War, the twilight of empire and the thrust to independence led to hasty moves by Rome to Indianise the hierarchy, which up to then had been largely European. This had seemed preferable to Rome under the British Raj, but was clearly embarrassing under an Indian government. In the light of the teachings of the Second Vatican Council, the now Indianised hierarchy founded and funded a National Biblical Catechetical and Liturgical Centre at Bangalore. It became a centre for study and experiment, where once again attempts were made to come to terms with Indian culture and civilisation. Scholars delved into the history of India, so bound up with the Hindu religion. They studied her art and architecture and music and dance, studied the teachings of Hindu scriptures and holy men. They sought to show that Christ in India was not the unknown but the unnamed. One of the successful experiments was to adapt Indian *bajans* or religious songs for Christian use. Simple melodies and words repeated over and over again help to create an atmosphere of calm and contemplation.

The Centre went further, designing Indian prayers and preparing readings from the Hindu scriptures for use in churches – not to displace the Christian readings, but to add to them. An Anaphora, or Eucharistic Prayer was also prepared. And the letters of complaint went to Rome and the whole cycle of inquisition started up again.

Condemnation

In 1975, His Eminence Cardinal Knox, Prefect of the Sacred Congregation for Sacraments and Divine Worship, sent a letter to His Eminence Cardinal Parecattil, President of the Indian Episcopal Conference which put an end to most of the experiments – especially this use of the Hindu scriptures and the Indian-style Eucharistic Prayer drawn up at the Bangalore centre.

This condemnation was the fruit of a campaign by conservative laity and clergy who found a receptive audience in Rome. Commandant Benedict Mascarrennas, retired from the Indian army, was one who disapproved of the liturgical changes.

> Some of the innovations I feel are not acceptable to a large number of Catholics, both among the clergy and the laity, and I would go further to say that they have had an adverse effect on many. Take for instance, the introduction of a particular type of brass lamp that has been used in Hindu worship and has got particular connotations. Or the practice of garlanding the priest and offering an 'Arati' before he goes to celebrate the Mass. Then again, the cosmic tree and the cosmic dance, and things like that which are incomprehensible to, I would say, 99% of the people, and even those few who know something about it, they are not compatible with the God of the Christian religion. Consider then the introduction of the word 'Om'. I could quote Dr Radakrishnan, our previous president, and a great philosopher. He defines the word 'Om', as a mystic meaning for the triad, Brahma, Vishnu and Shiva, representing the one-ness of the three Gods. Now, I just fail to understand how that can be substituted for the Holy Trinity. Now things like that are certainly confusing – not only confusing, but scandalising to many. To me they are.

The condemnation was reproduced with much satisfaction in a conservative Catholic magazine called *Laity* – along with a cartoon showing Cardinal Knox sweeping a cloud of dust off the the the altar. Written in the cloud of dust were the words, 'Indian rites, Indian Anaphora, Non-biblical Mass readings, Further experiments'. All swept away!

The downside of centralised government

While the history of the church shows many benefits flowing from centralised church government, it also provides us with a collection of horror stories. What happened in India is unfortuately only part of a long saga in the history of what is nowadays called 'indigenisation' – that is the attempt to wed Christianity to the local culture. An even more damaging case was the so called 'Chinese rites controversy'. One would have thought that the church might have learned from this tragic story, but incidents like the 1975 letter of correction to the Indian bishops seem to show that little is ever learned, and similar mistakes are made by succeeding generations of Vatican civil servants.

The Chinese Rites controversy

By the middle of the sixteenth century, Europeans had circumnavigated the globe and few mysteries remained, apart from one – China, the sealed empire which rigidly excluded all foreigners. In the end, the first person to mediate China to the West was an Italian Jesuit, Matteo Ricci.

Ricci gained the esteem of the Chinese through his knowledge of European science. He was a tolerant prudent man who tried to adapt Christian thought and worship to fit as far as possible into the Chinese cultural tradition. With this careful approach, he won many converts to Christianity. After his death in 1610, his successors continued this policy. A German Jesuit, Adam Schall von Bell, was appointed President of the Board of Mathematics at the court of the new Tartar dynasty which replaced the Ming dynasty in 1644. For the next hundred years Jesuits played a leading role in court. They were entrusted with the mapping of China, with negotiations with the Czar Peter the Great, and helped to cure the Emperor, K'ang Hsi of malaria with 'Jesuit bark' from South America – the original quinine. In 1692 the Emperor rewarded their faithful service with an edict of toleration for the Christian religion.

The centre of the world

The word 'China' comes from an anglicisation of the pronunciation of two Chinese symbols which means 'centre platform', or in a better looser translation, 'the centre country in the world'. China had a sophisticated culture when most people in Europe were, so to speak, hanging from the trees. Ricci was wise enough to see that Christianity could never have any place in China as an exotic import from Europe. It must somehow be engrafted into Chinese culture and interpreted, so far as possible, in Chinese symbols and ways of thought. In line with this policy, the Jesuits accepted two important elements in Chinese tradition as compatible with the acceptance of Christianity – namely the veneration of Confucius and the paying of respects to dead members of their family.

Disputes within the Christian family

With 300,000 converts, and official toleration by decree of the Emperor, other religious orders like the Franciscans and Dominicans were encouraged to enter the new mission field. Despite the fact that they had little exposure to Chinese culture, and often no knowledge of its language, they forbade any cultural concessions to their converts and condemned the Jesuits to Rome. The Jesuits were accused of permitting quasi sacrificial superstitions like offering gifts of food to the dead, and genuflection before the ancestors. They pointed out in reply that children in China genuflect before their living parents, while offering food was the Chinese way of showing affection and gratitude. Nobody expected the ancestors to eat it. One might as well condemn a European for leaving flowers on a grave because it suggests that the dead had a sense of smell.

The Jesuits obtained a document from the pen of the Emperor K'ang Hsi, which they hoped might decide the matter.

> Honours are paid to Confucius not as a petition for favours, intelligence or high office but as to a Master, because of his magnificent moral teaching which he has left to posterity. As for the ceremony in honour of dead ancestors, it originates in the desire to show filial piety. According to the customs observed by Confucians, this ceremony contains no request for help: it is practised only to show filial respect to the dead. Souls of ancestors are not held to reside in the tablets; they are only symbols which serve to express gratitude and keep the dead in memory, as though they were actually present.

Rome makes its decision

Giovanni Francesco Albani (Pope Clement XI) was the pope to whom it fell to make a decision. His reputation is that of a charitable, mortified man of devout life, a good organiser, popular with the people of Rome, but who always had the interests of the church at heart – at least as he saw them. His importance in the history of Christian mission is that he was responsible for what appears to have been – as far as fallible human beings can judge – one of the most disastrous decisions of all time. Clement appointed nine Italian cardinals to settle the Chinese Rites issue. None of them had ever visited the East. They declared the veneration of Confucius and the dead ancestors superstitious, and therefore prohibited.

Clement's constitution *Ex illa die* (1715), required all missionaries in China to sign an oath that they would observe the decrees of the Holy Office prohibiting all Chinese converts to Christianity from taking part in ceremonies to honour the Chinese philosopher Confucius, or ceremonies showing respect to their ancestors, or to use certain Chinese words to express the notion of God.

The decree is enforced

Charles de Tournon, a young zealous, tactless Frenchman who knew no Chinese, was sent to inform the Emperor and enforce the decree. He chose as his interpreter a conservative French bishop who understood Chinese imperfectly, but was opposed to the approach of the Jesuits. At their interview, the Emperor exposed mercilessly the bishop's ignorance of Chinese language and culture, and expressed astonishment that people as ignorant as Tournon and the bishop should claim to decide on the meaning of texts and ceremonies from Chinese antiquity.

If the Emperor judged that Roman Christianity was not the universal religion within which Christ wishes all men to be saved, but a narrow local Italian cult, who could condemn him? And so the Emperor decreed that all missionaries in future would require an imperial permit, only issued to those who accepted the Ricci tradition. Eleven years after Tournon's visit, Christianity was outlawed in China. China, now if not then the largest nation in the world, was virtually lost to Christianity. It took 224 years before Clement's decree was revoked by another pope – Pius XII – which stated that it was lawful for Catholics to be present at these acts of honour paid before an image of Confucius, or his tablet in Confucian monuments or in schools – which is exactly what had been originally condemned! Like the rehabilitation of Galileo Galilei, it came a few hundred years too late.

Mass at Shantivanam

At Shantivanam Ashram, on the banks of the river Cauvery, morning begins with the celebration of Mass. Obedient to the Roman ruling, Fr Bede Griffiths takes the readings from the Bible alone and the prayers from the Roman Missal, but aspects of the ritual and ceremonies have a character that is unmistakably Indian. Before the Offertory, the participants mark their foreheads with the *tika*, the caste-mark, to denote their unity and brotherhood as they sit around the table of the Lord. After the bread and wine have been offered up, the sacred name of Om is invoked and the offerings are honoured with flowers and incense and light. The same signs of honour mark the elevation of the host and of the chalice.

East is East, and West is West, said the poet, and never the twain shall meet. But in places like Bangalore and Shantivanam, the twain have met and found a common ground that some never suspected – a shared belief in one God who has shown himself in many different ways, at many different times and places. Fr Bede summed up for us his own cosmic theology:

> The way I look at it is that Hinduism and Buddhism belong to the cosmic religion, the cosmic covenant – God revealing himself in the whole course of nature and in the human heart. The story of the Children of Israel brought into this cosmic covenant a new dimension of a historical reality, God intervening in history and the history of a people, leading that people to its fulfilment, and Christ coming as the fulfilment of history.

> Judaism, Christianity, and to some extent Islam, all belong to that latter tradition and I feel the future of the world is really the meeting of these two traditions, the Semitic with its own very special character, and the Oriental with its own diverse but also unified character. How exactly we're going to meet, nobody can say, but we have to be true to our own tradition and to be open to the other and then only the Holy Spirit can teach us how to meet, how to share, how to bring us to this fulfilment. Surely God is leading mankind to unity, to fulfilment, and we have to be instruments in that movement of grace which is carrying us forward.

2
THE TWO FAMILIES OF PETER RUSHTON
Family problems in the Catholic priesthood

Hobart, an attractive sea port of 150,000 people and capital of Tasmania, was home for the Rushton family when we visited them in 1978. Peter and Helen Rushton and their three children lived in the hillside suburb of South Hobart, beside the parish church. When the wall of your garden contains five stained-glass windows it can make life difficult for an active twelve-year-old boy, as David Rushton discovered to his cost.

> Well it started off when my brother and I were playing cricket and I was batting and my brother was bowling – he has got a tendency to bowl fast slick balls with spin. Anyway, we had a bit of an argument – but nothing much. I thought it was all forgotten, but he didn't seem to think so because he bowled a really fast spinner at my face and the only thing I could manage to do was a nice block and it just bounced off the bat and elevated up and went straight through the window. And it just so happened that it went through as the five o'clock Mass was about to come to an end! My father was walking down the aisle at the time and it landed about three or four feet in front of him and everybody stopped saying their prayers and everything was silent, including my father who just stopped and stared, looking at the ball. And then – well after they came out we had a bit of running and hiding to do!

At the time of the incident, David's father, Peter Rushton was the Roman Catholic parish priest of South Hobart. When he was ordained eight years previously, Peter was the first married Catholic priest in Australia, and probably the first in the English-speaking world. Formerly if a married man wanted to be a priest he had to separate from his wife and family. But in Hobart, priest and altar boy, father and son, celebrated Sunday Mass on the altar together.

Peter had been Anglican chaplain to the Australian air force and later a curate near Sydney. His wife, Helen was the first to become a

Catholic. After three months Peter followed her into the church. Fourteen years later he was ordained a Catholic priest.

Peter's wife Helen was, of course, consulted when the possibility of ministry in the Catholic church was mooted. We asked her did she have to do a lot of heart searching:

> No, I didn't, because I had always felt that my husband had a ministry and I knew that he was the sort of person that people would go and talk to if they were in trouble or had any problems or worries. And when the possibility of him becoming a priest first came up I was delighted. But I don't think I realised perhaps quite what was in store.

> And what was in store? You have had eight years experience of it now – what have been the problems?

> The biggest problem is to realise and accept the fact that he is no longer yours, he belongs to other people before he belongs to you and that one has to be prepared to take second place to the people he serves. And I think that was the hardest thing to learn.

> In practical terms how did that show itself?

> Demands on him – if somebody wanted him or needed him it had to come before us, and always has done, and we have had to be prepared to let it, and not to do it in a grudging spirit but to do it freely and willingly.

> So if you planned a night out together it might have to be jettisoned?

> Yes.

> Did that happen often?

> No, not very often. We don't often have nights out!

On Fridays the Rushtons used to leave their various jobs and converge on the family's holiday house at Gypsy Bay, an hour's drive from Hobart.

Here they were free from the incessant calls at the presbytery door and telephone for twenty-four hours at least. But the holiday house underlined the dilemma in Peter Rushton's life. In the situation where one is wedded on the one hand to his wife and family and, on the other hand, to his parish and the church, how does one sort out the priorities?

In terms of time, my prior commitment is to my wife. The church permitted me to extend that commitment. This is not to be seen as making a first commitment to the whole people of God and then narrowing it to one person. Rather it is making a commitment to one person and then broadening it to include the whole people of God.

In practical terms that must create difficulties.

It does indeed. It creates a good deal of tension. I find it difficult in the present circumstances to imagine a young man being able to raise a family because of the other demands upon his time and his emotional and spiritual energies. When the indult was given, the Holy See accepted my ordination, not just as that of a married convert clergyman, but a married man of mature years whose family are well on the way towards growing up.

I feel the pressures of the priestly life as we know it now would be just too much for a young family. Living in a presbytery is like living in a railway station. One can find a parallel of course with a busy doctor, but doctors have got the financial resources to erect barriers – which they do. Some for instance won't do night calls. I have never met a priest who is prepared to take a line like that. Living in a busy presbytery you are exposed twenty-four hours a day.

All the family made the effort to be at Gypsy Bay for the weekend whenever possible. Jim, at the time, was studying dentistry at Adelaide University. Ann was finishing an Arts degree at Hobart. These weekends away from the presbytery helped the family gradually sort out the conflicts and tensions that their unusual position imposed on them. Peter spoke about the effect of his ordination on his children.

I think there is no doubt that Ann found it very difficult, very difficult indeed. She was fifteen when I was ordained and sometimes, if she did something wrong, unwise teachers at school would say 'fancy you doing that when your father's a priest'. This made it difficult for her. Jim is a different type. He has just let it roll over him and it hasn't worried him a great deal. David of course has grown up with it and hasn't really known there was anything else. He has been the problem in the sense that he is the one that we have had to make time for more than the others, because Jim is twenty-one now. David is still only just twelve.

David did say, I believe, that the only way to see you was to sign his name on the visitor's book !

> Yes, yes, but that was some time ago. We had to take steps. Again, you see we were fairly old to be having a child of his tender years.

David himself seemed to be pretty sanguine when we asked him how he felt about having a priest-father.

> A few friends call me 'father' but its just a nick-name and I don't mind much. You get a few teachers who say: ' Just imagine doing that when your father's a priest', and they use my father as an example a lot.

> You see a priest's life much more closely than most people do. Do you think its a tough life?

> Yeah I think it is. I wouldn't like to be a priest, but I think they get their satisfaction out of it though. They help people and they feel pretty pleased – well my father does anyway. I can see that he likes helping people.

Fr Rushton couldn't afford to keep the family on his allowance as a priest. His wife Helen worked outside the parish, counselling people with emotional problems, and her salary paid most of the household bills. She made up her mind to keep away from parish councils and committees – with a full time professional job as well as a family, she had no time.

> I have always felt that the wife of a priest, even of a Protestant clergyman, shouldn't have a lot to do in the affairs of the parish. Maybe take part in a few meetings if she is able to, but shouldn't run them all. This should be left to the rest of the laity. And in any case here in South Hobart I hadn't the time nor the opportunity.

> Has it deepened your understanding of the Mass to see your husband celebrate?

> Yes I think it has. I am often aware of that when I see him up at the altar. That's when I become aware of the tremendous responsibility that I bear as his wife.

Sadly Peter Rushton died suddenly and unexpectedly a few years after this programme was made. However, others have followed in his footsteps, especially since the decision in the Anglican Church to permit women priests. (This, by the way, was not a one-way movement. Catholic priests also moved the other way, mostly because of the celibacy issue.)

The experience of married priests within the Roman church gives an opportunity to assess the practical problems that might be encountered if there were a change in the otherwise inflexible rule of celibacy for priests. Our programme about the Rushtons suggest that a married priesthood could give rise to new and different problems which must be faced in any discussion about a possible change in the law. Interestingly enough, a group of wives of married Episcopalian priests who took the path to Rome were surveyed by a sociologist from Loyola University, New Orleans. Two thirds of the wives thought that celibacy should *not* be optional for diocesan priests in the Catholic church!

Some of the kinds of practical matters to be considered, as suggested by the Rushton film, are as follows:

Unfair pressures on wives and children

A priest's marriage may put unfair strains on wife and children because priests are expected to be always available to their parishioners, and find it difficult to find the necessary time to meet family needs. Also because the young members of the family are put under pressure to be better behaved and feel they are judged differently because they are the priest's children. Wives also find that they are expected to act as unpaid helpers of their clerical husbands and have to fight against this notion.

Financial concerns

Every parish with a married priest would have to face doubling their contributions, such as Christmas and Easter dues, which provide the priest's support. If it costs £12,000 to support a priest now, then at least £20,000 will be required if he has a wife and family. Even then a wife may feel under pressure to earn and contribute, whether or not she wishes to work outside the home. The priesthood is not a job where one can supplement earnings for the little family extras by doing overtime!

And should a parish be consulted about whether they prefer a married or celibate priest? And if they get a married priest, might they object on the grounds that they can't afford to pay for him?

Problems about implementing at seminary level

If, as in the Eastern Orthodox Church, marriage can only be entered before ordination, and not after, the pressure on candidates approaching ordination would be immense, and the danger would be that some might hurry into unsuitable marriages.

Another pressure towards marriage may come if it becomes a common perception – as it might well become – that the secular seminarian who opts for celibacy when he is free to marry is in fact homosexual. Some who are celibate and homosexual may be happy for that to be in the open. Others who are heterosexual, or who do not wish to be typed either way, may be less happy about the public perception.

People speak of optional celibacy, suggesting it is something the candidate chooses. But how is that choice of celibacy to be exercised? In formal fashion as a promise for life made at ordination? Or simply by not marrying? Suppose a candidate makes this formal promise and ten years later changes his mind and seeks a dispensation – which has happened and will happen again. Must he be laicised and give up the priesthood? And if not, then why make a fuss about choosing an option for life which some may look to have dispensed later, while still continuing in the priesthood?

Married seculars and celibate religious

If there is to be any change in the celibacy rule, I feel it would probably have to be a complete change whereby marriage would become the norm for diocesan priests. Choosing the road of a lifelong commitment to celibacy would normally mean joining a religious order. The community life of a religious order can more easily provide the kind of comradeship and protection which prevents celibacy from becoming a burden. Anyway the structure of religious orders, at least as we know them, with the triple vows of poverty, chastity and obedience, makes marriage among members an impossible option. The tricky question would arise where a priest member of a religious order wishes to marry, gets dispensed from his vow of perpetual chastity, and then wishes to continue his priesthood. If permitted, it would clearly mean joining the diocesan priesthood.

Where vocations are concerned is celibacy the only problem?

In much of the 'top of the head' discussion of the dearth of vocations to the priesthood, it is presumed that celibacy is the problem. Maybe it is. But one would need to explain how non-celibate priesthoods, like Orthodox and Anglican/Episcopalian, also have vocations problems.

And whereas it seems likely that in some Latin American societies, abandoning celibacy might bring an influx into the priesthood, that is not at all clear in Western Europe or North America. Other churches who have a married clergy face similar problems about vocations as the Catholic church.

It is sometimes said that some clergy who become restless with their celibacy often have a hopelessly sentimental view of marriage. They see it in terms of sexual fulfilment and loving companionship. They seem to dwell rather less on the onerous responsibilities that follow from being a husband and father. Marriage may solve some problems for them, only to create new and more serious ones.

I can't answer many of these questions. Nor am I arguing for or against a married priesthood. I just want to make the point that changing the celibacy rule in the Roman tradition of priesthood may not be as simple as some seem to believe, and would require considerable thought and preparation.

And as for married women priests – well Pope John Paul says women priests there can never be, and Cardinal Ratzinger says his statement is infallible and the matter can no longer be discussed. So...

3
ARGENTINA:
THE CHURCH AND HUMAN RIGHTS

*The 'dirty war' in Argentina,
and the continuing controversy about the church's role*

The name 'Belgrano' will conjure up for many people in these islands the image of Margaret Thatcher and a sinking battleship – in which 368 naval officers and ratings in the Argentinian navy lost their lives. But the first Belgrano I came to know was a pleasant suburb of Buenos Aires. The local parish church was in the care of Irish Pallottine Fathers and dedicated, naturally, to Saint Patrick.

The private oratory of the Pallottines was conventionally furnished. The only unusual thing about it was the carpet, which had ten holes in the middle. Some two years earlier, on 4 July 1976, gunmen broke into the presbytery at two in the morning, tied up the community of five who were home at the time, and shot them dead on the oratory carpet. The carpet was cleaned but the bullet holes left to remind the visitors as well as the community that human rights were not valued by all in Argentina.

One of those killed was Father Alfredo Kelly, forty years old and the parish priest. In a sermon the previous Sunday he had said that the death penalty was a violation of human rights. Father Duffau, the only one of the five who was not of Irish origin, was in his seventies. A friendly father figure in the area, he was a threat to no one. And Father Leydon, local superior of the Pallottines, is still remembered in the area as a walking saint. The other victims were two young Pallottine students.

Who killed them? Passers-by saw a white Ford Falcon drive away from the house at two in the morning. The army generally use white Falcons, but then so do others. Nobody claims to have heard the gunfire and subsequent police investigations came to nothing. There were no survivors. Only one member of the community escaped death, and that was because he was away from the house at the time.

An Irish priest, Fr John Mannion had the difficult job of taking over the Belgrano parish after the slaughter. He was circumspect in his reply to the question whether those who murdered the priests and the seminarians left any indication of who they might be.

Yes, there were some slogans left on the door. One of the slogans read 'for poisoning the virgin minds of the young,' another slogan read 'for being members of the Third World Movement for Priests' and a third slogan read, 'for our dynamited comrades'. Now this last slogan must refer to the massacre which took place in the police dining room on 2 July 1976 when a bomb was placed and eighteen policemen were killed.

The military culture in South America

I once saw a T-shirt in Amsterdam. The legend read 'Join the army, see the world, meet other young people – and shoot them'. I thought it a fair reminder of what armies are about. Would to God that they all could be abolished! But if we have to have them, then the only tolerant situation is where the army is the servant of the state. Too often in the recent history of Central and South America the state would appear to have been the servant of the army. And even today, where some political leaders are elected, they still hold power at the whim of the military who in the not-so-distant past have shown that they are quite willing to take over elected governments – if *they* judge that it is in the national interest.

The military in Argentina

Argentina as I knew it back in the late seventies was one such state. Army presence was all-pervading. The speediest cars, the finest office blocks, the best equipped hospitals, the luxurious apartments, all went to army personnel. They were a privileged caste. And as a career it was that more attractive, being open to all classes and offering better chances of social advancement than any other profession. From what I have read since, not all that much has changed.

The military took power in 1965 and, with a few brief intervals, ruled Argentina until after the Anglo-Argentinian war over the Falkland Islands.

Previous to the military regime, the Catholic church had suffered under the government of Juan Peron. Some churches were sacked, clergy ridiculed and, more important, people lifted and liquidated without trial. General Videla, head of a military triumvirate, was a devout Catholic, so the church felt more comfortable with him than it had with Juan Peron. The problem, however, that the bishops should have faced up to and didn't always do so, was that the disappearances and liquidations continued under military rule.

The liquidation of two French nuns

On 8 December 1977, a group of women, mostly wives and mothers of missing persons, met at the church of the Irish Passionist Fathers in Buenos Aires. The purpose of meeting was to raise funds for an advertisement in the Buenos Aires papers stating the facts about their missing relatives. Two French nuns from an order specially devoted to working with the poor, joined in the meeting. There was a big crowd at the church for Our Lady's feastday, and after the Mass the people came milling around the grounds of the church for an open-air rosary. A few of them noticed that some of the women were taken away quietly and handcuffed. It was later discovered that thirteen in all had been lifted in this way, including one of the French nuns. Within a day or two the other French nun was also lifted from her home. They were never seen since. No one would give an opinion as to who took them but people in the area pointed out that terrorist groups don't usually use handcuffs.

The mothers of the Plaza de Mayo

On Thursday afternoons since 1977, a group of the wives and mothers of missing persons have walked in silent procession around the square in front of the presidential palace in Buenos Aires. Their weekly parade was a protest against a total lack of information as to where their dear ones were being held in custody. The mothers had no doubt that they were in military hands somewhere, if they had not been killed already. One would have needed a heart of stone not to be moved by the courage and determination of these strong women. Government propaganda labelled them 'the Mad Mothers'. Police cars patrolled their movements and sometimes they were forbidden to march. Amnesty International took up their case and claimed that there were as many as 15,000 people unaccounted for in Argentina. (Others have since said up to 30,000.) The military replied that less than 5,000 had been arrested under their special powers. In trying to tell this story, we interviewed a journalist and two bishops who spoke from very different backgrounds.

A courageous editor

Robert Cox was, for the times, a courageous editor of Argentina's English language daily, the *Buenos Aires Herald*. One of his front page stories, contemporary to our filming, was headed, 'Editor apparently kidnapped'. The story, which read as follows, was of the kind that might have led to him being kidnapped as well:

> Alberto Fontevecchia, the young editor of *La Semana*, was last seen on the corner of Virrey Ceballos and Cochabamba when he was forced to stop and bundled face down into the back of a cream coloured Ford Taunus. *La Semana* is one of Argentina's leading news magazines – an aggressive newcomer to the field of publishing with a reputation for printing controversial articles – particularly a two-part interview with fugitive ex-labour leader, Casildo Herreras.

Robert Cox had so far survived kidnapping, he himself felt, only because he was English, and therefore his disappearance could cause an international incident.

> A lot of journalists in Argentina have disappeared. A lot of them have been murdered. And in most cases, you just have no idea what the reasons are. If it was just being arrested, that would be the normal thing that one accepts as part of life, but it isn't that. It's the inexplicable disappearances of journalists that is very worrying, and the feeling that anything you write might upset somebody who has a gun, and he might be a left-wing terrorist who doesn't like the fact that you say that you don't approve of what the Red Brigade are doing in Italy and he might decide to shoot you and kill you. There is less danger of that now, thank God, because we have a more secure situation, but there is certainly a lot of danger from the right.

A concerned bishop

Bishop Jaime De Nevares, Bishop of Nequén, spoke to us about what the bishops were doing in 1978 to stem these manifest abuses of human rights.

> We asked the government especially to take steps to localise or find out where these thousands of disappeared persons are, if alive or dead. Because in a very great proportion of these disappearances there are proofs that they were abducted by people of the armed forces. After that then we tried to ensure that those who are in prison be judged and, if there is no cause, that they be freed. However none of our documents, public and private, have received the response we expected – indeed the situation (with regard to human rights) in our country has not changed.

A military bishop

The other bishop we interviewed, Archbishop Adolfo Tortolo of Parana, head chaplain to the Argentinian forces, was perhaps more typical of the Argentinian hierarchy than Bishop De Nevares. Between the three armed services the head chaplain had 217 priests working under him. As one might expect from somebody in his position, he made light of the human rights problems.

> The government doesn't put lists in the newspaper but there are groups under arrest being released more or less every week, in such a way that the minister of the interior told me that, maybe by the end of the year, the whole situation will be normalised.

But there are still maybe 5,000 people who don't know where their relatives are?

> No, no, not 5,000, much less than that. Mainly because of what I said about people being released and going back to their homes – I know that because here in Parana they come to see me, to say hello, and thank me for my help in securing their freedom. This is happening to such an extent that the number you mention is not correct. But we have to take into consideration that among those missing, some are missing for other reasons. For instance, certain organisations which are quasi-communist also kidnap and they also kill. So we cannot say that somebody who is missing is missing because the government have put them under arrest. There is a lot of vengeance in the different sectors, a lot of vengeance.

The truth begins to emerge

But even in 1978 the truth about the 'dirty war' was beginning to emerge from the army itself. General Augusti who had just retired, commented guardedly at the time, 'the military government must not commit the same mistakes as the terrorists', which could only be interpreted as admitting complicity in crimes and killings. Bishop De Nevares however commented, 'Naturally that is hopeful to hear him say that. But one doesn't understand why he didn't say it before he left office'.

The full dirtiness of this 'dirty war' in Argentina only began to come out in 1995, when Captain Adolfo Francisco Scilingo became the first to talk to the media about how prisoners of the military were treated. His story was featured in *Time* magazine.

> They were unconscious – we stripped them, and when the flight commander gave the order, we opened the door (of the aeroplane)

and threw them out, naked, one by one. That is the story, and nobody can deny it.' With these words, former Argentine navy Captain Adolfo Francisco Scilingo, 48, spilled one of the dirtiest secrets of the 'dirty war' that raged in his country from the mid 1970s through the early 80s.

As a twenty-eight-year-old lieutenant, Scilingo was appointed to the Naval School of Mechanics in Buenos Aires, just a year before our visit. The school was a notorious detention centre for those rounded up by the military as subversive. According to his story, fifteen to twenty prisoners were brought by truck every Wednesday to the Buenos Aires airport and put on a military plane. Prisoners were told they were being transferred to a detention centre further south and were given supposed vaccinations, which made them groggy. Once on the plane, they each received another injection which knocked them out completely. Then from a height of about 4,000 meters, they were thrown into the Atlantic ocean to provide a meal for the sharks. Scilingo estimates that between 1,500 and 2,000 people 'disappeared' in this manner from his base alone.

His first death-flight so disturbed Scilingo that he went to a navy chaplain: 'He told me it was a Christian death because they did not suffer, that it was necessary to eliminate them, that war was war'.

Pardon for crimes by the military

President Carlos Saúl Menen issued a controversial final pardon in 1990 for all those convicted of crimes during the 'dirty war'. This was another indication of how the armed forces manage to remain outside normal democratic control. Menen was afraid to apply the law to the military because the sad lesson of Argentinian history was that to do so would have threatened his political, if not physical survival.

But the pardon remains controversial. In the Autumn of 1995, the government fuelled the controversy by providing a certain Captain Alfredo Astiz police protection on the grounds that he had been attacked twice by angry citizens. Captain Astiz, also called 'the Blond Angel', was convicted *in absentia* in France for the kidnapping, torture and death of the two French nuns referred to earlier in this chapter, and is believed to have had a part in many other disappearances. Yet he remains a navy officer on active duty, and lives the good life, frequenting all the haunts of the idle rich.

Some lessons for the church to ponder

The revelations of military brutality proved very shocking to the church in Argentina, which found itself forced to examine its role during the years of military dictatorship (1976 to 1983). Questions began to be asked about the role of the Conference of Bishops, the nuncio, and the chaplains to the army.

From the church's point of view there are lessons to be pondered. The first is the danger of a church hierarchy failing to keep it's distance from the civil powers, and thereby becoming accomplices in evil. The second is the vexed question of the status of chaplains to armed forces – of which more later.

By and large the bishops as a Conference were too frightened and conservative to challenge the military, and preferred to turn a blind eye to what went on. Even in late April 1995 the bishops as a group found difficulty in agreeing on any statement on the matter from their bishops' meeting in San Miguel. According to a report in the *Tablet* of 6.5.95, five of them spoke out before the Conference, presumably because they felt something needed to be said, and the Conference as a whole was not likely to say it.

> 'During all our life,' they confessed, 'we will carry on our consciences the weight of not having done much more to impede the aberrations of the military'. Bishop Miguel Hesayne of Viedma acknowledged 'the very grave' responsibility of the armed forces, 'but also of the church', for atrocities during the military dictatorship. He said church authorities showed no scruple in dining with the torturers, and that the 'Mothers of the Disappeared' were shunted away from the front door of the plenary assembly of the Bishops' Conference after having waited an entire day in the rain. Last week, for the first time in twenty years, these mothers were received by the Bishops' Conference: they met its vice-president and secretary general and delivered a document in which they denounced 'the shameful participation of many priests during the military dictatorship'. But, after a ten-day meeting, the Bishops' Conference felt it needed more time to draft a statement.

The role of the nuncio

Archbishop, now Cardinal, Pio Laghi was nuncio to Argentina during the military period. He was accused by *Pagina 12*, and other Argentinian newspapers of playing tennis frequently with Admiral Emilio Massera, commander of the navy and principal architect of the 'disappearances' during the military regime. Massera himself was said to direct a torture centre in Buenos Aires. Others accused Laghi of hearing the confessions of the worst of the torturers.

Emilio Mignone, who wrote a book called *Church and Dictatorship*, tells us that he was one who asked Pio Laghi to help trace his twenty-four-year-old daughter Monica. In May 1976 she was dragged from the family apartment by a group of armed men and never seen again. Her only known sin was to work with a progressive Catholic group in a Buenos Aires slum. According to Mignone's account, the nuncio told him he himself was very afraid because he had been threatened. To this, Mignone replied in stern fashion, 'In the last analysis, if they kill you, you should rejoice, because as Jesus told us the good shepherd gives his life for his sheep. You are a pastor before you are a nuncio.'

Mignone also faults Laghi for giving Holy Communion to a general at the funeral Mass of the three priests and two seminarians – the story of whose death opened our programme – even though he knew the military were responsible for the murders.

However, Robert Cox, in a letter to his old newspaper, the *Buenos Aires Herald* supported Laghi as one of the few people who strove to prevent people who had disappeared from being murdered. According to the *Tablet* of 1.7.95, Cox testified that Pio Laghi

> With his courageous secretary Mgr Kevin Mullen, tried to help relatives and friends of people who were sucked into the maw of the military's killing machine. He offered advice and did his best to intercede with the military commanders. He had scant success. As Mgr Mullen once put it to me 'Every time we ask about some-one we meet a stone wall ...'

We talked to Kevin Mullen about the disappearances at the time – Kevin was of course Irish – but neither he nor anybody at the nunciature were willing to be interviewed for television. Apart from the delicacies of the human rights situation, they were very much taken up at the time with mediating the controversy between Argentina and Chile over the Beagle Channel, where war had been threatened.

The role of the bishops

As became clear to us back in 1979, the bishops were at best nervous and ineffectual throughout the dirty war period. Even after sixteen priests and two bishops were killed by the military, the hierarchy, according to Mignone, refused to challenge the dictatorship because it bestowed economic and political privileges on the institutional church, including government salaries for bishops, heads of religious orders and seminarians, as well as state pensions for bishops and a government subsidised mansion for Cardinal Aramburu! According to Mignone, as reported in the *National Catholic Reporter* of 27 November 1987, the military decree authorising government salaries for bishops was drawn up shortly before the crucial meeting of Latin American bishops in Puebla in 1979. The military paid for the bishops' airfares to the meeting. It is not surprising therefore that at Puebla the Argentinian bishops publicly defended their military government.

The record shows that the bishops continually refused to receive organisations representing relatives of the disappeared. One bishop for instance, Carlos Mariano Pérez, then Bishop of Salta, was quoted as saying, 'The Mothers of the Plaza de Mayo should be eradicated'. The mothers remember with bitterness how the doors of the cathedral were always barred to them, particularly when they were trying to escape from the batons of the riot police. And how the letters they wrote to the bishops' conference asking for help were never answered.

When a delegation of the Organisation of American States visited Argentina in 1979 to investigate human rights abuses, numerous bishops protested, claiming there were no violations in Argentina. The penalty for speaking out could of course be severe. Of the five bishops who did so, two were killed. Enrique Angelelli, the Bishop of la Rioja, was killed in a fake auto accident which a penal judge later proved to be premeditated murder.

The Mothers of the Plaza de Mayo today

The brave and persistent mothers still demonstrate before the president's palace in Buenos Aires every Thursday. The banners nowadays read, 'We don't seek the list of the martyrs. We want the list of the assassins of our children'. When the controversy about the church's role was at its height in 1995, they handed in a tough message to the Bishops' Conference.

> In the name of God horrible crimes were committed. In the name of God people were savagely tortured. But it was always with the blessing of the church. The priests who collaborated with the administration in the torture and extermination camps should no longer be offering Mass. They cannot go on lifting up the Eucharist with hands stained with blood.

Dr Death

June 1995 saw one of the most bizarre twists in the story of the 'Dirty War'. Genetic testing has established that a seventeen-year-old boy brought up by a naval lieutenant is in fact the son of a couple who are believed to have been tortured and murdered at a navy detention centre. Carlos Rodolfo Luccia, the boy in question, has had to face the gruesome fact that his adoptive parents were associated with the killers of his father and mother. They have been arrested for 'suppression of identity and forging of public documents'. Dr Jorge Berges, a gynaecologist who is alleged to have tortured opponents of the military government, is the 'Dr Death' who is now accused of selling babies born of murdered detainees to childless military couples. Fifty-six children of such people have been traced and human rights activists suspect there may be up to five hundred.

The wider issue of the church and the military

Repeated suggestions that the military chaplains in Argentina were somewhat less than firm in their adherence to Christian principles during the 'dirty war,' prompts one to consider the wider issues relating to the church and the military.

The role of the chaplains

Soldiers who are Christians have every right to have the service of priests and ministers, and in the circumstances of war where they may face death as a daily possibility, their need is clearly greater than the normal citizen. But there are different ways this service could be provided. One way is to take the clerics into the army, train them in army ways, give them a uniform, officer status, and by clerical standards, a handsome salary. The other is to attach the clerics to army units, but to insist that they retain their independent status, and that the church not the army provides their income. This kind of status is recognised in the case, for instance, of Red Cross personnel who work alongside the army, but are not part of it.

The problem is that clergy, like all human beings, are naturally influenced by the company they keep, and the status they assume – for instance, by wearing army uniform. Fr Peter Collins OP was an Irish chaplain to the Argentinian army when we interviewed him in 1979. He did his best to be even-handed.

> I think many of us at home in Ireland will sort of look askance at the idea of what we would call a military dictatorship and we

would say well why don't they have democratic rule. My answer, and it's personal, is I don't think Argentina is ready yet for democratic rule. I don't think the world really realises the tremendous cruelty of the guerrilla movement here in Argentina. That's not to deny that many of them may have been very idealistic and everything like that. But it got out of hand and it became very Marxist, very Marxist.

How did the soldiers that you met react to the guerrillas?

With the young soldiers – these would be conscripts of about eighteen years of age – I would say they just didn't have any opinion. But talking with the young army officers I often mentioned to them the fact of the necessity of not torturing or anything like that and being careful about whom they fought against. But they said to me in a very simple way, they said, Father, look we agree with you but what do you expect us to do if your best friend is shot down in cold blood with his wife and his child? How do you expect us to react? And I have no doubt that there were abuses, even President Videla has said that there were abuses. He has recognised it. But is there any war in which there aren't abuses?

Making God Head Chaplain to the forces

Christians are always pleased to see their leaders acknowledge the existence of God. However, unfortunately this acknowledgement can involve God's name being invoked for political purposes. During the Gulf war, for instance, when the US forces opposed Iraq, President George Bush proclaimed a national day of prayer, and called on 'Our Heavenly Father to watch over and support the courageous members of our armed forces … From our very beginning as a nation, we have relied on God's strength and guidance in war and peace. Our cause is moral and just!'

One doesn't doubt that George Bush was sincere. But what if the God of his prayers were to see some contradictions when he remembered the US invasion of Panama, and Grenada, and military interventions in El Salvador, Nicaragua, Guatemala, Iran, and numerous other countries?

A long history of army chaplains losing their detachment

There is a long history of army chaplains becoming involved in conflicts and losing their detachment and objectivity. God and country may not always be comfortable partners. When a chaplain at Pearl Harbour urged a navy gun crew to 'praise the Lord and pass the ammunition' the sentiment seemed worthy enough to turn it into a popular song, if not a prayer. And one old engraving I treasure shows the Reverend Thomas Mooney, chaplain of the (Fighting) 69th New York Regiment during the American Civil War, 'baptising' a large canon gun with holy water, dedicating it to the defence of the stars and stripes, and naming it 'Hunter,' in honour of Colonel Hunter, Commander of the Brigade!

The practice may vary in different countries, but a chaplain in the US Army is legally obliged as an officer to defend national policy. American army manuals during the Vietnam war spoke of the chaplain's role to 'supplement and reinforce the total instruction of the troops in the Code of Conduct by his spiritual and moral leadership, and his personal presence during combat and combat training'. According to a report in *Time* magazine of 30 May 1969, some chaplains in Vietnam went a lot further than spiritual and moral leadership.

> One chaplain for instance likes to take a turn firing M60 machine guns from Huey helicopters. Another wears a shoulder holster and a .45 even when in Saigon. A third, with more honesty than relish, admits that 'I could kill a man in a second. After you see how vicious the V.C. can be, it's hard to separate yourself from it'. Some genuinely heroic acts, on the other hand, are forced simply by the nature of the war. The Rev Jerry Autry, 28, a Baptist chaplain from Princeton, SC, once landed near a Viet Cong village with a platoon of green soldiers commanded by an equally green lieutenant. When they froze, Autry rallied them and led the charge. Autry carries a weapon only because he has to. Like many chaplains who go on patrols or fly on combat sorties with airborne troops, he has discovered that his unarmed presence can make the men jittery.

So much for unarmed combat!

Conclusion

It is reasonable for the church to provide spiritual care to army personnel. But the question to be faced is, does the status of commissioned officer compromise the pastoral role of the priest/minister? In practice is seems that sometimes it does, partly because chaplains inevitably get absorbed in the military culture and begin to think like the people they live and sleep and eat with.

Before the Gulf War the American Bishops' Conference sent a letter to President Bush saying a war would likely violate Catholic 'just war' teachings. Some of the American bishops went further and held that the war was certainly unjust. One of these was the President of Pax Christi, Bishop Joseph Sullivan who also said he believed chaplains 'have to form their own consciences and not just be automatons for the military. They are moral leaders, and I think they have an obligation to reflect on the moral dimensions of this war.' But even if US chaplains to the Gulf War forces found the war difficult to square with their conscience, it's not easy to see what they could have done about it, being bound by the military code not to undermine morale. Indeed some army personnel who filed as conscientious objectors said they did not find the majority of chaplains supportive or helpful.

The alternative to the present system of military chaplains is for the local conference of bishops to arrange for priests to serve the spiritual needs of army personnel without entering the military structure and wearing military uniform. This is the way it once was in the US, but a long time ago – before the Revolutionary War. Most of the chaplains in the Civil War were commissioned and took salaries, but some preferred to stay out, and just followed the troops to serve them wherever they camped. However, armies like to have chaplains under their control, and in uniform, and hierarchies don't want to have to pay for the support of chaplains if the military is happy to do it for them. So we are not likely to see any change.

4

NEWS FROM THE VATICAN

How the Vatican communicates,
with some thoughts on the church's central government

Peter Hebblethwaite, the author and journalist, died in December 1994. Anyone in the English-speaking world interested in understanding what was going on in the central offices of the Church of Rome very much regrets his passing. A year and more later there seems nobody to replace him. Certainly no younger person could easily gather the range of experience, or indeed the contacts gathered over a lifetime which provided the basis for his informed comment. One vital part of that experience was built up in the early 1960s. As a young Jesuit priest he had the good fortune to attend the last session of the Vatican Council and report it for the Jesuit publication *The Month,* of which he afterwards became editor. The experience of the Council was of course, in church terms, the defining experience of this century. In 1974 Peter was dispensed from his vows to marry Margaret Speaight. Friends say about him that while becoming a loving husband and father, he never really left the Jesuits! He certainly never lost his passionate interest in the church, and there are some fifteen significant books to testify to that abiding passion. Like the best critics, he was basically conservative. He didn't want to get rid of Pope or bishops or even the Curia. He just wanted to help them perform better.

News from the Vatican was a programme about the Vatican organs of communication, which include a radio station, a newspaper and a press office. But it was also a programme about how writers and journalists relate to these services, and because Peter knew more than most about them, we naturally spoke to him at length. The following are some excerpts from the filmed interview.

Reporting on a monarchy

Reporting on the Vatican is immensely difficult given the international nature of the organisation, and given of course the special status of the papacy in the church as an authority. I mean, this is the last monarchy in the world – it's not quite an absolute monarchy but it's not very far from it in some respects and that makes it very difficult. It would be like trying to report the court of Louis XIV. I don't think he'd have welcomed journalists!

Theory and practice in church communications

We have got a perfectly good theory about communications in the church – the Pastoral Instruction published on the mass media in 1971 talks about the need for writers to have access to people, talks about intelligibility, talks about the fact that unless there is communication in the church we have no right to talk about the church as a community, because communication is the measure of community. Now this is perfectly wonderful doctrine but it seems in practice to be addressed to others – to civil governments who should give right of access, but not to the central government of the church itself.

Most news comes from unofficial sources

An American researcher did a study on sources of news from the Vatican and he showed that 85% of news came from unofficial sources. Now in some ways this is not a bad situation because it means that at least if you have access to these unofficial sources you can build them up – even if it takes years to do it. In fact your list of telephone numbers is your most important possession. You can get at what is going on – not in the higher ranks of the Curia because we all know cardinals don't want to talk to such riff-raff – but chiefly in the middle rank of the Curia where there are extremely good people who are possibly frustrated and invariably celibate, and this combination together makes them always ready for a yarn for relief ... I wouldn't like to say more than that lest I burn them up, as it were!

The *Sala Stampa*, or press office of the Vatican, is housed in a massive building on the edge of St Peter's square. The technical facilities are superb – simultaneous translation, telephones, telex, fax, whatever is needed – yet for the most part journalists leave it as disappointed men. Hebblethwaite again:

Too much information and not enough news

I think that the main problem in reporting Vatican events is that there's too much information and not enough news. By which I mean that every day there are masses of documents which are nearly always speeches of Pope John Paul II – but that's all you get. Now to get an interesting story out of a speech you have to be very ingenious and newspapers often are. There is a recent example when the Pope at his Wednesday audience remarked that to look at a women with lust was sinful and to look at your own wife in this way could be sinful! 'Pope lashes lascivious looks' was the headline in one American paper. But that's the sort of levels to which people have to descend to wring an interesting story out of this material.

The press officer issues denials rather than positive interpretations

You never get any comments on events that are happening from the Vatican Press Office, and maybe the good reason for that is that if you did, then the press officer would be participating in the teaching authority of the Pope himself and so he doesn't interpret things. The main thing that the press officer does is to issue denials, he says this or that is a scandalous invention by a sensation-mongering journalist who ought to be ashamed of himself. This usually in fact draws attention to the incident that nobody else knew about, but that's just one of the hazards in this profession.

Vatican Radio

Vatican radio has an interesting history in so far as Marconi, who is credited with the invention of radio, was a close friend of Pius XI and took great pride in putting this new technological miracle at the service of the Pope and the church. Broadcasts today come in 33 different languages and are prepared by a staff of some 250 people. Vatican transmitters are among the most powerful in the world. The quality of what is transmitted however is variable. Peter was a little scathing.

Vatican Radio, in its Italian news bulletins, does seem to me to be a little excessive. I remember when the Pope went to visit a shrine in the Dolomites there was a long description of the ski kit which he was wearing – it was of course white in colour with red edges and the excited commentator said thus John Paul II becomes the first Pope to recite the Angelus above the height of 10,000 feet!

The Vatican newspaper

Osservatore Romano, the Vatican newspaper, is published in the major European languages. It's origins go back to 1861 when the Pope, having just lost most of the papal states, began to feel that he wasn't being fairly reported in the international media. Nowadays people mainly take the Osservatore to have the official texts for papal addresses and Vatican documents. It is not highly rated among journalists.

I would say about *Osservatore Romano* what Pope Paul VI said about it, that is, that this newspaper does not present what happens but what it would like to have happened – that is its fundamental fault. But this is a fault that any house organ is going to have – it is the newspaper of the Holy See and so things are filtered a bit. Again it has improved recently but its main function is to defend the Holy See and of course all its polemical articles and its editorial articles are very conservative indeed. They always defend the most conservative positions. I mean even being generous about how one defines conservative! It's as though there were no other voices in the church except one sort of voice, and that all the others were made up by long-haired, irresponsible, probably sexually deviant intellectuals!

Our programme dealt mostly with the external communications of the Vatican, but I think the problem of communication in the church is at a rather deeper level. In the Roman church the papacy and its executive arm, the Vatican Curia, are at the heart of the organisation, so any study of communications problems must begin there. Peter Hebblethwaite devoted most of his later life to that study. I don't find that hard to understand, for the Church of Rome remains the most interesting, intriguing, contradictory, awe inspiring and maddening institution in the political and religious history of the world for twenty centuries. That's a substantial claim – but there are extraordinary facts to support it.

Twenty centuries of Peter

Nobody has ever bothered to question the pre-eminence of Simon Peter. In the Scriptures he comes first in the lists of the apostles, generally acts as their spokesman, and is repeatedly treated as their leader by Christ. If such a leadership arrangement was willed by Christ, it seems reasonable that his followers should continue the arrangement in succeeding generations under a designated successor. And even if there is no absolute proof that Peter was buried in Rome, there is neither any good reason to question it. The early church clearly recognised Peter's leadership role, so it is not likely that people would forget where he was buried. No other city or town in the Roman Empire has every put down a counter claim. And when Constantine came to erect the first St Peter's basilica in the fourth century, why would he take enormous trouble to remove a considerable part of the Vatican hill, and build the altar over a first century tomb – except that he was confident the tomb contained the bones of Peter?

Peter's earliest successors were not afraid to claim his authority

St Clement – probably the third in the line of succession to the apostle Peter – wrote a letter to the people of Corinth in Greece around the year 96. Some would like to think that the Bishop of Rome only gradually came to gather power and authority to himself, but there is certainly no evidence of it in this letter written less than thirty years after Peter's death.

> If one of you should not obey what Jesus has spoken through us, let him know he commits a grave sin and lays himself open to dire peril … You will give us great joy if, by obeying what we have written in the Holy Ghost, you cast off the unrighteous vehemence of your anger, according to the admonitions which we have expressed in this letter in favour of peace and concord.

There have been some 260 bishops of Rome since Clement – 126 since the first millennium. This latter group were a mixed bunch, largely administrators who exhibit the full range of human virtues and failings. But of these 126 only five have been dignified with the title of saint. Some may be surprised by that fact. But if we relate it to the New Testament account of Peter, perhaps one shouldn't. For while Peter's leadership position is clear, much of what else we know about him is unflattering – the very detailed account of his triple denial being the most obvious example.

Twenty centuries of human history: The Vatican Archives

Without getting lyrical – as so many do – one cannot help marvelling at the papacy's ability to survive strong and vibrant and intact through difficult times. It was twice as old as the Constitution of the United States of America is today when the Pope sent St Patrick (or was it Palladius?) to Ireland in 432. No contemporary institution has been more intimately, or more continuously involved with the religious and political development, not just of Europe, but also of the Orient and the Americas.

Much of that history was made in the city of Rome, and most of the records – written on velum, paper and stone, in frescos and paintings – are stored in a small area of Rome surrounded by a medieval wall which we call the Vatican.

The Curia or papal civil service

From the very beginning of the papacy, the incumbent bishop of Rome has had people around him to receive and write letters, prepare documents, make some of the lesser decisions, and advise on the big ones. That group is known collectively as the Curia, a word once used to describe the Senate house in ancient Rome. The Roman Curia as structured today is largely a creation of the Council of Trent, which in turn was both a purifying and 'battening down the hatches' council in the wake of the Protestant Reformation. So the present Curia was designed to impose decisions and assure uniformity rather than to encourage dialogue.

The size of the Curia

The Curia is surprisingly small and efficient. In 1987 it had 1,800 – lets say 2,000 employees – carrying on the business of a church which now claims roughly one billion members. So the ratio between curial employees and members of the church works out as roughly one curialist for each half a million Catholics. This could be compared with the United States where the federal government in Washington employs 300,000 people to serve a population of roughly quarter of a billion – or one federal employee for every 800 citizens. It isn't perhaps a fair comparison, but if the US federal government were to be run on Vatican lines there would be 500 federal employees instead of 300,000!

How does one get to work in the Curia?

If one is satisfied to be a secretary or gardener or maintenance engineer or Swiss Guard, one can work in the Curia and remain in the lay state. But if you are thinking of going further you must become a priest, because clerics hold all the important positions. Ideally you should have been born in Italy, though it's a bit late to say that now. The best seminary to enter is the Roman seminary, but some come from elsewhere in Italy – and the rest of the world. Become well-known in the seminary for a spirit of obedience and a love of Canon Law. Become proficient in more than one language, and get a postgraduate qualification, preferably from a Roman university. After that it is a bit like the joining the CIA. You might ask your bishop to recommend you if you think he will spare you, or, as is more likely, you will be brought out to dinner by some well-dressed cleric and asked wouldn't you like to serve the Holy Father for five years in a special way. After that, keep the head down and find some patron who appreciates your worth and will forward your career. Forget about 'the loyal opposition' bit. If you are thinking of the diplomatic service there is a special school called the Pontificia Accademia Ecclesiastica in the Piazza della Minerva where, presumably, one learns how to present one's credentials to monarch or president, throw a cocktail party, and eat a soft fried egg without letting it go all over the plate.

People who join the Curia and make its service a career

Giovanni Battista Montini is a good example of how one moves through the system. He was born into a comfortable family – his father was a banker, newspaper editor and member of parliament. Giovanni studied in Milan and at the Gregorian University in Rome, where a Monsignor Pizzardo was impressed with him and arranged his posting to the Curia. He went to the Accademia, and got his first and last diplomatic appointment in Poland. The cold winters didn't suit his delicate health so he got sent back to the Secretariat of State. The influential patron with whom he came to work most closely was one Eugenio Pacelli, who became Pope Pius XII in 1939. Pius was his own Secretary of State, but Montini became one of his two most senior assistants. In 1954 he went to Milan as archbishop and acquired some pastoral experience. In 1963 he became Pope on the death of John XXIII, calling himself Paul VI.

Irish members of the Curia

There have never been many Irish working in the Curia. John Magee, a missionary, was helping out in Propaganda in Rome when he impressed Archbishop Pignedoli, a friend of Paul VI. When Paul wanted a secretary for his English correspondence, Pignedoli knew the very man for the job. I doubt if there have been many other Irish who became secretary to a reigning Pope.

Monsignor Diarmuid Martin of the Dublin diocese has come to prominence in recent years, being mentioned regularly in dispatches around the time of the UN Conferences on ecology in Rio in 1992, population in Cairo in 1994, and women in Bejing in 1995. Diarmuid is now secretary of the Pontifical Council for Justice and Peace and could become our first curial cardinal of the 21st century. The last one was Michael Browne OP. During post graduate studies in Rome, Diarmuid stayed, not at the Irish College but in the Teutonic College where he came to know Joseph (later Cardinal) Ratzinger. His mentor in recent years however has been another cardinal, Roger Etchegaray, who just *might* become next Pope. Fr Tom Stack and I visited Diarmuid a few years ago in his apartment in the Holy Office – Diarmuid once spent a summer many years ago as a clerical student working with Radharc. For some reason the electric power failed shortly after we arrived at this venerable building beside St Peter's. We were wandering around one of the upper balconies in the dark when another of the inhabitants came out of his rooms looking for a box of matches. In the circumstances and the place, Tom couldn't resist wondering *sotto voce* about which liberation theologian was about to be burnt at the stake!

Reforming the Curia

Peter Hebblethwaite used tell a relevant story of Benedict XIV. When the Pope was informed by some mad priest that Antichrist had been born in a village in the Arbuzzi, he asked how old he was, and on being told three years of age, he graciously replied: 'In that case I can leave him to my successor'. Like any other human organisation, the Curia needs periodic reformation. Unfortunately Popes in this century have been loath to tackle it – there is always the temptation to leave problems to their successor.

Pope Paul VI defined the Curia's task as 'to listen to and interpret the voice of the Pope and at the same time not let him lack any useful and objective information, or brotherly and pondered counsel'. One might have hoped that he would have included among their tasks listening to the other bishops, if not to the faithful: after all the Council that he presided over not so many years before had decreed that 'The universal body of the faithful who have received the anointing of the Holy One, cannot be mistaken in belief' (*Lumen Gentium* 12).

Paul brought about some changes – including retirement at seventy-five years of age – but neither he nor any other Pope in this century was prepared to tackle substantial reform of the Curia: or even contemplate retiring at seventy-five themselves. Pius XII largely ignored the members of the Curia, and in consequence their problems. John XXIII had enough on his hands setting up the Vatican Council. Paul himself had been too much part of the system to be prepared to take hard-nosed decisions that might hurt old colleagues and friends. John Paul I hadn't time to do anything and John Paul II probably likes the Curia just as it is!

What are the criticisms of the Curia that a reforming Pope or Council might have to take note of?

1. The Curia is too small and too overworked to be able to make decisions on all the matters which it claims competence to decide.

The one thing that everybody in the Curia will agree on is that they are all overworked. The comparison between the Curia and the US federal government mentioned above helps put the problem in a certain perspective. The number of people employed in the Secretariat of State is hardly much more than the number of countries with which the Vatican has diplomatic relations. Furthermore – unlike the diplomatic representative of a secular state – the Vatican representative has a double role *vis-à-vis* both the state and the local church – which includes a close involvement in the crucial question of the appointment of bishops. This double role adds to the work of the diplomatic service. So people haven't time to really study problems, or time and money to travel to distant countries and spend time listening to and learning from the churches about whom they are making decisions.

2. The system of recruiting and promotion encourages subservience rather than independent judgement.

Because they are celibate, and often have few if any interests outside their work, curial prelates are inclined to identify themselves, not just with the Curia, but with the church – the two become one. Then the Italian custom of choosing a mentor leads to sycophancy and the formation of groups bound by special loyalties. There is a further complication in the case of a monarchy – in addition to the regular route to the top, there is the backstairs. The backstairs in recent years has been crowded with Poles!

3. The Curia is a number of independent fiefdoms.

In practice this means that there can be different ways to get a permission or decision from the Curia, and depending which way the question is routed, the answer may be yes or no. If Cardinal Ratzinger, for instance, is known (as he is) to be unsympathetic to national bishops' conferences, then it would be important to avoid the Holy Office over which he presides when trying to push any measure in their regard through the Curia. To some extent the importance of this factor depends on the Pope in office, and how much he wants to exercise overall control.

4. The bishops are also vicars of Christ and successors to the apostles, yet the Curia always seems to wish to diminish their role.

The curialists have been consistent, and so far successful, opponents of collegiality between Pope and bishops, because deep down they believe that power shared is power lost. The late Cardinal Ottaviani typifies this attitude. In reply to a question as to whether the twelve apostles ever acted as a college, he once made the sarcastic comment that the only occasion he could think of was in the Garden of Gethsemane – when the evangelist adds the postscript, 'and then they all fled!'

The two most effective rearguard actions of the Curia after Vatican II were the maintenance of the prohibition on birth control against the wishes of the majority of bishops, and the evisceration of the original concept of a Synod which would carry on the collegial process that Vatican II had begun.

5. The Curia has too much say in papal elections.

The Curia controls all the files, and can therefore make or break a cleric, including cardinals who are in the running at a papal election. But their influence begins much earlier because they have a large say in the selection of bishops, and probably have a considerable influence on who is promoted to the cardinalate. I wrote elsewhere that 'the Curia is a civil service and perhaps the best way to understand it is to remind oneself of the popular BBC series, *Yes Minister*. This was a comedy programme, but a good comedy programme because the humour was rooted in a deep understanding of the particular foibles of human nature which emerge in the civil service situation'. Paul Eddington – who played Jim Hacker in the series – died in November 1995 when I happened to be writing this chapter. In his memory the BBC re-ran an hour-long episode about how he became Prime Minister. The plot involved Sir Humphrey, the archetypal civil servant, who becomes secretary to the British Cabinet shortly before the sitting Prime Minister chooses to resign. Sir Humphrey is naturally deeply concerned about the succession, and decides with his mandarin friends that among the possible candidates, Jim Hacker would be malleable and cause them the least trouble as Prime Minister. So they institute a search of the MI 5 files to find dirt to kill off the other candidates. One was found drunk driving, another was found to have been dallying with a lady from Argentina, while the third was involved in legal, but politically damaging financial transactions. This information was then used – with delicacy, but to maximum effect. And surprise, surprise, Jim is elected Prime Minister!

6. The Curia exercises unwarranted control of access of persons and information to the Pope.

Part of the role of the Curia is to help keep the Pope informed. Inevitably this leads to a certain filtering process depending on who decides whom or what the Pope is to see or read. On the question of access, it is well known that during the period when Paul VI was making up his mind about the birth control question, the ultra conservative Cardinal Ottaviani saw him at least once a week, while liberal bishops couldn't get near him. Even Cardinal Villot, the

French-born Secretary of State, was anxious about the control that conservatives in the Curia were exercising over Paul VI in the run up to the decision about birth control. Cardinal Suenens wrote in his biography.

> This lightning trip to Rome (March 1968) was a pretext to meet with the Holy Father; Cardinal Villot had insistently been asking Cardinal Doepfner, myself, and probably others as well, to go and see the Pope – in order, he said 'to offset the local influences', which tended to point in a counter-conciliar direction.

7. The Curia is Italian in thought and style, and unsuitable for an international church.

One reform that Paul did attempt was to bring in some non-Italians to work in the Curia. This is easier to talk about than to put into practice. Bishops in the main want to keep their good men, and don't like sacrificing them to work in the Curia. When asked to spare somebody for the service there is always the temptation for them to unload one of their personnel problems! Priests on their part would generally prefer to do pastoral work in their own country or on the missions rather than push paper around in Rome. Which is the great paradox – that if a priest really wants to work in the Curia one must be suspicious of his motivation, while the clerics best fitted to work there are those that don't want to! A further problem often noted is that foreigners working in the Curia tend to become more Roman than the Romans themselves – probably because as outsiders they feel the need to identify. Far from adding a liberal element to the mix, they tend to become more deeply conservative!

8. The Curia is conservative to the point of being reactionary.

While one would wish and expect the Curia to be conservative, it is far more deeply conservative than the church as a whole, and therefore unrepresentative. Which is why the first action of the bishops at the Vatican Council was to reject the preparatory documents proposed by the Curia and put in their own men to write new ones. Peter Nichols, Rome correspondent of the London *Times* during the Council summed up the situation.

> The Curia resented criticisms, just as it resented the claims that the bishops were to make for a share in responsibility in governing the church. As the Pope's executive, the Curia's members had grown used to basking in the sun of papal power, while identifying much of their own activities, by an easy sleight of mind, as

virtually blessed with papal prerogative. The curial atmosphere was exotic and close, reflecting little awareness of what was happening outside those sacred walls. Thus, the lines of battle were traced, inevitably, before the great pageant began. This was unfortunate. As events have shown, the Curia is left untouched by frontal assault. Only in the most glaring instances, such as over the procedures of the old Holy Office, did angry protests from the Council floor against the structure and customs of the Curia bring change, and this was scarcely radical reform.

Everything for the good of the Church!

I pointed out in the Preface that one reason for calling this book 'No Vipers in the Vatican' was to make it clear that in criticising the Curia, I am aware at the same time that I am criticising better men than me – men who believe as I do in the value and importance of a centralised authority in the church. The main difference between us would appear to be that, whereas I believe that authority would be strengthened by power sharing, they see it being weakened. I could elaborate on this point, but prefer to quote Peter Nichols again, who speaks with more authority, having lived in Rome and reported on the Roman scene for a number of years.

> Everything that is done by the Curia is done for the good of the church. This is a motivation that should not be forgotten however hypocritical the expression of it may seem to be. It is certainly not forgotten by curial prelates themselves when evolving policy or engaged in the less dignified activities – on occasion, one can say intrigues – to which they are liable to descend. Sometimes it is a cause for marvel, sometimes of genuine sorrow, but as often as either it is just thoroughly puzzling how much they mean by these assertions of convinced, dedicated purpose, even when involved in what, from the outside, looks like unscrupulous adventure. It is not hypocrisy. It is not self-deceit. It is the natural acceptance of any reasonable means available for making a particular point prevail. They might be better civil servants if they and their methods were otherwise constituted, but they would be poorer priests in their own eyes were they to fail to defend or promote what they understand to be right. This sublime self-confidence of the Curia sets a blank wall across the path of the reformer.

I always feel a Christian must be a confident optimist. To be otherwise seems to suggest that God doesn't know how to run his own show. And the people I most admire are people like John XXIII who really trust in God. Having said that, I see no human hope of the Curia being reformed without, as it were, an accident spoiling their carefully laid plans. Even another Council would make only a temporary difference. Because the liberal bishops – and there aren't that many left – will come faithfully to the Council, make their contribution as before, and leave. The Curia will remain as before to undo much of what they may have achieved. Edmund Hill, in *Ministry and Authority*, put the problem succinctly when talking of the aftermath of Vatican Two.

> The proposers and supporters of collegiality were naïve enough to hand over its implementation to its most committed opponents, who being anything but naïve, have done their best to neutralise it ever since.

There seems to me only one thing that could change the current depressing scene, and that is a vigorous young Pope of the mind of John XXIII or Gregory X who would remain in office long enough to copper fasten substantial reform of the Curia. A Pope who would have time not only to make reform work, but make it be seen to work, so that even a conservative successor will not wish to reverse the changes. Humanly speaking, that at the moment appears to be an impossible option. But then we Christians believe that nothing is impossible – with God!

5

WHERE THE POPE IS A COMMUNIST AND THE BISHOP A GUERRILLA

How the US has subverted democracy in Latin America

A Benedictine brother told me this story in Coban, Guatemala, which helped to explain something of the relationship between the rich and the poor in Guatemala, and gave us the title of our programme:

> Here in this past year, we were having special celebrations for the Holy Year in different centres. Well in this one particular village there is a farm plantation and the people there asked their owner (*sic*) if they could come to a certain hamlet for the celebration of the Holy Year. And the owner asked the delegate, the lay minister, 'Well, who is telling you to do that?' And the delegate said, 'Well the Pope is – he started the idea of the Holy Year, and he wants us all to celebrate in a proper way, and all that – so we decided to go there'. And the landowner said, 'Well he's a Communist'. Then the landowner continued to ask, 'And who around here is asking you to go to that celebration?' And the delegate replied, 'Well the bishop is – he's encouraging everybody around here to celebrate the Holy Year'. And the landowner said, 'Well the bishop – he's a guerrilla'. So they really couldn't go.

I have made films in El Salvador, Nicaragua, Guatemala, Mexico, Cuba and Grenada. That is not enough to make me an expert on Central America, but it has given me memories and images which leave me permanently shocked, sickened and with feelings of anger. In Guatemala in the 1970s and 80s people were being clubbed to death, dismembered alive, burnt alive, buried alive. Girls were raped in front of their parents, young children dashed against rocks and trees. There were even reports of cases of cannibalism by the military under the terrified gaze of the people's relatives. How could one forget hearing so many vignettes of evil, as for instance this one drawn for me by Fr Basilio, a Benedictine priest, and prior of his monastery in Guatemala?

We were in a meeting with several of the army people and we

were discussing various problems that were taking place. And this fellow was one of the men out in the field that had to direct the units that do what they call 'a clean-up'. And he said that one of the basic rules that they used is that if they found a band of armed men in a country area, and especially if they had machine guns and heavy equipment, then they would simply decide that anybody in that area, men, women, children, would be wiped out, because they would all in some way or other be involved in helping the guerrilla movement. And so they would simply kill everybody. For example, the kids, the reason why they wouldn't want them around is because they would be able to tell other people what had happened, and who was there, and all kinds of other things. In other words, they'd be witnesses – which the army wouldn't want. The women would be involved in making food and feeding the guerrillas, so they'd be guilty. And so, since it's just impossible to decide that this person, that person, would not be guilty, they would just simply wipe out everybody. And from a military point of view, you can see that such a simplistic attitude is very easy to follow and you can tell your men what to do and very easily they can do it. But from the viewpoint of justice and human rights, of course, it's terrible.

There was more than a little of this mindset behind the killing statistics: between 1980 and 1984 somewhere between 50,000 and 75,000 largely innocent people were tortured, mutilated and killed by the Guatemalan army. The figure today is over 120,000 and still climbing.

Another priest, Fr Bernadino, was chaplain to a hospital:

When I was in the hospital one time visiting people during the time when they were bringing in all kinds of people, some wounded and a lot of dead – around 25 people or so that they found killed every day. There was a wounded boy, 15 years old, that joined up with the army. And he was saying, 'You know,' he said, 'I killed all kinds of guerrillas'. But he was just like a little boy playing a game.

Another day a person came up behind me and started speaking Spanish. He wanted to talk to someone. And he was from the National Guard in Salvador who fled, and he was in the torture part, and he said that they would put people between two jeeps and pull them apart. And he said that they would stick their bayonet in a person that would be keeling down before them. And, he said, when he cut off the guy's head, he realised he was doing something wrong to his brother, and he had a conversion.

An Irish Sister working in Guatemala talked about the resulting terror among innocent people:

> The effect of the killings was the insecurity of who would be killed next. People said to me, 'we leave our home, and we don't know what will happen when we are away'. Also some of those people were taken off buses, and so they fear even to come to market and sell the things they need to sell to make money to buy clothes or keep the children at school. They fear to do that because maybe in the process they will get killed. I think the fear of even having children – people with a culture that appreciates children saying, 'why should we have children now because if we have children, especially boys, maybe they are just going to be killed in the future, and that's going to be suffering for us?' So there was a change in their own culture pattern from a rural trusting people to a people who felt that, for no reason, they could be killed.

The Civil Patrols

One of the evil but effective methods of the army was to force every able bodied man in the rural areas to carry arms on at least one day a week. Seven hundred thousand peasants were enlisted in this way. Part of their duties was to set up road blocks, check passing traffic, guard installations and so on. They were effective because they knew failure to do what the army insisted meant death. If they guarded a bridge and the bridge got blown up, the guards forfeited their lives. If the electricity supply to a town was destroyed, thirty of the civil patrol were killed. The effects of this violence on local communities was horrific. It often amounted to the deliberate destruction of affections and loyalty. Families were put under enormous pressure to report on the activities of their neighbours. Brother forced to kill brother – the penalty for non-compliance was torture and death. All of which helps to explain the civil patrols' reputation of shooting first and asking questions afterwards.

I met Brother Jaime Steinbeck up in the Peten, the northern part of Guatemala. He brought me to see the magnificent Mayan city of Tikal. We were stopped at a checkpoint by one of these civil patrols. I noticed a car in the ditch just beyond the checkpoint, riddled with bullets. Jaime told me that it had been shot up the previous Thursday, that the owner lived just down the road, and that he must have been well known to the people who shot him. It may be that the civil patrol shot him because he didn't stop, while he didn't stop because he felt they knew him. Either way there wouldn't be any enquiry.

Press Gangs

Jaime told me that in Flores, the town where he lived, the army had come on two nights of each month for the previous three months and set up outside the disco bar and the school. If any young people couldn't prove what they were doing as students, or didn't have proper identification papers, they were taken off into the army. Some of the young people press-ganged like that naturally protest and get beaten up. Most just sit there quiet. 'Mom may be frantic and dad off his nut, but I am going to sit here and do as I'm told because I want to live.' Jaime also mentioned a village 30km away where two youths got mad with the army and shot at a truck of soldiers. The soldiers wiped out the whole village and everyone in it.

The church amidst social chaos

The church found itself powerless to do anything in this awful situation. The disruption was enormous, with one and a quarter million people uprooted from their homes. The prior of the Benedictines spoke about the parishes in rural areas which they used serve from their monastery in Coban.

> I found it very difficult to decide whether I could go to say Masses, or whether I would only endanger the people by having meetings where they would be gathered together. Everybody knows that a Mass is going on in a certain area, so that it is a good time when the army could catch the people and cause trouble. One of the parishes in another part of the diocese here has had 2,000 people missing in one year.

Delegates of the Word were particularly at risk. Sr Francis spoke about their work.

> The delegates are very special people – they are volunteers and they work for their local community. There are many mountains in Guatemala and so the priest cannot always go in to celebrate Mass; maybe he can only go two or three times a year. So the delegates take training and they go and evangelise and arrange a 'Celebration of the Word'. Many of these delegates suffered because they had helped the people to realise that maybe they didn't always have to be poor.

In 1981, after the murder of many catechists and several priests, attacks on religious houses and convents, and death threats against himself, Bishop Gerardi Conedera, head of the diocese of Santa Cruz del Quiché, decided to close down the diocese, and told all religious personnel to leave. There are few examples of such extreme action in twenty centuries of the Christian church. Bishop Flores Reyes, of the neighbouring diocese of Vera Paz Cobán, commented to us.

> I believe that pages have been written on the subject of martyrdom in our country, that are dramatic, exemplary, and important, whether it refers to the thirteen priests who've been assassinated, plus two who have disappeared, or the hundreds of catechists and committed Christians who have fallen victim to the violence and overall repression suffered in our country.

In May 1982 the bishops as a whole issued a very stark statement expressing profound concern about the massacre of the peasantry: 'Never in our nation's history have we been at such a grave point,' they said. 'These assassinations are now catalogued as genocide.'

The essential cause of instability

The essential instability in Guatemala is the result of the poor *campesinos* struggling for a minimal share in the resources of their country, while the rich, aided by the United States, use every means in their power to prevent them having any share. One or two figures may help to explain. In Guatemala in 1988 an estimated 98% of the 3.6 million indigenous people were either without land, or with insufficient land for their subsistence. 2% of farmers own 65% of the total farmland in Guatemala. At the other end of the scale, 40% of farmers own 1.4% of the land. This is the end result of the abolition of communal tenure of Indian lands and their seizure by the ruling classes in the last century.

The responsibility for all this suffering

Much of the responsibility for this human suffering in Guatemala must be laid at the door of the United States. And much though I love and admire the United States of America, its Constitution and its people, I think history will judge their record in Latin America in the latter half of this century as perpetuating extreme injustices and causing human suffering on a vast scale.

The tragedy of Latin America for the forty and more years of the Cold War was that conflicts which, by themselves should be seen as the result of legitimate striving for reform by oppressed people, were seen by successive US governments as giving scope to the Soviet Union to establish a presence in the United States' backyard. Even efforts at limited reform came to nothing, particularly in

Central America where the US consistently supported dictators and oligarchies.

One sad example of this immoral and illegal interference was the US organised overthrow of Jacobo Arbenz, the lawfully elected president of Guatemala, in 1954. Arbenz tried to introduce a very limited land reform, which included the appropriation of idle and unused lands belonging to the US-owned United Fruit company – with compensation. But the United Fruit called the compensation inadequate and Arbenz a communist. Working through the US Secretary of State, John Foster Dulles – who was a stockholder and director of United Fruit – the company convinced President Eisenhower that Arbenz was a puppet of the Soviet Union.

That assessment of communist influence was grossly exaggerated. Christopher Andrew, Professor of Modern History at Cambridge:

> Arbenz was neither a communist fellow-traveller nor a potential Castro. Party members played a part in his land reform agency, but they were excluded from his cabinet, from the national police force, and from most departments of government ... the preconditions for a communist coup did not exist.

After the removal of Arbenz – which involved bombing Guatemalan cities with US warplanes – constitutional politics in Guatemala degenerated rapidly with the increasing domination of the military, and a succession of rigged elections. Political parties in Guatemala had to be registered with the Ministry of Defence, and as a first step had to submit a list of their members. In the case of opposition parties, this has frequently been the prelude to political assassination.

'Hitherto acceptable rules of conduct do not apply'

A month after the Guatemalan coup, President Eisenhower commissioned a report on covert activities by the United States. The report makes chilling reading:

> It is now clear that we are facing an implacable enemy whose avowed objective is world domination by whatever means and at whatever cost. There are no rules in such a game. Hitherto acceptable norms of human conduct do not apply. If the United States is to survive, long-standing American concepts of 'fair play' must be reconsidered. We must develop effective espionage and counter-espionage services and must learn to subvert, sabotage and destroy our enemies by more clever, more sophisticated and more effective methods than those used against us.

Training the military and the police

After the coup, the United States set up and trained the Guatemalan police. Five years later the US Embassy, no less, reported to the US State Department that this police force was 'employed in the investigation and harassment of political opponents and in the carrying out of this or that unsavory assignment. This body is feared and despised by virtually everyone in Guatemala except those whom they serve'.

The US also had fifteen military advisers in Guatemala in 1959 – even though there were no known subversives or guerrilla activity in Guatemala before 1960. In the 1960s and 70s, the Guatemalan army received $63 million in US military aid. 2,300 Guatemalan army officers were trained by the United States in counter-insurgency tactics. The price that the people of Guatemala have since had to pay as a result of military control of the government makes awful reading – even in cold statistics.

Slaughter by the military and the police

Between 1966 and 1970, around 10,000 civilians were killed during the course of a military campaign against an estimated 350 guerrillas. Between 1980 and 1984, the Guatemalan army and the army/police death squads killed approximately 50,000 to 75,000 people, in many cases after horrifying torture and mutilation. The total deaths during the 80s is given at 120,000. A million people were displaced from their homes. In 1995 a UN human rights report confirmed that organised killing was on the rise again. In two days of February 95, 22 mutilated corpses turned up along highways, most showing signs of torture. Among the victims were a university professor and three university students, and a government inspector. The report presents extensive evidence of military involvement.

US involvement in other Latin countries: Chile

President Eisenhower was not the only president who worked to overturn a democratically elected government. On 15 September 1969, President Nixon summoned his closest advisers to the Oval Office asking for a plan of action to keep Salvador Allende out of office in Chile – where he was expected to win a democratic election. Nixon promised $10 million to the project and more if necessary. David Phillips, the head of the secret Chilean task force of the CIA, charged with organising a military coup, is on record as wondering 'Should the CIA, even responding to a president's ukase, encourage a military coup in one of the few countries in Latin America with a solid functioning democratic tradition?'

The very day after this Oval Office meeting about Chile, Nixon told an audience at Kansas State University :

> There are those who protest if the verdict of democracy goes against them, democracy itself is at fault, the system is at fault – who say that if they don't get their own way, the answer is to burn a bus or bomb a building. (Or pay $10 million to organise a coup, one is tempted to add.)

A coup was attempted by the CIA in Chile, but it collapsed. The CIA are known to have spent at least $8 million secretly financing Allende's opponents in the three years between his election and his death during the storming of the presidential palace. They knew about the impending military coup weeks ahead, but did not inform Allende. On the day after the coup, the leader of the army Junta, General Augusto Pinochet, held a secret meeting with the US Military Assistance Advisory group.

In March 1991, the Chilean Commission on Truth and Reconciliation gave its report on the Pinochet years to the current Chilean government – Pinochet remains to this day commander of the Chilean army. The report gave details of 2,279 who were executed for political reasons, died under torture, or were 'disappeared'. These are only the clearly confirmed killings, so they are known to be a considerable underestimate. No information is given on non-fatal cases of torture, arbitrary imprisonment and other excesses of Pinochet's military dictatorship.

The School of the Americas

If there were spare Nobel Peace Prizes around, I would give one to Fr Roy Bourgeois, who has served over two years in jail for protesting as a lone figure against the so-called 'School of the Americas'. He describes the School as 'a symbol of the age-old attempt by the United States to impose its political and economic will upon Latin America by maintaining the lucrative gap between the rich and the poor' – which in my experience would appear a pretty accurate description. The school at Fort Benning in Georgia is run by the US army and trains army personnel from all the countries of Latin America. Over the years it has trained 58,000 soldiers from 23 countries, including virtually all the leaders throughout the region who have since been held responsible for massacres, death squads, and every known abuse of human rights. To honour graduates who reached senior ranks in their militaries, the State Department and Pentagon each year select Latin American generals for a Hall of

Fame. Among the two dozen inductees whose framed pictures hang in the school's main foyer are men who have 'certainly not been sterling examples of democracy,' according to an embarrassed US officer, as reported in *Newsweek* magazine. Graduates of the school include the following:

Guatemala

General Manuel Antonio Callejas y Callejas, chief of Guatemalan intelligence in the late 1970s and early 1980s, when thousands of political opponents were assassinated.

General Romeo Lucas Garcia, Guatemalan dictator 1978-82, whose bloody reign saw at least 5,000 political murders and up to 25,000 civilian deaths at the hands of the military.

Argentina

Leopoldo Galtieri, ex-head of Argentine junta responsible for the 'disappearances' of 15,000 people – at a conservative estimate – in Argentina's dirty war.

Bolivia

General Hugo Bánzer Suáez, Bolivian dictator 1971-78, who brutally suppressed progressive church workers and striking tin miners as dictator of Bolivia.

Columbia

In 1992 a coalition of international human rights groups issued a report charging 246 Colombian officers with human-rights violations; 105 were former students of the school.

El Salvador

Roberto D'Aubuisson, the late Salvadoran death-squad leader, plotted assassinations, including, many believe, the assassination of Archbishop Romero.

Nineteen of the twenty-seven officers that a UN Truth Commission implicated in the murder of six Jesuits in the Central American University, their housekeeper and her daughter in November 1989. This group included General Juan Rafael Bustillo, former Salvadoran air force chief, who was cited in the 1993 UN Truth Commission report for helping to both plan and cover up the Jesuit massacre.

Honduras

General Policarpo Paz Garcia, who presided over a corrupt regime in Honduras in the early 1980s. Humberto Regalado Hernandez, who as Honduran chief of staff was linked to Colombian drug dealers.

Four of the five senior Honduran officers accused in a 1987 Americas Watch report of organising a secret death squad.

Panama

General Manuel Noriega, ex-dictator of Panama, who is now serving a forty-year sentence for drug trafficking.

Peru

At least six Peruvian officers linked to a military death squad that killed nine students and one professor at a university near Lima last year were graduates of the school.

School of America alumni like the above have attained positions of prominence which include 10 presidents, 15 ministers of national department, 23 ministers of defence, and many others senior positions. So according to its own brief – which is to extend US influence in Latin America – the School of the Americas has been enormously successful. Unfortunately most of this success has been achieved at the expense of the lives of hundreds of thousands of defenceless people.

Cowboys and Indians

In 1993, 38,000 US citizens died from gunshot wounds. In 1994-5 more Americans were killed by guns inside the US (60,000) than in the whole of the Vietnam war! The medical cost of handgun injuries is nearly a billion dollars a year. Every 14 seconds some US citizen is the victim of a gunshot. An estimated 100,000 kids go to school each day with a gun.

There are 1,800 gun manufacturers in the US, subject to virtually no restrictions, and 284,000 licensed gun dealers. A gun is made every nine seconds in America, and another is imported. Six million guns are added yearly to the estimated 212 million in private hands – nearly one per citizen. In a 1991 Gallop Poll, 80% favoured hand gun registration, and 93% approved of a seven-day waiting period for handgun purchase. Yet the National Rifle Association, with the help of vast political contributions, has been able to prevent curbing legislation.

The US is the world's number one merchant of death, selling weapons to 142 of the world's 180 nations. According to The Centre for Defence Information, 40% of sales are for delivery to authoritarian governments. The nation's top arms manufacturers employ about three million people.

Solving problems by shooting people has become a pervasive quality of popular American culture, and this suffuses the whole society – and its foreign policies. The six-gun tradition, wedded to a kind of chauvinism, led to the uncritical acceptance of such actions as the invasion of Panama in 1989 in which somewhere between 4,000 and 7,000 innocent Panamanians died, and the ridiculous invasion of Grenada in 1983, together with a total lack of concern for the quite disproportionate sufferings of the people of Latin America at the hands of military governments trained, armed and supported, and in the case of Guatemala, actually imposed by the US establishment.

6
BOMBS IN THE BACKYARD

*Some US citizens who actively opposed the arms race,
and some who suffered for it*

Fr Jack Morris is an activist for peace with a clear understanding of his own motivation. We met him on a farm in Oregon where he and a group of like-minded people organised seminars to inform and conscientise people with respect to the nuclear arms issue. How to turn swords into ploughshares was for him the vital contemporary Christian issue.

The arms race isn't simply about militarism, it's about one's relationship with God. And if the bishops and the Holy Father himself have called this 'the gravest moral issue of our times', then it's about sin, it's about redemption, it's about spirituality, it's about salvation. And when the church does not address that, we are failing in our mission. So I have to be involved, for my own salvation.

I walk this way but once, and I feel God is love, and he's holding me in his hands. But I'm frightened that I could end my life and he'd say, 'Well what were you doing about this arms issue?' I'd say, 'I talked about it'. And he'd say, 'You did what? Where are your wounds? You haven't got any wounds in your hands and your feet and were you willing in some way to follow me?' And that's what church is about, if you want to be like Jesus you follow Jesus. And it just seems to me that Jesus lived under a military government, the Romans – he lived in an occupied country. He was killed because he was monkeying in politics.

Thirty-five thousand atomic warheads

Bombs in the backyard was about people who were trying to do something to halt the nuclear arms race. The programme opened with the explosion of an atomic bomb, followed by one of the most telling visual aids I ever came across in my film career – an acre or so of missile models standing upright in rows in a public park in Washington DC. It's aim was to bring home to people – ordinary people as well as legislators – the sheer craziness of the whole nuclear weapons industry. In the 1980s the US was reported to have had 35,000 atomic warheads – enough to destroy the whole world several times over. If America were to explode one of these bombs every day, it would take 96 years to use up 35,000 warheads. And even in the future, after the cold war has long ended and all the promised decommissioning has taken place, the US will still have ten to twenty thousand warheads.

Modelling nuclear weapons

Barbara Donaghy was the leader of a group of concerned people who made these thirty-five thousand scale models of missiles and nuclear submarines, and set them out in rows on the green grass with the Capitol buildings visible in the distance. The missiles had crisp clean-cut names like Titan, Tomahawk, Cruise, Minuteman, Poseidon; when armed with atomic warheads, each one was capable of vaporising a whole city and every living thing in it. Barbara Donaghy talked about the experience of making the model missiles as a help to try and understand the psychology of people working in the armaments industry.

> We spent eight months casting warhead replicas every day. We started to forget what they were – at the end of the day we felt we had a good day, we made three hundred warheads, or we had a terrible day, we broke sixteen missiles! And you just get really involved with the one thing that you are doing and lose track of the total picture. And every once in a while someone would be working and kinda feel overwhelmed all of a sudden with the reality of what they were making.

Giving up one's job in the armaments industry

Bombs in the backyard was in part about people who worked in the arms industry and whose conscience forced them to leave. Two of them formerly worked at the Trident submarine base at Bangor, on Puget Sound – which is the entrance to the port of Seattle, in Washington State. The Trident missile system is the most expensive, and potentially most destructive weapons system ever developed. One submarine packs enough explosives to kill perhaps 200 million people. Mona Seehale used to be in charge of co-ordinating the training programme for the strategic weapons facility – the outfit that assembles the nuclear weapons.

> I used to have feelings of nausea when I looked at the place where they have the actual buildings in which the weapons are assembled. It used be forest like this but there is nothing there now, it's

completely bare except for the guard towers, and the fences with barbed wire. The buildings have no windows, and it's a very scary feeling. If you ever touched a bomb as I have, then you know it exists. But I think most people can't really believe in the reality that's there – it's 'deterrence,' or something theoretical, it's not real. I think the people who work there don't really think about the fact that what they are doing is preparing for the destruction of the world. If this actually came home to them they would probably all resign.

Mona had no job when we met her, but she wasn't in a position to forget her old one. The fence at the bottom of her garden was the one surrounding the Trident base. Al Drinkwine was another casualty of conscience who used to work at the base, and whose family suffered as well:

The day the first Trident submarine came in, I knew I could no longer work for the Department of Defence. I heard comment so often on the base, that what we need now is a good war to stimulate the economy and I just couldn't go along with that type of philosophy – you know, it's a first strike force that seems to be being built in this country right now.

The kids miss vacations the most – we used to go on vacation every other year. And allowances and that sort of thing, and we sold a lot of our household stuff. It's just been a real bind telling the kids we can't buy clothes now, or we can't go to the movies and things of that nature – things we took for granted before.

Bill Wall, a well-paid military doctor also chose to leave the services.

I just became more and more astounded by the development of this gargantuan concept of limited nuclear war. I just had to take responsibility for doing something about turning the thing around, and the first person that I had to turn around was myself.

We met Bill at a house called Ground Zero – a meeting place for a number of Christians who live near the Trident submarine base. Their main aim is to draw public attention to the sinister presence of nuclear arms in their backyard.

The tactics of 'Ground Zero'

The opposition of the Ground Zero group to the Trident programme first hit the national headlines in 1981. Jim Douglas, who became the inspiration for the group, realised that the great white train that went past his house twice a year into the Bangor base was in fact laden with nuclear warheads. The navy had been secretly transporting as many as fifty nuclear warheads at a time from the Pantex plant in Texas by a roundabout route to the Seattle base. The ghostly train had passed thousands of homes on each journey with its harvest of death, and nobody had known. Peaceful protest in as many places as possible along the tracks of the train became the object of the Ground Zero group. Their protests, and the efforts to defeat them by the railroad company who varied the route and even altered the speed of the train, became a kind of bitter game between the supporters of Ground Zero throughout the country and the nuclear arms industry, which earned the anti-nuclear cause valuable publicity.

The military culture

Some of the deepest misgivings about the military culture have been expressed by military men themselves. President Eisenhower worried about what the cold war was doing to America in 1961 when he said, 'this conjunction of an immense military establishment and a large arms industry is new in the American experience'. George Washington spoke more strongly in 1796 of 'Overgrown military establishments, which under any form of government are inauspicious to liberty … are to be regarded as particularly hostile to republican liberty'.

Since World War II the military has unfortunately become a powerful and seemingly permanent feature of American life. Patriotism has taken on a military connotation. American success or failure is military success or failure. To be critical of the military role in Vietnam or the Gulf War was, and is, unpatriotic. The victorious general Colin Powell was hailed by many as a probable future president if he could be persuaded to run. He has declined for personal reasons, at least this time. To oppose the military mentality in the US is clearly countercultural. But it is one of the most serious demands on the Christian community at this awesome moment in history when men have the power to wipe out most living things on this planet.

The cost of militarism to poorer countries

In the Third World, there are six times as many soldiers as there are physicians.

The average expenditure for maintenance of one soldier is 25 times higher than expenditure on the education of one child. In 1992 the developed countries exported $18 billion worth of arms to poorer countries. Most of these arms had to be paid for – eventually by the poor themselves. In 1992, despite the end of the cold war, global military expenditure exceeded $600 billion.

The United States – armourers of the world

The US hold top position in general arms sales – more than half the global value in 1992. Between 1989 and 93, the US sold $116 billion worth of arms to 160 nations – including 39 in Africa and 38 in Latin America. The US spends twenty times more on military research than research to protect and improve the environment.

The cost of militarism for the US taxpayer

The US Defence Department, with a budget of $291 billion, spends almost $1 billion each working day of the year. In 1997, there will still be 1.4 million Americans on active duty. In the next five years the US will spend $1.3 trillion for military objectives it does not need and cannot afford. (A US trillion is a million million.)

Military spending has made the US the world's biggest debtor nation. As a result, more of each tax dollar goes on paying the interest on the national debt than goes to all housing, education, social welfare food, employment, transportation, energy and environmental programmes combined. Is it any wonder that the US government services came virtually to a halt for several weeks in 1995?

In 1991, 36 million Americans were classified as poor. While the military budget increased by 50% in the 1980s, the federal programmes directed towards reducing poverty were cut by 54%. The US, which ranks first among the nations of the world in overall wealth, ranks only 21st in infant mortality rates and only 22nd in the number of physicians per head of population.

Wastage

On 16 May 1995, a Senate Committee was told that the Department of Defence were unable to account for $28 billion, spent or lost during the previous ten years. Just suppose that it had been a welfare programme which lost such a sum! That same day down the hall, another Senate committee was considering a $60 billion contract to build thirty attack submarines. Who does America plan to attack in the late nineteen nineties?

The cost to others of US militarism

57,900 American troops were killed in Vietnam, which is in it's own way a horrifying figure when one considers how little they accomplished by their deaths. But American casualties fade into insignificance as compared to the cost to the Vietnamese, Cambodian and Laotian peoples. 2,200,000 of their people died in the war, and 3,200,000 were wounded. In all 6,600,000 tons of bombs were dropped – twice as much as the Allies dropped in the whole of the Second World War. 19,200,000 gallons of Agent Orange and other poisonous herbicides were sprayed from the air.

The landmine problem

Landmines kill or mutilate 2,000 people every month, mostly innocent civilians, and many of them children. It is estimated that there are about 100 million mines in place in the world and another 100 million stockpiled for possible future use, although no one really knows for sure. A land mine, which costs $5 or less, can blind a person or blow a leg off, but to clear it once it is laid may cost anything between $300 and $1,000. For every thousand mines cleared, there is, on average, one accident. And the problem gets worse.

According to a recent report by the UN Secretary General, twenty mines are still being laid for every one lifted. Only 100,000 mines were cleared last year by UN agencies whereas they estimate that another two million were laid. It would cost an estimated $33 billion to clear the mines already buried around the world. Statistics, statistics, but ones which hide an awful human reality of suffering and pain. And just one more to bring us back to nuclear arms: after all the commitments for reduction have been met, the world's nuclear stockpiles will still hold more than 900 times the explosive power expended in World War Two. Can no one shout 'Stop'?

Ending the scourge of war

Taking into account the history of the human race to date, it seems utopian to hope for the banishment of war. Yet it was 'to save succeeding generations from the scourge of war' that the UN was founded. And, as Barbara Ward pointed out in 1972, we have to a certain extent banished killing as a means of deciding conflict *within* civilised states (with some well known recent exceptions).

> Disarmament, far from being unusual and impossible, is the normal state of civilised man inside his own community. All the procedures proposed for disarmament – elimination of private control over arms, subsidisation of police forces, courts of law, mediation, arbitration, and all other methods of settling disputes peacefully – are in fact practised every day inside domestic society.

The trouble is that we do not connect this now perfectly normal method of human behaviour with any unit larger than the nation state.

The need and the will to re-deploy labour in the armaments industry

When Jerry Brown became governor of California many years ago, he thought he could render down the armaments industry. But it didn't happen that way. Too many voters were working in the industry.

Any interference with the business of America's merchants of death must be painful. Lockheed, Boeing, General Dynamics and similar powerful corporations are among the nation's top arms manufacturers, and employ slightly more than three million people, most of whom have wives or husbands and families to feed. Apart from the children, they all have votes. There are enormous pressures for America's arms merchants to develop new markets abroad, now that the end of the cold war is cutting into the home market. Permission to sell abroad can be denied by the federal government, but political factors, if the past is anything to go by, will inevitably lead to the granting of the required permissions.

Bombs in the backyard was about people in Seattle who thought about the arms issue, were prepared to put their jobs on the line when the chips were down, and who suffered for it. One of these was a bishop. But since there were a number of very different issues special to his case, we made his story into a separate programme called *The Auschwitz of Puget Sound* – which is the title of the next chapter.

7

THE AUSCHWITZ OF PUGET SOUND

The humiliation of a US bishop by the Vatican,
and the backlash that led to his reinstatement

In 1981 Raymond Hunthausen, Archbishop of Seattle, Washington, spoke about the arms race to students of Gonzaga University, in Spokane:

> I live in the area of Puget Sound where what may be the most destructive weapon in history – the Trident submarine and missile system – is about to be deployed. That will not happen in silence.

> For seven years now, a non-violent campaign has been going on in resistance to Trident. I have joined in that campaign because I cannot stand aside from it and claim to be proclaiming any good news. The good news of Jesus today is that, through a way of non-violence, nuclear war can be stopped. Trident can be stopped. All nuclear weapons can be stopped. The good news of Jesus is that we can choose a world of peace and justice – the kingdom of God: and that God will give us the power to live out that kingdom now. The kingdom of God is at hand.

> Last summer in a public talk, I identified Trident as 'the Auschwitz of Puget Sound'. I believe God calls us to name the evil our society has embraced so wholeheartedly in our nuclear arms, and to do so clearly. Trident is the Auschwitz of Puget Sound because of the massive co-operation required in our area. The enormous immoral complicity that is necessary for the eventual incineration of millions of our brother and sister human beings. I say with deep sorrow that our nuclear war preparations are the global crucifixion of Jesus. What we do to the least of these through our nuclear weapons planning, we do to Jesus. That is his teaching. We cannot avoid it, and we should not try. Our nuclear weapons are the final crucifixion of Jesus, in the extermination of the human family with whom he is one.

> My dear people of God, as all of you know, I have spoken out against the participation of our country in the nuclear arms race

because I feel that such participation leads to incalculable harm. Not only does it take us along the path toward nuclear destruction, but it also diverts immense resources from helping the needy. As Vatican II put it, the arms race is one of the greatest curses on the human race and the harm it inflicts on the poor is more than can be endured. I believe that, as Christians imbued with the spirit of peacemaking expressed by the Lord in the sermon on the Mount, we must find ways to make known our objections to the present concentration on further nuclear arms build-up. Accordingly I have decided to withhold 50% of my income taxes as a means of protesting our nation's continuing involvement in the race for nuclear arms supremacy.

We were not present to film this address by the archbishop, which was delivered some years before. However we used part of a tele-recording of it to open the programme. I found myself moved by his presentation, which was obviously the result of much prayer and reflection by a deeply spiritual man. Hunthausen continued, quoting Jesus in the gospel:

'Happy are you when people hate you, drive you out, abuse you, denounce your name as criminal on account of the Son of Man … This was the way their ancestors treated the prophets.'

I do not have the feeling that Jesus was describing me when he addressed these words to the crowds standing before him. I'm not poor and hungry. I'm not weeping because of my condition. I've not been driven out. I'm not abused. I've not been persecuted for the faith which I profess. I'm not treated with contempt, hatred and suspicion as were the prophets of old.

Raymond Hunthausen was soon to find that the prophets of today get treated just like the prophets of old. While many of his flock felt that their archbishop's courageous Christian approach to problems of war and violence was something one might expect his church to honour, that was not to be. Two years after his Auschwitz speech, the Vatican sent in an inquisitor to investigate his running of the diocese. Two years later the Pope imposed an auxiliary bishop on Hunthausen with power to overrule him in certain sensitive areas.

The Hunthausen story is certainly one of the more dramatic church stories of the 1980s. And it all happened to an unlikely person, and in an unlikely place.

The man

Raymond Hunthausen, known to his friends as 'Dutch', was born in Anaconda, a mining town in Montana where his father ran a grocery store. Anaconda of course was built from scratch by an Irish emigrant miner and millionaire, Marcus Daly. Raymond became Bishop of Helena, a quiet trouble-free diocese in Montana, in 1962. Things went smoothly during his thirteen years in Helena – Hunthausen's pastoral rounds included morale boosting visits to US army installations, which is ironic in retrospect. When he came to Seattle in 1975, he chose as his motto 'Justice and Peace' – perhaps a dangerous motto for an archbishop of a diocese where so many people are employed by either the armed forces or the arms industry.

His diocese

Seattle is in the Pacific North West, an area which has the lowest religious membership and church attendance rate in the US. But among the Catholic population in the Seattle archdiocese in the mid-1980s, two thirds of the faithful attended Mass, as opposed to half on average elsewhere. Infant baptisms were double, and adult conversions treble the national average. Vocations were steady where elsewhere they were in decline, and money was pouring in for pious causes. Large diameter buttons were for sale on the streets with the legend 'I love Hunthausen'. A happy diocese – the Pope must be pleased, you might well say.

1983: The investigation

But the Pope apparently wasn't pleased, because in 1983 the Vatican announced that it was sending the conservative Archbishop of Washington, James Hickey, to Seattle to investigate criticisms regarding Hunthausen's pastoral ministry. Hunthausen remained in his two-roomed apartment throughout the investigation while 120 people were interviewed by Archbishop Hickey. He was not informed of the charges being made against him, nor was he asked to respond to them. The series of events over the next few years was as follows.

1985: The findings

Two years later Hunthausen hears the result of the investigation from Cardinal Ratzinger who was critical of his administration. He is further informed that a Fr Donald Wuerl will be ordained by the Pope and sent to Seattle as an auxiliary bishop.

1986: The disquiet

Bishop Wuerl overrules Hunthausen in a difference of opinion. Rome confirms in writing that Wuerl has authority to do so. Laity and clergy of Seattle rise up in support of Hunthausen. The Hunthausen controversy dominates the autumn meeting of US bishops in Washington.

1987: The resolution

The Vatican appoints a new commission of three US bishops. Bishop Wuerl is transferred to Philadelphia and Bishop Thomas Murphy, a friend of Hunthausen, appointed coadjutor bishop. Full authority is restored to Hunthausen.

Why this public humiliation of a bishop ?

1. Rome was anxious to make an example of an American bishop.

'The Catholic Church in the United States would appear to have been singled out by Rome for correction. The evidence seems inescapable.' Such was the opinion of the leader writer in the *Tablet*, 27 September 1986. '… almost every week has brought news of fresh action against this church: imprimaturs withdrawn from books and catechisms, priests and theologians disciplined, religious called to account, bishops investigated … But the American Catholic church has huge intellectual vitality and impressive pastoral outreach, and it can handle innovation, change and dissent. Here Pope John Paul II's pontificate, a pontificate without nuance, is bound to create difficulties.'

2. Right wing opposition to Hunthausen provided the opportunity.

In 1983 the hierarchy issued a pastoral letter called 'The Challenge of Peace'. One much respected scholar and diplomat, George F. Kennan, called the pastoral 'the most profound and searching enquiry yet conducted by any responsible collective body into the relations of nuclear weaponry and indeed of modern war in general to moral philosophy, to politics and to the conscience of the national state'. Hunthausen, as the bishop who had been most outspoken on the subject matter of the pastoral, became a particular target for its enemies. One powerful enemy was the armaments industry. Another was Ronald Reagan. Reagan's Catholic supporters hurriedly formed committees of prominent right wing writers, politicians and church people to debunk the pastoral, and undermine the credibility of the bishops believed to be primarily responsible – one of whom was Hunthausen.

3. The Vatican was co-operating with the Reagan administration on Poland.

Pope John Paul II and Ronald Reagan met in June 1982. According to the account in *Time* magazine of 24 February 1992, the Secretary of State, Al Haig, and the National Security Adviser William Clark met with Cardinal Casaroli and Archbishop Silvestrini to tie up the details of 'one of the greatest secret alliances of all time' – nothing less than 'a clandestine campaign to hasten the dissolution of the communist empire' which would begin in Poland. There is much evidence that the Pope and Reagan – two men who had a common experience in surviving attempted assassination – got on well together, and this relationship continued throughout the Reagan administration, and developed down the line. William Clark tells of dropping in on the Vatican nuncio, Archbishop Pio Laghi, in Washington for breakfast. 'I'd speak to him frequently on the phone and he would be in touch with the Pope.' The Nuncio, according to *Time*, developed a close relationship with William Casey, the Director of the CIA. Pio Laghi is reported as saying 'Occasionally we might talk about Central America or the church position on birth control'. While according to one cardinal who was present at a meeting to prepare for the 1985 synod, Pope John Paul opened the discussion by telling Cardinal Bernardin of Chicago that he did not understand why the US bishops did not 'support your own President's policies in Central America'. Now the Reagan administration was anxious about opposition among the American bishops to government policies on armament as well as on Central America. So add all that together!

Why did the Vatican pull back?

In the end the Vatican had to retreat publicly on a disciplinary decision with regard to Hunthausen – which it rarely ever does. It did so, I suggest, for the following reasons:

1. The American bishops as a body were concerned for their own position as well as for Seattle.

What Rome did to Hunthausen it could as easy do to others. As individuals the bishops were weak, but as a body – all three hundred and fifty of them – they were formidable. Rome was left in no doubt about the strong feelings within the Conference, and reminded that their dioceses contribute a quite disproportionate part of the annual collection for Peter's Pence.

2. Despite facing surgery for cancer, Hunthausen impressed the other bishops with his defence of his actions and policies at the US Bishops' Conference in 1986.

Hunthausen told the bishops that he had never been allowed to see the formal visitation report, or the testimony against him, or the appraisal made by Archbishop Hickey. All the witnesses had been placed under secrecy, not just guaranteed confidentiality. And he continued:

> such unwitnessed private questionings with no opportunity for the subject of the questionings to face his accusers, to hear or to be informed of their allegations, or to defend himself, are not a *just* manner of proceeding. This kind of an approach seriously wounds the community of faith and trust that is the church. The action taken as a result of the visitation could hardly be interpreted as anything other than punitive.

Among such judgements for which he had not only been called to task but deprived of his episcopal responsibilities, were the allowing of general absolution under certain conditions, preparing children for first communion before undertaking the formal, structured catechesis for first confession, ministering to homosexuals, and the employment in teaching positions and for service in the liturgy of priests who had left the active ministry and/or had been laicised.

The archbishop replied to all these charges, including the one which had aroused most ire among his conservative critics – the question of ministry to homosexuals.

> Although church teaching is abundantly clear on the matter of the specific immorality of homosexual acts, and I have always made it plain that I stand in full accord with that teaching, church *practice* with regard to the best ways to minister to these members of our community is nowhere near as clear, and, I suppose, it never will be.

Pastoral discretion is required in what are often 'no-win choices'. With regard to his decision in 1983 to allow the members of 'Dignity' – a homosexual group – to have a Mass in his cathedral church, he claimed it did not 'differ *in kind* from the decision made by many bishops to allow local Dignity groups to celebrate Mass in one or another church on a regular basis'.

3. Theologians, who would of course include some bishops, were concerned at the theological implications of this interference in a diocese.

In his submission to his fellow bishops, Hunthausen said:

> It is my hope that you will see the apostolic visitation of the church of Seattle as an ecclesial matter with serious theological implications which touch very directly and profoundly on our individual role as bishops and on our corporate responsibilities as members of the College of Bishops ... how does a diocesan bishop, who is himself the vicar of Christ in his particular church, carry out his role with the degree of independence which this role implies while at the same time doing so in full union with and under the rightful authority of the supreme pontiff?

Because the Pope appoints bishops, many assume that the bishop's authority also comes from the Pope. They understand the bishop's role much as a manager working under a chief executive with authority to hire and fire. That however is not the Catholic understanding of the office of bishop. Once bishops are duly appointed to a diocese, their authority comes from the fact that they are considered successors to the apostles. The Pope may appoint them, or the clergy of a diocese elect them, but their authority is from God. As the Second Vatican Council declared of bishops:

> The pastoral charge ... is entrusted to them fully, nor are they to be regarded as vicars of the Roman Pontiff; for they exercise the power which they possess in their own right, and are called in the truest sense of the term prelates of the people whom they govern.

For Rome to appoint a second bishop to Seattle with power to overrule the first didn't fit very well, to say the least, with official church teaching.

4. The clergy and laity of Seattle gave massive support to Hunthausen.

The strong feeling in the diocese was summed up in an open letter signed by 83% of the clergy. The following is an abbreviated version:

> We deplore the confusion and division that have arisen in our church because of the apostolic visitation which was undertaken here in 1983 and because of certain actions that have been employed here in its aftermath. To serious confusion and division, these actions have added the even weightier burden of grave scandal that may well take more than a generation to overcome or offset.

With our archbishop, we do not hold ourselves or our ministry above evaluation. In fact, we would welcome a fair and careful evaluation. In the case at hand, however, we believe that our archbishop has been evaluated improperly, inadequately, and unjustly, according to procedures which have been called into question by the professional association of canon lawyers of this country...

5. The Pope was due to visit the US in the Autumn of 1987.

Papal visits are world media events, and the possibility of the Pope being embarrassed by public protest in the US about the treatment of Hunthausen was very real unless some satisfactory resolution was found in time.

A note on conservative targeting of the Vatican

One of the weaknesses of the Vatican's system of government is that it governs, and has always governed, in the main in response to written information. Vatican congregations are bodies designed to process letters and submissions, and make reports and recommendations on which higher committees meet to make decisions. The files of the Vatican, which go back so many centuries, are primarily files of letters. And since people tend to write more often to complain rather than praise, there is an ever-present danger that decisions tend to be over-influenced by negative information. So when groups organise to influence the Vatican and frighten it by telling it its authority is being flouted, their effect can be more significant than their numbers or credibility would justify. One such group, calling itself 'Catholics United against Marxist Theology', ran newspaper advertisements urging Catholics to protest against Hunthausen by reducing church donations. The group's spokesman, an employee of Boeing, one of America's largest arms manufacturers, is reported in a Seattle newspaper as saying that the aim of his organisation was to create a national network of opposition to Hunthausen that would send complaints to the Vatican.

Another group is associated with an American Catholic magazine called *The Wanderer*, which, according to reports, airmails two dozen copies weekly to the Vatican. In one year alone, *The Wanderer* published fifteen articles critical of Hunthausen. On 10 March 1988, for instance, the lead editorial as quoted in the *National Catholic Reporter* suggests that its readers write to the Vatican about their dioceses. The Holy See, the editor said, appreciates this information. He quoted a statement by Cardinal Joseph Ratzinger which recently appeared in the New York diocesan newspaper to the effect that personal letters 'provide us with a reflection of typical Catholics ... who are preoccupied with the thought that the Catholic church should remain the Catholic church'.

The editor also recalled that a similar call to *The Wanderer* readers two years ago sparked over 10,000 letters and postcards mailed to Rome in support of its decision to censure US Catholic theologian Father Charles Curran. (I wonder who in the Vatican counted the letters and reported back!)

This time the editor of *The Wanderer* suggested a wide range of subjects to write to Rome about:

> Is the celebration of Mass and the sacraments in your parish done with reverence and in accordance with the liturgical laws of the church? That is worthy of mention. Conversely, are there abuses in the celebration of the liturgy? Certainly, these could be enumerated in detail. What about homilies? Do they reflect sound orthodox teaching, or the personal, social and political views of the priest? Is the religious education in your parish solidly orthodox or does it reflect modernist and heterodox opinion?

> If you are familiar with the operations of one or more diocesan offices – the tribunal, education department, pastoral office, newspaper – or have specific knowledge of a particular situation, such information might be quite useful to the Holy See. And what about the public statements and policies of your bishop? What impact do they have on Catholics?

And once the information is assembled, what next? The editor tells his readers to name names, be specific, detail aberrations, send in supporting evidence and testimonies. Then type, or have typed, the file and send it to: Most Rev Giovanni Battista Re, Congregation for Bishops, 10 Piazza Pio XII, Rome, Italy.

Some general reflections on saying 'no' to Rome

Two weeks before he died in August 1994, Bishop Michael Harty told a friend of mine that he and another bishop had recently agreed on what was one of the core problems in the Irish Catholic church: The bishops hadn't said 'No' to Rome early enough and firmly enough.

It seems to be a very difficult thing to do. Several cases come to mind since the Vatican Council, where substantial people tried to stand up to Rome and, for whatever reason, caved in. When the Vatican appointed Adrian Simonis as bishop of Rotterdam in 1970, the then leader of the Dutch Church, Cardinal Alfrink, stood out against the appointment because Simonis had been a prominent leader of the right wing opposition in the Dutch pastoral Council who resolutely opposed every move towards a more open church. The cardinal had tremendous support from the Dutch laity and priesthood, but under sustained pressure from the Vatican he gave in and accepted Simonis. From then on the Curia had free reign, and took advantage of it to appoint a string of conservative bishops – most of whom have since been in trouble or had to resign for one reason or another before their time.

Archbishop Quinn of San Francisco tried to make a stand on *Humanae Vitae* at the Synod on the family in 1980, but in the end he beat a hasty retreat. Robert Blair Kaiser, in his authoritative history of the contraception crisis *The Politics of Sex and Religion*, describes the occasion. At the beginning of the Synod, Archbishop Quinn made an intervention on behalf of the US bishops that might have won him accolades at Vatican II. He called for 'a completely honest examination of the serious problems which fidelity to the teaching of the church creates for individuals, for pastors and for the world'. Within twenty-four hours, according to Kaiser he was stuttering an apology and insisting he hadn't 'challenged' the Pope over *Humanae Vitae*.

The importance of being a bishop

If journalists – clerical or lay – criticise the Pope or the Vatican Curia, they might get a disapproving letter from their bishop, but the Vatican is not going to take action against such small fry.

If theologians don't toe the line they can and will be removed from their teaching positions. If they make public declarations criticising the Vatican, such as the Cologne Declaration with 163 signatures – only one of many such public protests by theologians – the Vatican notes the signatories to make sure they never get bishoprics, and sails on as if nothing happened. Theologians may be ignored – they have no mandate to teach except in so far as their superiors permit them.

But when a bishop doesn't toe the line, that is quite a different matter. Why? Because in the church's understanding of herself the 'magisterium' or teaching office is something which is passed down from the apostles to their successors. Candidates for bishoprics may in the current practice be appointed by the Pope. But their authority, their mandate to teach doesn't come from the Pope but directly from God (Canon 375 #1). All bishops – not just the Pope – are 'vicars of Christ'.

Provincial captains and Roman generals

It is clear that the Vatican Curia often treats bishops as if they held their authority by Rome's grace and favour, but it's bad theology. And many of the Curia's actions in dismissing or demoting bishops have been theologically very questionable at least, and most probably indefensible.

So the Vatican insists more and more on absolute control over the appointment of bishops, because the best way to prevent independent bishops is to screen them out beforehand. That is also why the Vatican surrounds bishops with oaths of loyalty and fealty and whatever – to make it difficult for them to demur in public. And why any questioning bishop is attended to immediately at the highest level.

The cashiering of Bishop Gaillot

The most recent public cashiering of a bishop was that of Jacques Gaillot, Bishop of Evreux, in France, whom the Pope dismissed from his diocese in January 1995. We interviewed him in Haiti in 1991, and again in Paris in 1994, and found him an unassuming, honest, intelligent man. I have not heard or read of anything he has ever done which cannot be reconciled with the example and teaching of Christ. Fifteen to twenty thousand of his admirers are said to have attended his farewell Mass in the diocese – most of whom had to stand in the rain. Tens of thousands sent messages of support. The Archbishop of Cambrai said his dismissal was a source of misunderstanding for the poor and all those who put their trust in the church. The Archbishop of Toulouse said Rome's action threatened to create divisions and misunderstanding in the church. The Archbishop of Rouen, President of the French Bishops' Conference, said he had pleaded with Rome to have patience, but to no avail.

It may be difficult for the French hierarchy to oppose Rome on this matter because Cardinal Lustiger, Archbishop of Paris, is one of Gaillot's severest critics and a close friend of the Pope John Paul – who personally signed the dismissal order. But if the French bishops allow the dismissal to stand, they will be contributing to the erosion of the office of bishop and to undermining the traditional theological understanding of how authority is exercised in the church. Many of them must understand that.

The American experience

The American hierarchy seem to be particularly feared by Rome for their democratic tendencies, and as a result have been treated with a heavy hand in recent years. Apart from the Hunthausen affair, they have often had to take insulting behaviour on the chin and say nothing. Nothing public, that is, until June of this year when 12 bishops drew up a 5,000 word document of protest (which another 30 bishops endorsed) outlining many of their frustrations with Rome.

The fact that some 40 bishops should support this remarkable document seems to me extremely significant. It is the first time since Vatican II that any group of bishops has voiced substantial criticisms, however politely, of the growing centralism and dictatorial attitudes of the Roman Curia. About one third of the document deals with relationship with the universal church. It gives several examples of growing interference from Rome. (The headings in the following extracts are mine, the text from the document.)

Concern about curial interference in the preparation of documents by the US Bishops' Conference.

One senses a growing feeling that as a conference we aren't accomplishing what we need to accomplish. We somehow miss the opportunity to have open exchanges that reflect the thoughts and feelings one hears privately among the bishops themselves. Why do major and pressing concerns seem so often to go unaddressed?

When formulating documents in the past we did not submit them to Rome until we had fully discussed them, completed them, and voted. Now they are frequently submitted beforehand by the committee chairperson, and upon receiving the results, there is no dialogue. The response from Rome is treated as a directive. The document on *The Teaching Ministry of the Diocesan Bishop* was sent to Rome for approval before it was even presented to the conference!

The letter that Cardinal Ratzinger wrote to the committee drafting the pastoral on women's concerns significantly influenced the outcome of that document. This, however, was without the knowledge and participation from the rest of the conference who had never and still haven't seen the letter.

The bishops feel ignored on vital issues of a patoral nature

On vital issues of a pastoral nature, the bishops sometimes feel ignored. A recent example was the English translation of the *The Catechism of the Catholic Church*. This was taken completely out of our hands and the hands of other English-speaking conferences. The English draft that we saw earlier appears to have been 'intercepted' by a small group who succeeded in reintroducing sexist language, at considerable delay, all this without consultation with us. We patiently waited, almost like children. This is cause for some wonder and suggests the need to develop a more mature, adult, collegial relationship with Rome.

The *Directory of Priests* was sent out by the Congregation of the Clergy without input from conferences of bishops. If there is any matter on which the local bishops should be consulted, surely it is this one. The *Ex Corde* document on relations with institutions of higher education came from Rome, without consulting conferences.

Likewise, the recent apostolic letter, *Ordinatio Sacerdotalis*, was issued without any prior discussion and consultation with our conference. In an environment of serious questions about a teaching that many Catholic people believe needs further study, the bishops are faced with many pastoral problems in their response to the letter. The questions now being raised by women, theologians, ecumenists and many of the faithful as a result of this new apostolic letter present an immense pastoral problem that might have been prevented had there been more regular and open communication from us to Rome.

Concern about Roman documents trying to reinterpret Vatican II

There is a widespread feeling that Roman documents of varying authority have for some years been systematically reinterpreting the Vatican II documents to present the minority positions at the Council as the true meaning of the Council. The above-mentioned 'Letter to the Bishops on the Meaning of *Communio*' would be a specific example. It interpreted *communio* on the vertical level, emphasizing the bonds between individual bishops and the Pope, and de-emphasizing the collegiality of national conferences. This is a very particular interpretation or reinterpretation of *Lumen Gentium* (and other council documents as well) into a vertical ecclesiology.

Concern about Synod procedures

Finally, Synods are one of the most ancient exercises of collegiality, and one of the important ways we relate to the Bishop of Rome and the whole college of bishops. One hears concerns about the procedures relative to Synods. There is a rule of secrecy imposed on the conferences and on the publication of individual interventions. For example, response to *lineamenta* [preparatory documents] by national hierarchies cannot be shared with one another. We don't know what other English-speaking conferences wrote in preparation for the last Synod, much less other conferences. There is also some concern about the procedure by which delegates are selected. All this, it would seem, is appropriate material for a discussion at the conference level.

Concern about the appointment of bishops

There are many different styles of good leadership, but one thing is certain: A bishop is called to be a leader ... It is undoubtedly a caricature, but there is a feeling afoot that among the criteria for selecting bishops, leadership qualities are considerably overshadowed by a concern for characteristics that would identify a candidate as 'safe'. Yet, a leader is precisely a person who will take risks and be creative and who is not afraid now and then to make a mistake ... The church is in a competitive arena to capture the minds and imaginations of people in building the future. Bishops, individually and as a conference, have a particular call to be transformative leaders, articulating a vision of the kingdom that attracts people, that deepens their relationship with God and encourages them to make real their love for God and others by their lives and ministries of service.

Conclusion

In the way things are presently ordered in the church, the only members who can do anything directly to ameliorate or change this ethos of authoritarianism are bishops, singly, or preferably in groups. The rest of us can only give them encouragement and support – and remind them once again of the passage in the Epistle to the Galatians: 'When Peter came to Antioch I opposed him to his face, since he was manifestly in the wrong'. That is the way it has to be, Paul and Peter, bishop to bishop.

8
CHURCH AND STATE IN NICARAGUA
How a dream of the liberal church never came to be

When we arrived at the tiny village of Las Colinas, the smell of smoke was still in the air. Five houses scattered around a gentle hillside were burnt to the ground, another scorched, a dispensary and shop looted and burned. The little schoolhouse was wrecked – the desks and schoolbooks strewn around after an unsuccessful attempt to start a bonfire. Most of the people wandered around looking stunned. The frame of a bed and a half-burnt chair stood out in the middle of a floor without walls. A woman told us what happened.

> The Contras came from over there while we were still in our beds. It happened at six o'clock yesterday morning. They were firing wildly – the first house to be attacked was that of Jesus Mendoza. Three years ago they killed my husband and just seven months ago they took one of my sons and killed him. This time no one was killed because, thank God, the army came and gave them the run.

Another man spoke on behalf of himself and his wife:

> We were still in bed when they came into the house. I tried to escape but what they wanted was to set fire to the house with us inside it. This isn't the first time it happened to us – we were living over the other side of the valley when they attacked us the last time. We were left barefoot, almost naked, just like the day we were born. We plead with Ronald Reagan to stop this bloodbath. We've had enough bloodshed. What we want is peace.

We visited a hospital where injured children were being treated. Paul Laverty, a young lawyer from Scotland working on human rights issues, brought us around. He told us about two poor unfortunate children whom we filmed – not a pleasant thing to do in the circumstances, but it seemed necessary if we were to suggest the human tragedies involved.

> Jaime is seven years of age, and just a couple of days ago he was injured by a Contra land mine. You can see that he is actually pep-

pered with shrapnel. In fact he was very lucky to survive. His three brothers were also badly injured. One broke both his legs, another lost four fingers on each hand.

Jorge here was injured by shrapnel from a bomb which actually entered his abdomen and broke one of his arms – he also has shrapnel in the other arm. In the same incident his sixteen-year-old brother was kidnapped and his ten-year-old brother killed. The US government has consistently hidden the fact that many of the Contra targets are actually civilians.

Who are the Contras?

The Contras were a fighting force of approximately twenty-five thousand men who opposed the Sandinista government in Nicaragua, and who had been trained and funded by the Untied States. The war they initiated led to 14,000 deaths before it finished, and left the Nicaraguan people with debts of eleven billion dollars.

How the US got involved

The US first got involved in Nicaragua in the nineteenth century when the shortest route to California included a land crossing of Nicaragua – this was of course before the transcontinental railroads and the Panama Canal. The United States later occupied Nicaragua for nineteen years of this century. They even organised 'elections' way back in 1912, which US Marine Major Smedley Butler – the Oliver North of his day – described in a letter to his wife: 'Nicaragua has enjoyed a fine free election with only one candidate being allowed to run … to the entire satisfaction of our US State Department; the Marines patrolled all the towns to prevent disorder'.

Before they left, the US marines trained a national guard whose leader later became President of Nicaragua, General Anastasio Somoza. The Somoza family, father and son, and the National Guard, basically ruled Nicaragua for over forty years – backed by the US who saw them as a bulwark against the spread of communism in Central America. The Somozas fed like vultures on the Nicaraguan people. When a disastrous earthquake destroyed the capital Managua a quarter century ago, killing twelve thousand people, the Somozas are said to have pocketed most of the international aid collected to help the victims. But then the elder Somoza once said 'Nicaragua es mi finca' – Nicaragua is my personal estate. Another story told of Somoza relates how President Franklin D Roosevelt noticed his name on a list of heads of state to be invited to Washington and said 'Isn't that man supposed to be a son of a bitch?'

'He sure is,' replied his Secretary of State, Cordell Hull, 'but he is *our* son of a bitch!'

It took a revolution, with 40,000 people killed and 100,000 injured, to dislodge the Somozas. All this in a country with a slightly smaller population than the Republic of Ireland. Ex-President Somoza left for Miami with his family, the contents of the Nicaraguan banks, and several shiploads of possessions. A revolutionary Sandinista government took over Nicaragua.

Why the US Government became hostile to the Sandinistas

The record seems to show that any government anxious to promote reforms which threaten US commercial interests in Central and South America is labelled subversive by the power brokers in the United States.

Thomas Monaghan, the conservative Irish American Pizza King who supported the Contras, and since gave $3 million to Cardinal Obando y Bravo to build a new cathedral in Managua, said in interview with the *Conservative Digest* that failure to support the Contras would threaten the US.

> Talk about dominoes if we lose! It's going to be El Salvador, it's going to be Panama, it's going to be Mexico. We could have a Soviet client state along our Southern Border.

President Reagan told the US Congress in 1983:

> The national security of all the Americas is at stake in Central America. If we cannot defend ourselves there, we cannot expect to prevail elsewhere. Our credibility would collapse, our alliances would crumble.

How the US fought the Sandinistas

President Reagan persuaded Congress to provide $300 million aid to the Contra forces. However this was only a part of the aid provided. $400 million was spent in Honduras on bases for their operations. An unknown amount of aid was supplied without the knowledge of the US Congress. According to the final report of the Special Prosecutor in the Iran-Contra investigation, Lawrence Walsh, both President Reagan and Vice President Bush supported the policy of secret aid to the Contras, and were regularly briefed on its implementation, but lied to try and cover up their involvement when the scandal erupted.

The CIA involvement in covert aid also came to light after the

Contra war ended. In 1991, Alan Friers, head of the CIA's Central America taskforce, pleaded guilty to two counts of lying to the US Congress about illegal diversion of funds to the Contras. He had been ordered by the CIA's deputy director to deny any knowledge of the transfer when he originally testified before the House Intelligence Committee.

What was the attitude of the US media?

Generally the US media were subservient to US policy. For instance, the Sandinista government held elections in 1984 where they won 67% of the votes. The White House termed them 'Soviet-style sham elections'. The *New York Times* echoed this view, accusing the Sandinistas of 'refusing to subject their power to the consent of the Nicaraguan people ... only the naïve believe the election was democratic or legitimising proof of the Sandinista's popularity'.

If this was the view from New York, the view from Nicaragua looked different. An Irish parliamentary delegation including Bernard Allen, Michael D. Higgins, Liam Hyland and Shane Ross reported that 'the electoral process was carried out with total integrity. The seven parties participating in the elections represented a broad spectrum of political ideologies.' New York's Human Rights Commission called the elections 'Free, fair and hotly contested'. Some years later, however, the *Washington Post* published parts of a 'secret-sensitive' memo from the National Security Council (Oliver North and Co.) outlining a 'wide-ranging plan to convince the Americans that the Nicaraguan elections were a sham'. US officials are reported to have told the *New York Times* that 'legitimate elections' would have been bad for the Contra cause. So the media obediently lied.

Much importance was also given in the US media to the suppression for a time of the Nicaraguan newspaper *La Prensa* by the Sandinistas. They did not report, according to a US group called FAIR (Fairness and Accuracy in Reporting), that '*La Prensa* editor, Jaime Chamorro, admits receiving $250,000 in essential US government funds,' or that 'the CIA began financing *La Prensa* in 1980'. Or that the editor left to join the Contras!

What was the attitude of the Nicaraguan hierarchy to the Contras?

In public the Nicaraguan hierarchy are represented by the Cardinal Archbishop Obando y Bravo of Managua or his deputy. None of the other Nicaraguan bishops ever seem to speak independently to media. The attitude of the cardinal is perhaps best expressed by the leader of the Contras as reported in the *Irish Times* of 7 July 1990:

> Speaking at the close of the demobilisation process, Commander 'Ruben' of the Contras praised the role of Cardinal Obando y Bravo in supporting his fighters over the previous ten years. 'In our darkest hour,' he said, 'the cardinal was always there, encouraging us to keep up the struggle'. Cardinal Obando blessed the ceremony ...

When compulsory military service was introduced in 1983, in response to the Contra menace, and even though conscientious objection was permitted for seminarists, 'Radio Catolica' called on young people to desert, while the archbishop began referring to the Contras as 'a national military and political force'.

When the archbishop was made a cardinal in 1985, he was fulsomely congratulated by President Reagan. Significantly he said his first Mass as a cardinal on the American continent for Contra leaders in Miami, whereas he refused to meet the President of Nicaragua, Daniel Ortega, at the airport on his arrival back in Managua. At that point, Cardinal Obando launched a campaign against the government, touring villages on the feast days of patron saints, and removing priests 'tainted' by liberation theology.

During the trial of Clair E. George, former chief of CIA's clandestine service, former aide Alan D. Friers said he helped the late CIA Director, William Casey, defy congressional restriction by using corporate connections – by implication W. R. Grace of New York – to funnel payment to the Catholic church in Nicaragua. This Casey operation, according to a *Washington Post* article quoting 'informed sources' was designed to support 'the anti-Marxist activities' of Obando y Bravo in late 1985 and 1986.

During our visit we filmed the cardinal at an ordination ceremony. There were five camera crews present. The 'sermon' was mostly about the release of political prisoners, and afterwards the Cardinal held an impromptu press conference in the sacristy during which we heard him say, 'I will be delighted to contact President Reagan at the end of this week. If I can phone him directly, I'll be delighted to do so. If not, I'll contact him through some cardinals in the US who are friends of mine.'

Fr Miguel D'Escoto, Nicaraguan Foreign Minister :

> Isn't it sad, for example, that when President Reagan made his

final pitch to the nation a few years back when he was asking for a hundred million dollars, to continue killing people in Nicaragua, that a key to his speech were the quotes from one of the Nicaraguan bishops? And he ended that speech that appealed to the people of the United States for more money to continue the war in Nicaragua by saying to the bishop, 'Rev Bishop, your plea will not go unheeded'.

The action of the Archbishop of Managua and his auxiliary in many other countries might well have been treated as high treason.

What was the attitude of the Pope and the Vatican?

When Pope John Paul visited Nicaragua in 1983, he described the Sandinistas as 'wolves in sheep's clothing.' When the crowd at the papal Mass asked him to pray for the sons of the motherland killed in the civil war, he cried, 'Silence, Silence!' and declined to do so. So clearly the Pope was very unsympathetic to their cause. There were several reasons for this. One was undoubtedly the presence of four priests within what the Vatican had decided was a Marxist government. Fr William Boteler, superior general of the Maryknoll Fathers, the religious congregation to which the Nicaraguan foreign minister, Fr Miguel D'Escoto, belongs, said in 1985 that the Vatican authorities who insisted on the minister's suspension from his priestly functions are convinced that Nicaragua has an 'out-and-out Marxist government, with no redeeming values'.

The other main reason was that the Pope and President Reagan became closely involved together in helping to undermine the communist government in Poland, and naturally influenced and became influenced by each other in other areas. *Time* magazine reported that on 17 June 1982, Reagan and Pope John Paul II met at the Vatican library for the first time and agreed to undertake a secret campaign to keep the outlawed Solidarity movement alive and destabilise the Polish government. A far-reaching covert network was established by the church, whereby the Solidarity movement in Poland received supplies, money and advice.

After the *Time* report of the dealings between the Pope and Reagan (24.2.92), William Wilson, the first US Ambassador to the Holy See spoke freely about his own role, in an interview published in the *National Catholic Reporter*. He told how he often spoke with the Pope and Vatican officials over a broad range of affairs, including the Central American issue, 'which involved Nicaragua most of the time I was over there'. He said he had 'to explain to the Vatican what our policy was, what our concerns were and what our goals were in whatever we were doing in Central America'.

The issue of liberation theology, he said, spilled over beyond Nicaragua into other South American countries. Liberation theology he added, was 'more of a political problem than a religious problem, though it's both'. Talking about liberation theology was 'an opportunity for the Vatican to explain to us what they were trying to do to offset the problem'. Ultimately the Vatican 'quieted the priests down who were talking about that,' Wilson said.

The Reagan administration collaborated with the Vatican on other issues as well. In response to concerns of the Vatican, the State Department in 1984 announced a ban on the use of US aid funds for the promotion of birth control or abortion. The US withdrew funding from Intentional Planned Parenthood Federation and the UN Fund for Population activities. Wilson said that the US acquiesced to the Vatican because the US was concerned for Third World countries and 'one way to be effective in those countries was by working in collaboration with the church'.

What was the attitude of the US bishops to the Contra war?

Mixed, as one might expect. According to a report in the *National Catholic Reporter* of 28 February 1992, the Auxiliary Bishop of Detroit, Thomas Gumbleton, who visited Central America several times during the 1980s, said the *Time* article's revelations of papal politicking in Poland angered him. 'Why does the Pope then come down so hard on the people in Nicaragua and priests?' Particularly troubling to Gumbleton was the CIA connection.

> When this thing started in 1982, that was the very time that the US government was mining the harbour in Nicaragua and heating up the whole low-intensity conflict in Nicaragua. For the Pope to work in concert with Reagan and the US government to do something about Poland and by that very fact to condone what at the same time it was doing in Nicaragua, I find very contradictory and very wrong.

Cardinal O'Connor of New York, on the other hand, took the opposite view when he once commented that 'the US bishops should not pit their knowledge against the knowledge possessed by the State Department'.

Archbishop, later Cardinal, Pio Laghi, nuncio to Argentina during the rule of the generals, moved to Washington in time for the election of President Reagan. According to the *N.C.R.* of 11.9.92, 'He did much to align Vatican policies in Central America with those of the US Administration. He supported the Contras against the Sandinistas in Nicaragua. He was rewarded by seeing his office transformed from that of a mere apostolic delegate into a Pro-nuncio.'

What were the feelings of the religious orders, foreign clergy and lay workers with respect to the actions of the hierarchy?

In my experience, foreign clergy, members of religious orders and lay workers were almost uniformly pro-Sandinista. We interviewed Caesar Jerez SJ, Rector of the Jesuit Central American University in Nicaragua:

> The official position of the hierarchical church is affecting very much the practice of the youth. For many will tell you that they are very happy with God, they don't have any problems with the gospel, but really they do have some problems to understand the position of the hierarchical church *vis-à-vis* the Nicaraguan revolution.

> The fear of some Catholics or Christians here in Nicaragua and mainly abroad, that the Sandinistas have already taken over education and are manipulating and indoctrinating students through education, in my opinion is not a rational fear. I am working in a university and I can tell you that we are enjoying freedom to teach whatever we like, and in the way we would like to do it. And my impression is that the same is true with primary and secondary education.

Mrs Kathy McBride Power, a North American, was working with basic Christian communities in Nicaragua.

> The role of Cardinal Obando y Bravo has been a role of abandonment of the people that are committed to this revolution. He has never denounced the war – he wouldn't even accept that there was a war existing in Nicaragua financed by the US government. And there are many priests in Nicaragua under the cardinal that would not bury a young soldier with a Sandinista flag – people that had died for their country.

> I think that in Nicaragua there is a maturity – can we say a theological maturity, because people recognise Cardinal Obando as the cardinal, as the bishop, but they also realise that he does not represent the interest of the poor or the interest of the Nicaraguan people.

Fr Molina was a Franciscan and parish priest of Our Lady of the Angels Church:

> The church is not a monolithic body, in my opinion. It admits and it has always admitted that there are various tendencies within it, in its thought and in its theology. Here in Nicaragua the divisions aren't because of doctrinal or theological reasons. It's not the faith which divides us but it's our position about the revolutionary process the country is living through. We have never wanted to make a different church, but rather it's like a vanguard which is trying to bring the church up to date, to have an 'aggiornamento' or a renewal in the church.

Fr Joe Mulligan, editor of *ENVIO*, a prominent journal of Christian comment on Central American affairs:

> As far as freedom of religion under a Sandinista government – that's recognised in the new Nicaraguan constitution. There is no state religion, and perhaps that upsets some of the church leaders. I think many church leaders in Latin America have gotten accustomed to governments giving some sort of support to the church and to the teachings of the church. But here there is freedom of religion even if there is no official religion. In the new constitution the preamble recognises the role Christians played in the insurrection against Somoza.

The defeat of the Sandinistas

Despite superior numbers, the Sandinistas couldn't match the sophisticated US armaments available to the Contras during the war. At one stage helicopters turned the tide in the government's favour – Contra bands were very much more obvious to spot from the air. Then the Americans supplied the Contras with Redeye ground-to-air heatseeker missiles, and the Sandinistas were forced to admit losing ten helicopters within a short period – the Contras claim to have shot down twenty-six.

Apart from arms, it is now public knowledge that the CIA supplied the Contras with detailed information on troop movements and targets in Nicaragua gleaned from spy satellites. Also with blueprints of dams and bridges built by US agencies which the Contras might like to blow up.

Eventually the Central American countries themselves brokered a peace plan to end the war and lead up to another election in which the Sandinista vote fell to 44% – a respectable vote, but not enough to keep them in power. A new government coalition came to be under Violetta Chamorro, the opposition candidate. This was not an unexpected decision, because people understood that the US would never accept the Sandinistas, and therefore a vote for them was seen as only prolonging the war which was devastating the country.

With the loss of the elections, the Sandinista party split amid accusations of some corruption. The two Cardenal priest brothers, Ernesto and Fernando who were ministers in the government, publicly announced their decision to leave the party, accusing a 'small minority of Sandinistas, including some high-up leaders, of appropriating goods of state for their own advantage' in the interval between losing the election and the hand-over of power in 1990. Fernando however claimed that the Sandinista revolution itself had been the most beautiful period of his life, and that he continues to believe that 'our dream is possible and that one day we will have in Nicaragua a society that is juster, more fraternal, more participatory, and – in a word – more Christian'.

How did the economy fare after the end of the Contra war?

Nicaragua is reported to have the highest per capita foreign debt in the world. The national debt stands at $11 billion with $260 million due in repayments annually. More than one third of that debt ($4 billion) is owed to countries from the former Soviet block. According to Fernando Cardenal, the Sandinistas never thought the Soviet Union was going to charge them for tanks and trucks to fight the Contras, but now they are looking for payment. Moreover to get further loans, the economy has to undergo 'structural adjustment'. In human terms this meant firing 63% of government employees – and they did not have unemployment benefit.

A publication from a group called *Witness for Peace* on structural adjustment in Nicaragua gave some figures of what this means for the population as a whole. In 1984, even though the war was at its height, the Sandinista government spent $42 per capita on education and $58 on health. These figures under structural adjustment declined to $13 and $17 respectively. Hospital beds have been reduced by half. Only 54% of Nicaraguans have safe drinking water, and only 27% have sewage systems.

Meanwhile the US Government has cut back on aid, and the right wing US Congress is trying to impose conditions, such as the reversal of land reform under the Sandinistas, and return of estates to those landowners (now mostly living in the US) who owned them in the time of the Somozas!

How did the official church fare after the Sandinistas were defeated?

President Violetta Chamorro has delegated 'moral guidance' to the cardinal, who chose the top three posts in the Ministry of Education, re-instituted his weekly televised Mass and expressed satisfaction that cabinet meetings now began with the 'Our Father'.

Cardinal Obando y Bravo has directed his energies since the end of the war to building a cathedral on land donated by the government. It is a massive square concrete building topped by small domes. The price now exceeds $4 million, three million of which is reported to have been contributed by Tom Monaghan, the Dominos Pizza magnate, owner of the Detroit Tigers and member of the Knights of Malta. Critics say the cathedral is a symbol of the cardinal's priorities in a war stricken country with 60-70% unemployment and the distinction of being the second poorest country in the Western hemisphere after Haiti.

The Sandinista revolution in retrospect

What accusations did the hierarchy make against the Sandinistas?

During the Contra war, Cardinal Obando Bravo once asked the UN for help and described the 'state of persecution' being suffered by the church in Nicaragua. He accused the Nicaraguan government of the interrogation of priests by security forces, harassment of church institutions, 'harsh censorships', and of forcing Catholics to sign documents containing 'falsehoods and calumnies against the honour of church persons'.

Meanwhile, more than 100 pastoral agencies of the church in Nicaragua issued a statement denying religious persecution in Nicaragua. The statement pointed out the unusual circumstances caused by the economic blockade of Nicaragua and the guerrilla war which was being financed by the United States. The emergency imposed by the government was not to 'punish the people, but to protect their interests'. 'We reject the interpretation that this is to impose a Marxist-Leninist dictatorship'.

There are indeed various possible indices of persecution of the church. Many will remember the six Jesuits and two women shot together in cold blood in El Salvador in 1989 – just one dramatic incident among many in which hundreds of priests and lay workers were kidnapped, tortured and killed in Guatemala, Honduras and El Salvador. The only priest to be killed in Nicaragua under the Sandinista government was blown up by a Contra landmine.

What were the real and perhaps hidden issues involved?

1. With the US

Miguel D'Escoto said to us that when peasants ask him to explain why the US was acting like it was, and why it was so fearful of Nicaragua, he reminds them of the landowners who owned the big estates before the revolution in 1979. They would remember that when they wanted to talk to the landowner about any matter they would have to wait until he visited the estate, because normally he didn't live there. If they were lucky they might get a few minutes of his time. This wouldn't be inside the house, but outside. They would come up to him, take off their cap, go down on one knee and speak in a very humble way, and hope he might graciously answer their request. Then imagine one day if one of these peasants came up with his big dirty boots on, just walked into the house, sat down in a chair and began to talk to the landowner in familiar form (2nd person singular in Spanish). The landlord might be angry, but he would more likely be frightened, because his position would be threatened. The poor *campesino* would be telling him, now I am your equal. That is what the landlord would fear because other peasants who saw this might be tempted to follow his example. And then the whole control structure would crumble. This is what Nicaragua is doing today. Having been under the thumb of the United States, which created and brought down governments at will, Nicaragua began to ask for an equal relationship with the US. Suppose other countries in South America were to do the same? US freedom to do what it willed in Latin America would be compromised. D'Escoto quoted a book published by Oxfam the previous year which said 'the threat of Nicaragua is the threat of good example'. Latin America wants to move on to a relationship of equality with the US because that is necessary to enable them to do things to benefit the majority in their own country. And that makes the US, like the big landowner, afraid.

The United States versus liberation theology

According to a report by Fr Luis Perez Aguirre SJ in *The New Keyhole Series* published by LADOC in Lima, Peru, 30 September 1988, Nelson Rockefeller told President Nixon in an extensive document reporting his tour to Latin America, 'that the United States should support fundamentalist Christian groups or churches like that of Moon or the Hare Krishna as a way of resisting the new liberation theology' and he added 'the Catholic church has ceased to be a confidant of the United States and the guarantee of social stability on the continent'.

Poverty and Power, a publication of Cafod, London, who again are a reputable source of documentation, makes similar allegations.

The notorious Santa Fe document, drawn up in 1980 by right wing academics as a primer for the Reagan administration, identified liberation theology and its supporters as an enemy of US policy. Finally Central America in the 1980s provided plentiful evidence of attempts by the Reagan White House and the right to use evangelical and Pentecostal churches to combat the influence of the socially active wing of the Catholic church.

Cardinal Arns of Sao Paulo expressed corroborative views when we interviewed him in Sao Paulo.

The Pentecostal churches are increasing – certainly. They are growing with the money that comes from North America; they also grow because of the influence which the military regime had in not allowing missionaries from various countries to enter the country but importing ministers from all the cults to favour the growth of the sects against the Catholic church because she (the church) defended democratic government.

What were the real and perhaps hidden issues involved?

2. With the Nicaraguan hierarchy

It's often said that the church in Nicaragua is two churches, the church of the rich and the church of the poor. In a more essential sense, I believe the structure itself is divided another way into two churches, the church of the indigenous secular clergy and the church of the religious and foreign missionaries. I was told in Nicaragua in 1979, shortly after the revolution, that 70% of the clergy in Nicaragua were foreign born, the majority from the United States. The support for the Sandinista revolution, the support for liberation theology and the basic Christian communities came from this group. They were highly motivated people, most of whom would have come from relatively comfortable backgrounds, and did not need to live in a slum in a tropical country without many of the comforts of western living. They came to serve the spiritual and material interests of the poor in the spirit of the gospel of Jesus.

They can have no clerical ambitions, because their nationality pretty well rules them out from ecclesiastical preferment.

The indigenous church, on the other hand, is heir to a Spanish colonial tradition where church and state work in a cosy relationship, the lower clergy serve the needs of the middle classes who pay their stipends, the higher clergy achieve the equivalence and influence of noble status, and the poor cling on to what remains of the initial colonial effort at evangelisation.

I think Obando y Bravo is a man who, like most other men, prefers where possible to be on top of the heap. He took a significant part in legitimising the revolution against Somoza in 1979, but then when priests came into government he had to take a back seat. Priests in government put the whole hierarchical structure in disarray. In the army of the church, priests are privates and bishops are officers. Privates don't tell officers what is best. Then the hierarchical structure in the form of the Pope/Reagan axis put him under pressure in two ways. As a bishop he is tied by oaths of loyalty to the Pope who, with the background of his Polish experience, is sternly opposed to any hint of flirting with Marxism, and who adopted the CIA's view of the Marxist nature of the Sandinista government. Obando had little choice therefore but to oppose it. It must also have been clear to him that support of the Pope/Reagan stance might bring some personal rewards, and so it did. Nicaragua is a small country and the Archbishop of Managua has never before been elevated to the cardinalate. Friendship with President Reagan and wealthy right wing Americans is obviously personally satisfying, and has helped him achieve his ambition to build a new cathedral.

The church of the poor

The collapse of the revolution, and all it's hopes and enthusiasms, the suffering of the war, the economic collapse, and the vast increase in poverty has brought about much disillusionment and shock among missionaries, lay and clerical, working with the poor in Nicaragua. The basic Christian communities have largely disintegrated because the dioceses insisted on licensing catechists and lay leaders, and because of general frustration with the church, and under the pressure of people absorbed in trying to survive.

Christians throughout the world had seen Nicaragua as an exciting example of how the preferential option for the poor could be put into practice with the active sympathy of the government of a third world country. In fact, it developed into a struggle between the United States, the Pope and the hierarchy on one side, and the priests, ministers and grassroots church on the other. And a bitter struggle it was. The Sandinistas were particularly angry that the cardinal refused to condemn even the worst of the Contra atrocities, and there were many. Neither would he condemn US support for them, as he considered the war against the Sandinistas a just war.

It will be interesting to see what historians will have to say about the role of the hierarchy and the papacy in this civil war twenty years hence when the anger has subsided and the major participants retired or passed on. From what I have written, it will be clear why I fear it may appear to be a very inglorious one.

9

THE POPE'S BRIGADE

The temporal power of the Pope is no more,
but some of the trappings remain

An old man in Kerry in 1950 recalled a ballad he heard in his youth.
I quote four verses of it because they may give some flavour of the
enthusiasm generated in Ireland in 1860 by the Pope's Brigade.

Our Irish boys with courage bold they left their friends and home;
Their hearts were free of terror when they were facing Rome;
They placed their trust in Mary, their mother and their hope,
To put down each wicked demon who conspired against the Pope.

At Castlefidardo well they fought upon the battle plain,
Against twenty-five thousand infidels and the Sardinian train,
Till Reilly with his Irish boys he made their foes to dance,
With the Marquis of Pimodan and the gallant sons of France.

At Loreto and Spoleto each Irish heart awoke,
And then Perugia's mossy plain amidst fire, blood and smoke;
Two thousand was the strength of our brave band as you may
     plainly see:
Against thirteen thousand for six hours they fought them man-
     fully.

Shed not one tear for them that's gone for heaven is their home,
They suffered as the martyrs did before in ancient Rome;
They fought the cause of heaven with their Pope and Holy See,
And may they rest forever blessed through all eternity.

Grand Uncle Peter

The first I ever heard about the Pope's Brigade was when my Uncle
Joe told us as children about his Uncle Peter. Great Uncle Peter was
an engineer who spent most of his life prospecting in Australia
where, according to family lore, he dug a lot of holes in the ground
and buried considerable sums of my grandfather's money! There is
a photograph of him in the family album sitting on the steps of my
father's home in Sandymount surrounded by nieces and nephews,
and looking just like a miner should – weatherbeaten, bearded,

with a drooping moustache and slouch hat. He said once that he could have bought the Broken Hill Mine – in it's heyday, the largest silver mine in the world – for $600, but unfortunately he thought the ore there was lead! In between his engineering studies and mining in Australia, he joined the Pope's Brigade. I'd like to be able to report on his great bravery in battle, but I haven't found his name mentioned in any account so far.

Having a great uncle in the Pope's Brigade is not a sufficient reason to make a film about it, but I suppose one's interest has to start somewhere. Maybe I would never have otherwise read about this fascinating, somewhat bizarre, but ultimately significant event in both Irish and papal affairs – which is hardly mentioned in many history books.

The Pope and the Papal States

The story of the Brigade began early in the Spring of 1860 when Count Charles MacDonnell came secretly to Ireland to raise an Irish battalion of volunteers to help defend the Papal States. Throughout most of Christian history, what we now know as Italy was divided into different states and kingdoms ruled by monarchs, dukes and doges whose political power rested on control of the important towns and cities like Venice, Milan, Ancona, Florence, Perugia, and Rome. One of these rulers was the Pope, who had held political control over much of central Italy for a thousand years. Pope Pius IX was convinced that the Church could never be free if the Pope had to live subject to another ruler. Indeed the disastrous period in the fourteenth century, when Popes were forced to live in France under the thumb of the French king, seemed evidence enough of that. But the Pope had only a token force to protect his independence – the Catholic powers of Europe were expected to defend him against outside aggression. In the late 1850s however the Emperor Napoleon III drove Austria out of north western Italy and did a deal with King Victor Emmanuel of Piedmont which left the Italian king a free hand to attempt the unification of Italy. In desperation Pius looked to the rest of the Catholic world to help defend his territories.

Enthusiasm for the papal cause in Ireland

Pius IX was popular in Ireland. He had shown much concern during the time of the Great Famine, and given extraordinary honour to the remains of Daniel O'Connell when they were brought to Rome. The changing political climate in Ireland at the time was also more favourable to the formation of a military force. The failure of the constitutional movement for repeal of the union with Britain, and the death of O'Connell who had been resolute against the use of force, led to a renewal of interest in what might be achieved by armed struggle. The Young Irelanders, and particularly Davis in the *Nation* newspaper, focused a great deal of attention on the Irish abroad. The glories of the Irish Brigades who fought in the armies of Spain, Austria and France were carefully chronicled. So the climate was ripe to whip up enthusiasm for an Irish Brigade to fight for the Pope. And that enthusiasm was by no means diminished when the British government came down firmly on the side of the Pope's enemies.

Caution on the part of the Irish bishops

The Irish church at the time was dominated by Archbishop Paul Cullen, later to become cardinal, who was friendly with the Pope and anxious to appear sympathetic to his cause. However he was also a realist, and did not believe the Papal States could be defended by a papal army. Furthermore it was illegal under British law to raise troops in Ireland for a foreign power, and Cullen wasn't one to tweak the Lion's tail. On 26 February 1860, Cullen wrote to Monsignor Kirby in the Irish College in Rome:

It is nonsense to talk about getting men in Ireland – it would require two years to train them – the people don't know how to fire a gun, and without training they could do nothing.

Later in the year he wrote again to Kirby, 'Probably the whole affair will end up a fiasco – like some of the crusades'.

The path to Rome

1,300 Irishmen eventually made their way to the Papal States to fight for Pius IX. To say the least they were a varied group. They included medical students, engineers, shop assistants, and a group of sixteen boys from Kerry who, it was said, the local parish priest was delighted to get rid of from his parish. It wasn't easy for them to get to Italy, because the normal route was through France and Piedmont – enemy territory! So the men were recommended to find their own way somehow through England, Belgium, Holland Prussia, Austria, and from Trieste to Ancona, to reach the far off country they set out to defend. When they arrived at Ancona there was nobody to meet them. They couldn't communicate because they knew no European language. There were no tents, no blankets, so they slept under the stars at the Ancona citadel. Other Irishmen arrived at a staging post in Spoleto, where they slept on scanty straw which was four months old and full of insects. They had been promised a shilling a day and received the equivalent of a penny-halfpenny!

A divided army

From the beginning, the Irish were split between Spoleto and Ancona, and this was a source of great discontent. They wanted to form a strong united Irish contingent and win glory like the Irish brigades of old who fought for Austria, Spain and France. In fact the two Irish contingents never met until they were shipped home together after the war.

Looking for a leader

Originally the Irish military commander was meant to be a Major Fitzgerald, an experienced soldier from the Austrian army, but he left after a row, and the Irish bishops were asked to find a replacement. They chose Myles O'Reilly, a farmer and horse breeder from Meath, a student of military affairs, but with no military experience. He accepted, although it can't have been convenient – among other things he had just married a wife! On the 22 July, Myles, now Major Myles O'Reilly, arrived with his new spouse, and took up residence in the castle of Spoleto.

Training the troops

His immediate task was to try and weld the odd mixture of recruits, few of whom had any military training, into a fighting force. Little did he know at the time that in less than two months his men would be blooded in battle. Drill began in the courtyards of the castle: serious military training was more difficult, because they had few guns, and these were of the old smooth-barrelled muskets type which were short ranged, very inaccurate, and no match for the enemy rifles. Judging by the messages Myles O'Reilly sent to the General-in-Chief in Rome, he and his men seem to have been short of everything.

> The Irish in Spoleto are getting on well. However they are short of 200 pouches, 492 haversacks, 100 cloaks, 185 vests, 75 caps, 403 belts, 300 shirts, 300 pairs of drawers and 500 Mass books. Send everything as fast as you can, and don't forget some examples of the new uniforms.

The new green uniforms specially designed for the Irish Battalion of St Patrick, as the group was now officially known, never arrived, and apart from a few officers who may have had their's tailor made,

the Irish fought in their own clothes, or papal uniforms made for
Italians half their size.

The approach to war

Meanwhile the conflict was hotting up. South of Rome, Giuseppe
Garibaldi, a freelance general in the cause of Italian unification, had
invaded the kingdom of Naples. Sicily fell in a few weeks to his red-
shirts: on 18 August he crossed the Straits of Messina and marched
on Naples itself. His very success spurred on King Victor Emmanuel
to military action – to prevent this independent maverick claiming
credit for the unification of Italy. It was no secret that as soon as
Garibaldi had taken Naples, he intended to march on the Papal
States, so Victor Emmanuel decided to forestall him. All he needed
was a pretext.

In the end, the king used the formation of the papal brigades as the
excuse to go to war. The rest of the world was told that the Papal
States were being repressed by foreign mercenary troops, and that
the Piedmontese were coming in as deliverers and restorers of law
and order. On 11 September the king declared war. 'Soldiers,' he
proclaimed, 'I am leading you against a band of drunken foreigners
whose thirst for gold and desire for plunder has brought them into
our country'. Needless to say, the Irish were not impressed with
this estimate of their motivation.

The Brigade is blooded in Perugia

Victor Emmanuel's army, seasoned by the campaign which drove
Austria out of north-western Italy the previous year, invaded at
three different points. General Cialdini with 17,000 troops headed
for Ancona, General Cardona for Gubbio with 7,000, and General
Fanti for Perugia with another 12,000 men. Fanti headed for the
cathedral square where the bishop's palace and the municipal
buildings were situated. 145 Irish troops had been previously sent
to Perugia from Spoleto to face this formidable enemy force.
Despite the fact that the papal army in Perugia was outnumbered
ten to one, it was decided to put up a fight to show that the Pope
was not giving up his authority over the city, but was being driven
out by the invaders.

Half the Irish party in Perugia were commanded by Corporal
Allman, a medical student from Cork. He led his men in a running
fight along parallel streets – every time they cleared a crossroad
they received a volley. Eventually they were caught in a street with
the enemy at both ends. Allman led one group of men in a final

charge but was shot in the heart. Tynan, Power and McGrath and two others were wounded, while the rest of the group were captured. Another group was caught hiding in a house, and surrendered after a fierce gun battle on the stairs. In the official report of the battle, General Schmidt reported dissatisfaction with some of the defending troops but added, the Irish company and the second line battalion alone showed determination to do their duty.

Defending a future Pope!

One of the many anecdotes told after the war relates to the battle of Perugia. Aloysius Howlin was one of the Irish soldiers detailed to protect Vincenzo Pecci, the local bishop. Pecci went on to become Pope Leo XIII and Howlin went on to become a Patrician Brother in Mallow in Co Cork. Later in life he went back to Rome on a visit, where he met Leo and reminded him that only for the Irish Brigade he might never have lived to be Pope. The Pope, we are told, was impressed, and forthwith gave permission to the Patrician Brothers to wear a green sash, which they still wear on important ceremonial occasions!

Preparing to defend Spoleto

After the fall of Perugia, Orvieto and Viterbo were given up without a shot being fired. It remained to be seen what Major O'Reilly could do in Spoleto. O'Reilly had about 330 Irish and 400 others, a mixture of Swiss, Bavarian, Austrian and some local troops.

He asked for instructions from the Minister of War in Rome, Monsignor de Mérode, who sent him this extraordinary message in reply.

> If this telegraph conveyed tears there would be some of mine on this. I can only say do your duty. The true reward is not for the stronger. I say do your duty neither more nor less. Signed Mérode.

O'Reilly wrote in his diary, 'It told me we fought without hope but it did not tell me what I wanted to know – to what extremity I was to carry the resistance'.

O'Reilly brought in as much food as he could for the troops in the castle, sent up a few cases of preserved meat and a couple of flasks of brandy to his own quarters in the tower, and kept an eye out for the invaders. He also noted in his diary that the Irish spent the night before the battle in dancing and singing. No authority could get them to bed, they were so excited at the prospect of a fight.

At dawn on the day of the battle, an Italian officer came up to the gate to demand that the Irish surrender the castle. Major O'Reilly went outside to meet him and declared in the name of Pius IX that he would not surrender. (He explained afterwards that he went outside because he was afraid if he let the Piedmontese in they might see how weak the Irish defences were.) The attackers in this gentlemanly war agreed that the women who were inside the castle could leave, and so Myles O'Reilly's newly wedded bride, her maid, and an Austrian officer's wife were allowed to leave. They watched the battle from the safety of the town down below, and prayed for their menfolk.

The siege of Spoleto

The Rocca at Spoleto was strongly built, but there was only one six pounder in serviceable condition to defend the whole castle. During the battle they could only get it to fire three times. And when the enemy brought up artillery, there were very few places in the castle itself where one could mount a canon to return fire and make them keep their distance. The attackers were armed with new sophisticated rifles and they attempted to fire down on top of the papal forces from a hill overlooking the castle. The papal forces, on the other hand, had old antiquated muskets and even though they tried to lob their shots across the valley, at the end of the day when the battle was over they found that not one single shot had reached the enemy lines!

At 3 o'clock in the afternoon, when the bombardment seemed to be having little effect, the Piedmontese general determined to storm the gate. Fourteen of his men died in that unsuccessful episode. Meanwhile O'Reilly was running short of ammunition, so both sides were happy enough to call a halt to the fighting on honourable terms.

The Race to Ancona

At this stage, the papal commander in chief, General de Lamoricière had only one major strategy left. If Ancona could be held for several weeks, public opinion might shift to the side of the Pope and force one or other European government to come to his assistance. So starting 12 September, de Lamoricière marched at speed over zigzag roads through the Apennines to the town of Loreto, followed by his second in command, General Pimodan. The Irish group on the march, over 100 strong, were under the command of Captain Kirwan. This forced march through the mountains exhausted the papal troops. When they arrived at Loreto they were too tired to go further. Anyway it was clear that they had been forestalled by the enemy.

The battle of Castelfidardo

Loreto is only about 25 kilometres from Ancona, with one important obstacle, however, the river Musone. There were only two fords where an army could cross the river, and both were near rising ground where the Piedmontese General Cialdini took up position after his march south from Rimini. So there was now no chance of reaching Ancona without a fight. At the height of the battle the papal commander called for reinforcements, but seeing the extent of the bloodshed, the men refused to fight and ran away. In the report of the battle, however, the Irish were commended as having distinguished themselves in the fighting; but how many of them died is not known – the monument marking the battle only gives the names of the victors.

The last stand

Ancona was the final battle. General Cialdini moved in with an army of 34,000 and a small fleet of battleships against a defending force of less than 6,000. The battleships were in the end the deciding factor, blowing up the powder magazine and blasting the town's fortifications from close range. De Lamoricière surrendered, not to the army, but to the navy.

The heroes return home

The war now over, the exhausted troops were anxious to go home. But if the troops were exhausted, so also was the Roman treasury – there was just no money to pay the men's fare any further than Marseilles. So the Irish bishops were handed the problem, much to their annoyance, and had to charter a ship to get the men back to Cork. The bishops had been conscious from the beginning of the unsatisfactory manner in which the expedition had been organised through the barrage of complaints coming back to Ireland. They were fearful therefore that the men would hold the church up to ridicule when they returned.

In fact all the frustrations were forgotten when the men were greeted as returning heroes – the reception throughout the towns of Ireland, according to Archbishop Cullen, being 'enthusiastic to madness'. They were praised by generals on both sides of the war. They had acquitted themselves so well that people thought of them again as the old Irish Brigades of the eighteenth century. Special medals, showing the upturned cross of St Peter, were awarded by the Pope. Some years later, Myles Keogh, an Irish Brigade veteran wore his medal when he fought and died in Custer's last stand. Crazy Horse, the Indian chief, wore the medal afterwards as a memento of the battle.

The end of the temporal power of the Pope

The rest of the story can be briefly told. In 1870 the French troops protecting the Pope were withdrawn and Victor Emmanuel marched into Rome. With the seizure of Rome the unification of Italy was complete. The visions of the old glory of the Roman Empire stirred in Italian hearts, and victory monuments such as the Vittorio Emanuele in the heart of Rome were calculated to nourish this romantic ideal.

The Pope retired to the Vatican palace where he and his successors remained as virtual prisoners until the Lateran Treaty of 1929.

The consequences for Ireland

What happened in Ireland and Italy in 1860 was of deep consequence – both for Ireland and for the papacy. The consequences for Ireland were well summed up by the American historian, Emmet Larkin:

> The launching of a national agitation, the inaugurating of the Peter's pence, and the raising of a papal brigade by the bishops and clergy all resulted in the Irish people's thinking and acting more in national, and less in regional terms ... This developing Irish-Catholic consciousness was further hardened, meanwhile, by the English reaction to it. The undisguised delight of the English at the imminent demise of the temporal power of the Pope, and their unconcealed contempt for everything Irish and Catholic, caused the Irish not only to become more aware of themselves as a people but also to perceive more clearly how profoundly different they still were as a people from the hereditary enemy of their nation and religion.

The consequences for the papacy

The consequences for the papacy turned out to be the opposite of what its opponents predicted. Before 1870, the view accepted by most Catholics was that the independence of the papacy and the support it needed to function as a world church could only be secured if the Pope held on to the Papal States. Indeed that was the view of the Pope's enemies as well – when Victor Emmanuel invaded they rubbed their hands in glee and anticipation of the imminent demise of the papacy, in both its spiritual and temporal capacity.

In the event, the problem of the Pope's freedom and independence was overcome with the guarantee by Italy of the independence of the tiny Vatican State – the so-called Lateran Treaty agreed between Mussolini and Pius XI. The problem of revenue for central church administration was overcome by the establishment of 'Peter's Pence' – an annual collection held throughout the Catholic world to help meet the expenses of running an international church – in addition to a later financial settlement under the treaty itself.

In the end, losing it's power as ruler of much of Italy was probably the best thing that happened to the papacy in the nineteenth century. The church had to thank her enemies for bringing about this liberating change – which all her friends opposed. If any dictator were to try now to force the papacy to take back the Papal States, I think it is fair to say that the papacy and the whole Catholic community would fight the proposal tooth and nail.

Yet it took fifty years for the papacy and its Curia to accept the *fait accompli*. The Pope rejected a law passed in the Italian parliament in 1871 guaranteeing the political independence of the Holy See, and offering to indemnify the papacy for the loss of property. What was much worse – the Pope forbade Catholics to take any part in the new Italian government, thus leaving control of Italy's destiny in the hand of anti-clericals, freemasons and agnostic politicians who had a free hand in bringing in offensive legislation.

And despite the fact that the head of the church was no longer a head of state, the Holy See continued to exchange diplomatic representatives, receive heads of state, and make concordats as if there had been no change.

Irrelevancies that impede the church's mission

What happened in 1860 needs to be mulled over, studied, and kept continuously in mind, because the church is still encumbered by irrelevancies which impede its mission. The Papal States and the papal army have gone – except in the form of the ceremonial Swiss Guards – but the papacy still retains and augments its diplomatic corps as if it were a powerful secular state. Indeed in Catholic countries the Vatican insists that the nuncio be dean of the diplomatic corps, and take first place among ambassadors of all other states.

Up to recently the Vatican representative was called by the reduced title of 'pro-nuncio' if and where the privilege of the first place was not granted. Many people who love the church feel that this elaborate and expensive diplomatic machine has little to do with the message of Christ, and should have been dismantled with the Papal States. Where contacts with governments are required, this could be as well conducted through the local church. But to suggest this to Pope John Paul today would be a bit like suggesting to Pius IX in 1860 that he should voluntarily surrender control over the Papal States.

The church is that unique organisation which always seems to gain power by losing it, or better still, by giving it away. Pope John XXIII, in my opinion, will be judged by history to have been the most powerful Pope in the twentieth century. His power came from giving power away. Perhaps that is the essential paradox of Christianity. Christ gave life to others by giving his life away. When he humbled himself, he was exalted.

Nobody has ever claimed the Vatican's diplomatic service is of divine origin, so its existence and operation are obviously open to questioning and evaluation. When the service is questioned or criticised, it is usually under one of the following headings.

1. Nuncios are imposed on, not welcomed by, the local church

a. Ireland

The newspapers of 24 November 1995 report that Mr Desmond O'Malley TD suggested closing the Irish embassy to the Vatican on the grounds that it was wasteful to have two embassies in Rome when we had no embassy in important places like Brazil. In light of this intervention, it is amusing to note the overriding importance that the first government of the Irish Free State attached to opening this embassy – despite the known opposition of a number of members of the hierarchy, among whom the Archbishop of Dublin, Edward Byrne, was the most prominent.

Patrick McGilligan, Minister for External Affairs, made all the arrangements to open diplomatic relations in secret and went to Rome with Joseph Walshe, Secretary of the Department, to seal the agreement in 1929. This agreement was accompanied by a specific request from the Vatican to the government *not* to inform the bishops. In fact the government decided only to tell the Archbishop of Dublin of the *fait accompli* within twenty-four hours of publication of the decision. Walshe wrote in a letter back to Dublin about his meeting with Mgr Duca, the Vatican Under-Secretary of State.

> Each time that Mrg Borgongini Duca speaks of the exchange of diplomatic relations he does so with evident delight at the thought of the bishops' discomfiture concerning the new control which is about to be suddenly exercised over them.

Sensitive to the opposition among the bishops, the Vatican took its time to implement the agreement. Charles Bewley was appointed as Ireland's ambassador to the Holy See six months before the Vatican appointed Monsignor Paschal Robinson, an Irishman, as nuncio.

Monsignor John Hagan, rector of the Irish College, wrote to Archbishop Byrne on 27 November that Robinson was 'a sort of compromise or better still a manoeuvre to disarm opposition by making it appear that the Holy See is anxious to show deference to Irish feeling by appointing one of themselves'. He mentioned the example of the first nuncio to Bavaria, Andreas Frühwirth, who 'was the first, and of course the last, of the natives chosen'.

Bishop John Duignan of Clonfert wrote to Hagan early the following year.

> The nuncio has arrived. His actual coming came, I think, as a great surprise to the episcopal bench. I knew nothing about it until I learned of it in the press. From an ecclesiastical or rather spiritual point of view, the church in Ireland might get on just as well without a nuncio; in the past we had no nuncio or delegate and the church was as flourishing as in countries blessed with nuncios – and trouble, serious trouble dangerous to the faith, might easily arise if there is any undue interference with bishops, priests or laity. How the appointment will affect us politically I have no idea. It is possible it will be to our good, but the contrary is more likely, I fear.

b. USA

In 1892, Pope Leo XIII determined to give the Catholic church in the United States something it had tried long and hard to avoid – an apostolic delegate. This is the equivalent of a nuncio in a country like the USA which did not formally recognise the Vatican – at least until recently. When the Vatican first mooted a delegate, the US bishops suggested that they might send a delegate of theirs to Rome instead, but the Vatican ignored the offer. In the end, Pope Leo didn't consult the US hierarchy before acting because he knew they would oppose it. Instead he sent a friend of his, Archbishop Francesco Satolli, as legate to the Colombian Exhibition in Chicago in 1892 which marked the fourth centenary of the European discovery of America. Satolli then arranged to attend the annual meeting of the archbishops on other business, and announced to them at the end of their meeting that he had been charged by Leo XIII,

> to inform the Metropolitans that, according to the traditional policy of the Holy See to appoint delegates to reside permanently in countries wherein the hierarchy is well established, it was the Pope's heartfelt desire that now a permanent apostolic delegation should be established with the kind concurrence of the Most Reverend Metropolitans.

Satolli would stay on as apostolic delegate, The Pope directed the bishops to give Satolli 'aid, concurrence and obedience in all things'. Not all the bishops were willing to accept this apparent *fait accompli* without demur. John Lancaster Spalding, Bishop of Peoria went public in a press interview.

> There is, and has been for years, a deep feeling of opposition to the appointment of a permanent delegate for this country. This opposition arises in part from the fixed and strongly rooted desire ... to manage as far as possible one's own affairs. (American Catholics) are devoted to the church; they recognise in the Pope Christ's vicar, and gladly receive from him the doctrines of faith and morals; but for the rest, they ask him to interfere as little as may be.

Later, in a private letter to the Pope, Spalding pulled no punches, pointing out that the presence of a delegate simply encouraged those who subscribed to the belief that the Catholic Church is a foreign intruder. Furthermore, public criticism of the delegation was bound to destroy little by little the authority of the Holy See. Satolli's inability to speak English or German or French, together with his ignorance of the country and its customs had left him simply an instrument in the hands of an unworthy clique in the hierarchy. And so on. But the die was cast, and barring the bishops kidnapping Satolli and putting him on a boat to Europe with a one-way ticket, there was no way they could avoid a permanent 'eyes and ears and mouthpiece' of the Vatican in their midst.

2. Nuncios introduce unnecessary tensions

One of the tensions between nuncio and hierarchy may arise in relation to the meetings of the Episcopal Conference. Canon 450 #2 makes it clear that nuncios are not *de jure* members of the Conference. However, there may be a grey area where nuncios seek to establish some right by custom to attend meetings, while the bishops try to keep that attendance to a minimum in order to preserve their freedom of discussion. Dr Gerada, the nuncio who retired recently, attended the first part of the Maynooth meetings, whereas his predecessor Dr Alibrandi normally only attended an opening Mass.

Sometimes tensions between bishops and the Vatican representative become quite public, as they did in Australia in Archbishop Mannix's time. There are many amusing stories still told which illustrate the strained relations between the two ecclesiastics. Archbishop Giovanni Panico (known to the Australian clergy as 'Panicky Jack') was speaking at some function when he said he looked forward to the day when the Australian hierarchy would be Australian born – which was a dig at Mannix, who was of course born in Co Cork. Later Mannix had his turn to speak, and said he too looked forward to the day when the Vatican's representative to Australia would be Australian born – Panico was of course Italian!

It is said too that Mannix made fun of Panico's poor grasp of English. One day when they were at a function together and Panico was struggling through a speech saying how much he loved Australia 'with its glorious sunshine and, and ...' Mannix whispered up to him 'moonshine'. 'And its glorious moonshine' repeated Panico – to the great amusement of all except the speaker himself who only learned afterwards of the import of what he had said!

3. Nuncios may be the eyes and ears of the Vatican, but one must worry about what, in the nature of things, they see and hear

Cardinal Suenens in 1969 called the nuncios, 'spies on the local churches'. Spies have to gather information, so the question is 'Who does the nuncio speak with?' It is unfortunate but true that a nuncio must suspect any priest and most bishops who make friends with him as having ambitions to move up the ecclesiastical ladder. And indeed history shows, and common sense would suggest, that friends of the nuncio have a much better than even chance of becoming bishops. That is not a good basis for a meaningful friendship, or more importantly a good basis to hear the truth.

Some nuncios make a point of moving around in different circles and/or inviting a range of people to meet them. However language is often a problem. Most nuncios are Italian, and Italians are not renowned as polyglots. Archbishop Alibrandi was here twenty years, and although he improved, he was never really comfortable in English.

Letters are very important to nuncios, and apart from what they read in the press, or learn from church sources, they are probably the principal source of their information. But people are more likely to send letters of complaint and condemnation rather than praise. And the Vatican, it seems, pays more attention to blame than to praise. When conservative people write to their nunciature in the reign of Pope John Paul II, they know they are writing to a conservative administration which will, likely as not, be sympathetic to their point of view.

4. *Nuncios sometimes get involved with local issues*
   which might be better left to the local bishops

In October 1994, Archbishop Alibrandi, now retired to Sicily, gave a remarkable interview to John Cooney which was printed in the *Irish Press*.

In relation to the first referendum campaign to remove the constitutional ban on divorce, Archbishop Alibrandi said he was appalled to learn that many religious were supporting the Taoiseach, Dr Fitzgerald, on the grounds that individual Catholics could in conscience vote for divorce. 'When I saw the danger I became very busy,' Alibrandi recalled. 'I was very strong. I phoned the various heads of the religious orders and I told them that, if they were supporting divorce, they were going against the Holy Father. I also told them they were in danger of falling into mortal sin. Not only were they acting against the Holy Father, but God himself ... I could not withdraw from the challenge laid down by Mr Fitzgerald.'

One anecdote told after that press interview relates to the reaction of the Pope when his attention was drawn to the interview. 'What's gotten into him,' said the Pope, 'does he need money?' 'Holy Father,' said the surprised official, 'Do you not know that Archbishop Alibrandi is a Sicilian Prince?'

5. *Having a diplomatic service suggests to the world*
   that the church is analogous to a political power

Cardinal Casaroli, a former Secretary of State, claimed that the church can play a useful political role because the Holy See, not having any political, territorial or military interests of its own to defend, is in a position to see with greater objectivity the reality and implications of international problems. Sometimes the Vatican has acted as a neutral force and helped to resolve a political controversy. A good example of this mediation was in the Beagle Channel dispute between Chile and the Argentine in the late 1970s. It is not clear, however, why this mediation service might not be provided just as efficiently by an envoy of the Holy Father as by a local nuncio.

6. *The main charge against having a diplomatic service is*
    that diplomatic considerations inhibit or even contradict prophecy

Jean-Bertrand Aristide was a priest who worked with the Haitian poor. Despite the fact that the majority of priests and religious admired and supported his actions, Rome insisted that he be expelled from his Salesian order. When the army was temporally forced out of power in 1990 and there was a chance for free elections, the poor had no credible candidate to represent them except Fr Aristide. His friends persuaded him to run, and he won two thirds of the votes. Within a year he was forced into exile by another bloody military coup. Some three thousand of the Haitian people died under the consequent military reign of terror. The only state in the world to appoint a diplomatic representative to these military usurpers was the Vatican. (See Chapter 12.)

7. *Nuncios, being for the most part Italian, can give the impression that the*
    Catholic Church is an Italian national church with colonial pretensions

The first apostolic delegate appointed to the US church in 1893, Francesco Satolli, was a native of Perugia. His successors were Archbishops Martinelli, Falconio, Bonzano, Fumasoni-bondi, Cicognani, Vagnozzi, Raimondi, Jadot, Laghi, and Cacciavillan – the present incumbent. All Italian except Jean Jadot, a Belgian. All former nuncios became cardinals except Jadot (1973 to 1980). Yet Jadot is the one who is almost universally praised as the best delegate ever. According to the *National Catholic Reporter*, Jadot transformed the US hierarchy. 'He introduced a type of bishop that became the benchmark against which all future bishops were measured – by those American Catholics who bother about such things.'

8. *Nuncios exercise too much personal power in the appointment of bishops*

Dr Alibrandi was nuncio for the appointment of most of the present bench of bishops. In all, 44 appointments were made in his twenty years service in Dublin. It is difficult to apportion responsibility for appointments, but Alibrandi is quoted as saying that the Vatican always accepted his recommendations. And when he gave his interview to the *Irish Press*, he certainly gave the impression that he played the significant part when it came to appointing bishops.

'Bishop Daly accepted Down and Connor because I pushed him into taking the post ...'

'I promised Bishop Daly two auxiliary bishops to help him with the difficult task in Belfast and this I did with the appointments of Bishop Patrick Walsh and Bishop Anthony Farquar ...'

'I chose Father Clifford because I thought he was the right man with the right qualities for one of the four senior posts in the Irish church ...'

'I allowed Bishop Michael John Browne of Galway, Bishop Austin Quinn of Kilmore and Bishop Neil Farren of Derry to stay on until they were 80 ...'

'I made Dermot Ryan Archbishop of Dublin, but the great Archbishop of Dublin was Kevin McNamara ...'

9. The overriding aim of the diplomatic service seems to be to defend institutional rather than gospel values

One curial defender said of the diplomatic service, 'When we extract from a government some concessions in favour of the freedom of the church in the nomination of bishops, Catholic schools, influence over youth, we save more souls than when we preach or hear confessions'. The principal aim of the Vatican, some of its critics maintain, often seems to be to defend the institution rather than to preach the gospel. However this is an easy brick to throw. An institution is surely needed if we are to continue to preach the gospel, and institutions often need to be defended!

10. As representatives of the poor fisherman, nuncios mix with the wrong people

As dean of the diplomatic corps, a lot of the nuncio's time has to be spent at diplomatic cocktail receptions on the occasion of national days, royal birthdays, visits of dignitaries to the host countries. The nuncio's world is the world of the powerful and the rich. When I was in El Salvador in October 1979, I was told a story of how ten priests wrote to the newspapers saying that they were tired of seeing pictures of the papal nuncio at this or that cocktail party or diplomatic reception, and hoped in future they might see his picture visiting one of the poorer *barrios*. Their bishop suspended them from saying a public Mass for six months, which also meant they received no salary.

Our ideas and outlook are inevitably influenced by the ideas and outlook of our own milieu, of the people we mix with. If, as in Haiti, or El Salvador, the nuncio in his actions reflects the ideas and thinking of the rich and the powerful, should we be surprised?

11. The ambience in which nuncios traditionally live often seems inappropriate for representatives of Christ's church

Up to Alibrandi's reign as nuncio, the nunciature was the only other embassy apart from the American residence to be housed in the Phoenix Park. The Irish Government provided the former under secretary's lodge at a rent of £1 a year, and in practice looked after the maintenance of the house and gardens as if it was a state residence. It was a very beautiful house with a delightful conservatory, but it grew old, and would have needed a lot of work to make it fit for a possible future papal visit, and so Dr Alibrandi decided to move. As the then director of the National Office for Communications of the hierarchy, I was consulted about a move to Dublin 4, where most embassies are located. I gave my opinion in January 73 that property adequate to the apparent needs of the nunciature would only be available in embassy land (centred on Ailesbury Road) at a cost which would likely give scandal, and that it would be better if the nuncio moved to a contiguous but less fashionable area like Sandymount or Merrion, where one of the convents might give him a patch. But convenience would suggest he move to the southside, where all the other diplomats seem to gather. Eventually Alibrandi decided to stay on the northside, got land from the Dominican nuns in Cabra for free, and built a large embassy there of about 10,000 square feet. His successor Mgr Gerada found it inconvenient on the northside and made some attempts to move again to embassy land in Dublin 4. He put his eye on a house in Ailesbury Road, and the Cabra nunciature was surveyed with a view to sale. The swop might not have cost that much, perhaps another £100,000, but somebody with clout obviously decided that the scandal aspect was material, and the move was abandoned.

I am sure there are some modest nunciatures, but I have never seen one. I think for instance of the one in Buenos Aires with its great semicircular staircases – a veritable palace. Or Haiti where the nunciature was situated among the houses of the very rich – up in the cool of the hills, with magnificent views over the surrounding countryside. Or even the London nunciature – which a correspondent in a recent *Tablet* describes as that 'splendid residence opposite Wimbledon Common'.

According to my 1992 copy of the *Annuario Pontificio* (it's the most expensive single volume I ever purchased so I don't buy one every year) the Holy See is represented in over 140 countries by a nuncio or apostolic delegate – with some doubling up in the case of smaller countries. A typical nunciature will have a counsellor in addition to the nuncio, a secretary/telephonist, a housekeeper, and maybe a driver and handyman/gardener.

12. Their duties could be entrusted to presidents of episcopal conferences, who are anyway better informed about the nuances of the local situation

This is the situation that in the long run most hierarchies would prefer. They would like Rome to trust them, to accept that they are as concerned about the universal church as any Italian – or Sicilian.

13. Inevitably the lifestyle of the celibate diplomat isolated in a foreign land is not such as calculated to inspire confidence in his judgements

The fact that most members of the Vatican's diplomatic service are Italians is not necessarily something one can easily rectify. Italians have a tradition of working for the papacy, but very few priests in other countries seem to want to join them. It has always been difficult to find foreign clergy willing to work for the Roman Curia.

Humanly speaking, the job of the clerical diplomat is not very attractive. For much of one's life one is being moved around the world as a faceless secretary without any public position. Eventually, if one perseveres, one becomes a nuncio and receives ecclesiastical honours with the title of archbishop, and a better than average chance of becoming a cardinal. One receives power over the church one has been appointed to, and an important say in the appointment of bishops. One lives a comfortable lifestyle with a small staff to carry out one's wishes. But the life is lonely, without the friendship and support a priest would normally have from the laity in his parish, or colleagues in a religious order.

14. Their function would be better done by lay people

Maybe this might be possible in a different kind of church, but certainly not in the one we know and love. Besides, the whole diplomatic service must be very costly as it is, without having to support spouses and families.

Conclusion

It is sad that institutions don't seem to be able to give up power even when by giving they gain. And it is doubly sad that where institutions are concerned, it usually requires a painful crisis before there can ever be substantial change.

The Pope needs a good information service if he is to lead the church wisely and well. Whether he needs to send scores of Italian archbishops around the world and maintain them in diplomatic style to achieve this purpose is, however, another question.

There are arguments in the secular world about the need for ambassadors nowadays when instant intercommunication between governments has become normal and natural. One could argue further that in the case of the church the system of diplomatic representation by the Vatican in the present form and on the present scale confuses spiritual and temporal power – with too much emphasis on the latter. However the system is likely to remain as long as the Curia can hold on to it – just like they held on to the temporal power so long as they were able.

A few years ago, when the Vatican seemed to be in financial trouble, some thought that the creditor bankers might be the Victor Emmanuel of today who would move in to trim the diplomatic service down to size, as the Piedmontese trimmed the Papal States. Fortunately or unfortunately, the financial crisis seems to have been averted, so the reformers must look to some future day, or some other way.

10
ASIA'S QUIET WAR

*Military dictatorship continues in Burma
while the hopes of ethnic minorities are crushed*

We arrived in Kanchanaburi – about 130 kilometres from Bangkok – to stay at a non-touristy hotel to meet people we didn't know who would bring us to the rebel student military camp somewhere in Burma. Nobody turned up, and there was no message. It was a bit disconcerting. The rooms were hot, and the mosquitoes active and plentiful. But we waited. The students turned up the following day. We expected them to accompany us into Burma, but no, they had to go on business down to Bangkok. Arrangements had been made to hire a four-wheel drive vehicle for us, but when the time came it wasn't available. The only transport on offer was a partly enclosed Toyota van, well used, with wooden seats in the back. Apart from lack of comfort, there was one very serious possible problem. It was the beginning of the rainy season, and if there was heavy rain we could be stuck in a tropical forest, unable to get out because our transport, designed for Japanese tarmac roads, couldn't make it through the muddy jungle.

It was a simple decision. Scrap the whole programme, or risk it and go. We decided to go. The party included Michael Kelly, an Australian Jesuit, Rossi, from the Jesuit Refugee Centre in Bangkok who was our interpreter, Peter Kelly of Radharc, and myself.

The back door into Burma

The journey took about six hours not including breaks for filming. There were reasonable roads to the border where two Thai guards manned a little hut with a window and counter – like a small shop or kiosk. The guards inquired whether we had any camera. We had a cine camera and two stills cameras. I produced one of the still cameras. They said they would have to hold on to it as it was forbidden to take cameras into Burma – we could collect it on the return journey. After that there was some paperwork to be completed, and Rossi and I co-operated meekly standing at the office counter – where incidentally the guard had left down our camera. Just before we'd finished, and when the guards weren't looking, Rossi picked

up the camera, and handed it to me, motioning me to return to the
van. I admired her coolness, as she followed me, nonchalantly wav-
ing to the guards. And off we went into Burma. (Its military rulers
now call it Myanmar, but most people still use the old name.)

Scarred landscapes

Everybody has seen documentary pictures of the destruction of the
rain forests – scarred landscapes, mud, and stumps of scorched,
dead trees – and a strange stillness, because there are no wild animals, or birds, or insects. The reality is far worse than the picture
because the picture is finite, while the reality seems infinite, mile
after mile after mile of destruction, broken every now and then with
storage areas, where trunks of hardwood trees, some 3-5 feet in
diameter, wait for the rainy season. When the rains come, the rising
water in the rivers will float them down to the coast, and over the
sea to the First World, where people bemoan the destruction of the
rainforests, screw the developing countries for repayment of debt
and offer high prices for the mahogany and teak which is one of the
few products that the poorer countries are able to sell to pay off
their debts.

Eventually we got beyond the destruction, and into the cool of the
forest itself. There had been some rain, and there were tense
moments when it was not clear that we could get beyond some
watery craters in the mud road. I well remember those little lakes,
because when the van plunged into them, a cloud of butterflies
arose, filling the air around us like thick snow, catching shafts of
afternoon sunlight that filtered through the trees. They had been
drinking at the pool, and I hoped most of them were agile enough
to escape being crushed under our wheels.

It was near evening by the time we arrived at the student camp – a
clearing on high ground with a river nearby which provided water
and bathing facilities. Perhaps it is time to explain why three thous-
and Burmese university students were hiding in a forest near the
border with Thailand, and why we should be interested in filming
them.

A military dictatorship

It is now thirty-five years since the Burmese army ousted the elected
government and seized control. Since then they have held on to
power by imprisoning, torturing and killing large numbers of their
citizens, and destroying every social, political and economic structure in the country. They have helped finance their policies with

payoffs from the drug trade. Half of the world's heroin comes from Burma. They have also prosecuted a ruthless war against their ethnic minorities.

With few exceptions, foreign journalists are rigorously excluded from entering Burma, so there is no pressure on the military to restore civil and human rights. In political terms it seems unfortunately true that what goes unreported in the world's media might as well not be happening.

The Revolution of 1988

Civil unrest in the cities came to a head in 1988. Apart from the protests about army oppression, there was widespread anger at the way the country's economy was being mishandled. In September 88, General Saw Maung suppressed the pro-democracy movement by ordering the army onto the streets of Rangoon where half a million people were protesting. 3,000 demonstrators were gunned down. 10,000 students fled to the protection of the jungle forest along the border with Thailand. In the words of one of our student interviewees:

> Among those fleeing were students who were anxious to continue the revolution, and others who were simply afraid of what the military might do to them. The revolutionaries have formed the All Burma Students' Democratic Front, which has continued the fight for the past two years. We have no faith in any military governments, and we have no intention of returning to our homes until this one is completely overthrown and a new government installed which shows respect for human rights. When that happens the student revolution and the people's protest will come to an end.

A report from Amnesty International dated May 1990 accused the army of operating 19 torture centres, and routinely brutalising political opponents by beating, electric shock treatment, and forcing prisoners to crawl over broken glass. 18,000 common criminals were thrown out of jail to make room for up to 8,000 political prisoners. The students know they are facing one of the most brutal regimes in Asia – a regime that fired indiscriminately into crowds, a regime that shoots first and doesn't even bother to think later.

Night in the camp

We bedded down that night with the officers in their bamboo and palmleaf hut. We were provided with mosquito nets, but I was thankful to have my own to put underneath – the one proffered had enough holes to satisfy any half inquisitive mosquito.

I felt at the time, and in retrospect probably correctly, that health-wise, this was the most dangerous place we had ever been. We had been told that many of the students suffered from malaria, and some from cerebral malaria, which is the most dangerous kind. Furthermore the mosquitoes in the Burmese jungle carry the para-site *Plasmodium falciparum* which is particularly resistant to quinine and its derivatives. And to some extent this was born out when we filmed next day in the hospital where several young men were in a pitiful state, suffering from cerebral malaria – without the modern drugs which might have helped them to survive.

Morning on the barrack square

Next morning people got moving before dawn, and soon after the sun appeared, some fifty or so uniformed soldiers, women as well as men, began limbering up on what passed for the barrack square. Three hundred students were based at the camp, of whom all but sixty were away fighting. The day began formally with the raising of the flag and singing of an anthem, followed by various marching exercises, mock attacks and so on – with bamboo guns!

The students looked very young. One of them – 'the smallest com-rade' as his friends called him – was just fourteen years of age. Indeed the whole exercise had something of the flavour of Boys' Town, or a summer scout camp. One had to remind oneself that there was a serious purpose behind all this – despite the bamboo guns. 310 students had been killed in the fighting so far. The Burmese army was not far away. Their comrades were away on patrol with real guns. And this camp was the only student camp that the Burmese army hadn't got around to attack so far.

Later that morning we photographed a group being instructed in the assembly and dismantling of a Browning machine gun, which we were proudly told had been used to shoot down a Burmese mil-itary plane. It soon became clear, however, that the lesson was a ready-up for the camera, because the so-called instructor didn't seem to know much about the weapon, and there were indications, such as rust in vital places, which suggested that the gun hadn't been used for some time. With very limited financial resources, the students found it difficult to respond to the firepower of the regular army.

A jungle university

After lunch a number of students repaired to an open barn-like structure to attend lectures. When they first fled to the jungle they hoped it would only be for a short period. Now the months were lengthening into years. So they were trying to make up for the missed semesters at the university by sharing among themselves whatever learning and talents were in the group.

Students of law, commerce, science, or medicine are ill-equipped to hack out a life in the jungle, and those who found it too much, either made their way back home and risked imprisonment and torture or, more likely, drifted into Thailand and further abroad. But 3,000 or so, according to reliable estimates, were remaining in the forests, pledged to fight. In that of course they were not alone – these wild and remote areas of Burma are the territory of the ethnic minorities, tribal forest people who have been fighting the Burmese for forty years.

The Karen

When the students first arrived in the Autumn of 1988, the local people were very suspicious of them. After all, they were lowland Burmese, and the tribal peoples had all suffered greatly at the hands of the Burmese Army. It took a little time for the Karen people to realise that the Burmese army doesn't represent the Burmese people.

Apart from the Burmese proper, there are ten ethnic groups in Burma, adding up to about a third of Burma's population. They mostly live in the border regions surrounding lowland Burma. The Karen claim to be the largest ethnic group, numbering eight million, although the Burmese dispute that figure.

The Karen population is 15% Christian. In 1948, the British promised autonomy for the Karen – but that promise was never kept. With a population larger than that of neighbouring Laos, the Karen felt entitled to nationhood. They had their own language, their own culture, even their own government Within the year 18,000 Burmese army regulars had shelled nine major Karen strongholds. Tita village, which we visited, was the last unscathed outpost for the 4,000 strong Karen National Liberation Army. The Secretary of the Karen National Union put a brave face on a deteriorating position.

Saw Maung (the Burmese military dictator) declared that he would completely destroy all resistance by the ethnic minorities within two years. But due to the increased support from the civilian population, and the fact that the students are with us, we, the Karen National Union in Mergui/Tavoy, are neither beaten or bending. Moreover we have become much more mobile, and can penetrate more deeply into enemy held territory than we could, say two years ago.

In their forty-year struggle for independence, the ethnic armies traditionally fought to defend secure positions. But the extensive incursions on the part of the Burmese army forced a change to guerrilla tactics – patrols, ambushes, harassment by shadows who disappear into the forest. We came across a patrol of Mon, ethnic neighbours of the Karen, returning to their village which was almost hidden in a deep valley in the jungle. It was pouring tropical rain. Two boys were running though the puddles playing with a home-made wheeled toy at the end of a stick, seemingly oblivious to the downpour. A little girl held an umbrella over a tiny child with a swollen tummy, who didn't really need it because he was naked. The patrol included a number of beautiful women who kept the business ends of their guns dry under a swinging cape. A unit of Burmese commandos, they told us, was camped just a half hour's march due east of the village.

Ethnic minorities and the timber issue

The Mon had recently suffered great territorial losses. Their headquarters at Three Pagoda Pass was captured by the Burmese army in February 1990 and thousands were forced to flee into Thailand. 1990 was a crucial year for the ethnics, now faced with their greatest threat – the Burmese government had sold logging rights to large tracts of the forests in the ethnic territories to Thai logging companies. With logging now banned in Thailand, Burma is the only country in the region with teak reserves. Nai Hong Sa, joint general secretary of the New Mon State Party, spoke about the new situation.

When Saw Maung and General Chavalit of Thailand began to co-operate with each other, the Burmese army got Thai support in exchange for access to Burmese timber and fishing resources. One side is selling the forest, and the other is oppressing us! The Mon at the border now cannot return to their territory At present around 7,000 Mon refugees are short of the basic necessities for survival. We have divided them among four refugee camps, and are trying to help them in the midst of our own difficulties. But they need international help.

The ethnic minorities always treated the rainforest as part of their patrimony, cutting selectively and allowing the forest to regenerate. The logging companies from Thailand, on the other hand, cut down everything. In the past the ethnic population always enjoyed a five month reprieve from war during the rainy season, when conditions in the rainforest made it too difficult for the military to fight. But when the logging companies built roads to take out the timber, the army gained access to areas previously cut off during the monsoons. This factor, along with the availability of supplies from the logging companies, the presence of Burmese government officials on the border to monitor timber output, and, of course, the cash generated to fund the military campaign, all accelerated the offensive and undermined the ethnic minorities' security.

We eventually found the President of the New Mon State Party, Nai Shwe Kyin, on a jungle road. He had been educated in England many years ago, and while his English was convoluted, he spoke with a perfect upper class English accent, and it wasn't too hard to understand what he was saying,

> In our struggle for statehood the first thing is – you can get it as a gift. That is out of the question now. Secondly by force of arms. We have been fighting forty years. They can't put us down, we can't put them down, so it is almost on a level. The third thing is by force of circumstances. We rely on you media people, the United States and other organisations in this. Refugee relief organisations are very sympathetic to our cause so we look forward to this falling together of circumstances.

Slave labour

The Mon and Karen told us they had been shocked recently by the arrival of small groups of Burmese, all telling horrific tales of mistreatment. We met some of these people who had very recently escaped at Three Pagoda Pass, some twenty miles away, and arrived a few hours before, obviously still very distressed by their ordeal. They were civilians kidnapped by Burmese soldiers – part of a group press-ganged while waiting for a bus. They were forced to work like pack animals, chained together carrying supplies and ammunition, and sometimes as human mine-sweepers. The porter fatality rate was said to be at least 50%. Many were shot while trying to escape.

The military call elections

It was generally believed that when the military in Burma called elections for 27 May 1990, they would be nothing more than a farce. The opposition were refused access to the state-controlled newspapers, radio and television. Campaign signs were banned. The public were warned not to attend rallies, while Daw Aung San Suu Kyi, leader of the National League for Democracy (or NLD), and other opposition leaders, were placed under house arrest. But contrary to every expectation, the voting was free and reasonably fair and the NLD, which was the main opposition party, won a landslide victory, gaining 86% of the vote. The military won only ten of the 447 seats! On 29 June the NLD demanded that power be handed over immediately and all political prisoners be released. The military ignored the demand, and have carried on since as if there had been no elections.

Aung San Suu Kyi was held under house arrest for six years, and was only released in July 1995, but into a society where the rights of free speech and assembly are still denied. Any significant political action is regarded as illegal. It is said that the new constitution promised by the military will have provisions which would make it impossible for 'The Lady', as she is called in Burma, ever to be president.

Burma today

As I write in late 1995, Burma is still in a mess with inflation rates soaring, and the country short of cash. Per capita GDP is $235, half of India's and below that of Bangladesh and Nigeria. Only 10% of homes have electricity, heroin is the country's largest export, and Rangoon University, once the best in Asia, is now probably the worst.

The army still imposes its will by violence. The Mon and the Karen have had to give up the struggle, and the students with them. 90,000 members of ethnic minorities are refugees at the border with Thailand. They fled because their villages were attacked, or to escape slave labour. Human Rights Watch claims that at least one million people have been put to work for no pay in appalling conditions in order to rebuild Burma's long-neglected infrastructure.

There are over half a million illegal immigrants from Burma in Thailand. Numbers work in the brothels of Bangkok, and bring back the AIDS virus to their homeland. It is said that most of the heroin consumed in New York originated in Burma. The International Committee of the Red Cross announced on 16 June 1995 that it will close its office in Rangoon after it failed to gain access to Burma's detention centres, or to find any way to rescue civilian victims of Burma's internal conflicts.

Mairéad Maguire, Archbishop Desmond Tutu and others from a group called the Burma Action Group, have appealed to the British government in December 1995 to change their policy and not do business with this corrupt and repressive regime, but not so far with any success.

That then is the tragic story of a people in the grip of a military dictatorship, a suffering people whom the rest of the world has done little enough to help.

Why go half way around the world to make documentaries about problems which do not affect Ireland or Irish interests, and where one can do little or nothing to improve the situation? There are two answers to that. The first is that it is important to people who fight for justice and against tyranny to feel they are not alone, that elements in the world outside are aware of their plight and support their cause. That is one of the things the Mon president tried to tell us. The second reason is that dictatorships have perforce to respond to international pressures, and these pressures come from political and commercial considerations which are influenced by information supplied by the world's media. Television documentaries can be one influential source of that information. Our Radharc/RTÉ programme was shown on television in Ireland, Austria and Australia, while the video was used by interested groups in Canada and elsewhere. It may not add up to anything immediately measurable but, who knows, it may have influenced somebody who someday, whether in the Australian Parliament or in the EEC Commission, may be in a position to help bring about change. One does what one can.

Communications technology will eventually defeat the dictators

In the long run, however, the development of mass media must make dictatorships like the one in Burma more difficult to impose and maintain. Authoritarian governments were possible in the past because they could control information – they had to if they were to stay in power. Which is why Soviet Russia continued for so long to jam foreign broadcasts at staggering cost. New technology including broadcast satellites made that kind of control of information no longer possible – which was one important reason for the fall of authoritarian government in Russia.

There are only a few places in the world where oppressive regimes continue to exist. These are relatively poor countries with controlled internal media and little access to free broadcasting. Burma is one such country with a military regime which has remained in power by keeping educational standards low, driving out the international media, and exercising tight control over its own people.

The events in 1989 in Tiananmen Square, when the Chinese old guard shot down about 1,000 people in the full glare of television, will remain forever a turning point in Chinese affairs. Because of media presence, it remains a much more significant event in the public imagination than the much bloodier student revolt in Burma in 1988 in which nearly 3,000 were killed in Rangoon. The television cameras weren't present to send the pictures around the world, and therefore people are hardly aware of the slaughter.

We all know by now that satellites with high definition television cameras can photograph the earth below in great detail and pinpoint, for example, mass graves in the former Yugoslavia. Broadcast television pictures can be taken with tiny cameras and sent in digital form down telephone lines. Wherever the personal computor penetrates, one can have open communication via Internet. In the long run, these and similar developments in communications technology must make it more difficult to maintain oppressive dictatorships like one finds in Burma today. Which is something to celebrate.

11
A COUNCIL
IN THE LIKENESS OF POPE JOHN
The arguments for more democratisation in the church

The church is not a democracy

When I published *No Lions in the Hierarchy* in 1994, my archbishop reminded me that the church was not a democracy. 'The hierarchical church is of divine not human origin,' he pointed out. 'To present it in a light that requires it to conform to a democratic political institution is to create a distortion that inevitably leads to error.' And that indeed is the Catholic position. Popes, bishops, priests and deacons derive their authority, not from winning elections, but from a call from God and a mandate from Christ. The truths of our Catholic faith are not determined by vote or sociological survey.

I would go further and say that many if not most of the organisations that impinge on our daily lives do not conform to democratic political institutions either. RTÉ, for instance, is not a democracy, decisions are made by a Broadcasting Authority which is appointed, not elected. CIE is not a democracy – the workers don't elect their chairman or chief executive. Nor do university students elect their president or governing body. So the fact that members of the church don't conform to a democratic political institution does not make the church particularly unique within the framework of a democratic civil society.

The pressure towards 'democratisation'

To say the church is of divine not human origin does not of course mean that it is a divine society! From Reformation times the Catholic teaching has insisted that the church is a visible human society with a human structure: it is not, as the Reformers once taught, an invisible relationship between the individual believer and God. But if it is a human society with human structure, then many of the same rules that apply to other human structures will likely apply to it. And no matter how they are constituted, it seems that most institutions nowadays cannot avoid coming under pressure to *democratise*. Take RTÉ for instance. In 1995 – for the first time ever – RTÉ staff were permitted to elect one of their members to the RTÉ Authority. Previously the government had appointed one member of staff, and previous to that the staff were not represented at all. One could pick other examples. A student – in practice the elected head of the Students' Council – is now appointed to the governing body of UCD, and there is talk of widening this representation. That is different from when I was a university student there. CIE trade unionists elect four members to the board – the other eight are appointed by the government. Many other industries have in recent times introduced a form of power sharing, and found the well-being of the workers and the efficiency of operations much improved. Everything indicates that the church is no more immune than any other society to this pressure to democratise. A survey, for instance, in the US indicates that two thirds of all the Catholic laity under fifty-five years of age favour more democratic decision making at every level of their church from parish to Vatican Curia. Archbishop Connell himself has recently instituted a Women's Forum in the diocese so that women's concerns may be better heard. So even if democracy is out, by definition, *democratisation* may still be in.

The Vatican Council

The Vatican Council provides a very interesting case study of this democratising process within the upper echelons of the Catholic church. And whereas it wasn't the prime purpose of *A Council in the likeness of Pope John* to make this point, many of the interviews illustrated it.

Wilton Wynne is an American journalist who reported the Council for *Time* magazine.

At the first meeting of the Council the agenda had been drawn up by the arch-conservatives in the Vatican and Pope John knew it wouldn't hold up. And in fact the agenda was practically disregarded in a few weeks. John called the bishops of the world in, he told them to practice holy liberty in their discussions and he made clear to them that there would be no pressure on them from the top – it was what we call in America an 'open convention'. And as the bishops realised this in fact was the case, they conducted their debates in a framework that you could only call holy liberty.

The evolution of democratic procedures

Fr Ralph Wiltgen, who was involved in press relations at the Council, spoke about the evolution of democratic procedures.

As the Council evolved, whenever a Council father would make proposals to amend a document and the new draft of the document would come back, the responsible commission for revising the text in view of the proposals would always indicate why they accepted the amendment or why they didn't accept it: or perhaps they would indicate where this matter had already been covered elsewhere in their document or in some other document. It gave the Council fathers the feeling that they as individuals were important, and what they had to say could then eventually become part of a Council document, and this is what actually happened.

The involvement of other Christians

Dr George Lindbeck, a Lutheran observer from the United States, remembered with enthusiasm the involvement of Protestant observers in the decision making process.

One had a situation in which the observers not only had greater knowledge, greater access to what was happening within the Council, but also in many respects greater input than the bishops themselves! That is to say the Secretariat for Christian Unity was constantly asking us for our reactions to various drafts and then sometimes the observers would hear their suggestions repeated by the bishops in their speeches before the Council. One observer, Oscar Cullmann, is reported to have been responsible for as many changes in the Council drafts as any other single individual. Well this naturally made us feel very important: but more than that we also were received with extraordinary warmth.

Consultation and collegiality

Francis Sullivan, a Jesuit theologian at the Gregorian University, remembered how theologians felt involved as well.

One of the great events of the life of the church since I've been in Rome was the collaboration that took place between bishops and theologians during those four years of the Council. And it was evident that a great number of bishops felt the need of the counsel and help and advice of theologians, and not only the ones they themselves brought with them. So there was a great deal of consultation.

One of the most prominent issues in the documents that were approved by the Council was the role of bishops – what is so often called 'collegiality'. In other words, the bishops as a whole college have a role to play in the life of the whole church, in the government, in the decision making. Not all the answers can come from Rome. The bishops are there and the Pope really has to work with them as a group. In the second session, 1963, there was a crucial vote on collegiality. The vote made it perfectly clear that a very great majority of the Council was in favour of a strong position on the collegiality of the bishops.

It is interesting to note that when Paul VI requested the Council fathers to include a statement in the schema on the church saying that the Pope was answerable only to God, they refused. The Pope may be head of the college of bishops, but bishops as successors to the apostles are co-responsible with the Pope for the unity, legitimate diversity, and freedom of the world church. And that by divine institution (according to Canon 375) – not because the Pope appoints them.

Dissatisfaction with the Synods

The memory of the openness of the Council made it more difficult for the bishops to accept the renewed curial control exercised in the post-Vatican II synods. Bishop d'Souza from India attended the Council and subsequent Synods.

The Synod of bishops, as it was conceived by the fathers of the Council, was of a completely different complexion to what is now taking place. Matters that are absolutely harmless are being brought into the Synod. The bishops meet, they talk, and then what happens to the discussions? We are not even aware of the resolutions, the discussions. What we envisaged at the Council was that the Synod should be a more effective way of involving people from different parts of the world in the administration of the church.

The ethos of democracy

The Vatican Council is a striking example of what some like to call the ethos of democracy – the ethos which encourages mutual respect, a readiness to listen to others and participate with others in decision making. But the Council did more than that. It also provided statements and definitions which give a major impetus to democratisation in the wider church. For instance, it changed the notion of 'church' from the kingdom of God, holy without spot or wrinkle, and in no need of reform or change, to the notion that the church has to be constantly reformed or changed to remain true to itself in a changing world. The buzz word of the Council was 'aggiornamento', which means 'updating'.

Updating on democracy in civil society

The *Decree on the Church in the Modern World* speaks about democracy in civil society with favour, even if in a rather convoluted fashion.

> It is fully consonant with human nature that there should be politico-juridical structures providing all citizens without any distinction with ever improving and effective opportunities to play an active part in the establishment of the juridical foundations of the political community, in the administration of public affairs, in determining the aims and the terms of reference of public bodies, and in the election of political leaders. (75)

This certainly was updating the church's teaching, bearing in mind that Pius XII was the first Pope ever to say that Catholic social teaching supported democratic forms of government. Pius's teaching was in turn a major update on *Libertas Praestantissimum*, an encyclical of Pope Leo XIII written only 83 years before. Leo then called the theory of separation of church and state an absurdity, and condemned free speech and freedom of the press because the law must protect 'the untutored multitude from error and falsehood'.

Updating on democracy within the church

The Vatican Council's *Dogmatic Constitution on the Church* tells us that those who are reborn in Christ are finally established as 'a chosen race, a royal priesthood, a holy nation ... who in times past were not a people, but now are the People of God'. Each member of this People of God participates in the priesthood of Christ and shares 'a true equality between all with regard to the dignity and to the activity which is common to all the faithful in the building up of the body of Christ'. 'By reason of the knowledge, competence or preeminence which they have, the laity are empowered – indeed sometimes obliged – to manifest their opinion on those things which pertain to the good of the church.' (*Lumen Gentium* 9, 32, 37)

Granting that selective quotation from Council documents can support different points of view, it still seems the inescapable message of these and similar texts that the Council fathers at least believed that the People of God should have a role to play in the church which is greater than the traditional pay and pray.

Summing up the Council

1. It seems fair to say that a democratic collegial approach to decision making fits better with the church's self understanding after the Vatican Council than an authoritarian approach.

2. A democratic approach within the church fits better with the church's present teaching on the need for democracy in the civil society.

But apart from mining Council documents, there are other ways of exploring the concept of democratisation in the church. One can look to see how far there has been a democratic tradition at different stages of its history. One can enquire what Christ had to say about how he wished his followers to act. One can see what thoughtful Christians have had to say about decision making. And lastly, one can examine the roots of authoritarian leadership and see whether they are sourced in the teaching of Christ, or in models devised by ancient pagan societies.

1. *Evidence for a democratic tradition*

The New Testament

One familiar quotation from Jesus is quite dramatic in its rejection of authoritarian rule: 'You know that among the pagans their so-called rulers lord it over them, and their great men make their authority felt. This is not to happen among you ...'

In the New Testament, the Greek word we translate as *church* is '*ekklesia*' (from which comes English words like *ecclesiastic*). The original meaning of this Greek word is 'a democratic assembly of full citizens'. Surely that is a significant choice of a word by the sacred writer!

The early church

At the height of the Roman Empire the apostle Paul spoke of a remarkably democratic ethos in the infant church, equating Jew and Greek, citizen and slave. 'For just as the *soma* (a political term meaning body/corporation) is one, and has many members, and all the members of the body, though many, are one *soma*, so it is with Christ. For by one Spirit we were all baptised into one *soma* – Jews or Greeks, slaves or free – all were made to drink of one Spirit.'

When it came to choosing leaders in the community, the Acts of the Apostles records that the whole assembly participated in the selection of Matthias to replace Judas among the apostles(1:15-26), and also in the choice of the seven men after the Hellenist dispute (6:1-6). The popular election of ministers thus became a paradigm for the early church. The election of Ambrose, governor of Aemelia-Liguria, as Bishop of Milan is one of the better known examples from the fourth century. The laity insisted that on the death of the

Arian bishop Auxentius, Ambrose should succeed him, even though he had not yet even been baptised!

Involvement and consultation of the laity

At the beginning of his episcopate (c 248) St Cyprian writes to his presbyters and deacons, 'I have decided to do nothing of my own opinion privately without your advice and the consent of the people'.

The fact that the laity were actively involved in councils of the church from the Council of Carthage in the fourth century to the Council of Trent in the sixteenth, is often overlooked. The emperor Constantine summoned the Council of Arles in 314 when he was invited by churchmen to intervene in the Donatist dispute. An important precedent was thereby established. One tends to forget that it was the emperor, a layman, and not the Pope who went on to convoke the seven great councils of antiquity, the only ones recognised by both the Eastern and Western churches.

The medieval church

When Gregory VII, Hildebrand, attempted to reconstruct the hierarchy and remove it from the control of Italian groups in the eleventh century, he recalled the old traditional manner of electing bishops by the priests and people of a region.

After 1305, the Avignon papacy, having no tax basis in France, used the granting of bishoprics as a means to generating revenue. Local rulers chose the candidates, but the Pope insisted on approving them – for a substantial fee.

Scandal and schism and the problem of having two and then three claimants to the papal throne, led to the calling of councils at Constance and Basle in the first half of the fifteenth century to try and sort out the problems. These councils provided an opportunity for some democratic thinking in the wake of the scandal brought about by a totalitarian and corrupt papacy. The councils insisted on freedom of speech, free and equal voting power, and committee systems to help with decision making. Constance decreed by perpetual edict 'that general councils should be held every ten years forever'. Unfortunately they weren't. Unfortunately too, the conciliar movement in the church failed, not because it was wrong, but because the Popes returned to a policy of absolute monarchy as soon as it was feasible for them to do so. I say unfortunately, because if the more democratic decision making process of councils had become the norm, who knows but that the divisions among Christians in the sixteenth century might have been resolved without schism.

The Reformation and after

The effects of the reformist teaching of Luther and Calvin was to challenge the legitimacy of papal and even episcopal leadership. The church reacted by reinforcing the pyramidical structure – laity-priests-bishops-Pope. The violent upheavals in secular society as it moved away from monarchical government in 1789 and 1848 also seems to have engendered a fortress mentality which didn't begin to melt until after the second great war in this century. The Second Vatican Council, as we have seen, laid the groundwork for a more democratic church. However, its promise has not been fulfilled due to a powerful conservative reaction in the Curia.

Popes are still elected

Election of bishops by local clergy was normal well into the middle ages. Indeed the election of the Pope by the College of Cardinals is a relic of this practice, since the 'cardinals' were simply the priests of the cardinal churches of the diocese of Rome. Nowadays cardinals come from all around the world, but the tradition remains of appointing them as titular priests of churches in Rome itself.

Elections of religious superiors

Abbots, abbesses, superiors of religious orders are normally elected, and this is a long democratic tradition. Indeed, some religious orders have carried democratisation to extreme lengths since Vatican II, one of the penalties being endless meetings and painful tardiness in reaching decisions!

Trusteeism

European Catholics who emigrated to America in the eighteenth and nineteenth centuries brought ideas which led to the establishment of parishes run by lay trustees. Indeed, an Irish bishop from Cork, with the inappropriate name of John England, provided the intellectual underpinning for the system – which was killed later in the nineteenth century with the movement towards centralising authority in Rome.

The church's social teaching

Pius XI, in his encyclical letter, *Quadragesimo Anno* (1931), stated that the principle of subsidiarity is 'a fundamental principle of social philosophy, fixed and unchangeable'. In simple terms this principle states that it is wrong and unjust to transfer authority to larger and higher bodies which can be properly exercised at a lower level. Larger units of government should only take over functions when individuals, voluntary groups and local governments are not able to deal with the issue. While addressing a group of new cardinals in 1946, Pius XII noted that the principle of subsidiarity 'is valid for social life in all of its organisations and also for the life of the church'.

Should not this principle of subsidiarity then be applied to the church government as well as to civil government as Pius suggested – for instance in the matter of appointment of bishops? Obviously it could, because it has been that way in the past. And taking into account the church's self-understanding as the 'People of God', perhaps it should.

2. How can the church become more democratic?

Very easily. Many of the structures are there, and only need to be activated. For instance:

1. *The Synod of Bishops:* The Synod of bishops should set an example of power-sharing in the church. But before it can do that, the following reforms would have to be implemented at the very least:

a) The Bishops' Conferences must be permitted to interchange among themselves – and publish for the priests and laity – their response to the *'Lineamenta'* or theme document proposed for each Synod. This would open up the document to discussion and mature consideration.

b) The bishops should be free to bring theologians and experts for advice and consultation – as they did during the Second Vatican Council.

c) The procedures at present prevent the bishops making any decisions or even voting between alternative propositions. Nor do they have any control over the final document that is supposedly issued from the Synod. This is written by the Curia in the name of the Pope, and as many bishops have said, often bears little relationship to what was actually said in the Synod. If the Synod of Bishops were allowed to function freely, and not under the autocratic control of the Curia, then that would be an immense step forward.

2. *Conferences of Bishops.* Bishop's Conferences have made a marked contribution to democratisation. The US Conference in particular has initiated a system of consultation with priests and laity before

issuing policy documents which set a headline for other conferences. The general tendency of Vatican pronouncements however
has been to downgrade the importance of Conferences of Bishops –
again one suspects because the Curia prefers to deal with bishops as
individuals rather than as a group who might queer the pitch of the
centralised authority.

3. *Councils of priests.* Clergy are reasonably served with fora to
express their views. In Ireland most, if not all, dioceses have a council
of priests. In addition, priests have a National Council of Priests with
direct elections from the dioceses and religious orders. This body
tends to be more independent in its activities – they recently elected
Professor Enda McDonagh as chairman, which suggests that they do
not contemplate a conservative agenda in the immediate future.

4. *Pastoral councils.* The Second Vatican Council expressed the wish
that pastoral councils, embracing priests, religious and laity, be set
up everywhere. Canons 511 to 514 expand on the details, and declare
that members of a diocesan pastoral council 'are to be selected in
such a way that the council truly reflects the entire portion of the
people of God which constitutes the diocese'. Canon 536 speaks of
pastoral councils at parochial level. National Synods of clergy and
laity are also supposed to be encouraged, but very few ever came to
be, presumably because of the Roman reaction to some of the early
attempts – such as the first Pastoral Council which was held in the
Netherlands. Its aim was 'to foster the cohesion of all Dutch
Catholics in the development of a common pastoral strategy'. Rome
however made clear its view that many matters of pastoral policy
were not matters for discussion by priests and laity, and the Dutch
bishops capitulated. So nothing came of a movement which at the
time galvanised the whole Dutch church – except great frustration.

There has been mention recently about the possibility of a National
Synod to review the present state of the church in Ireland – some
say crisis, but I think that is too strong a word. My own view is that
there is no point in holding a Synod until there is a more relaxed attitude in Rome, and evidence of a greater willingness to share power in
decision making. Otherwise expectations will only be raised, followed
by frustration when the synod finds it has no power to change anything, and it's recommendations are totally ignored.

But clearly new structures aren't needed to bring about democratisation – at least immediately. Just the will to let the old ones function with the freedom of the children of God!

12
PRIEST, PROPHET, PRESIDENT
How a priest became the first elected President of Haiti

Slow boat to Haiti

We started with one, and now there are four filing cabinets full of large brown envelopes with the flap cut off and filled with ageing bits of paper. When a programme is completed, the full typed interviews and shotlists and scripts go into an envelope with the subject and catalogue number written on the top. The envelope disappears into the file, to be rarely ever opened again. Back in the early days of Radharc I started a special drawer for programmes which were still just ideas, which we reviewed every year. One envelope was simply marked 'Haiti', and it contained a single page that I had typed out of a book in the early 1960s. It gave an outline of the careers of Toussaint L'Ouverture and Henri Christophe – romantic tragic stories that I longed to have some excuse to tell. In the end it wasn't Toussaint or Henri Christophe who brought us to Haiti but a modern story, hardly less exciting and dramatic – the story of a little man, son of a widowed washerwoman, who became a priest, and then a champion of the poor, and then a fiery preacher against injustice, and then a thorn in the side of the military and the Americans, the object of hate, assassination attempts, the despair of the church hierarchy, and President of Haiti. His name was Jean-Bertrand Aristide. We went to Haiti for his inauguration.

The president is inaugurated

The inauguration was to begin at 8 am in the parliament house. The press officer was a big horse-faced woman with a light skin and reddish hair. We pleaded, we cajoled, we threatened not to leave her office without a ticket. When it came to giving stick she gave as good as she got. 'There's no room. There's only going to be two television crews. You should have written months ago, and not asked at the last minute' and so on. We retreated, tail between the legs, before her onslaught. But on reflection I decided we shouldn't do it anyway. The Mass in the cathedral was more important to us, and it took place immediately after the inauguration. Whatever hope the president had of getting from the parliament house to the cathedral on time, it was clear that nobody else stood much of a chance. So we decided to arrive early at the cathedral, get a good place and set up the camera. Then we would at least cover that part of the celebration well.

Not getting the picture

We were half an hour early and the presidential party was about half an hour late. So we got a good place. But for the next hour every nook and cranny around the altar filled up with some few professional TV crews, many amateur video makers and lots of other serious looking gentlemen who were obviously journalists, or if not, making a good attempt at pretending to be, so they could justify pushing in front of us. Our carefully chosen vantage point was soon useless. When the new president appeared (at something under or around five feet, the word 'appeared' is perhaps an exaggeration), all one could see was a commotion passing up the aisle, with, we presumed, the president in the middle of it. At the same time the pushing and shoving around us reached a climax. I certainly didn't get a picture. In fact the Mass was nearly over and I still wasn't sure we had any usable footage. There are limits to what I will do to get a picture and it seemed to me that I had already passed those limits. At one stage I had tried to balance on top of a railing between two pillars, one hand clutching the pillar, the other trying to keep the camera steady. It didn't work. We had come all this way at great expense, and the big moments were slipping away. Finally the sound recordist and I forgot decorum and dignity and walked over choir stalls, edged around pillars and pushed through people until we got to a position where something like a real picture of the new president looked possible. I quickly switched on the camera, and found a whole array of unwanted technical information written across my viewing screen. Down the years I had always used film camera, and we had only recently switched to professional video so I had no idea what had happened. I tried to shout to the engineer struggling with his microphone some distance away, but he couldn't hear me through the crowd. So there was nothing to do but go ahead and hope it didn't matter. It didn't – but I only learnt that an hour later. It seems that pushing though the crowd some of the switches were tripped on the side of the camera, which now told me a lot of technical things which I neither wanted to know nor understood. In the end I got good pictures when the bishops went in procession to greet Aristide, which from our point of view was probably the most piquant moment in the ceremony. So that was fortunate. And we got some great pictures when the whole choir and sanctuary filled with excited people who danced and sang alleluias in vibrant exultation after the formal ceremony.

A man of unique charisma

The excitement of the inauguration and the enthusiasm of the common people for Aristide was something unique in my experience. The man himself has an extraordinary ability to play a crowd like a musical instrument. His inaugural speech was subtle, grave, dramatic, tough and comic. And at all times the crowds were in his hands. Two days later, the poor and the blind and the lame were invited to have breakfast in the presidential palace. It was at the same time a pitiful and a joyous scene, this spectacle of wounded humanity – many hobbling on crutches, entering a place in which they would have been shot for setting foot a few weeks before. Aristide walked among them, and spoke to them of his hopes and fears – all through dialogue. His way was to bring some cripple forward from the crowd and conduct a three-way conversation, with the people adding their comments and roaring out answers to his questions. I was moved at the time by the scene, and terribly impressed. After the speechifying there were refreshments and a band played under the trees. A young man was singing a song about freedom called 'O La Liberté' when he looked around to see who was singing beside him. It was the president himself.

The very strength of the enthusiasm for Aristide in one way made me fearful and sad. One so wanted the first ever elected leader of Haiti to succeed and bring some peace and prosperity to the poorest country in the region, if not in the world. Even though he only promised them dignity, they must expect more. I felt at the time that no man, however selfless, however bright, no man could produce dramatic economic effects in Haiti. The problems were just too vast. So what comes when Aristide fails to deliver? As he must fail to deliver in his short term of five years. In the end he didn't have time to fail. Seven months later an army coup forced him to flee.

A tradition of violence and death

One day driving though Port-au-Prince, we noticed a small crowd gathered at the side of the street and stopped to see what was happening. A man lay face down on the street. Blood oozed through a bullet hole in the back of his shirt. A woman talked in agitated fashion with a reporter from some local radio station. The rest just stood around looking at the body, and wondering if anything else would happen. Death can be close to anyone in Haiti. Aristide himself escaped death by a whisker seven or eight times.

Jean-Bertrand Aristide first came to public notice as the Salesian parish priest of the St John Bosco church in Port au Prince. The parish includes a vast slum area called La Saline, the salt marsh. The one-room houses in La Saline are packed side by side, with muddy pathways and piles of garbage in between. Living means getting by, earning a dollar or two with a street stall, stealing a bit of fruit, playing cards or draughts on the side of the street, sending the kids with a bucket on their head to get water to wash with, walking clear of the big black pig that roots around the piles of garbage. It is here that Aristide adopted an approach to mission informed by the theology of liberation which for him meant seeking justice rather than handing out bowls of rice. In his own words:

> Haiti is the parish of the poor. Beans and rice are hypocrisy when the priest gives them only to a chosen few among his own flock, and thousands and thousands of others starve. Perhaps that night the priest can sleep better thinking, 'Claude's eyes look brighter today'. Perhaps that will put the priest's mind at rest. Hypocrisy! Because for every Claude and Bob and Marie to whom the priest gives his generous bowl of rice, there are a hundred thousand more sitting on bony haunches in the dust, chewing on a pit of a mango, finishing their only meal for the day.

> So long as the priest keeps feeding the children without helping deliver the poor from poverty, the poor will never escape the humiliating fate to which they have been assigned by the corrupt system. When the priest only feeds the children, he is participating in that corrupt system, allowing it to endure.

The poverty and degradation of La Saline helped turn the quiet scholar into the fiery preacher, whose sermons proved to be such a scourge for the powerful and the wealthy. He spoke about 'a regime where the donkeys do all the work and the horses prance in the sunshine, a regime of misery'. When he spoke like that some of the horses got restive, so his superiors sent him out of the country for a while to Canada.

Horses who prance in the sunshine

The young Fr Aristide made some powerful enemies. Jean Claude

Duvalier, President for life of Haiti, feared him as one of the very few who challenged the Duvalier family's control of power and wealth. Colonels and sergeants and lieutenants in the army were angered when he spoke in his sermons about abuses they committed – and mentioned them by name. The Americans were annoyed because he said the US was responsible for training and arming and supporting the military, who had no enemy to shoot but their own people. The Catholic hierarchy were jealous of his large following and of the attention he attracted from foreign journalists. The wealthy feared him because he said the system by which they enriched themselves was corrupt and criminal, and that wealth would do better to be shared. But the poor people loved him and hung on his every word. They called him a prophet while his enemies said he was only encouraging people to spill blood.

A nation born in blood

Haiti has seen the spilling of a lot of blood. For more than a century the French tortured their slaves – rolled them downhill in spiked barrels, or stuffed gunpowder up their rectums and blew them apart. In 1791 in the first slave revolt, women were disembowelled, men cut in half and babies held impaled on pikes. 2,000 whites and 10,000 slaves died in that struggle. The colonial powers as a group were determined to undermine the new state – they didn't want their own slaves elsewhere following its example. In a final attempt to regain control, Napoleon sent a full army to the Caribbean in 1802. Forty thousand whites and sixty thousand blacks died in the ensuing campaign. It was out of such carnage that the first black state in the world was born. Its flag was blue and red – the French flag of revolution with the white torn out.

The Duvaliers and the Tonton Macoutes

The Haiti that Jean-Bertrand Aristide grew up in was ruled by the elder Duvalier known to all as 'Papa Doc'. The official catechism of the Duvalierist regime was said to begin with the invocation, 'Our Doc who art in the National Palace for life, hallowed be thy name, thy will be done at Port-au-Prince and in the provinces'. Papa Doc died in 1971 and was succeeded by his son, Baby Doc. Somewhere between 10,000 and 30,000 Haitians were killed during the 29 years of Duvalierism. Duvalier organised his own personal security force of thugs, the Tonton Macoutes, named after the bogeyman in Haitian fairy tales who carried off bad children in his 'macoute' or knapsack.

The church in the early 1980s

During the early 1980s the Catholic Church became the only effective voice calling for greater justice and democracy. As often when all political protest is suppressed, the church retains some immunity from state control. Clergy and laity took a lead from Pope John Paul II when he said, during a papal visit in March 1983, that ' Haiti has to involve itself completely for the good of all men and women but especially the most deprived. It is indeed necessary that things change here.'

Jean-Bertrand Aristide was one bright young cleric who agreed with him. Having earned a master's degree in psychology, Aristide studied in Rome, Jerusalem, Britain, Ireland and Canada, where he learnt English, Italian, Hebrew, and Spanish – to add to French and Creol, the local languages.

In February 1986 a popular uprising forced Baby Doc into exile and the long era of dictatorship seemed about to end. Even at this early stage Aristide was the most visible among a group of progressive priests and nuns who had helped organise opposition to Duvalier.

Military rule after Duvalier

With the fall of the Duvaliers, the army under Lieutenant-General Henri Namphy took over, promising elections, and then did what armies generally do in these circumstances – forget the elections and try to cling on to power. It was a period of great frustration and disappointment for the Haitian people.

On 26 April 1986, Fr Aristide helped organise a march to Fort Dimanche, a notorious prison. Three thousand of the Duvaliers' enemies had languished, starved, and died there – those who weren't actually tortured and executed. Aristide had drawn up a petition and collected eleven thousand signatures asking that the prison be closed and turned into a museum. But the military junta wasn't interested in petitions, and treated the demonstration in the old Duvalierist way.

After a shouting match the soldiers opened fire. Aristide was there with a reporter in a radio jeep and broadcast the incident live for Radio Soleil, the Catholic radio station. People who listened to the broadcast said they could hear the bullets flying around him. Six people were killed and more than fifty wounded. Aristide's open condemnation of this army brutality turned him into a national hero.

At the end of July Fr Aristide's superiors – it is said under pressure from the Vatican nuncio – decided to change him to a church on the outskirts of Port au Prince. The area was a Duvalierist stronghold. His supporters judged that this was inviting assassination, so they took over the cathedral and organised a hunger strike. After six days the church authorities were forced to give in, and Aristide stayed in the parish of Don Bosco.

Peasant massacres and attempted assassinations

One month later Aristide was in trouble again when a massacre took place near the city of Jean Rabel. Peasants seeking land reform were ambushed and hundreds died at the hands of thugs in the pay of local landowners. Aristide attended a commemoration ceremony for the victims, and when he rose to speak, four or five men in the crowd opened fire, but the bullets missed him. He was returning with three other priests to Port au Prince – under a blanket in the back of a Volkswagen – when the car was ambushed near the town of Freycineau. Fr Antoine Adrien, who was present, described the scene for us.

> The mob was there with sticks, with rocks, with guns, and they were telling us, 'Here they are the communists. Here they are the communists, where is Fr Aristide?' They asked us to get out of the car and I said 'No. Nobody is going to go out of the car. We have been checked already by authorities at Freycineau'. So we refused to get out. Well a lot of things happened. The car was destroyed, people throwing rocks – it was horrible.

When the attackers were distracted by another car coming in the opposite direction, the driver shot forward and they escaped. Their wounds were treated at a remote Protestant mission where they stayed the night. It was late the following day before people knew they were still alive.

As the military regime became more violent and more oppressive, Aristide's preaching became less veiled. He spoke of anger in the veins, in the gut. He spoke of when the winds of hunger blow, and the storm of injustice is raging, of a people weighed down by all this human and inhuman suffering who will become a people marching toward justice, and the subject of their own history.

Murder in church

By September 1988 Aristide seemed to be the only voice left to challenge the military. One Sunday, while he was offering Sunday

Mass, a band of thugs entered the parish church. Maggie Steiber, an American photographer preparing a book on Haiti, was in the church at the time and spoke to us of her experience.

> About 30 or 40 men burst through the doors of the church which had been locked and they had guns and pistols and machetes and some clubs with spikes on the ends and they just started chasing everybody. At that point there was great pandemonium. I was up by the altar and people sort of realised what was about to happen, so some young men in the congregation ran up and surrounded Aristide and basically carried him out the sacristy door. There was a great deal of panic and people were running everywhere. The pews were crashing. There was a lot of screaming and shooting ... I ran right into the arms of one of the men with a machete and at that point he grabbed me by the shoulder and he had his machete raised and I thought I was going to be killed. But if I can say this without being over dramatic – there is something about looking into a man's eyes who is about to kill you, you really look into the eyes of death I guess, and it's that fear more than the fear of death itself that made me react. I turned and pulled away from him with all my force and I think it surprised him enough so that he lost his grip on my shoulder although he did keep my dress and it tore all the way down to the small of my back, and so somehow I managed to get away. We broke out a window and jumped down to the street, at which point I saw that my car had been burned. A little bit down the road there's a military complex and there behind the wall there were soldiers just sort of watching everything that had gone on without lifting a hand to help the people in the church.

Attempts at banishment

Thirteen people were killed, eighty injured, and the church burned. It was two weeks before any protest came from the hierarchy, and then it didn't mention either Aristide or even the name of his church! Aristide himself was terribly shocked, confused, and saddened by the loss of life and agreed under pressure from his superiors to go abroad. But when the news broke many thousands of young people marched to Petionville, where Aristide was being kept at another Salesian house, chanting 'we don't care if Archbishop Ligondé, who sucks up to dictators leaves, but Aristide must stay'. Protesters blocked the roads to the airport. The banishment was rescinded.

Expulsion from the Salesians

A few months later, the Salesian order expelled Aristide. Now a priest without a pulpit, Aristide took up residence in a home that he had founded earlier for homeless boys. Eighty-three Haitian priests issued a formal statement supporting Aristide and that was some consolation. But his own brothers in the Salesians had rejected him. The communiqué from Rome had said that the commitment he had assumed was in serious conflict with the clear will of the founder. It accused him of incitement to hatred and violence and the exaltation of class struggle which go directly against that fidelity to the teachings of the church that forms a living part of the Salesian spirit. Aristide filed an appeal in Rome against expulsion. He got no reply.

Many Salesians were sad to see how swiftly their Order in Rome expelled Aristide without that due process that is appropriate in a church which so often speaks to others about justice and human rights. One of them told us:

> Here in Haiti the Salesians don't know what happened. I think that it was the bishops who spoke to Rome and in Rome they told our superior to put him out of the congregation.

Marjorie Michel is a family friend.

> But for Aristide it was very very hard because I think all those years he expected that the Salesians at least would understand, because he loved the community a lot and it was very difficult for him to accept the fact that the community put him out. And this was one of the times I saw Aristide very, very, how can I say, very down you know. He was very down because he had the feeling and the wish to be part of a community and he couldn't understand what he did wrong.

Choosing the first democratically elected president

Army repression continued till March 1990, when the then current military dictator, General Avril, was persuaded to fly to the US. The move to oust him was spearheaded by a group of priests led by Fr Antoine Adrien, who co-ordinated twelve political groups in negotiations with the United States. The new leader of the army, General Abrahms, agreed to install a woman lawyer as interim president and arrange free elections. But when Roger Lafontant, former head of the Tonton Macoutes, returned to Haiti and wasn't arrested, many people feared the worst. The only hope seemed to be to find a candidate for president who could not be beaten. There was only one.

Fr Adrien, leader of the priests who had helped to set up the elections, and probably the most respected cleric in Haiti, said to us, 'Aristide's candidacy was the only answer to the threats of the Macoutes. We had no choice, it was a necessity.'

His election campaign was extraordinary in so far as the candidate hardly appeared because his supporters were afraid he would be shot. But he didn't really need to – once he became a candidate, the majority poor of Haiti had already decided their vote. There were over a dozen candidates. Aristide got 67.7% of the total vote.

Diplomatic congratulations poured in from all sides. The Vatican however, and the Catholic hierarchy remained silent. Rome sent Aristide a private note asking him to step aside as a priest while he held political office. He declined, saying he would only leave if the Vatican ordered him to do so.

Church opposition

In a Mass broadcast for the New Year, the Archbishop of Port-au-Prince, Francois Ligondé commented on the result of the election.

> Are we heading for a regime of authoritarian politics with a leftist orientation carrying the defrocked bolshevism rejected by the countries of the East? By the year 2,004 people will be eating rocks.

It was an outrageous rejection of the democratic voice of the people. Less than a week later, Roger Lafontant, former head of the Tonton Macoute, appeared on TV and announced he had seized power. For ten anxious hours the future of democracy in Haiti was at stake before the army made up its mind to go with the people and storm the palace. The conspirators were quickly overcome.

The anger of the poor

Large numbers of people went out on the streets of Port-au-Prince to protest against the coup. Archbishop Ligondé's sermon was interpreted as having at least given encouragement to the leaders of the coup, if not indicating church involvement. The crowd sought Ligondé, and when he fled the country before them, they vented their anger on the church institution as a whole, burning the old (unused) cathedral, part of the archbishop's palace, the bishops' conference office and the nunciature, where they suspected Ligondé was staying. The nuncio escaped, but his secretary was caught by the crowd and beaten. Although the Vatican sent a new chargé d'affaires less than two weeks after the attack, the position of nuncio was left unfilled while Aristide remained as president.

We drove up to the nunciature. It was situated in a wealthy neighbourhood, up on a wooded hill to catch the cool breezes which can
moderate the tropical heat. Panoramic windows looked over the
city. I walked though it with a camera, which was easy because it
was what one might call 'open plan'. Every window frame, every
fitting, ever stick of furniture had been removed. The remains of a
massive bonfire filled part of the driveway. Filing cabinets with
mangled drawers and half-burnt contents spilled out over the tarmac. A picture of the Pope moved slightly in the breeze. I picked up
a half-burnt newspaper cutting with a photo of Fr Jean-Bertrand
Aristide, who one day later was to be inaugurated as the first democratically elected President of Haiti.

The Vatican seems to have held Aristide responsible for '*le dechoukaj*'
of the nunciature – though he denied hand, act or part in it. The
people were so angry with Archbishop Ligondé that it is unlikely
that Aristide could have controlled them – even if he knew what
was going on. The president-elect was of course hiding from would-
be assassins in this interim period before inauguration.

On 7 February 1991, Aristide, still a priest, was installed as Haiti's
first president. He lasted eight months in office before the army
decided once more to intervene and take over the government.
Diplomatic intervention helped to get Aristide out of the country
before he was shot. He was in exile for a full three years. And how
did Haiti fare while he was away?

Haiti without Aristide: A view from outside

The World Council of Churches

In 1993 a World Council of Churches delegation confirmed reports
of gross violations of human rights in Haiti, and of widespread
killing and torture of supporters of Aristide. The delegates estimated
that 3,000 people had been summarily executed since the *coup d'état
in* 1991, 4,500 illegally detained and 2,000 wounded by shots or
blows. There had been damage to 2,000 houses. Approximately
400,000 people were thought to have left the capital, Port-au Prince,
to take refuge in rural areas. They thought about 40,000 had fled the
island by sea, where 2,000 had perished.

The US Drug Enforcement Administration

In 1993, the US Drug Enforcement Administration said the amount
of cocaine passing through Haiti has reached 4,500 kilos a month,
more than double what it was before the coup, while Howard

French, an American journalist, pointed out in the *New York Times* how significant amounts of money were being made – not only by senior officers in the Haitian army, but by lower grades too.

A US bishop's view

Bishop Thomas J. Gumbelton, Auxiliary of Detroit, visited Haiti in 1993 on behalf of Pax Christi, and wrote about his experience afterwards. He quotes an editor of a newspaper who asked him, 'Do you know a country where they pull people out of church and kill them, and no bishop speaks out?' Gumbleton continued:

> The Catholic church is really two churches: the church of the elite and the church of the vast majority of the people – the church of the poor. And the bishops are almost without exception tied to the church of the rich. That happens so frequently in so many parts of the world that most of the time I am not too bothered by it. But in Haiti a couple of weeks ago I felt strongly the contradiction between our words as a church, and our actions.
>
> On 11 September 1993 one of the most blatant acts of violent repression happened in Sacred Heart Church in Port-au-Prince. Antoine Izmery, a businessman and supporter of exiled President Jean-Bertrand Aristide, was dragged out of the pew where he was attending Mass with his family. As he lay on the street, a soldier pressed a gun against his head and fired it. Izmery died within minutes.

The Holy See

In a leading article entitled 'An outrageous Vatican appointment in Haiti', the *National Catholic Reporter* expressed strong views with respect to the appointment of a nuncio who presented his credentials to the discredited and illegal military junta shortly after they ousted Aristide.

> This is the government born in blood that the Vatican recognised after shunning Aristide, prophet of the poor … The military government naturally praised the Holy See's positive attitude and said it showed 'much understanding toward the Haitian people'. But the Haitian people have been clubbed out of the arena. What the Holy See is rubbing shoulders with now, after ignoring the will of the people and abandoning the priest who preached and tried bravely to live the gospel of the poor, are the forces of oppression and corruption, exploitation and terror.

Radio Vatican

Radio Vatican put out a programme in 1993 highly critical of Aristide's 'reign of terror'. One month later, Fr Ebêrhard von Gemmingen, in charge of the German-language output of Radio Vatican, apologised for the programme admitting that 'even Radio Vatican makes mistakes' and that 'human rights violations have been worse and more numerous since Aristide's time than during his term of office'.

The Pope

In the summer of 1994, the Pope's only remarks on Haiti were to lecture its citizens on the evils of voodoo.

Aristide's comment

Referring to the leaders of the coup that ousted him, Aristide said in a speech to the UN General Assembly in September 1993:

> Rejected by all the states of the world, these criminals are still recognised by the Vatican – the only state to bless the crimes it should have condemned in the name of the God of justice and peace. What would Pope John Paul II's attitude be if Haiti had been Polish?

The view from inside Haiti

The laity send a cry to the Pope

Five thousand Haiti Catholics signed an open letter to Pope John Paul asking for his help in recognising their right to live in freedom.

> We have approached our bishops in the hope that our pleas would be heard but nobody listens. Where is the Pope in the middle of this crisis which stifles us?

'We have proof,' said the open letter, 'that pastors of the church in Haiti, helped by high-up religious leaders, worked behind the scenes to achieve this new government of oppression, brought in with the help of the army in the presence of the apostolic nuncio, the Archbishop of Cap-Haitien and the Auxiliary Bishop of Port-au-Prince. Some people in Haiti are persuaded that it was the nuncio and some bishops who demanded a purge of priests, religious and lay people opposed to the provisional government.

The purge of priests: two weeks of army activity

In late May 1992, Fr LeRoy from Petit Rivierie was forced to leave his church after soldiers stoned the parish. On 2 June, Fr Marcel Bussels was arrested and held for two days at military headquarters in Cap Haitien, and then put under house arrest. Fr Dennis Verdier, head of Caritas in Les Cayes, was arrested on 1 June while driving to his office and imprisoned until 6 June. Br Jean-Baptiste Cassius of the Sacred Heart Order was apprehended on 2 June and released the next day. Fr Gilles Vanroc of the Order of Preachers, a French citizen (whom we had previously interviewed) was arrested on 6 June in Verrette with seven lay people, and held until the following day. Yet despite all this oppressive activity against church personnel, the bishops remained silent and there was no official church protest.

The bishops make a statement

The bishops eventually issued a statement after their October meeting that year. They said the sufferings of their people didn't leave them indifferent, and that 'the Lord will not let his people fold up under the burdens they bear'. And they urged the faithful not to forget their rosaries. Despite the turmoil around them, they offered no criticism or comment on the political situation whatever.

Priests talk about their bishops

Fr Jean-Yves Urfié, CSSp: 'When I see the Vatican being the only state in the world to officially recognise the killers of the people in Haiti, how can I sleep with my conscience? It's a shame for the church. Of course, we should respect the authorities of the church, but the authorities of the church will be even more respected when they respect the gospel.'

Rev Gerard Jean-Just: 'Most of the bishops have sold their souls to the devil, and now fear that retribution is on the way, either at the hands of their flock or Fr Aristide ... People don't forget, and that is why the bishops are scared.'

Fr Jean-Marie Vincent, a Montfort missionary priest who was until recently director of Caritas in northern Haiti: 'While dozens of priests, nuns and even a bishop are threatened, imprisoned and persecuted, the hierarchy with the notable exception of Bishop Willy Romélus of Jeremie, have said nothing ...'

Death of Fr Jean-Marie Vincent

On 28 August 1994, the same Fr Jean-Marie Vincent's car was stopped in the driveway of the Montfort Fathers, the door pulled open and the priest shot dead at the steering-wheel.

At the Requiem, neither the celebrant nor the bishop who said the prayers before burial mentioned the circumstances of his death – they simply read the liturgical texts. It was left to the Montfort provincial superior, who preached the homily, to remind the congregation that the priest was a victim of state terrorism.

One of the prayers of the faithful was a plea that 'in the same way that the first killing of a priest awakened the conscience of Archbishop Romero of San Salvador, so may the killing of Jean Marie awaken the conscience of those responsible for the church'.

The congregation who heard these words knew that three weeks earlier the Haitian bishops' conference had issued a pastoral letter condemning any foreign intervention in Haiti to help restore Aristide as 'illegal and murderous' and making us 'tremble with indignation'.

Aristide and his priesthood

One of the questions that most interested the foreign press when Aristide became president was whether he could or would remain a priest. We put the question to different people and made a little montage of their replies.

BISHOP GAILLOT. If today Rome declares Aristide is no longer a priest, that would be to do an injury to the people. That would not be what the people had voted for.

FR. ADRIEN. He always said people don't need Aristide, they need Fr Aristide. That is why he was so upset by the fact that the hierarchy seem to want him out of it. He has said that 'if it is the price I have to pay for peace with the church I will pay it. But it is a difficult one for me to swallow, and I will accept only if the hierarchy publicly state that is what they want.'

BISHOP GAILLOT. The Bishop of Rome is a head of state and everyone accepts the situation on the part of the Pope. The Pope often gives political discourses. Nobody reproaches him. But if any other cleric says something political, people reproach him !

MARJORIE MICHEL. Aristide is a priest. He will always be a priest. And he is a priest because he cannot live without thousands of people. You know when you are married to somebody, you have to be married to that one person. But Aristide is married to a thousand people, and he cannot live without this feeling of loving thousands of people.

Aristide himself answered the question for us when we spoke to him a few days after his inauguration.

> What I am doing today as a president is in fact what I was trying to do as a priest, sharing life with people, loving people, putting the law of love into practice. So if I continue to do the same – even if the place from where I am doing it is different – people will realise that there is no contradiction between who I was yesterday, and who I am today.

Leaving the priesthood

On 17 October 1994, Aristide wrote to Archbishop Francois Gayot of Cap Haitian, head of the Haitian Bishops' Conference:

> You have asked me to leave the priesthood for the growth of harmonious relations … between two heads of state: the head of state of the Vatican and the head of state of the Republic of Haiti … I have decided, Excellency, to agree to your request.

Something over a year later, the following paragraph appeared under the heading 'Milestones' in *Time* magazine, 29 January 1996:

> Married. Jean Bertrand Aristide, 42, Haitian President; to American Mildred Trouillot 33; near Port-au-Prince. The relatively simple ceremony – no music, no bridal gown – was designed to mollify his countrymen, who had believed the former priest would remain theirs alone.

Many people in Haiti remain very disappointed that the church would not permit a compromise over Aristide's priesthood and make a temporary exception in the unique circumstances of the poorest country in the Western world. And so died part of a dream.

Some thoughts on the wider problem of involvement of church personnel in political affairs

The problem of church personnel being involved in politics may be at three levels – broad political involvement, running for elected office, and lastly, accepting ministerial responsibility.

1. Broad political involvement

When the Pope and Ronald Reagan planned together to give aid to Solidarity and destabilise the communist regime in Poland, the Pope was certainly acting politically. When bishops criticise new legislation which has a bearing on moral issues, they act in the political arena, but again the church has no problem about that. However, there is one gloss to be added here. Popes and bishops give themselves far more licence in this kind of political action than they will normally permit to priests. Part of this I have no doubt has much to do with the authoritarian structure, where bishops prefer priests to know their own place, which is under the bishop and not in an independent power structure where the bishop might feel threatened.

In the past, priests and sisters in the United States have had a substantial political role. Fr Theodore Hesburgh, ex-President of Notre Dame University, estimated once that over a period of twenty years about 20% of his time was spent working in federal posts. He is credited with playing a key role in the Jimmy Carter administration after the president's election, helping him choose cabinet and other high ranking officers. President Carter hired Sister Victoria Mongiardo, as co-chairman of his 'ethnic desk'. Bishop, now Cardinal, Roger Mahony headed the California Agricultural Relations Board for a period.

2. Elective office

Sister Claire Dunn was elected to the Arizona state senate as a Democrat in 1974. She spoke then about her motivation:

> When we make the gospel present in the wilderness of politics, we bring hope to the poor, the weak, the powerless, the voiceless – to those without political clout and professional lobbies. We show that there are those who care about the powerless where decisions are made that affect the quality of their lives, who believe that they are not expendable and their rights barterable.

Fr Robert Drinan SJ was a very successful congressmen in Washington in the reign of Pope Paul VI, and is generally held to have wielded a lot of influence and done much good. Come the pontificate of John Paul, however, the pressure was put on him to resign, which he did, but purely in obedience to the Pope's wishes.

3. Ministerial office

Before Aristide came to prominence, the other well-known examples of priests being involved in politics were to be found in Nicaragua, where four priests took prominent roles in the Sandinista revolutionary government. We met and interviewed three of these on several visits to Nicaragua – Fernando Cardenal, his brother Ernesto, the poet, and Miguel D'Escoto, then foreign minister. Each of their cases is complicated and different, and each has its own poignancy.

Fernando Cardenal

Fernando Cardenal is a Jesuit who, at the end of his studies for the presthood, lived for nine months in a slum in Colombia.

> I felt the poverty of the people was insufferable, that it was unjust. It became unbearable for me, the misery, the sadness, the constant suffering of those who lived alongside us. I made a promise before leaving – I would fight for the liberation of the poor.

Cardenal joined the Sandinistas in 1970 and, when they formed a government, he was asked to be minister in charge of the literacy programme. Literacy was a Sandinista priority, on the grounds that the exploitation of the poor was made easier by the fact they could not read or write. In a remarkable countrywide effort, the secondary schools were temporarily closed, and sixty thousand young men and women descended on the rural areas to teach the *campesinos* to read and write. The index of illiteracy was reduced from 50% to 12% in five months – surely a remarkable achievement. Improving the standard of literacy and abolishing illiteracy altogether became a harder task with the Contra war and the subsequent economic collapse. The Contras killed 400 of Fernando's teachers.

The law of the church

Canon 285 par. 3 in the law of the church says: 'Clerics are forbidden to assume public office whenever it means sharing in the exercise of civil power'. Fernando was initially given permission to continue working with the government by the Nicaraguan Conference of Bishops in June 1981, but by way of temporary exception, and this was later withdrawn. In the course of a long letter to his friends in 1984 he said:

> I believe that Canon 285 is valid, and I am not against it. I also believe that today more than ever the exception for the priests in Nicaragua ought to be renewed because today more than ever the church ought to give witness to being on the side of the poor at a time when there is a desire relentlessly to attack and destroy their hopes.

Cardenal gives one the impression of a deeply serious, perhaps over-scrupulous man. He said at the time that he had devoted a lot of time to discernment and spiritual direction, always involving a lot of prayer, and eventually came to the conclusion that he would be committing serious sin if he were to abandon his priestly option for the poor of Nicaragua through his work in the Sandinista revolution. He spoke too of a bond of blood linking him with the many who died in the original struggle – some 40,000 people – amongst them his brother-in-law and three nephews. Their cause which he saw as 'just, noble, beautiful and holy' was not something he could lightly abandon, especially when he felt the poor of Nicaragua would see that as a betrayal.

Why did his superiors move against him?

Cardenal quotes a letter from his Jesuit superior in Rome in which he seems to admit that the only reason for asking him to give up his work is that the Pope wants it. The letter reads:

> Though it is possible to exercise a real apostolate in a position like the one you hold, the Holy Father has over and over manifested his will that such offices not be performed by priests and he hopes that the Jesuits will be an example of obedience in this matter. It is necessary, therefore, that we follow the will of the Holy Father promptly and in a spirit of faith.

> I realise I am asking you for a very difficult act of obedience, one in which the human reasons can appear to be insufficient; but I am sure that God will reward your faith and make it apostolically fruitful. You can count on my prayers for this, on my admiration and on my help in all that is within my hands.

From what Fernando said to us in 1988, it would appear that the Vatican was satisfied with the formal expulsion from the Jesuits in 1984, and did not hunt him out of his community, where life went on pretty much as before.

> These were ecclesiastical sanctions, but since then they have left us in peace. We continue to live our priesthood in private. I live in a Jesuit community – I celebrate Mass there, and also in other private places. The three of us (ministers in the government) continue living as priests, fulfilling all the obligations of the priesthood including celibacy. But our fundamental task now is to help our people through the revolution in the post that we have been given. We can say that since 1984 our lives have been peaceful in regard to the problems that we had before with the Vatican.

Miguel D'Escoto

Miguel D'Escoto is a Maryknoll priest, whose father was a Nicaraguan diplomat. The young Miguel was educated in the US, and worked as a missionary in Chile and in communications for the Maryknoll

Fathers, a New York based missionary order. His diplomatic family and his communications experience, added to his early support for the Sandinistas, probably help to explain his appointment. His position as foreign minister inevitably brought him into conflict with the Archbishop, later Cardinal, of Managua, who supported the US backed Contra forces against the Sandinista government. According to D'Escoto himself, his own order supported him and refused to dismiss him when he was foreign minister. Then at the height of the Contra War, he got a letter from the Vatican giving him fifteen days to withdraw from his post or be *ipso facto* suspended from priestly faculties. He believes this is the first case in history of the Vatican suspending a religious priest over the heads of his superiors.

No longer foreign minister, he is now national co-ordinator for the Communal Movement, a non-governmental organisation involved in the struggle against poverty – leadership training, medical aid and all such things that may be relevant in what now is the second poorest country in the Latin America (after Aristide's Haiti).

According to a report in the *Tablet* of 2 September 1995, D'Escoto has a letter from the Vatican which refused his request to have his priestly faculties restored on the grounds that he was not sufficiently repentant, the proof of this lack of repentance being his work for the slum dwellers – a letter which he says he hopes to show to God on the day of judgement!

I've met D'Escoto three times, one of which was a long session. I've read about him and watched him since we first met in 1979. I don't know how good a foreign minister he was, but he certainly was every inch a pious priest trying to do good as best he saw it, but having to work in the circumstances of a divided church with a conservative hierarchy in league with the national enemy.

Ernesto Cardenal

Ernesto, the minister of culture, the third priest holding ministerial appointment, is a poet in Spanish of international reputation. I don't think he was ever bothered much about what the hierarchy or the Vatican thought of him. His picture however may be more widely known than that of either his brother Fernando or Miguel d'Escoto. A photograph taken during the papal visit of 1983 which shows the Pope wagging his finger at Ernesto kneeling before him on the tarmac at Managua airport, repeatedly turns up in religious books and magazines – why, I dont know. Maybe because editors think it a characteristic pose of Pope John Paul!

Conclusion

So should priests get involved in party politics? As a general rule, clearly no. Even the priests who have been involved say that. But should there be exceptions? There should – and particularly where gospel values are involved, which means, like Christ, being on the side of the poor. And maybe people like the priest's immediate ordinary to whom he is directly responsible should decide what circumstances justify it. The Jesuit superior would never have expelled Fernando Cardinal, or made a good man suffer so in his conscience. The Vatican, not the Maryknolls, suspended D'Escoto. And if I have the feel of influential Salesian priests I have met, I don't think they ever wanted to expell Fr, now Mr (much against his will), Jean-Bertrand Aristide.

Postscript

Aristide returned to Haiti on 15 October 1994, and resigned from office on 7 February 1996. It was the first time in Haiti's 192 year history that there had been a peaceful transfer of power. Even though Aristide was forced to spend three years of his term in exile, he did not try to overturn the ruling in the Haitian constitution which only permits a five year term.

And what about citizen Aristide? Nobody expects him to disappear into the woodwork. Clearly he will remain a power in the background of Haitian affairs.

Freed from the constraints of high office, he may well return to the role he played so consistently before he became president – the scourge of the enemies of the poor.

13
SEPARATE OR TOGETHER
A cold look at integrated education, and some alternative strategies

When eleven people died in the bombing at Enniskillen on Remembrance Day 1987, the wave of revulsion helped to bring Catholics and Protestants together in an effort to overcome differences, which in their extreme form had led to the horrible tragedy. One of these initiatives was the founding of an integrated primary school in Enniskillen where Catholic and Protestant children are educated together.

Lagan College, the first ever integrated school opened in Belfast in 1981. Its parent body were a group called All Children Together, or ACT for short. The motto they chose for Lagan was *Ut sint unum -* that they may be one. The school badge displays two doves of peace, and the bridge which the school hopes to help build between the two communities.

Integrated education is something that appears to have wide support. Most leaders in the community speak well of it, or if they don't, keep quiet about it in public. Yet there are only nineteen integrated primary schools out of a total of 1,000, and nine integrated grammar and secondary schools out of a total of 250 in Northern Ireland.

Sr Aideen Kinlen was principal of St Catherine's College in Armagh when we made this programme. Before she became a Sacred Heart sister, she was a practising barrister in Dublin. Law is in the family – her brother Dermot is a well-known member of the judiciary. She told us that her interest in integrated education was what really brought her to accept the post in Armagh.

> In the 1970s, before I came to Armagh, I was convinced that integrated education was the obvious answer. I was from the south, living in Dublin, reading about and hearing about the troubles and felt it was so stupid to be divided in this way when we don't need to be. But I've had to revise my opinions a little bit since I came here eight years ago. I see it as far more difficult than I had anticipated.

Difficulties in the way of integrated education

Difficulties: No. 1. Legal considerations

The easiest difficulty to remove involved changing the law about government aid to schools. The first moves were made by Lord Dunleath in 1978. He helped to bring in legislation enabling state schools – which in Northern Ireland are *de facto* Protestant schools – to become integrated while retaining their 100% government funding.

With this enabling legislation, All Children Together were confident that the Church of Ireland, the Presbyterian and the Methodist Churches, which had committed themselves in public to the support of integrated education by resolutions at synods, assemblies and conferences, would now move to integrate at least some of their schools. However, genuine as opposed to verbal support for a policy is only tested when the aims of that policy become achievable. It soon became clear that the Protestant churches aimed to do nothing about integration, so ACT decided to move on its own and set up Lagan College, the pioneer among integrated schools.

The hierarchy of the Catholic Church, on the other hand, has never been equivocal about its anxiety to preserve its own schools – and indeed down the years Catholics have had to pay dearly for the privilege. Up to 1930 Catholic schools only received minimum subsidies for heating and cleaning. Between 1930 and 1944 they received half their capital and maintenance costs. After 1968 this was increased for most Catholic schools to 85% of capital costs and 100% maintenance. While Protestant, and now integrated schools receive 100% funding, Catholic schools have still to find 15% of their capital funding – which is nearly half a million on a three million school extension.

In 1988, the Minister of Education set out a programme of legislation designed to encourage the growth of integrated schools. This programme offered 100% funding, as well as priority in the allocation of funds. The legislation, passed in 1990, was strongly criticised by leaders of all the main churches, as well as by educationalists like Paul Hewitt, headmaster of the Royal School, Dungannon.

> Where I have difficulty is that these schools are going to be funded from part of the normal education budget. In doing that, you're making a special case for the schools, whether they are popular or viable or not, at the expense of the established schools. Money in

education is hard enough to come by now, but to take what little there is away at a time of great educational change, to me seems a very harsh and unworkable principle. In fact I would say it annoys people about the very idea of integrated education, not because of the principles of integrated education but the way it's being fostered.

But the main provision, perhaps, that worried Catholic educators was the possibility of a forced take-over of some Catholic schools. Sr Aideen explained the point.

The Minister for Education has encouraged integrated schools and has given any group of parents who want to set up such a school a *carte blanche*; he'll give them a hundred per cent funding for capital expenditure and indeed a school whose parents want to change its status can do so, simply by a majority vote at a meeting. Now the bishops were very worried about this; they felt that Catholic schools could be hi-jacked by some fanatical group or other, that it was a very arbitrary and highhanded way of moving and I certainly would see it that way myself.

The fear of take-over perhaps more than anything else brought the bishops to seek legal opinion as to where they would stand if the matter had to be tested in court. The late Cardinal Ó Fiaich explained their reservations shortly after the Bill was published.

We felt that this again was being unfair to the whole parish community who in general would have contributed to that school, because if it becomes an integrated school, then in some parishes you would have no Catholic school left and it was being unfair to the trustees who in fact are the legal owners of the school.

Difficulties: No 2. Physical and social division

However, it wasn't the legal problems that forced Sr Aideen to revise her hopes for integration.

I see it as far more difficult than I had anticipated. First of all it's difficult to run an integrated school unless you have a very big city with a sufficiently large number of people able to support a school. For the most part, the towns are small in Northern Ireland and they're backed up by a rural population which is very, very polarised. Here, for example, we have a bus coming in from the country and the bus carries Protestant and Catholic children together. And regularly I have to go up to the headmaster of the local (Protestant) secondary school with an apology for the behaviour of one of our girls, and indeed, *vice versa*, he has to come up here and apologise for the behaviour of his boys or girls to our pupils. Now that's 50 in a bus; multiply that into a school of 800 and you may find that you're not solving a problem, you're only making it worse – that's one example of the kind of difficulties we're up against.

The *de facto* polarisation of communities more than anything else is what discourages many people interested in integrated education. Armagh is a town of about 17,000 inhabitants, 40% Protestant, 60% Catholic. The division is strict. West Armagh is republican and Catholic. The graffiti on the walls tell you so – 'IRA' in large capitals with hooded men pointing their guns out from behind the letters. Flags in green white and orange. 'Up the Provos,' painted small and large. East Armagh, on the other hand is loyalist. The graffiti there which I also photographed – with a little trepidation – said 'UVF,' 'No Pope here', 'Armagh True Blues', and 'God save the Queen'. The divisions run so deep that I was told that few Catholics in Armagh would ever have visited this particular housing estate, and would still be too afraid to do so. Sr Aideen again:

> This school here is a Catholic school and it's situated in a Catholic housing area. Now the nearest Protestants living would be about two miles away from us here. Similarly all the Protestant schools are over near the Mall which is two miles or so from here. So they wouldn't be coming here.
>
> I think another difference would be that there's a certain social distinction between Catholics and Protestants, going back to times when the Catholics didn't have employment. Linked with that there is the desire to better yourself. Protestants aren't going to come to a school with Catholics because that would be lowering themselves. You would have the rare occasion of Catholics wanting to go to a Protestant school, but you wouldn't have *vice versa*. Now I think the same kind of misgivings would be operating even in an integrated situation. It would be social climbing by the Catholics and social descent by Protestants – unless they were very much still in the majority.

This idea seemed to be confirmed by a student of Dungannon Royal.

> Catholics probably think we are better off, better jobs you know, maybe, you know, a class higher, upper class or middle class.

Q. Do you think they are justified in that?

> Well most Protestants seem to have fancier cars, fancier houses.

Difficulties: No 3. The morality of social engineering

When people find fault with their society they often turn to education – both to blame it for existing defects, and to use it to promote the brave new world they aspire to. Critics of this view describe it as social engineering and argue that education ought to reflect, rather than try to define, the norms of society.

Among supporters of integrated education, the belief is implicit that contact between two people with opposing views is likely to help each of them, if not to change his or her own view, at least to better appreciate the point of view of the other. Critics on the other hand argue that while this may happen with children of liberal parents – the kind who send their children to integrated schools – it could just as well have the opposite effect where children of prejudiced parents are concerned. A student of Dungannon Royal expressed this view fairly bluntly to us:

> If you look at America, they have integrated schools in which blacks and whites go to school together – and it is just as bad as if they didn't go to school together because they fight like anything in school. You know it can be worse if you have two different types of people together; they will start to resent the other type being there and you sometimes get ferocious fights.

Several headmasters expressed the worry that if there were an integrated school nearby, it would tend to cream off the very children who were an important leaven within their own school community. Thomas Duncan, headmaster of the Armagh Royal School:

> One slight worry I have with the promotion of the integrated schools movement is that perhaps it is removing from the average community school the liberalising influence of those parents who have actively pursued an integrated education, and perhaps the extremists, or the people at each end of the continuum, are being left in the community schools and in the local schools.

Paul Hewitt, Headmaster of Dungannon Royal School, echoed similar sentiments:

> One of the things that worries me is that some children who are removed from our schools by parents who want to have an integrated ethos are the very children who would add salt and light to our own school atmosphere. We need those children to act as salt and light in their own communities and without them I think the task becomes more difficult.

Difficulties: No 4. Harmonising cultural identities

Perhaps the major problem that the integrated school has to face is the question of identity. For instance, in a Protestant school on the Queen's birthday, it would be normal for the minister to give a homily to the assembled students about Her Majesty and the good works she carries out on behalf of her loyal subjects. In a Catholic school the good lady would most likely be ridiculed if remembered at all. And the integrated school? One student at Lagan felt sore on this point:

> Well, I can remember the Catholic students didn't show us a lot of respect, you know. I can remember – it was just when it was her 60th birthday, people were sort of making a lot of fun about her and showing a lot of disrespect ... yes some people, I am not saying everyone did.

Q. Did that annoy you?

> It did annoy me a bit. I mean if you don't consider her as the Queen, you should still show her respect the same way as we would show respect to the Pope or anything like that.

Many nationalists – among them fierce critics of the Catholic church – oppose integrated education on the grounds that schools are the only place in Northern Ireland where nationalists still have control over their own lives. Integration for them means being absorbed in official Britishness. Mr Tipping is a teacher in a Catholic school.

> One of the two ethoses has to surrender to the other. Now let me put it this way, supposing a Catholic from any part of the Catholic community in NI decides to join the RUC. He has to sublimate his nationalism towards the ethos he's entering. He has, for example, to wear a British uniform with the emblem of the British crown. He has to salute the British flag and stand for the British national anthem. In fact he has to become a kind of unionist in a sense, and he's not allowed to exhibit or display or to live his nationalism within the order of the RUC.

> Now it seems to me that a sort of parallel applies in the educational sphere. If you go into the ethos of integrated education, would the school that you're entering fly a Union Jack? What national anthem would they play at the end of school functions? That sort of thing – these may appear to be minute points but they're not so much points as pointers to the feeling in the nationalist community that integrated education demands a surrender

on the part of the Catholic community rather than a coming together of both communities into some sort of new Ulster identity or some sort of Unionist/ Nationalist/Catholic/Protestant identity. I think that's the main fear, that *they,* in the sense of the unionists, are going to try and 'unionistise' the Catholic nationalist population rather than cheerfully and gladly and joyously enter into some kind of new Northern Ireland hybrid identity.

Some of the most interesting studies relating to the segregated/ integrated schools question have emerged from the Centre for the Study of Conflict, a cross disciplinary unit set up in the University of Ulster, Coleraine. The Centre aims to promote research and contribute to the public discussion of conflict and its causes in Northern Ireland. Professor Seamus Dunn, its present director, spoke to us about identity:

> The question of identity is of particular relevance to the integrated schools, because they have to start to generate a sort of common curriculum which takes account of the Protestant and Catholic, unionist and nationalist versions of the past – and of the present. So they have a hard job to create a school which celebrates both of these traditions and both of these cultures and both of these histories, and that's not easy and there isn't much precedent. There isn't much about that helps them. But they're not in the business of assimilation, they're not in the business of getting the two to look alike, they're trying to keep them separate and yet to celebrate the differences.

If integrated schools could demonstrate that they could achieve this celebration of the differences in the average community, there would indeed be cause for optimism. But it is difficult to see how they can at this stage of political development in Northern Ireland – except among an already tolerant minority.

Difficulties: No 5. Harmonising religious identities

If you pass though Armagh and find a school with a statue of the Sacred Heart in the grounds and images of the saints in the corridors – or even if you only see the name 'St Catherine's' on the gate, you have a sure marker that this is a Catholic school. In an integrated school, on the other hand, you will find an understandable absence of religious symbols, which would be very noticeable to the average Catholic parent, though perhaps less so to a Protestant.

Religion is important to both Catholics and Protestants in the

North. They see it as part of the school environment, and not just a class subject which can conveniently be consigned to a 'religious' period. So the simple act of saying a prayer becomes problematical when different Christian traditions have to be considered. The Hail Mary, for instance, could hardly be used in an integrated school. Paul Hewitt, headmaster of Dungannon Royal:

> We believe that our society is founded upon Christian principles, and whether it's in medicine or in law, or in the arts, you have got a basic Christian culture and it's vital for children to learn about this and see where it fits into place. You cannot put religion in a little compartment on the side, on a Sunday or in a particular slot in an RE period; it pervades the whole of our education in the western world and particularly in Northern Ireland, and I think that that's what parents want.

Integrated schools are not by any means secular schools. In fact they generally have a strong religious programme running through the syllabus. Mr Agnew, vice-principal at Lagan College:

> We have a very active support of a wide number of chaplains from all the Protestant denominations and from the Catholic church. These chaplains come in and provide pastoral support on top of what we put the children through in terms of their daily subjects. They draw the children into small groups and provide an appropriate support in the denomination concerned. We also involve the parents in the religious pastoral programme as well.

Lagan College has since gone further and now funds two full-time chaplains, one Catholic, one Protestant.

Brothers and nuns, and to a lesser extent priests, have traditionally been very involved in teaching roles, and perhaps this is part of the reason why one rarely finds Protestant children in Catholic schools. And whatever about nowadays, in the past when Catholic education was not state funded, or only funded to a meagre extent, this involvement was very necessary. Seamus Dunn from the Centre for the Study of Conflict had an interesting observation to make here:

> It may seem paradoxical but one of the things that has made the integrated schools more acceptable is the absence of clergymen associated with them. If you ask a Catholic parent to send their child to a Protestant school which has got Protestant clergymen on their management committee, naturally they're a bit worried about that and *vice versa*, the Protestant children and Catholic clergy-

men. But if you've a school which deliberately sets out as a matter of policy not to have clergymen involved in the management of it, that means that neither side has any reason to be anxious about it from a religious point of view, and so it makes it more acceptable to both.

Difficulties: No. 6. Muted enthusiasm on the part of the churches

Whereas many clergy support integrated education in principle, it is often a desire akin to that of the young St Augustine, 'O Lord make me good, but not yet'. David Lapsley, a thoughtful and liberal Presbyterian minister and former moderator:

> It is a very complicated subject for me because I believe in what it stands for totally, and I think it must at some stage be part of the Northern Ireland scene. Whether you start with it or you work towards it is the big question. I am not convinced you can start with it at the present moment. I would like to see it but it is at what part you start is the big problem.

The impression is commonly given that Catholic bishops are the only ones who drag their feet when it comes to integrated schools. In fact their attitude seems to be reflected throughout all the main churches. Protestants naturally prefer to retain a segregated system in the Republic in order to maintain their own identity. This makes it difficult for them to actively support integration in the North where they are a majority, without seeming illogical. Unionists also have political reasons to oppose integration, in so far as integration of the two schools systems might be a step towards integration at a political level. Seamus Dunn:

> Since the troubles began, both of the main Protestant denominations, the Church of Ireland and the Presbyterian Church at their General Synod or General Assembly, have said that they are in favour of experiments in integrated education. They've expressed this quite strongly in 1971 and they've repeated it in later years. But they haven't done anything about it.

Shortly before he died, Cardinal Ó Fiaich gave an interview for this film, setting out, among other things, the Catholic position as he saw it:

> The church has always placed great emphasis on educating its flock in the faith and therefore, no matter what country you go to, you'll have Catholic schools there, all over Ireland, Britain, Europe, United States and even the mission countries. So I think

it's in that context that one can understand the desire of so many Catholic parents to have Catholic schooling for their children. But within that context, one has to see certain cases where various types of integrated education might be either acceptable or justified.

In fact he gave two interesting examples from his own experience.

Some years ago, a state school was in danger of closing in my own diocese. The numbers had gone down because Protestants in that area were rather thin on the ground, and some of the local Protestant farmers came to the local parish priest and said, 'Look, our school is going to close if we let it go on like this. Could you arrange to have Catholic children from certain townlands come to our school, and we'll be able to have two teachers and the second one we assure you will be a Catholic?' So the parish priest asked the parents to send their children to this school and the second teacher who was a Catholic was appointed and everything moved along happily.

I think in order to have a closer coming together, that it can be best done within local friendships and local situations. I have one school for instance in a large town, and when I went up to Armagh I discovered that many Catholic parents were sending their children there because there was no Catholic school in the area. They had moved out at the beginning of the troubles to this particular area. It was a Protestant school with one Catholic teacher out of twelve or thirteen. So I said to the headmaster, 'would you not consider if you're going to have a lot of Catholic children, appointing some Catholic teachers as well?' And he has now increased the number to I think about five or so. And the Catholic children from that area are going to that school. Now for all practical purposes that is an integrated school. A school attended by both Catholics and Protestants – it has grown up in a natural context, it has grown up within the friendliness of parents in that particular area, and I think that is much better than trying to force the thing, you know, against the wishes of the parents.

The cardinal also pointed out that we sometimes forget there is a large measure of integration already.

We're all together in Queens and in the University of Ulster – in fact Queens is now half and half, which means that a considerable number of Catholics have got to Queens in recent years who mightn't have got in in the past. Technical education is integrated already. The colleges of technology and so on are integrated. The only sections therefore which are not for the moment drawing from both sections of the population, are the grammar schools, secondary schools and the primary schools. But even among these there is a considerable amount of co-operation already.

Alternatives to integration

1. Linking schools within the current system

Integrated education is an area of special interest for the Centre for the Study of Conflict in Coleraine. In a survey of teachers and principals, their researchers found that almost all of them said that integration was not a viable option as a general movement, and that the vast majority of children would continue to attend denominational schools. At the same time nearly all teachers felt that separation at school level was doing some kind of social harm. The intelligent response, therefore, seemed to be to put the bulk of resources into minimising that harm in the wider community, rather than spending the money on what can only be a relatively insignificant growth in the integrated system. Two strategies were suggested. The first was to harmonise the curriculum so that children study the same kinds of things with the same resources in both kinds of schools. The second strategy is to encourage schools to cooperate and forge inter-school links across the religious divide.

Perhaps because the Catholic and Protestant schools feel somewhat under threat from the new legislation, they have set new emphasis on forging links between each other to counter the charge that they are divisive. Cardinal Ó Fiaich suggested going further:

> There are plenty of other things one could think about – an exchange of teachers between schools for instance, just as some teachers from the 26 counties go off to America for a year. I don't see any reason why an exchange programme between Catholic and Protestant schools couldn't be arranged in the North.

In the course of making the film we came across a variety of different programmes to bring children together, for instance, Catholic and Protestant schoolchildren singing together in a community choir. On a more intellectual level there are other organisations promoting contacts between schools – perhaps the best known is the Corrymeela community. The Kilbroney Centre at Rostrevor is another example: it brings schoolchildren of all ages together for communal activities, discussion and debate. Even the RUC organise an annual walk in the hills for pupils of the different schools in Armagh!

Participation in these cross-community contacts has increased annually in recent years, and now involves a third of primary and over half of post-primary schools.

Since 1992, two themes related to the issue of community have to be included in the NI school curriculum – education for mutual understanding (EMU) and cultural heritage. According to teacher guidance material, EMU is about self-respect, and respect for others, and the improvement of relationships between people of differing cultural traditions. While the themes are a mandatory feature of the curriculum, cross-community contacts with pupils or teachers from other schools remains an optional strategy which, however, teachers are encouraged to use.

2. The role of sports

Sporting meetings between Catholic and Protestant schools can foment rivalry, and push people apart rather than bring them together. The Royal School in Armagh, however, has been aware of this sporting problem and found an interesting solution. Alan Duncan was a member of the senior rugby team:

> Our school has an association with Glenstal Abbey for ten years now. We've visited them and they've visited us for a long weekend to play a match. And this year we decided to go on tour together: fifteen boys from their school and fifteen from our school, and we played seven matches in Canada altogether, with some of the boys from the Catholic school and some from our Protestant school on each team. So it was multi-denominational sides that played in Toronto, Calgary and Edmonton, and we won the majority of the matches!

It would have been perhaps preferable if the Royal School could have gone to Canada with another school from the North rather than the South, but the fact is that most Catholic schools in Northern Ireland play gaelic football, while Protestant schools play rugby. Another ecumenical problem!

It can be argued that this forging of links is cosmetic, papering over the cracks, and that the only worthwhile approach is to go the whole hog for integrated education. But even if this were true, the great majority of children will for the foreseeable future continue to be taught in religiously segregated schools. So if one wishes to impinge within a reasonable time scale on the problem of community division, there is no option but to do it within the existing system.

Leadership from the churches

Sr Aideen would like to see the churches take a lead together.

> Ideally it would be wonderful if the churches could set up an integrated school run by the churches together; it would take a lot of organisation but it would be a great step forward. So I think that there's great scope but I do think it needs to be very carefully handled and prepared and I think possibly the churches in the future need to work to prepare staff for a genuinely ecumenical school. And by ecumenical, I mean with a religious base to it. Not just a sociological or political one.

The integrated versus segregated schools debate has many different strands. It is a debate about the importance of the school in passing on the belief and practice of one's own religious tradition. It's a debate about whether one can, or should, try to integrate the community through the schools – and which comes first, the chicken or the egg? It is a debate about the best use of resources – whether to promote a new integrated schools system, or spend time, money and effort on bringing Catholic and Protestant pupils together in the existing one. It is a debate, some would say, as to whether integrated schools are possible where they are needed, or needed where they are possible.

I leave the last word with Sr Aideen:

> When I see young children walking along the mall or walking along here in a Catholic area and see their innocent faces, and think that they're going to be conditioned into divisions and prejudices and mutual ignorance and fears coming out of that, I think history will judge us harshly.

14

MEDICS, MITRES AND MINISTERS

Dr Noel Browne and the Mother and Child Scheme

My generation was all brought up on a simple understanding of the Mother and Child controversy. Dr Noel Browne, a knight in shining armour, is thrown from his horse by episcopal dragons and stabbed in the back by his own political colleagues. Whereupon he goes to join the media gods, about whom nobody dares utter a critical word without drawing down the ire of enlightened progressive people (to whom most of us wish to belong).

This appears similar to the version that Dr Browne himself accepts. As late as 1993 he wrote to the *Irish Times*:

> The miracle drugs … associated with a free health service, early diagnosis, mass radiography, ready access to isolation in fully equipped sanatoria with later rehabilitation services and depend-ant allowances, eliminated TB in the Republic from 1948 on … virtually none of these facilities were available to the average con-sumptive when I took over the Department of Health. They were all there when I was compelled to resign for disobeying the bishops of Rome in 1951 over the start of the free, no-means-test Mother and Child Scheme.

The modern historians

Dr Browne's own view of his role seems to be generally accepted in the written history of the period. R. F. Foster, in *Modern Ireland 1600-1972*, refers to '… the dynamic socialist minister Noel Browne, already responsible for the near eradication of tuberculosis … But once the bishops denounced state health-care for all mothers and children as "a ready-made instrument for future totalitarian aggres-sion" … Browne was abandoned by all his cabinet colleagues'.

Dermot Keogh, in *Ireland and the Vatican*, tells us that 'By the Autumn of 1950, it was made abundantly clear to government that the hierarchy opposed the Mother and Child Scheme root and branch. Within a few months Browne was abandoned by his fellow ministers and by his own party leader, Sean MacBride. He resigned on 12 April 1951 as the government 'obediently' capitulated before outright episcopal intransigence.'

Doubts about the simple scenario

That simple scenario was first undermined for me when I saw Sean MacBride interviewed on RTÉ and was quite astounded at the time to hear him say that Noel Browne told him that he would use the Mother and Child Scheme to bring down the government.

Some years later, I met Louie O'Brien, who had been MacBride's personal secretary during the controversy. In her understanding, the failure of the Mother and Child Scheme had much more to do with Noel Browne's ambition to take over Clann na Poblachta than with any problem about the bishops.

Then there was Ruth Barrington's book, *Health Medicine and Politics in Ireland, 1900 to 1970,* published in 1987, which showed how Dr Browne antagonised the medical profession to the extent that one doctor told her that the profession would have brought in Lucifer if they could have brought down Dr Browne.

Two years later Dr James Deeny, Chief Medical Adviser in the Department of Health, published a book on his side of the story. What he had to say in *To Cure and to Care* might be summed up as follows: 'I planned the Mother and Child Scheme, I gave it it's name, and I had to sit there and watch Noel Browne wreck it'.

So it struck me that here was an issue of importance in the history of church and state where many of the subtleties of the story seem to have been missed, and where it would be worthwhile to gather some of them together in a programme before all the participants passed on. And that was the genesis of *Medics, Mitres and Ministers*.

In retrospect, I was happy that we tackled the subject, but at the same time I was somewhat disappointed with the programme in the end. We knew beforehand it had to be a talky programme, but if it was going to involve the viewers there would need to be some conflict of views and ideas. Dr Browne could be expected to say what he thought, and so indeed he did. When we came to interview Mr MacBride, however, we found him obviously in poor health, and as it turned out, not far from death. Then our tape recorder broke down a short way into the interview – the only time I ever remember this happening in my long experience. We arranged to come back, but his health got worse and he died a few weeks later. So a lot depended on Dr Deeny, who had expressed some strong

views in his book. We went down specially to Wexford to interview
him, and he was there as arranged, but when the questions were
put to him he danced around them and eventually said, and I
quote, 'I am not going to discuss Browne, to tell the truth'. With that
I got a bit testy and said if that was the case, perhaps we should not
be wasting his and our time. Later he admitted that when he told
his wife what the interview was to be about she forbade him to
speak about Browne because anything to do with Browne only led
to trouble and dangerous controversy! To give Deeny his due, he
did phone us up a day or two later to say he had thought about it
since and realised that we felt let down, and that if we wished he
would give another interview in Dublin; which indeed he did.
However, we didn't feel we could press him as hard as we might
have liked in the circumstances. His wife's fear of Dr Browne's pen
was by no means unique. Professor Joe Lee spoke of his portraits of
his cabinet colleagues as 'etched in vitriol' and seen through 'jaun-
diced, but piercing eyes'. Friends of Sean MacBride used upbraid
him for letting Dr Browne away with statements they believed
untrue. But MacBride would always say, 'There is no use taking on
Browne. He has the press in his hand and they will always come
down on his side no matter what'.

The following reflections are based mostly on interviews recorded
for the programme by Darach Turley, research material such as the
Dáil reports of the time, and some few observations of my own.
Before going into the meat of the chapter, however, one should per-
haps say something of the people involved. Dr Browne was
Minister for Health from 1948 to 1951. Noel Hartnett was once
director of elections for Fianna Fáil, but fell out with De Valera and
helped found the Clann na Poblachta party, where he was Dr
Browne's closest colleague. Sean MacBride was leader of Clann na
Poblachta and Minister for External Affairs. John A. Costello was
Taoiseach in the first coalition government. Dr Ruth Barrington is
the author of *Health, Medicine and Politics in Ireland, 1900 to 1970*,
which is universally praised as the authoritative work on the subject of her title. Louie O'Brien was Sean McBride's personal secretary throughout the period of coalition government. Dr James
Deeny came out of the shadows when his autobiography got extensive pre-publication coverage in the *Weekend Supplement* to the *Irish
Times* of 25 February 1989. Ruth Barrington spoke to us about
Deeny.

The normal practice in the Department of Health was for the chief medical officer to be appointed from the most senior medical officers, but in Dr Deeny's case, he was recruited by open competition, and he impressed the interview board because of his experience in general practice and the outstanding research that he carried out on tuberculosis, gastro-enteritis, and vitamin C deficiency. So he stood out from all the other candidates and he was appointed on the basis of his experience.

When he came to the department he arrived in at a time when there were very serious health problems facing the country: tuberculosis was a scourge, a number of infectious diseases were still rampant, typhus, typhoid, gastro-enteritis had claimed over a thousand children's lives in Dublin in 1941. And the deprivation of the war really was taking a major toll of the health. So I think to summarise Dr Deeny's impact in the Department of Health, he was a model builder, he was able to take disparate ideas about what ought to be done and to wield them into a coherent programme and get political will to implement that programme.

The following then are reflections which question some of the received wisdom about aspects of Dr Browne's tenure as Minister for Health, and particularly with the Mother and Child scheme.

1.Who should get the credit for building hospitals in the late 1940s and early 50s?

BROWNE. I had been able to use the Sweep funds to build hospitals wherever they were needed. We doubled the existing hospital complement in the country in that 48-51 period. We built hospitals everywhere, so we had a physical infrastructure. All we needed then were the services and the Mother and Child was the most important first step towards a good national health service – free – no means test, of course.

DEENY. You must remember that every hospital institution barring two or three for which he [Dr Browne] could claim responsibility, we had started them all. We'd bought the sites, we'd started the building, the thing was moving.

O'BRIEN. When Browne went in to the Department there was already a full Fianna Fáil TB plan, with architect's hospital plans, etc., all ready to go, but there was no money. Then when Sean MacBride arranged for the Sweep millions to become available to the Department of Health, the officials were ready to start working on their plans immediately. A cardboard cut-out could have been put in place as minister for all the in-put that was necessary.

2. Who should get the credit for the Mother and Child Scheme?

DEENY. I put up the Mother and Child Scheme in 1946. And the minister and the civil servants, my colleagues, we turned this into a Bill and we wrote a white paper. The white paper said, 'This is what the government is going to do. We are going to provide a Mother and Child Service.' One day I was walking up a quay, going up to Bewley's for my lunch, and I was walking with my colleague, J. D. McCormack and I said, 'I've to label this thing,' and I said 'I've thought of a name for it. I'll call it the Mother and Child Service. Nobody can attack a mother and child service,' I said, 'That's safe.' Well I was wrong. We put this in and it was put into a Health Bill in 1947. And that became law, and this whole thing was all done. Browne came in 1948 and the whole thing was done before he came near the place. People adored him, they loved him, but you see he had never done any maternity and child welfare. He was a sanatorium doctor from a small sanatorium.

3. Did Dr Browne give credit to the fact that the doctors might have genuine worries about the Mother and Child Scheme ?

BROWNE. I made no judgement about the medical profession at all. I simply went to them and said the law is here and that we – I intend to implement the law, because it is a marvellous piece of health legislation.

BARRINGTON. There is always a tension between any Minister for Health and the medical profession, particularly a very active Minister for Health, but in Dr Browne's case, it went much deeper than that. Dr Browne nailed his colours to the mast early on as Minister for Health by saying that he wanted to create a state medical service and the doctors feared that this would mean that they would all be enrolled as civil servants as they called it; they'd lose their private practice and their professional independence, and they were determined to fight this by any means.

4. Did Dr Browne give credit to the fact that the bishops might have genuine worries about his bill ?

DEENY. Now when people talk today about politics, don't think that their fathers and their grandfathers weren't just as concerned – I mean men went and fought and died! Then we had to do something in creating a new country, and there was an enormous amount of thought given to the kind of country we were trying to create. All over Europe you had Franco trying to create one kind of place, you had Hitler, you had Mussolini, you had the Emperor of Japan. The Irish were trying to create a society of their own. Now the bishops wanted to create a vocational state, they were scared of a centralised authoritarian totalitarian state – you had it in Germany where Hitler infiltrated everything, and controlled everything and if you weren't a member of the party you're out and you're hungry. People were afraid of state control in education and health.

The concerns of the hierarchy with regard to the moral implications of state control of medicine began to be made known to the Taoiseach, Eamonn De Valera, as early as 1946, so nobody in government could fail to know about them.

Archbishop's House
Dublin N.E.3
24th January 1946

Dear Taoiseach,
At the recent meeting of the Standing Committee of the Hierarchy, concern was expressed, as the result of representations made by Bishops, in regard to certain provisions of the proposed Public Health Bill, 1945.

While fully admitting that the State is acting quite correctly, when it takes due and opportune precautions to safeguard public health, it is feared that the unusual and absolute power of medical inspection of children and adults, by compulsory regulation, and, if needs be, by force, is a provision so intimately concerned with the rights of the parents and the human person, that only clear-cut guarantees and safeguards, on the part of the Government, can be regarded as an adequate protection of those rights.

The Standing Committee of the Hierarchy has requested me as Chairman to bring to your notice these serious considerations, in the full confidence that you will be able to safeguard the fundamental rights in question and allay an anxiety that is widespread in Catholic circles.

With much respect, I beg to remain, dear Taoiseach,
Yours sincerely,
John C. McQuaid,
Archbishop of Dublin, etc.

5. Was it wise of a minster to so antagonise the medical profession?

> BARRINGTON. There was a document circulated which maligned the motives of doctors in treating tuberculosis patients and claimed that they were only interested in the fees that they were collecting. The medical profession claimed that this document had come from the Minister for Health, Dr Browne, and they employed a private detective in order to establish whether it had come from the minister's office or not, and they claimed to have established that it did come from the minister's office. My own research, I discovered this, yes, in fact, the minister had written this document, but it certainly didn't help his relations with the profession.

The document referred to likened some of the medical profession to scum on a muddy pool! Deeny in his book also recalls a meeting of a students' society in the College of Surgeons where Dr Browne was to speak on 'Unknown medical heroes of Ireland,' but instead launched into a vehement attack on the medical profession – to which Dr Leonard Abrahamson, Dr Bob Collis (of Christy Brown fame) and a string other senior people who were present replied just as vehemently.

6. Was it wise of a minster to so antagonise the experts in his own department ?

The department officials were upset because they felt Dr Browne threw away the support of all the people who were needed to implement the legislation.

> DEENY. One of the attributes of a really good politician is wisdom and judgement – particularly judgement. Now take it from a judgement point of view: If you're going to introduce a scheme you don't proceed to fight with the doctors, the men on whom you depend to run the scheme for you. You don't fight with the people who conceive the scheme in the Department of Health, who are there to help you and to work for you. You don't fight with your colleagues in the cabinet on whom you're dependent for support and who'd already committed themselves to the scheme, and you don't fight with them because they are going to have to put up the money. And you don't fight your own party, you don't fight with your own leader. So I mean if you get a crusader who proceeds to fight with five different groups, on whom he's dependent, his judgement isn't very sound.

Deeny was also upset because Dr Browne developed a little court of PR and administrative people around himself, and – in Deeny's estimation – effectively fired the best people in the department, including Theo MacWeeney, who was snapped up as Regional Adviser on TB for Asia in the World Health Organistion, and eventually Deeny himself.

> DEENY. I tried to do my best to advise Dr Browne. Dr Browne decided he didn't need my advice. And I went out to do a national TB survey which was the main factor in ending TB in this country.

7. Was it wise of a minster to so antagonise the cabinet of which he was a member ?

Professor J. J. Lee, in *Ireland, Politics and Society*, mentions that in relation to the Mother and Child controversy, Sean Lemass 'later surmised that Costello and MacBride greeted the affair as a God-given, or at least bishop-given opportunity to dispense with Browne, whose temperament left even sympathetic observers with no illusions about the difficulties ... colleagues must have faced in their dealings with him'.

A recurring theme among his fellow members of the cabinet seems to be that Dr Browne kept changing his mind. He would make a decision one day and change it the next. Or worse, deny he ever made it. This was put down by Sean MacBride to the influence of Noel Harnett, who MacBride believed to be Browne's closest adviser. One instance of this was when Mr Norton (according to Louie O'Brien) persuaded Dr Browne to accept that the scheme would be free to all earning less that £1,000 a year (the equivalent of £20,000 in 1996, measured by the consumer price index). Browne agreed, and the whole cabinet breathed a sigh of relief. But he came into Iveagh House the following morning to tell MacBride he had changed his mind.

Dr Browne probably also aroused a lot of jealousy in cabinet with his effective publicity machine. Clann were the first people to use film in an election campaign. Noel Harnett wrote the script. It could be said in modern parlance that Dr Brown brought in the first spin doctors – people like Aodh de Blacam and Frank Gallagher who, along with Harnett, made a very effective publicity team for the minister. Dr Deeny spoke of Dr Browne's political contemporaries.

> DEENY. All those men had gone through fire and the sword, some of them had been in the GPO, some of them had been in jail together,

some of them condemned to death. Mr Cosgrave ran his show as a team. It was the same in Fianna Fáil, Mr De Valera ran his team – mind you he was the captain, but still he ran it as a team But the idea of one man going out and building himself up as a kind of a national figure – it upset all the other politicians you know, and that's one of the reasons they couldn't stand him, because they got very annoyed at this strange young man coming in and being built up as a national saviour.

And if even a small amount of the scorn that Dr Browne pours on his cabinet colleagues in his autobiography appeared in contemporary dealings in the party or the cabinet, it is not hard to see why they might have wished to get rid of him.

8. Was it wise of a minster to so antagonise the hierarchy in an area where there could be moral implications?

DEENY. When the Mother and Child Scheme came out first there was practically no opposition to it. Archbishop McQuaid told Dr Conor Ward TD that this was a good scheme. (Dr Ward had been given special responsibility for public health matters within the Department of Local Government and Public Health in 1944.)

The archbishop wrote to Dr Ward as follows on 6 February 1946 – this was of course two years before Dr Browne came into the ministry. His letter gives a clear indication of the importance the hierarchy attached to public health, which the archbishop put on a level with national defence during the wartime emergency:

Dear Doctor Ward,
It has escaped me that opposition was being made a party politics scheme. Nothing said at the Hierarchy's meeting had allowed me to know that fact. I regret very much that fact, because Public health seems to me to be on a level with National Defence. On the latter basis, in an emergency all parties had found it possible to unite. It is a grave pity if all parties cannot be induced to do so again, on a major issue of national importance.

I have already explained to the Taoiseach, as you must know, that the Bill is substantially good, in my opinion. Much ignorant and irrelevant criticism has been spoken and written concerning the Bill. It remains to alleviate the widespread anxiety, which the Bill has caused among ordinary people, who have no means of understanding the vagaries of the party-politics opposition, but who genuinely fear the terms of the Bill under certain headings.

Having met Dr Browne, and having some experience of Dr John
Charles McQuaid, I have no trouble in understanding how the
chemistry between them was not likely to bring a meeting of minds.
Consider this one little piece from our interview:

> BROWNE. Dr McQuaid had some links with the medical profes-
> sion and I think it would be natural for our hierarchy – I think
> quite unnatural for people who profess serious Christianity – but
> our hierarchy appeared to feel they had the responsibility to
> defend the rights of the medical profession rather than the rights
> of the mothers and children and I assume that they were in collus-
> ion, yes.

Dr Browne was a Trinity College graduate at a time when Catholics
were forbidden to attend Trinity without ecclesiastical permission.
These were pre-ecumenical times when Catholics generally
believed that Trinity was controlled by Protestant interests who
were determined to keep control and were largely unsympathetic
to what they called 'the Free State'. I can remember as a schoolboy
being in College Green when a group of their alumni burnt the Irish
tricolour on VE Day 1945.

> BROWNE. I spent a number of years in England and religion
> doesn't weigh as heavily in England as it does here, particularly
> the Catholic religion. The Catholic religion is virtually dismissed
> as an important religion in England, and even though I was at a
> Catholic school and therefore ... no it didn't bother me what the
> bishops thought about Trinity at the time. I was quite happy to
> go, delighted to go and become a doctor – I didn't give it a
> thought.

> BROWNE. I didn't see why I should have to go and see the arch-
> bishop. However I was told by my colleagues, my senior cabinet
> colleagues, Sean MacBride, Mr Costello and various others, that I
> should go and see the archbishop. I did. But I have to say that
> when I went into the room I wasn't the slightest bit intimidated –
> to me there were three people sitting around, Bishop Browne,
> Bishop Staunton of Wexford and then the archbishop, and my
> conversation with them was the same as my conversation with
> you now. I listened to what they had to say, where I differed from
> them I said I differed and where I agreed I agreed, and where I
> could concede I compromised – where I felt I should compromise.
> When the meeting was over we had tea, I got up and walked out
> and that was the end of it as far as I was concerned.

THE TAOISEACH. His Grace of Dublin had told me in connection with the interview on 11 October ... that he (Dr Browne) had refused to discuss anything other than the question of education, brushed the other matters aside and walked out. *Dáil report 12.4.51.*

BROWNE. If you hand over your education, the education of the electorate, to one powerful political socio-political institution, this predicates the kind of attitude that the electorate is going to have, and therefore if you hand the electorate over to the Muslims or the Hindu or the Roman Catholics or the Protestants, you are depriving yourself as a democrat of the right to make decisions on behalf of the people, because the people will already have had decisions which are taken by somebody over whom you have no control.

Now there may be many readers who would share Dr Browne's sentiments. So be it. All I am trying to point out here is that some-body with his cast of mind was not likely to communicate easily and comfortably in the early nineteen fifties with Dr John Charles McQuaid, or indeed Bishop Browne of Galway.

9. Was it wise of a minister to so antagonise his party leader when trying to push through important legislation ?

MACBRIDE. For the last year, in my view, the Minster for Health has not been normal. I do not want to go into greater details.

FLANAGAN. Is that an insinuation that the minister is insane?

MACBRIDE. Might I qualify that – normal in the sense that he has not behaved as any normal person would behave or be expected to behave. *Dáil Report 12.4.51.*

Louie O'Brien, who was Sean MacBride's personal secretary during this period, believes that Noel Hartnett was an important and con-tinuing influence on Browne, and had much to do with turning him against MacBride, the party leader.

O'BRIEN. Hartnett was one hundred per cent a political animal. Originally he was one of de Valera's favoured sons (with Tod Andrews, Aodhgan O'Rahilly *et al.*). He had worked in Radio Éireann, he was Director of Elections for Fianna Fáil, he had entrée to De Valera at all times.

On 10 May 1946, Sean McCaughey, former head of the the IRA, died on hunger strike, naked and in solitary confinement. At the inquest, Sean MacBride asked the coroner if he would let a dog die in such circumstances: the coroner replied that he would not. It was only then that de Valera realised that one of his own, Noel Hartnett, had been MacBride's junior counsel. Immediately Hartnett was barred from all contact with de Valera; he lost all his work in Radio Éireann; he was barred from the Fianna Fáil head office; he was desolated. When MacBride was organising Clann na Poblachta with Con Lehane and Peadar Cowan, Hartnett was delighted to join; he was back in politics!

When the coalition was formed in 1948 and the inexperienced Browne got the health ministry, Hartnett, the politician, took Browne under his wing. Browne was the total neophyte: he hadn't a clue about politics. This is when MacBride made his first mistake. Everybody had taken it for granted – including Con Lehane himself – that Lehane would get this second ministry, not Browne. The next mistake MacBride made was to give the Senate seat to Denis Ireland; because Hartnett thought it was his. The result was that MacBride had two opposing camps in his executive, one led by Harnett and the other by Lehane – with both camps opposed to their leader.

So the period of the coalition government was not a peaceful one for Clann na Poblachta or its leader. Con Lehane and the Old IRA opposed MacBride because they had a grievance – they felt that MacBride was favouring the Browne/Hartnett faction. They expected that if MacBride were deposed, Lehane would automatically become leader, so they supported Browne in the effort to depose MacBride – until it slowly dawned on them that the scheme was to make Browne the new leader, not Lehane. So in the end they voted against Browne's resolution to depose MacBride.

10. At the time of Dr Browne's resignation, why did he not blame the bishops in the way he did at a later stage?

In his Dáil resignation statement, Dr Browne was very clear in putting the blame on his cabinet colleagues, not on the hierarchy.

BROWNE. While as I have said, I as a Catholic accept unequivocally and unreservedly the views of the hierarchy on this matter, I have not been able to accept the manner in which this matter has been dealt with by my former colleagues in the government. *Dáil Report 12.4.51.*

THE TAOISEACH. … the underlying and vicious suggestion in all this controversy, that I and my colleagues in the government roped in, if I may use that vulgar expression, the hierarchy in order to get us out of the difficulty of being ensnared in a scheme we did not like. That suggestion underlies the entire speech of the former Minister of Health today. *Dáil Report 12.4.51.*

Dr Browne also emphasised that he thought the hierarchy were satisfied as a result of his interview with them. It is hard to see how this could be, but it is interesting that he should say so at the time.

MACBRIDE. In the light of the numerous conversations that I had with Deputy Dr Browne, in the light of Deputy Dr Browne's own admission in the presence of numerous witnesses and in the light of that letter, how can Deputy Browne seriously ask this House today to believe the he 'had no reason to believe that the hierarchy was not fully satisfied'? *Dáil Report 12.4.51.*

11. Could the Mother and Child Scheme have failed, not because of the difficulty of reaching an accommodation with the bishops, but because Dr Browne decided to use the Mother and Child Scheme to bring down the government and oust Sean MacBride from the leadership of Clann na Poblachta?

Right or wrong, this was Sean MacBride's firm belief.

O'BRIEN. Sean MacBride was appalled by the whole thing, really appalled and thought it wasn't necessary. He kept on saying to Browne, 'You know, none of this is necessary. You could come to an accommodation with everybody if you really wanted to. But you don't want a settlement of it, do you?' Browne would never have an answer – he just didn't want a settlement of the Mother and Child Scheme with the hierarchy or with the doctors. And nobody could understand why – eventually we did understand why.

Obviously no one, not even possibly Dr Browne, can at this stage disprove the theories about his motivation which supporters of Sean MacBride believed at the time, and still believe. So the informed punter has to make up his or her mind as to who to believe.

O'BRIEN. Taking Browne's extraordinary popularity into account, Browne and Hartnett formulated a plan. Browne would resign over the Mother and Child Scheme. They would then together cause MacBride to be deposed. Browne would take over as leader. There would be a general election. He would head the poll and Clann would be returned with an increased number of TDs. De

Valera would come to Browne and Hartnett seeking coalition. Hartnett shivered with delight at the picture of de Valera coming to them hat-in-hand. And the scheme very nearly worked.

Sean McBride repeated to us what he had said in the original face-to-face interview on telelvision, that Dr Browne had told him he would use the Mother and Child Scheme to bring down the government.

MACBRIDE. There was a lull in the Dáil. We felt we could leave the Dáil for a couple of hours. I took him (Dr Browne) to dinner with me in the Russell Hotel. And he then unfolded to me what was his view of things, and that he thought that I was a hopeless leader, that Clann na Poblachta was useless, that the inter-party government was no good and he was going to try and bring it down, and bring down Clann unless he could control it. And that is a very summarised version of the effects of this talk. And this came to me as a complete bombshell or surprise at the time, and I made full note of that interview and gave it to the chairman of our executive, Donal Donoghue, because I felt once you are involved personally in the thing, once you are under attack yourself it is much better for somebody else to handle it, and Donal tried to handle it – he had several interviews with Browne and all that, but with no success.

O'BRIEN. I was there a lot of the time when Browne would come and attack Sean MacBride and say terrible things to him about how he was a bad leader; and he actually once said that he would depose him as leader, and that he would use the Mother and Child Scheme to do that.

Dr Browne however denies this scenario.

BROWNE. Well of course that is a complete fairy tale. I mean how could anybody rationalise a decision of that kind? I had worked in relation to tuberculosis, I had done that job, I had built the hospitals, … this was the logical conclusion to implement a piece of legislation which was on the statute book, and there couldn't have been anything more normal than doing that.

12. Was everyone agreed on the value or practicality – given the funds available – of a free for all scheme?

DEENY. Dr Noel Browne had a vision of providing free medical care, free care for all women and children regardless of the income. The richest person would get the same as the poorest person, and it was on that thing that he would neither listen to his own colleagues nor to me – because I wanted it for the poor.

O'BRIEN. Browne hadn't a clue when it came to financing a free Mother and Child Scheme for all. MacBride tried to explain to him that if the meagre facilities that existed were to be shared by those who could pay, it would be the poor that would suffer. MacBride was embarrassed to find himself, apparently, on the side of the bishops!

13. Dr Browne made much of his authority as a member of cabinet, but did he in fact always act with the cabinet's knowledge or authority?

BROWNE. I was answerable only to the people. I feel very strongly on that point. The essence of a serious democracy is that we are the representatives of the people and the people make the decisions, nobody else can take that authority away from the people or from the cabinet.

THE TAOISEACH. We heard rumours of a mother and child health scheme, free for all, and we were gravely uneasy. I can say this here and now that this scheme for the mother and child, free for all, no means test, which has been the cause of such acute controversy in this country, never came before the government as a government. The first time I personally heard of it was when a copy of the scheme was given to me by a person outside the government, who had got it I think from a doctor to whom it had been sent by the then Minister of Health. (Dr Browne) … That scheme was never brought before the government, ever considered by the government, or ever approved by the government. *Dáil Report 12.4.51.*

O'BRIEN. A free Mother and Child Scheme for all had not been on the agenda of any of the parties in the coalition. They were not against it in principle, but the cost was prohibitive. All were in favour of a free Mother and Child Scheme for all who could not afford to pay.

THE TAOISEACH. I had formed in my own mind, having regard to my experience over the last six months and the history of the affairs I have given in the barest outline, the firm conviction that Deputy Dr Browne was not competent or capable to fulfil the duties of the Department of Health. He was incapable of negotiation; he was obstinate at times and vacillating at other times. He was quite incapable of knowing what his decision would be today or, if he made a decision today, it would remain until tomorrow. It has been said he is inexperienced, but I regret my view is that temperamentally he is unfitted for the post of cabinet minister. *Dáil Report 12.4.51.*

14. In publishing the documents, was Dr Browne prepared to act against the national interest at the time?

IAN PAISLEY. I have nothing against individual Catholics as such. I have everything against the political machinations of the Roman Catholic hierarchy, demonstrated in your own country in the Dr Browne case. *RTÉ TV Interview.*

BROWNE. I said, Sean, I believe you are interested in the solution of the Northern problem, but I assure you that I have made arrangements to see that all the documents on this issue will be published. I had an arrangement with the editor of the *Irish Times*, Bertie Smylie, because the other papers could have refused to publish them, and he said, I will go to jail and publish them, so I had made arrangements to publish the documents because I felt it should be brought into the open and that the Irish public should understand that what they believed was representative parliamentary democracy was a charade, and that elections were a farce, and until that was cleared up, and until the Northern Protestant could be certain that Rome did not rule in our society, that we simply, as a society, we could not develop and I said I intend to publish those documents so it's a matter for you to make the decision, Sean.

MACBRIDE. This situation has already been, is being and will continue to be exploited by the enemies of this country in order to maintain the division of our national territory. I would like to make it clear that in my view the government of this country, this government or any other government, has a duty to hearken to and give weight and consideration to the views put forward by the leaders of any religious denomination recognised by the state, be that denomination Christian or Jewish. *Dáil Report 12.4.51.*

15. May Dr Browne's handling of the whole affair only have served to delay the Mother and Child Scheme and the benefits it was to bring to the poor?

BARRINGTON. If there had been more skilful political handling of the health issues involved in the Mother and Child controversy, I don't believe that this would have happened and I think the proof of that is the way in which Dr Jim Ryan, the subsequent

Minister for Health, implemented about 80% of what Dr Browne was trying to achieve with really the minimum of fuss. But he also showed that when the government was united in the face of the hierarchy, that they could in fact persuade the hierarchy that there was nothing to fear in a mother and child scheme.

DEENY. Dr James Ryan sorted it out with the bishops in a very short time, and we got the basic elements and essentials of the Mother and Child Scheme, and the proof of the whole thing is this, that it was working until fairly recently, and that … we have one of the lowest infant mortalities in the world.

16. May Dr Browne have had a rather limited understanding of democracy?

DEENY. Dr Browne said that the reason why he was prepared to risk his political career for this particular scheme was because he felt it wasn't good to have some pressure group exert power on the democratically elected government of the time. Now a democracy consists of pressure groups, it consists of people who walk up and down outside Leinster House, it consists of people who chain one another to railings, people who go and kick up a row about children, midwives, all the rest of it. On this thing the church has as much right to be a pressure group as anybody else. Now to give you an example. Where would Lech Walesa be without Cardinal Glemp and the Catholics in Poland? Where would the East Germans be that brought the wall down? It was the meetings that they held in the Lutheran churches and the Lutheran pastors and bishops that supported them. Where would the Rumanians be without that wee Calvinist pastor in Transylvania who was practically at the edge of death, fighting for freedom in the place, where would they be without these people?

Conclusion

If anybody has read this far, I want to make it clear that this is not an attempt to begin to write the last word on the Mother and Child Scheme. Or even write a defence of the bishops. What I did hope to indicate was that the Mother and Child controversy was complicated and other scenarios were possible in addition to the generally accepted version. If we are to believe Sean McBride, for instance, then the conclusion must be that Dr Browne used the Mother and Child Scheme in an attempt to bring down the government, oust McBride as leader of Clann, and enter a new coalition, possibly with Fianna Fáil. When that didn't work, he tried to cover his tracks by promoting himself as a martyr to the machinations of the hierarchy, which was a rather more gallant scenario to exit on. I don't say that is true – and Dr Browne denies it vehemently – it just depends who you believe. With regard to the bishops, I think it is quite clear that they found Browne confrontational. Now John Charles's father was a doctor and his closest friend was a prominent member of the medical profession, Dr Stafford Johnson. So he would have known what the doctors thought of Dr Browne. He was also friendly with both De Valera and Costello, and would have known of the cabinet's frustrations with Browne, and the bitter conflict within Clann na Poblachta. I would be sure too that he knew everything about the tensions within the Department of Health. So if the cabinet, the Clann, the doctors and the Department of Health would all be happy to be rid of Browne, it must have been very tempting to the bishops to give them a little help. Indeed it would seem to me that the episode of the Mother and Child debacle was more a case of *co-operation* between church and state, than confrontation. And that, interestingly enough, seems closer to Dr Browne's explanation at the time of his resignation (as understood by Mr Costello in No 10 above). The bishops however were, as often, very maladroit in the political sense: and as a result most of the egg ended up on their collective face.

There still remains a need to explain Dr Browne's enduring public popularity, particularly when some of it appears to rest on debatable grounds. Undoubtedly it has much to do with his appeal as a young campaigner with an aura of charm and quiet determination, and a genuine concern for the sick and the poor – qualities which we all respect and admire. However, it is my gut feeling that in addition to an original and manifestly effective publicity machine, it also has more than a little to do with the fact that he was the first man to thumb his nose in public at bishops like John Charles McQuaid and Michael John Browne – something which others, particularly in the newspaper industry, might like to have done, but didn't have the courage.

15
POOR CHOICE
Some who live Liberation Theology, and others who debate it

Living with the poor

Among missionaries and those who work in development aid to the Third World, I think the greatest heroes are those men and women who live with the poor, as if they were poor. One has to say 'as if they were poor', because of course they aren't poor, and never can be. Why? Because the genuine poor have no resources to draw upon in a crisis, no way out. If they are seriously sick they may die – simply because they can't afford expensive drugs, or surgery, or possibly even a visit to the doctor. If the government says they have no right to be where they are, and that their houses will be bull-dozed tomorrow, they have no solicitors to call on, or bankers to arrange a mortgage or a loan. To be poor is to be powerless. The missionary or aid worker is never powerless in the same way – there is always a powerful lifeline. Sick missionaries can be whisked away and given the best of care. If the pressure of daily living becomes too great, they can take a holiday, or return for several months to Europe or America, or simply return to a comfortable lifestyle. Nevertheless, I still think that those who choose to live with the poor of the Third World are brave to the point of heroism.

Steve McCabe is about forty years of age. He was brought up in Orwell Gardens, Rathgar, Dublin, and joined the Redemptorists who have their headquarters at Marianella, a metaphorical stone's throw from his home. He now lives in a shanty town in Fortaleza, on the coast of Brazil. The house has one room or three, depending how you wish to describe it – there are no internal doors. The dry toilet is off the tiny back yard. Steve is over six feet, so he has to stoop everytime he enters. Like all the houses around, it is built on sand, and when the wind blows hard, sand gets into everything. Steve reflected on his choice.

> You make an option to live among the poor, and as a result of that option, you have to make a number of sacrifices. You have no privacy at all in the house here. In a big parish house you'd have

your own room and maybe a shower or a bathroom – much more privacy for yourself. Here, as you can see, the house is open, you have a room but there is no door on the room so people can come in and out any time they want. They just come and clap their hands and say they're coming in, they want to have a chat with you. So that would be, I suppose, one of the big things – you have no privacy. You make an option to live a simpler style of life, simpler type of food, and we have moments here of prayer, moments of coming together here in the house to discuss things. We plan things out together – meetings and Masses. So it's an option that we've made as a group of Redemptorists to work among the poor and I personally feel very happy and fulfilled in this work because I think that's what the church is – it has to take this very serious position among the poor.

Different missionaries have told me at different times what they find most difficult about living among the poor. Some find it is the omnipresent dirt – soil or sand in the air that covers one's books and papers, food and furniture. Others find the necessity of sharing semi-public shower and toilet facilities the worst of penances. Still others fear sharing food, which good manners often requires them to do, food which was prepared without the hygienic safeguards that a westerner has come to expect. I remember Leo Staples, a Kiltegan priest who was the first missionary to work among the West Pokot people in Africa, telling me how he was often offered goat's milk out of a dried gourd. And so those who share the life of the poor often become prey to another of the many discomforts of the poor – parasites and worms and dysentery.

Rich and poor in Brazil

The economic facts about Brazil are quite bizarre, and Fortaleza provides some relevant images to convey them. When one walks down the miserable street past Steve's house and through the sand dunes, one can see on the horizon a group of high rise condominiums and hotels where the rich have their playground by the sea. For there are many rich in Brazil, which has one of the ten largest economies in the world. At the same time, other social statistics place Brazil among the least developed countries in the world. The national wealth is distributed so that one fifth of the population get 86% of the income, while the other four fifths (128 million people) have to survive on a share out of the remaining 14%. Half the population are undernourished, according to the Rome based Food and Agriculture Organisation. One is reminded of one of Archbishop

Helder Camara's witty sayings – wealth is like rain, there's plenty of it, but it is very unevenly distributed. So to chose the option for the poor in Brazil like Steve did, is to join the majority.

> I suppose a big part of our life is much given to listening to people. People want to come, they want somebody like us just to listen to them and show them that we're interested and we're concerned for them. A lot of people then come looking for help because they're hungry people. I won't say they're starving, but they're people who are just living maybe on a little bit of rice, maybe an egg, two eggs, that would be it. Maybe a bit of coffee in the morning time. People don't even talk about meat. So there is a very serious problem here with the hunger, which is linked with the whole problem of unemployment. People are in quite a desperate situation.

The majority of the poor are women

The poorest group in Latin America, as in most countries, are women. Women in Latin America collect 10% of the wages and own less than 1% of the property. They are generally paid half a man's wage for the same work. Steve McCabe spoke about this man's world:

> Brazil is very much what they call a macho society and the woman is seen very much as a slave to the man, and you see this especially in the family situation where the woman is treated as a person who is there to make the food, to bring on children – the woman is generally treated as a slave. A lot of the women who participate here in the community – we have a little basic Christian community – even have difficulty coming out to the regular weekly meeting. The husband very often will say, 'What are you going to the meeting for?' And they often throw out a remark like 'Are you going off to go courting with the priest or the sister?' – referring to whoever is running the meeting. So the women suffer an awful lot.

Many more sisters have chosen to live the option for the poor than priests. We met three religious sisters in Fortaleza who had left a comfortable convent for a roughly built wooden house in a hot dusty *favela* – which is what Brazilians call their shanty towns. Sr Norma was originally from the Philippines.

> I found it very difficult in the beginning but I feel good to be with the people, not as the head or not as the leader but be with them just while they struggle together. It isn't easy because I don't

know even if this really helps. But then most of them have made complimentary remarks, such as 'if you are here we feel secure' – even if we don't do anything, just by our presence. And when we are not around, they keep on asking 'where are the sisters, where are the sisters?'

Religious women have a kind of vow of poverty, but it's better to learn about poverty and simplicity of life from the people who are really poor – no big chairs or big furniture in the house, just simple things, no telephone, no phone calls and so on. But at the same time you see the hard life of the poor, and then you can understand why people are really reacting to this violent situation in the *favela*. There are lots of problems like drugs, and if fathers work for a week, they'd end up drunk, spending their money at the weekend.

Literacy and illiteracy

One day Sr Norma visited a house and found a group of women crying over a child who had come home from hospital, but now was clearly dying – mainly, it seemed to her, from dehydration. In fact the mother had been to a hospital and received written instructions how to treat the baby; but the instructions were useless because neither the mother nor any of her friends could read or write! So Norma called a meeting about it, and the women decided that whatever the cost in time and effort, they were determined to learn to read and write – if one of the sisters would only teach them. We filmed one of the study sessions while Sr Norma talked about her students.

Aside from the reading and writing, they tell their stories – how they are being treated by their husbands. Most of these women have been left by their husbands with five kids, with eight kids, and so they are acting like father and mother at the same time. Their kids are on the streets and so it's a hard time for them. And even during the time when they are studying here, the kids are around and it's very difficult for them to concentrate. And yet they say we have to learn, we have to read and write so that we know what is what, and so nobody can give us a piece of paper and say 'Write your name' and we don't know what it says …

The illiterate poor are open to the worst kind of exploitation when they can't read a public notice and never really know to what they are signing their name. Literacy plays a vital role in empowering women, making it easier for them to find better paid work, and to wade through the avalanche of printed information resulting from any contact with the state.

The labourers among the poor are few

The impression is sometimes given that South America is full of noble priests living like Steve McCabe. That is not true. First of all most of those who work with the poor are not men but women – perhaps 50% of women religious would be somewhat involved, but only 10% of men. Furthermore, most of the sisters and priests who embrace the option for the poor are foreigners.

In the nineteen seventies, many of the older seminaries in Latin America were abandoned in favour of a system whereby students for the priesthood were required to live among the poor, and study at a theological college, rather than be sent to live apart in a big seminary. This system did not however fit with the present provisions of canon law with respect to training for the priesthood. So when a canon lawyer from Rome was appointed as the new Archbishop of Olinda-Recife, a neighbouring Brazilian diocese, ITER, the theological institute in a poor part of Recife was closed, and two older seminaries at Olinda refurbished, one for diocesans, one for religious.

I was in both of these refurbished colonial buildings, and they are very beautiful. The Franciscan college in Olinda has a striking internal courtyard and a small aviary. The colonnaded ambulatory is decorated with ancient and probably priceless images from the life of St Francis in blue and white tiling. The library is ornamented with paintings of the great Franciscan scholars on the ceiling. Here students can study and pray and recreate themselves in cool and spacious and beautiful surroundings near the sea, far from the poverty and cares of the majority of the Brazilian people. Steve commented on today's seminarians:

> A lot of the Brazilian seminarians come into the seminaries from a very poor background, and suddenly they come up to ordination, they're ordained, and they don't want to hear anything about going back to a poor parish or a poor area like where they grew up, where their roots are, and they make an option for a parish that's very well structured, a traditional type of parish, and they don't want to hear anything about working in a poorer part of the city. It's something that we've discussed a lot at clergy meetings and with people responsible for formation in the seminaries. So they're aware of it, but unfortunately, this is the situation, the big majority of priests and sisters who work in the shanty towns are

from abroad, are foreign missionaries.

Cardinal Aloísio Lorscheider, who was then Archbishop of Fortaleza – he has since moved to a less demanding post because of a heart condition – said he would like to see more priests choosing to work with the poor, and to train seminarians with that in mind rather than coddle them with comfortable institutional living. Which would be possible if more decision making was allowed at local level:

> We here think that in fact it would be very good if there were more decentralisation. Rome signifies unity, signifies communion among all the churches. But every church has also a certain autonomy and is a church which is within a reality. To want to centralise everything results, after a certain time, in a kind of paralysis. It's exactly from decentralisation that the greatest dynamism of the church comes.

Models of church

Those who live the option for the poor often speak of the church in terms of models. The model of church which arrived with Columbus was a colonial church that saw little good in the conquered territory or its peoples. The successor to that model today is a church which seeks to dominate by imposing power structures and rules and thought-patterns of European cultural origin.

Those who live the option for the poor prefer a different model, but not in the sense of being a new or even parallel church. Rather they speak about a different *way* of being the same, universal, church. And they prefer a new model of theology, a theology of liberation, a theology that emerges from the experience of people's lives, which for most people in Brazil means a life of poverty and oppression.

Medellin and Puebla

The phrase 'option for the poor' was first coined at an international meeting of Latin American bishops at Medellin in Colombia in 1968. The official adoption of this 'option for the poor' was a triumph for the supporters of what came to be called 'Liberation Theology', and which was seen as a new driving force in the Latin American church.

Ten years after Medellin, at the next international meeting at Puebla in Mexico, conservative forces tried to row back on some of the more radical policies adopted at Medellin, with partial success. This pressure continued in 1992 at the third meeting in Santo Domingo.

One could say that since Medellin the liberation theologians have been under fairly sustained attack by the Vatican, allied to conservative bishops – all John Paul II appointees.

The theology of liberation in essence

I have read learned books on the theology of liberation, and understood them in part, and forgotten most of what I have read. But it is not too hard to hold on to the essential concept. In essence it is a belief and a theological method.

The *belief* is the rather daring one that God is among us, and takes sides. The God of our scriptures is not aloof. He is 'Emmanuel', God-with-us. And especially with those of us who are the last, the least, the lost, and the little. He is the God who scatters the proud-hearted, exalts the lowly, fills the hungry with good things and sends the rich away empty, as Mary says in her *Magnificat*.

The *method* is to start with what God has to say in the scriptures – as it were, God's story. One compares it then with one's own story, and thus a conversation begins between the Bible and one's life. And from that dialogue comes a better understanding of what God means in our lives, and what he wants from us.

Why does the hierarchical church so dislike this theology?

1. It is people power. People are encouraged to work out for themselves what God is saying to them rather than what the priest or bishop is saying to them. If and when the clergy trust the people, and cooperate with them, there should be no conflict. But that trust is often absent.

2. It can easily get religion mixed up with politics. If God brings down the mighty, and frees the oppressed, the presumption must be that he acts through men and women, and may need our help!

3. Some theologians have used a Marxist analysis in their writings. This was a powerful negative factor in the cold war period, but with the fall of the Soviet Union it is now a lesser problem.

Cardinal Lorscheider, who has lived his priestly life in Brazil, was appointed bishop in the reign of John XXIII. He is sympathetic to liberation theology. Bishop João Evangelista Martins Terra, Auxiliary Bishop of Olinda and Recife was appointed in the reign of John Paul II. He spent most of his priestly life in Rome, and is critical of liberation theology. In our programme we contrasted their views.

Bishop Martins Terra's interview seemed to divide up into five points (to which I have provided five headings).

1. Liberation theology is not South American, it is an import from Europe.

Liberation theology was never very native to Brazil. The great inspiration was the Peruvian, Gutierrez, who wrote his doctoral thesis on it. Then came the others in Brazil, above all, Father Boff. But all of the theologians of liberation theology in Latin America took their doctorates in Europe, above all in Germany. Boff in Germany, then his brother Clodovis Boff. Also Libanio, who did his doctorate in Frankfurt, as did Jon Sobrino. All of them were deeply influenced by political theology, and especially by John Baptist Metz.

2. It was only ever popular among a small theological elite

As a theology, it never in fact had a wide acceptance among the middle class in Brazil. It remained among a theological elite, restricted to some seminaries. The seminary of Sao Paolo, above all, and then here in Recife there was a very strong centre in ITER, the Theological Institute of Recife. One of the strongest centres of liberation theology, was, for a time, Petropolis, where Father Boff lived. From there, then, many publications came. They tried to publish a liberation encyclopaedia; an encyclopaedia of 70 volumes. This encyclopaedia dealt with all the problems of theology: dogma, moral, pastoral – but always had liberation theology as its base.

3. Liberation theology is Marxist, and therefore discredited since the fall of communism in Eastern Europe

I believe that liberation theology had a big influence in Brazil three years ago. Right now, after the problems of Eastern Europe and the failure of socialism, liberation theology, which always tries to change the regime – a capitalist regime to a socialist regime where there would be more equality, a greater distribution of land and all that – also suffered a big crisis.

Hugo Assmann was the most profound of all the liberation theologians. He identified to such a degree with Marxism that he became a Marxist and had a deep crisis of faith. He left the priesthood and the Catholic church.

4. Liberation theology re-reads the Bible from a political not a religious point of view

CLAR, that is, the Council of Religious of Latin America, tried to do a re-reading of the Bible, a five year project in preparation for Santo Domingo. And at the end of the pastoral edition of the Bible there's a vocabulary. This vocabulary is exclusively ideological. All the themes that appear in this vocabulary are 'oppression' and 'oppressors,' then 'slavery'. This type of vocabulary isn't typical of theology.

As this Bible is geared towards the people, it's a popular version. And because it was distributed almost cost free, it's in the hands of unlearned people. They are going to have this first meeting with the Bible from an ideological perspective which isn't a typically religious one. So the Holy See had to intervene.

5. Liberation theology's proponents set up a parallel magisterium or teaching authority, different from that of the Pope and bishops

There seems to be a type of parallel magisterium rising up; one orientation given by the bishops, another by the religious priests and sisters. An immense majority of catechists in Latin America are religious. There are more than 100,000 religious and all of them in CLAR would have this tendency to catechise in a way almost like a parallel magisterium, in a Bible course more socialistic than properly theological.

Cardinal Lorscheider was not asked to reply particularly to these criticisms, but some points from his interview offer relevant counterviews to Bishop Martins Terra. The question of whether liberation theology is of European or Latin American origin didn't interest him. The question was its relevance to Latin America. The headings then are the same (except that there is no number 1!).

2. It was only popular among a small theological elite

Among more conservative bishops there has always been a tendency towards a certain withdrawal of support for liberation theology and the option for the poor. A return to the past would really be disastrous, when our situation demands an even greater commitment to justice within the world in which we live today. In the past there used to be a big link between the church and the civil power, and there was always a lot of that in the idea of a 'Christendom'. Instead of looking on the gospel as a leaven in the mass, and the Christian as salt to the world, a light to the world, we looked much more on the Christian as an individual. For this reason there was created more of a devotional faith, than a really committed faith.

3. Liberation theology is Marxist, and therefore discredited since the fall of communism in Eastern Europe

Liberation theology in itself wasn't founded either in Marxism or in Communism. Liberation theology sets out to show, in the light of faith, how these liberating actions which we find among the people can be empowered, strengthened and consolidated, so that we may in fact succeed in having a world and society that are just, fraternal and in solidarity. So liberation theology isn't tied to communism. It wants to save this people for true Christian liberty. Naturally there have been theologians who wanted to establish a dialogue between Christianity and Marxism. That one can't deny. And even within liberation theology there have been theologians who thought that, for example, the Marxist analysis was an apt instrument for an analysis of the reality. But clearly today it is ever more evident that the path doesn't lie in that direction.

4. It re-reads the Bible from a political not a religious point of view

It is our situation here in Latin America, people aren't considered as human beings. And we need to achieve at least this; that every human person be valued in his or her human dignity. This is a Christian vision; people in the image and likeness of God, sons of God, brothers and sisters one of the other. The big question for us is how far have our attempts to evangelise in the past in fact penetrated. Because as well as problems of corruption, problems of divorce, of abortion, we also have the problems of the treatment of the indigenous Indians who practically have been killed off, a big part of them. And we have here in Brazil and in other Latin American countries the problem of the negros, whom we call the Afro-Americans. They also are discriminated against. How is it that we, as church, have not succeeded in evangelising better?

5. Liberation theology's proponents set up a parallel magisterium or teaching authority, different from that of the Pope and bishops

Today I think that Rome has changed its opinion in relation to liberation theology. As the Pope himself said to the bishops in 1986, in the letter which he wrote on 9 April, that liberation theology is not only useful but necessary within that great theological tradition of the church. I think that we should continue on our way of evangelisation, especially creating the small church communities, which we call the small basic church communities. They are necessary to create that spirit in which people know one another, in which people truly participate.

16
OUR DEBT TO THE AMERINDIAN

Western society owes much of its prosperity to the genius and labour of the original inhabitants of Central and South America

When I read that Bolivia has enormous debts owed to First World bankers, debts which remain even after three times the original amount has been paid in interest; and when I see the abject poverty many Bolivians have to live in, and realise that it was their forefather's labour and wealth that helped to make Europe rich; and when I go down a mine where, it is claimed, eight million Indians died mining silver for their Spanish colonial masters, I get emotional and angry.

When I think of places that I was fortunate to visit and photograph, like Tikal with its step temples, and Machu Picchu with its magnificent ruins and terraces, and the gold museum in La Paz and Bogota where some of the art of the ancient world is displayed; and when I think of how much of wonder and beauty was smashed and destroyed by Europeans in the selfish quest for riches, I get emotional and angry.

When I realise that half the people in South America have not enough to eat, yet some three fifths of the varieties of foods that we eat in the First World were developed by the Andean peoples, I get emotional and angry.

When I see people who have little or no childcare or hospital facilities when they are sick, and realise how much the world owes to the Amerindian for the discovery of many potent medical drugs like curare and quinine, I get emotional and angry .

And I think, if I had been born into great wealth, and with a charitable disposition (which seem to be a rare enough combination) I would devote most of that wealth to try and help the poor indigenous peoples of South America.

1. Silver from Potosí

On 1 July 1550 Domingo San Thomas, later Bishop of La Plata, Bolivia wrote in a letter:

It will soon be four years ago that, to complete the destruction of this land, a mouth of hell was discovered, through which a vast number of people passed each year, whom the Spaniards' greed sacrifices to their God. This is a silver mine called Potosí.

Potosí is a town in the Bolivian Andes dominated by a mountain peak called Cerro Rico, whose summit is 15,680 feet. 85% of the silver produced from the Central Andes during the colonial era came from this one mountain. Potosí's coat of arms, stamped on a silver coin, proclaims, 'I am Potosí, the treasure of the world and the envy of kings'.

Eduardo, a former miner from Potosí, told us the story of how the mine was discovered. A shepherd looking after llamas lost one of his animals and came to search the hill. When night fell it was cold so he lit a fire. Next morning he found the fire had melted silver out of the rock beneath. This was in 1545. Eduardo continued:

Potosí was transformed into an important mining centre, growing rapidly. At the start of the seventeenth century there were in this town 160,000 inhabitants, many many people. It had many people from Europe, many Spanish, and black slaves that the Spanish brought here.

Despite its unlikely setting at nearly 14,000 feet above sea level, Potosí became a mecca for gamblers and freebooters and everyone who hoped to get rich quick. By 1573 it was the largest city in South America, rivalling London and Paris in size. The great mint of Potosí that turned out billions of coins from the sixteenth century on into the twentieth is now silent, but it doesn't require much imagination to invest with life the giant wood and wrought iron machines.

The European hunger for gold

The first motivation for the Spanish conquest of a New World was not of course silver, but gold. Before Columbus discovered America, most of Europe's gold came from what we still call the Gold Coast in Africa. Europeans sought desperately for ways to increase the supply that trickled up from West Africa in a trade which was largely in Muslim hands. The gold trade was further disrupted by political unrest, such as the wars of Ferdinand and Isabella against the Moors in the fifteenth century. So Spain desperately wanted to find alternate sources. The greed for gold overshadowed all other considerations. Columbus's own account of his discoveries is frequently laced with the remark, *'I was anxious to learn whether they had gold'*.

Amerindian nations prized gold, but not in the same way as the Europeans. The Inca, Garcilaso de la Vega, said of his people's attitude to gold:

> There was neither gold nor silver coin, and these metals could not be considered other than as superfluous, since they could not be eaten, nor could one buy anything to eat with them. Gold and silver were esteemed only for their beauty and brilliance.

What one sees of Indian gold in America today is only a fraction of what once there was. The Spanish melted most of what they got their hands on into ingots for shipment, although some prize pieces were sent to the king. These were exhibited around Spain to glorify the monarch, but after public exhibition they were melted down and turned into coin. Between 1500 and 1650, the gold of the Americas added about 200 tons to the treasuries of Europe. However, the silver from the mines of Potosí and Mexico was in the end to have far more impact on Europe than gold ever did. Once extracted, silver was made into bars or minted into coins in Potosí itself before being shipped to Panama by sea, then across the isthmus by mule, and eventually in galleons to Seville.

The economic and political effects of abundant silver

Kings and emperors have always hoarded gold and silver, but the amount was limited by their scarcity. With the discovery and exploitation of mines like Potosí, however, Europe suddenly acquired massive amounts of silver. For the first time it became possible for ordinary citizens to collect coin. For the first time a money-fuelled economy appeared where individuals could acquire flexible capital in amounts undreamed of before.

Gold served for making jewellery, decorating palaces and churches, and making valuable coins; but for the thousands of millions of day to day transactions, silver provided a coinage of stable value for the small merchant as well as the large. Before it discovered the New World, Europe had only about $200 million worth of gold and silver. Just one hundred years later, the supply had increased eight times.

The new coins helped to wash away the aristocratic order where land was the only valuable commodity, and where money games could only be played by the privileged few. Charles V, King of Spain, had also been elected Holy Roman Emperor in 1519 and remained ruler of large territories in the Netherlands, Germany Austria and Italy until 1556. Spanish wealth did not stay in Spain but moved freely around his dominions. For the first time there was something other than land which provided a consistent standard whereby wealth could be easily measured, transferred and transported. An abundant silver coinage prepared the way for the new merchant and capitalist class in Europe that would soon dominate the world.

The Ottoman Empire, which stretched from Africa into Eastern Europe, had controlled much of the trade in Europe through its silver coinage. Once the wealth of Potosí came on stream, Europe no longer needed Muslim coinage, and so it very rapidly lost half its value. After centuries of struggle between Muslims and Christians, American silver probably did more to undermine Islamic power for the next 500 years than any of the Crusades.

South American gold destroyed the African gold market. African traders had now only one thing to trade with Europe for the cloth, beads, leather and metals on which they had become dependent, and that was slaves. With the opening up of the Americas the slave trade began to boom as part of that infamous three cornered trade – manufactured goods to Africa, slaves to the Americas, and raw materials back to Europe.

The cost to the Amerindian

In the first few years after the discovery of silver, the Spaniards brought in 6,000 African slaves to Potosí, but they didn't survive long working at the high altitude. So the Spanish imposed a system of forced labour on the Quechuan Indians which was most unjust. Not only were the men forced to work in the mines for one in each four years, their families were also required to provide them with food and candles. They entered the mine on Monday and did not emerge again until Saturday. Each man had to chisel out a daily quota of one and a quarter tons of ore and carry it to the main tunnel through narrow passages and up ladders.

Records show that, in the first ten years of the system, four out of five miners died during their first year of forced employment in the mines, while it is estimated that eight million Amerindians died an early death from disease or accidents in the following centuries. Cerro Rico is covered today with the rubble of centuries, and 5,000 mine entrances. The mountain of waste rock from the mines is called locally, *Huakajchi*, 'the mountain that cried'.

Potosí today

Every morning, before sunrise, Potosí comes alive as the miners head off to the mountain towering above. As they walk up the steep streets, they stop at little shops to buy the necessities for the day – a little bag of fresh coca leaves to chew, a length of fuse, some crushed stone (calcium carbide) for the acetylene lamp, and a few sticks of dynamite. It is odd to pass a stall on the street with sticks of explosives stacked neatly like candles wrapped up in brown paper.

When the men get to the mine they sit around, talk, and chew coca leaves for about half an hour before going down the shaft. This is one of the few pleasant social occasions during the day, for work in the mines is a lonely occupation.

The miners believe that chewing the coca leaves helps to overcome the lack of oxygen at the high altitude, and counteracts the effects of dust and fumes. But perhaps its principle function is to numb the pangs of hunger during the long day, because the custom is not to bring food down the mines. Most of the miners belong to a co-operative, where they share whatever profits occur. Eduardo, a former miner, brought us into the heart of the mountain, looking for miners to film at work. He spoke about their life in Cerro Rico

> They are working like in the colonial time, like in the sixteenth and seventeenth centuries – the same conditions. In some of these mines, for example, there are still mules working. It's like it was four hundred years ago, the same working conditions – it's very dangerous. The miners either die of silicosis or by accidents. They call silicosis *'mal de mina'* – it's the product of breathing all the dust and gases in the mines, in effect, poison to the lungs. Then the accidents – there are cave-ins all the time. But they have no choice, they have no other alternative, because there is no other industry – just mines. They have a short life, most of these miners are invalids when they are 40 or 42 years old from silicosis, and they start work when they are twelve, ten years. I'm not sure but I think the youngest miner is nine years old.

We walked for about half a mile into the hill, mostly by the light of acetylene lamps, because although we had powerful lights, we had to be careful to preserve the batteries for later when we came to film. The tunnels were low and narrow, and for the most part without ceiling supports. I remember only one or two junctions of tunnels where I could stand up straight. As one got deeper in the mine the temperature rose. There was no ventilation system, although presumably with 5,000 tunnel entrances air gets in somehow. Apart from dust and fumes, another reason for lung trouble is the fact that miners come straight out of the hot interior in winter into freezing Andean winds. For remember, the mine entrance is fourteen thousand feet above sea level.

I photographed men working at seams with hammer and chisel prising out small quantities of zinc and silver ore which their ancestors had left behind because they did not seem worth the effort of working. According to one estimate, ore which produced 46,000 tons of pure silver came out of this mountain in it's previous history. What is left is a low grade ore containing 10% silver, 30% zinc.

Rewards are minimal, but what else is there to do in Bolivia where 85% of the rural population live below the poverty line, and the country itself struggles under a foreign debt of four billion dollars? We asked Eduardo how he felt about celebrating the 500th anniversary of the arrival of Christopher Columbus.

> I don't feel happy. I don't want to celebrate the 500 years of the discovery of Latin America. I can't celebrate the bad things that the Spaniards did here. Eight million Indians died working here – how could I celebrate, how could I say cheers for these bad things? No. I don't want to celebrate.

2. Food

Machu Picchu is a special, breathtakingly beautiful place. I first saw a photograph of it in the *National Geographic* magazine when I was a child, and the picture has remained in my memory ever since. The train journey from Cuzco which follows the course of the Urubamba river is spectacular in itself. Cuzco was of course the former highland capital of the Inca empire, and one can see remains of the old Inca road as the train passes through long deep river canyons. As soon as the train stops in the villages it is besieged by bowler-hatted women in colourful dress offering rugs and wall hangings and other craftwork of real beauty for very little money. The journey itself would have been worthwhile even if it went nowhere. From the rail station at Machu Picchu to the entrance to the site is a steep climb of about 1,500 feet. Some travel on foot, but most avail of a local bus which meets the train. What one finds at the top is the remains of a town surrounded by steep parabola shaped hills. The well preserved stone buildings look down on terrace after terrace which cling to the steep sides of the hill, all the way to the valley floor, nearly 2,000 feet below.

No matter how familiar one is with Machu Picchu through photographs, it retains for the first time visitor an aura of grandeur and mystery which no representation can capture. Obviously it was a very special place. What has puzzled many experts since it was first discovered by Europeans in 1911 was why it was built. Why go to such tremendous effort to build a miniature city in such an inaccessible place which could support, at most, about five hundred people?

The public buildings in Machu Picchu surpass any administrative or religious buildings one might expect to see in a town of comparable size. Lacking any explanation, some have called the place the 'Sacred city of the Incas'. But the Incas who built Machu Picchu were not like the Aztecs who built massive temples to propitiate their gods, nor were they like the Mayas who built large observatories to study the stars. So there must be a better explanation.

Now the ancient inhabitants of Peru were the world's greatest developers of plants for food. Plant breeding is not a haphazard operation – it requires skill, organisation and considerable resources, as was clear to us from an earlier visit to the International Potato Centre in Lima, Peru. Its costs are underwritten by an international consortium of 31 donors who subscribe all of $20 million a year. Dr Carlos Arbizu is an expert on Andean root and tuber crops, employed by the Institute:

> In ancient times it is very probable that Machu Picchu had a very important role in the domestication of cultivated plants. Why? Because of the different ecological conditions. We can see in Machu Picchu variations from the climatic condition of the warm Andean valleys to a very cold condition on the top of the highlands, and in between there are ecological conditions in which root and tuber crops adapted to the our warm Andean valleys were domesticated.

The builders who built the terraces at Machu Picchu built them to last to near eternity. Because there is little soil on the sides of these mountains, it is clear that the labourers must have hauled up the rich earth from the river nearly half a mile below. There are hundreds of these terraces, all too small to permit any kind of large scale agriculture, but well suited to provide different conditions to carry out plant-breeding programmes. So this is one explanation that seems to fit the visual evidence. Machu Picchu may have been an agricultural station where it was possible to experiment with plants at different altitudes, different soils and differing amounts of rain and sunshine.

Indians of the Andes have cultivated the potato on their mountain slopes and valleys for a least 4,000 years. At the time of the Spanish conquest in the sixteenth century, they had already developed thousands of different varieties. Dr Arbizu:

> Andean people were very astute and very clever in such a way that they selected aesthetic qualities in potatoes as well. That's why they selected different colour potatoes, different shapes of tuber, different flavours and different colour of the flesh; Andean people wanted beauty – in addition to food value of course.

A world without the potato

It is difficult to imagine what the world might have been without the Amerindian potato. Before the discovery of America, the old world depended primarily on grain crops such as wheat, oats, barley and rye. But grain crops in Europe face many problems. Because they grow on high stalks, unseasonable wind, hail and rain can wreak havoc on the crop. This happened all too frequently in northern Europe, leading to regular famines. For as long as the old world depended on grain, the great populations and power centres tended to be in southern Europe where the weather was more reliable. The potato gave northern Europe an alternative food supply rich in vitamins, which produced nearly twice the calories from a given field, with half the work, and in nearly half the time.

The rise in population and power of the northern European states like Britain, France, the Netherlands, Sweden and Germany, has much to do with the introduction of the potato. The growth in population in Ireland was made possible by the potato. The unique problem in Ireland was that because of the great poverty, people could not afford grain or other alternative foods when the potato failed, while the government, some hundreds of miles away in London, neither understood the problem, nor had the political will to do much about it.

The International Potato Centre, Lima, Peru

Today the Andean tradition of developing new and better potatoes is carried on at the International Potato Centre in Lima, Peru, where ten thousand varieties of potatoes are grown and development work continues. One project in hands is to seek out strains among wild potatoes with resistance to potato blight, and breed the characteristic into the cultivated types.

As well as the common potato, other root crops first developed by

Andean peoples are studied here. The yam or sweet potato gave the Chinese a practical alternative to rice. China has now become the world's largest producer of sweet potatoes, where, like in Peru, it is the staple food of the poor. The sweet potato is currently grown in more developing countries than any other root crop. Farmers in the tropics can harvest potatoes within 50 days of planting, a third of the time it takes in colder climates.

The Potato Centre in Lima employs 300 people. The fact that such huge resources are needed to make even minor improvements in food crops grown today only highlights the achievements in plant development in the past. For without question the indigenous people of the Americas were the world's greatest plant breeders.

Indian corn or maize, developed from a wild grass by the Mayas, is another of the Amerindians' better-known gifts to humanity. They weren't satisfied to develop one plant, but gave us dozens of varieties. Corn can be had in a range of colours from red to purple and blue, and in many different forms like sweet corn, pop corn, and flint corn.

A prolific root crop, variously called manioc or cassava, is another gift from the Amerindian. Cassava is now an important food crop in Africa as well as in South America, though it is less well known in Europe, where it is only used in its derivative form, tapioca.

The Amerindians developed a whole range of grains which have not yet been exploited in Europe. Amaranth was highly prized by the Aztecs and is said to be the most nutritious of all grains, and has only been rediscovered in the West in recent years. It is now widely cultivated in Asia, but so far is little known in Europe.

The humble bean received particular attention. Numerous varieties – kidney beans, snap beans, string beans, common beans, Lima beans, butter beans, pole beans, navy beans, Rangoon beans, Burma beans, French beans, Madagascar beans – were all developed in America.

Three fifths of the food we eat were developed from the wild by the Amerindians. The list seems endless. Peanuts, pecans, cashew and Brazil nuts. Tomatoes, red peppers, chillies, squashes, avocados, cranberries, blueberries, passion fruit. We learnt from them how to make chocolate from cacao beans. The Andean people domesticated the sunflower, which gave Russia a reliable source of edible oil. Today Russia is the world's largest producer of Sunflower seed.

Scientists are still finding new varieties of plant foods grown in remote enclaves in the Amazon, in high Mexican valleys and along swampy creeks in Costa Rica. But despite all the plant improvements brought about by modern technology, the indigenous Americans remain the developers of the world's largest array of nutritious foods, and the primary contributor to the world's varied cuisines. For that we owe them a debt of gratitude.

3. Medicine

While European medical men talked learnedly about the balance of bodily humours, and Muslim doctors set leeches on their patients to suck out bad blood; while the physicians of China made potions of dragons' bones and rhinoceros horn, the Amerindians were until recent times the only ones to refine a range of drugs with any real physiological effect. Dr Fernando Cabieses, Director of the National Institute for Traditional Medicine in Peru, is an expert on traditional Andean medicine.

> The Andean people developed the understanding of how a plant can cure a disease and not only cure a symptom. Most of the knowledge of using medicinal plants is based on curing symptoms; this plant is good for cough, and this plant is good for diarrhoea, and this plant is good for pain, and this plant is good for nervousness – this is curing the *symptoms*. But when you find a plant that is good for a disease called malaria, then you change your whole understanding of medicine. When you find that an ethnic group develops a plant and understands that this plant called *Cephalaelis Ipecacuanha* cures amoebic dysentery, and when you find that another plant cures worms of the intestines – it doesn't cure only the diarrhoea, it kills the offending organism that *causes* the diarrhoea. This was not known by Europeans at all, and this understanding of disease, separate from understanding of the symptoms, is a tremendous step towards the development of modern medicine.

Strychnos, Quina and Coca, three herbs which yield curare, quinidine and cocaine have played a highly significant role in modern medicine. Curare, used by Indians on their spears, was first used in small quantities as a muscle relaxant, initially with victims of lockjaw. Quinidine, derived from quinine, is used to control irregularities in the heartbeat, while cocaine is still the basis for the most important anaesthetics used today. Dr Cabieses continued:

> Now if you consider only these herbs which were discovered by

an ancient healer in this country, you could not do a heart transplant without them right now. You need these three herbs to do a heart transplant which is one of the greatest assets of present modern medicine. Now there are at least one hundred different plants and drugs which were offered to the world by the ancient Peruvians, of which these are only three.

Malaria

For as long as there are medical records, it appears that malaria ravaged every part of Europe, Africa and Asia. Nobody had a cure. Malaria helped to kill Oliver Cromwell and Alexander the Great. One plant the Peruvian Quechua Indians specially valued for its medical properties was the bark of a certain Peruvian tree. They called it Quina-Quina, which in the Quechua language means the bark of barks – from which came our word 'quinine'. Quinine was introduced to Europe in 1630. It is ironic that quinine helped to make possible the colonisation of many countries by Europeans. The records of the Governor of Virginia in 1671 show that before the introduction of quinine, one colonist in five died of malaria in their first year. When quinine was introduced the deaths ceased. Quinine was mixed with gin by the British colonists to make it more palatable. It was gin and tonic that made it possible for Britons to colonise countries where they might otherwise have succumbed to the malarial mosquito. Dr Cabieses:

> Quinine was essential to building the Panama canal, to industrialise the Mississippi region, to stop malaria from destroying Rome and London, to really develop the health, good health of Europe which was being thoroughly destroyed by malaria at that time. So you will understand that there is a tremendous debt owed by Europe – shall we call it the debt that was never paid?

Until recent times, Europe gave nothing to American medicine. The first colonists did, however, present them with a number of European diseases to which they had no time to build up immunity. These included bubonic plague, tuberculosis, malaria, yellow fever, smallpox, measles, mumps, whooping cough and influenza. It is probable that 90% of the American Indian population died of persecution and disease in the first hundred years after the arrival of Europeans on their continent. The Western world destroyed whole Amerindian civilisations in its scramble to get rich quick. Everything of value which could be moved was pilfered. The people who survived the onslaught were enslaved. Now again, in the twentieth century, the people are enslaved – this time to Western bankers who pushed large sums of surplus oil money on largely military governments in the 1970s.

Since then the amount of the debt has been paid *three times over* in interest, and the poor have born the burden of the payment, and in so doing become poorer. In light of the injustice and suffering associated with the conquest, in the light of the historic debt due to the people of Central and South America for their contribution to our wealth, health and well being, this is surely a triple injustice that cries out to heaven for redress.

17

THE NOVEL IS THE STAINED-GLASS WINDOW OF MODERN TIMES

How a priest came to write novels, and what sociology has taught him about life and religion

Andrew Greeley, a priest of the diocese of Chicago, has written twenty novels and sold about twenty million copies. That's about 6,000 books ever day for the last ten years. Many an Irish author would be very happy to sell 6,000 copies of a book before it sinks into the remainder lists.

For most of his public life, Greeley had been known, not as a priest, or a novelist, but as a sociologist. So far as the sociology of the Catholic church in the USA is concerned, he has probably done more useful work than any other sociologist, living or dead.

The Greeleys came originally from near Ballyhaunis, Co Mayo, and Andy is passionately interested in Ireland, coming for a week at a time, at least once and sometimes twice a year. I first met him many years ago at lunch in Wynn's Hotel in Dublin with Conor Ward, then Professor of Sociology in UCD. Conor told me afterwards that if data came in from a survey which most sociologists would require six months to digest and write into a report, Andy would digest it and write the report in a month. For he has a quite unusual capacity to absorb and sift enormous amounts of data, intuit what is important, and get the facts quickly on to paper. In all he has published over thirty non-fiction works, mostly sociological, since 1963.

Andy does some pastoral work in parishes at weekends, but his office is the National Opinion Research Centre in the University of Chicago, and his home is in the Hancock building in the centre of the city, overlooking Lake Michigan. He bought the apartment many years ago when the Hancock was being built. Since then it has become the fashionable place to live in Chicago. If people ask him where his parish is, he tells them 'my mailbox'. One can't have as many readers as he has without a very large pile of correspondence. About half those who write to him would not go to church regularly, but they write to him not just as an author, but as a priest.

Andy told me once that he could write a novel in draft form in about a month. That kind of productivity requires management of time and resources. Andy does a lot of ordinary things, like going for a swim, or a meal in a good restaurant, and things that priests normally do, such as saying Mass and reading the Breviary. But he does not waste time like most of the rest of us do. Where others would sit in an aeroplane looking out the window, or thinking about the next free drink, Andy will be working at his laptop computer with which he can send and receive messages from his office by fax or e-mail no matter where he is – even up in an aeroplane. Everything about his life is well organised. He has a small staff working to him at the research centre in the university. He has a public relations consultant to look after all the details that surround the preparation and publication of his books, his media interviews, trips abroad, and so on. And because of the substantial income from his novels, he can afford to pay for the best and most efficient service.

Andrew Greeley the novelist

When he first began to write novels I, like many other priests, was a bit disturbed by what we heard. Firstly it seemed a waste of valuable time. Secondly it seemed undignified if not immoral for a priest to be writing imaginative fiction about sex and marriage. As a convinced celibate, and indeed vocal supporter of celibacy, he was not presumably able to write from experience; and if he wanted to stay celibate, he would probably do better to curb his imagination!

I was interested to find these attitudes reflected in a study of Chicagoan priests by Professor Ingrid Shafer. Of the one third of the priests who had never read a Greeley novel,

   42% felt them to be sleazy exploitation of the mass market,
   42% would discourage their congregations from reading them,
   64% thought they would cause loss of respect for the church.

However, among the two-thirds who had read some of them, only 14% thought they would cause loss of respect for the church. Greeley offered us this defence:

We're not archangels; so yes, we have to talk about sexuality. I think there is a fair amount of eroticism, mild eroticism in my novels, but the charge that one hears from some priests that they are soft core pornography can only come from people that haven't read them. Eroticism is a sacrament, I mean, if erotic feelings between men and women were not sacramental, then God made an awful mistake.

How did you respond to critics that would say, well what would a priest know about such things?

Well I'd say two things. A priest couldn't be writing about sexual feelings if (a) sex was evil, and (b) priests weren't human. But since (a) sex is good, not evil, and (b) priests are human, there's nothing wrong with writing about it.

Professor Shafer tried another experiment on Greeley's novels. She took a number of passages from contemporary novels and mailed them to college professors and book editors asking them to assess their literary worth. Such writers as Saul Bellow, John Updike, David Lodge, Robertson Davies, Irving Wallace, Edna O'Brien, Joyce Carol Oates, Harold Robbins, Robert Pen Warren, and Erica Jong were represented – in addition to Greeley. She sent out one batch which just said the quotations were from well known living authors, while another batch named the author of each piece. Where the assessors knew the authors, Greeley was at the bottom of the list, with people like Bellow and Updike at the top. But where the assessors did not know the authors, Greeley was very well represented at the top!

In the course of the programme we asked him why he, a priest, writes popular novels.

I write novels because I like to write them, they're fun, to begin with. But also I think they're the best way I know of, in the modern world, to talk about religion. Religion is story long before it's anything else. Jesus was a storyteller. If you want to get at the mind and the religious imagery of Jesus, you go to the parables. For most of human history, religion was passed on by stories. So my sociology led me to ask the question about fifteen years ago now – whether the popular novel might be the stained-glass window of the modern time, or whether you could talk about religion in the framework, in the context, of the popular story.

Do you get a lot yourself personally from writing a novel?

Well I find it the most rewarding of my activities. I get enormous positive feedback from the readers who understand the religious themes and say that it helps them in their spiritual lives and so that's very rewarding. Just the act of creating a story itself is lots of fun. A storyteller is something like God. You create these people and you fall in love with them, and then they don't act the way they should, and I think that's how God feels about us sometimes.

Greeley is very insistent that his books are religious stories – parables. And if any one challenges him, he can produce files of letters from readers which seem to indicate that they understood this aspect of his work. Filming with him on the streets of Chicago, people were continually coming up to him. 'Oh you are Fr Greeley! Oh Fr Greeley, I just love your books ...'

> Religion is poetic before it's prosaic. (Here the academic in Greeley begins to speak.) Religion begins with experiences that renew hope, then we encode these experiences in images we call symbols, and then we share those experiences with others by telling them stories. Sometimes we act out those stories in ritual. So you have religion as experience, image, story, community and ritual. Now because we're human and we're reflecting creatures, we have to reflect on religion, but the reflection comes after the religious experience, not before.

Do you consider them religious books?

> Oh yes, every one is a story about God; it's a story about second chances that God gives us. That it is the nature of our God that he gives us second, third, fourth and fifth chances in life: death and resurrection goes on all the time. In 'Lord of the Dance', this man who has been in prison in China for 20 years comes home and he complains to his niece about how hard it is, and she says, 'resurrection isn't supposed to be easy'. That maybe is the principle theme of all my stories.

Do you appeal to a particular audience?

> About three quarters of my readers in America are Catholic, which leaves a quarter who aren't. About three-fifths of them are women which means that two fifths are men, and the books sell more per capita in Ireland than they do in the United States, and of that I'm inordinately proud.

Andrew Greeley, the sociologist

Andrew Greeley fascinates me because he is one of the few men in the world of organised religion who has not just opinions, but facts to back them up.

It is commonly said that many Catholic clergy in the US are deeply troubled and unhappy in their vocation. I for one presumed that to be true until Greeley came along with figures to prove the opposite – that priests are just as content as married men and are more content than single men. But, even though they are happy in their own vocation, many of them think – wrongly as it turns out – that other priests aren't!

It is commonly said that more and more young people are leaving the church and that as a consequence the institution is dying. Greeley can produce facts, for the USA at least, to prove the contrary.

> There is a tendency for young people to drift away from the church, beginning in the middle teens, reaching bottom in the middle 20s, and then returning rather rapidly through the late 20s and into the 30s, so that in our research people in their early 40s are about as likely to go to Mass and to be devout and to pray as their parents were twenty-five years before.

The following quotes have been mined from the interviews filmed for the Radharc programme.

The church in the United States

Its assets are very strong parish life. We've tried for three decades to drive the Catholic lay people out of the church and they won't go. I mean the defection rate was fifteen per cent in 1960, and it's still fifteen per cent. Fifteen per cent of those who were born Catholic are no longer Catholic. So there's very, very strong Catholic life. But the institution is in terrible disarray. Bishops that are appointed generally are incompetent, and there's a shortage of priests which is a very acute problem. So you have the sort of paradoxical thing – a church which flourishes as community, and yet is very troubled institutionally. And also there is a tremendous financial crisis. Catholics are giving about half as much in terms of their real income now as they did thirty years ago.

The Catholic family

The big difference in Catholic families is that they have the enormous asset of the church's sacramental system which can sanctify the various rights of passage in family. The difficulty they have is that the church doesn't seem to understand the importance of intimacy in married life, that sex exists in humans to bind the husband and wife together – that what is uniquely human about human sexuality is its bonding propensities. You can procreate a higher order primate with a lot less inconvenience than we have in humans. Much of what is unique to human sexuality is for bonding the man and the woman together and I don't think the church comprehends that. It just thinks well, you know, husbands and wives shouldn't have all that much fun, they should be serious and responsible and sober about raising children instead of fooling around with one another all the time. But it is precisely the fooling around that makes the union between man and woman possible. It heals the friction, it renews the love, it's enormously important. I think the parish clergy realise this, but it often seems to me that the hierarchy and the Vatican don't realise it at all.

Religion and eroticism

I think one of the big improvements the church could make is to finally decide that St Paul is right when he says that marriage is the great sacrament. That is to say that erotic attraction between men and women is not bad, it's not dirty, it's not something we shouldn't talk about, but is a positive good. And the church should adopt as one of its major missions in life to help increase the amount of passionate love between husband and wife.

One of my friends came into my office, a Catholic friend, and threw something on my desk, in which the Papal Commission for the Family said that husbands and wives should be warned about the dangers of unbridled lust. He said, 'Don't the idiots know that the real problem is bridled lust? And if there was more unbridled lust in our lives we'd be a lot happier and we'd probably be a lot better Christians.'

We did a study the year before last of people who are married. It came out in a book called *Faithful Attractions*. They may have been divorced and remarried, but now at least, they're married people. And some of the findings were very interesting. Three quarters of the people said that they would marry the same spouse again. 87% say their spouse is their best friend. 65% say they're very happy in their marriage. 17% say that they're in a falling in love phase in the marriage. And interestingly enough, that proportion doesn't change through the duration of marriage. 17% of people in their 60s say they're falling in love with their spouses!

The strongest correlates we have of marital happiness is prayer and erotic play. So those people who pray together and take showers together – not necessarily at the same time – seem to have extremely high levels of marital fulfilment. Religion and eroticism, sex and prayer, are very strong predictors of a happy marriage particularly when they come together. Fr Peyton, the great Rosary priest, used to say the family that prays together, stays together, and I would, with all due respect to him, modify the dictum and say that the husband and wife who pray together and play together erotically tend to stay together. And I think the church, since it believes that eroticism is sacramental, should really celebrate that finding.

Ups and downs in marriage

Well our research shows – I guess everybody knows it but it lays it down precisely – that there are rhythms in marriage. There's times of ups and times of downs. The first couple of years are fine and the next three or four years are terrible. And then by the seventh or eighth year of marriage there is a rebound effect, so at the end of the first decade people are quite happy. The most fascinating finding of all is that the level of satisfaction for people that have been married fifty years is the same as for people that have been married for one year. So it suggests that if a husband and wife stay together long enough there will indeed be a happy ending.

Catholic schools

I think that combination of the neighbourhood, the parish, and the Catholic parochial school makes our neighbourhood parish one of the strongest communities that human ingenuity has ever invented. Catholic schools turn out to be high quality schools – they're better than any of the public schools in Chicago. And they are very successful religiously. I mean in a certain sense they pay for themselves because the people who send their kids to Catholic schools contribute more to the church. And then when the Catholic school kids grow up they'll be more generous and contribute to the church, and also they'll be more likely to go to church, more likely to support vocations for their children, more open on issues like ecumenism and social justice. The schools are tremendously successful in this country. I say that not as a priest but as a social scientist who spent thirty years studying them. Unfortunately I'm afraid that many parish priests have lost their faith in the Catholic schools.

The Mother of God

The Mary Myth was a very important book in my life because it helped me to think through the role of symbolism in religion. What persuaded me to reawaken my interest in, and my devotion to Mary, was that a Protestant theologian, Harvey Cox, had written a long chapter in one of his books about Our Lady of Guadalupe, and Harvey has one of the best sets of antennae of anybody I know. I figured if Harvey Cox had discovered the Mother of Jesus it was high time that a Catholic priest like me rediscovered her, and so I began to study the role of Mary, particularly in art and poetry and music, and it seemed to me that Mary's function in Catholic Christianity is to represent the mother love of God. It is perhaps the most impressive and important manifestation of the distinctively Catholic imagination that the whole world of creation is sanctified and is sacred; and the human body, motherhood, all of these things are sacred, and that woman tells us much about God, indeed that 'woman' is as adequate a metaphor for God as 'man'. Now I don't think that's been in the doctrine, but I think it's been in the poetry and in the music.

Happiness

Both women and men are happier when they're married, and the least happy of the four, if you divide people by gender and marital status, are unmarried men. Women are better able to cope with single state than are men. Celibates who are happy in priesthood and content with the priesthood are as happy as married men of the same age and educational background.

All the evidence points to the fact that the more religious people are, on balance the happier they are. For example, frequency of prayer correlates with personal happiness, marital happiness, family satisfaction, also with sympathy for condemned murderers and rapists. So prayer is good for you, religion is good for you, and those who say it isn't, who say they can do without it, well maybe they as individuals can, but the evidence in a number of different societies, United States, Ireland, England – each one of them with a lot of different religious cultures and heritages – is that the more religious you are, the more devout you are, the happier you are. Now I don't know which way it goes – maybe happy people pray more, or maybe there's some underlying orientation towards life and its purpose and meaning in the world around that leads to both frequent prayer and happiness. But in fact the more devout you are the happier you are.

18
THE CANDIDATE

*A portrait of Cardinal Martini, whom the Italian media
would like to see succeed Pope John Paul*

When the Italian media speculate about who will be the next Pope,
the odds-on favourite is Carlo Maria Martini, Archbishop of Milan.
And there is good reason for him to be the favoured candidate.
Behind the pomp and circumstance surrounding this Italian prelate
lies a biblical scholar of international repute. Cardinal Martini speaks
eleven languages, and is a former rector of both the Pontifical Biblical
Institute and the Gregorian University in Rome. He is an experienced
and successful pastoral bishop. Our programme attempted to take
a look at what kind of person lives inside this Jesuit academic who
rules the largest Catholic diocese in Europe, stretching into
Switzerland – with a thousand parishes and five million people.

The presence

Martini is a tall man. He moves swiftly with a straight back, head
forward, eyes looking over his glasses. His cardinal's biretta, which
he wears on formal occasions, is large and sits a little uncomfortably
on a tall face, accentuated by hair receding from the forehead. His
eyes are steady, and frame a well-shaped, aristocratic nose. He has
a pleasant, sometimes quizzical smile, but normally he looks a serious man. His voice has a guttural quality which is very marked in
English, but softens when he speaks Italian.

What the Jesuits thought of Martini

It is reliably said that when the Jesuits began considering a successor to Fr Arrupe, their much beloved Father General, Carlo Martini
was their first choice. The Pope appointed him unexpectedly as
Archbishop of Milan, however, thus removing him from contention.
Some Jesuits at least were annoyed, seeing this as a stratagem to
remove an independent candidate, so that the Pope could appoint
somebody less independent and more malleable to his will, which
in fact is what he did.

What the European bishops thought of Martini

When the Council of the European Catholic Bishops' Conference last
elected their president, they chose Martini.

What the Milanese media think of Martini

When a committee formed from the directors of the Milanese press, Radio and TV, met to choose the 1992 Milanese man of the year, they overlooked the politicians and industrialists and opera singers and chose the cardinal instead. The citation for the award was direct, if in rather florid terms:

> In the past year, in which Milan was rocked by a deep crisis that seemed to have made the city lose confidence in its own identity, Cardinal Martini, with the primacy of the Word, with the missionary impulse, with the exercise of charity, with an incisive and constant participation in the civil and political affairs of this city, with a strong teaching given from the chair of Ambrose and Charles (Borromeo) has infused courage and hope, but he has also recalled each person to responsibility and to personal and social duties in the spirit of a Christian love …

Moral leadership

The deep political crisis that first rocked the city of Milan, and then the whole of Italy in the early nineties is spoken of as '*tangentopoli*', perhaps best translated as 'Bribestown'.

Tangenti are the kickbacks that Italian politicians routinely pocket on all public works. Every one knew about it, but nobody spoke about it. Martini was one of the first to speak publicly about political corruption. People credited him as a prophetic voice as the scandals broke, and day after day the newspapers brought new revelations. Over a half dozen prominent people committed suicide, party leaders were forced to resign. Over two and a half thousand businessmen and politicians were arrested or put under investigation. It is said that if everyone involved were to be charged, 60,000 people would have to pass through the courts. One of the places we photographed – surreptitiously – in Milan was the prison where, we were told, Fiat executives, leading politicians and owners of soccer teams shared cells with convicted felons and drug dealers.

Publicly challenging the corruption in the then ruling Christian Democrat party as Martini did required courage, because the church had always been closely allied with the party since the Second World War. The cardinal however remains optimistic.

> We are in a very difficult moment in Italy, but there is a great desire of new things, of new mentality, and these are areas where the bishops can play a role of great leadership in our country.

Most of the more conservative bishops in Italy kept quiet about corruption, fearing a split in the Catholic vote, which was inevitable anyway, given the changed political conditions after the collapse of international communism.

Martini the communicator

From the first days of his episcopate, Cardinal Martini began to write and speak to his people on every social and religious issue, from business ethics to women's rights.

> There are so many problems that it is hard to make a list of them or to make a priority. But I would say that certainly one of the main problems is the size of the diocese – five million people. And then what you wonder is how can you reach all of them.

The use of radio has become one part of his strategy to reach these five million people. The archdiocese owns it's own radio station, and once a week the cardinal speaks to his flock on the airwaves about what concerns him, and what he feels should concern them. He has a microphone in one of the smaller rooms in his living quarters, and broadcasts from there.

Martini the author

Martini is more a writer than a broadcaster – indeed he is a publisher's dream! Since coming to Milan he has published fifty titles, selling about one million books in Italy every year. These include not only books on scripture and spirituality, but also publications on every kind of religious and moral issue, from family matters to business ethics, from problems of mass communications to questions of faith among young people. One wonders how all this creative activity can possibly fit in with the normal administrative work of a Catholic bishop.

Martini the administrator

With over 3,000 priests resident in the dicoese to chose from, Milan has always had a talented administration, and the means to organise itself efficiently and well. But much of this was in place before Martini came to Milan. What he has done is to give new inspiration to the organisation and freedom to those who work in it.

> Each diocese thinks it is unique and each diocese has its own good reason – we have reasons to think we are unique because we are so large a diocese. And in a sense this requires a different way of governing, of having in hand the diocese. And we are unique in

the sense that we have the largest body of priests in the world – more than 3,000. Therefore it requires special ways to have contact with them.

Cardinal Martini does not involve himself in some of the traditional aspects of a bishop's work which others might consider essential. He delegates to others the appointments of priests. He does not administer the Sacrament of Confirmation, his auxiliary bishops and episcopal vicars do that for him. All this is to free him for more important things, like visiting priests and people in one or other of the thousand parishes.

> I am very very happy with my collaborators – they are many – about fifteen vicars, and they work very hard in the different sections of the diocese. Therefore we are a very good team.

> Meeting people is easier than I had anticipated in so far as many people are longing to talk to the bishop, to see the bishop, to be in contact with him. So I am greatly helped by the people. Young people want to see me, to speak to me, and they come in thousands to meetings. And in these meetings, although there are many many people, it is as if you would speak to each one of them. I think there is a kind of communication which goes to many people but reaches each one of them if it is true and authentic.

The signs of the times

Cardinal Martini often speaks of what he calls 'the signs of the times', such as a renewed interest among young people in prayer and in spirituality. He believes that this interest is more than just a passing fad, but is in fact a sign of the times – a sign of the Holy Spirit working in the world. Shortly after he came to Milan, a group of young people asked him to help them to pray. His response was to invite them to come to the cathedral once a month and pray with him. In the beginning 2,000 accepted his invitation. This movement grew so that eventually there were 64 places around the diocese where every second Thursday of each month, 18,000 young people met to pray with the gospel.

Another great sign of the times that the cardinal believes is of special relevance is a growing interest in the scriptures. He has made a special effort to promote the prayerful reading of the word of God because he believes that from this many other good initiatives are born.

> If we don't start with the word of God, we build on a surface

which cannot resist the difficulties of the real life situations; therefore we want to dig very deep in the heart of young people with meditation on the scriptures. From the very beginning I attempted to bring young people to the word of God. And in fact we had a very good success – I am very proud of this group of young people. They are doing very, very well.

Two young students who attend monthly meetings of what Martini has called 'The School of the Divine Word' spoke to us of the movement with enthusiasm.

The gospel is for every day – there must be daily reflection on the word of God. These words are so beautiful and important for our daily lives. Our monthly meeting can help us to discover the beauty of the gospel, because our meeting is not just something for an occasion – it is something for every day.

Young people in particular, so busy in a city like Milan, need less words, more of the gospel, and more silence. It is a beautiful thing to be able to pray and study the word of God that goes back such a long way and that now is valued and appreciated, not only by monks and priests, but also by young lay people who meet with enthusiasm to pray in silence, together in the same place, in the same house of God, and return to their homes with greater strength and enthusiasm as witnesses of Christ.

Samuele and service to the community

Another initiative of the cardinal was to help young people think purposefully about their lives in the light of the gospel, and help them make decisions about their future rather than drift aimlessly. He called it 'Samuele'. For he sees this as another sign of the times, the willingness of young people to make themselves available for forms of service for the poor, the elderly, for catechesis, and even for development and missionary work. Partly because of initiatives like this there has been an increase in the numbers of young people willing to give both part-time and full-time service to the church in Milan.

We took a run out to Msnago, a rural parish in the archdiocese. Like almost all Milanese parishes, it has a parish centre where many activities take place. Anna Latini, a lay parishioner whom we met, is one of a small group who have dedicated their lives to serve the needs of the people of the parish. She has taken temporary vows of celibacy and obedience, and her superior is the cardinal. But she is not a nun.

We don't have our own house, we are out around the parish for whoever needs us, whether it be babies, young people, or the elderly. And we offer pastoral care and charity to the parish and the diocese. For us that is the most important thing.

Milan gets more than its share of immigrants, with the upheavals in the former Yugoslavia exacerbating the problem. Homeless and hungry, many turn to the church for assistance. Underneath – literally underneath – the Milan railway station, Fr Adriano Moro runs a refuge and night shelter with the help of seventy young volunteers. Andrea Passagnoli was one of them:

Our aim here is to get to know the reality of the lives of these needy people and perhaps help them in other ways. In fact near here in the parish there is a school to teach Italian to foreigners. Young people like us teach Italian to immigrants, so that they can have a better lifestyle, and achieve more in their work.

Cardinal Martini himself likes to drop in to the refuge every now and again, unannounced, and help to serve the food.

Collegiality in the diocese

In December 1993, the Milan diocese began a Synod of clergy and laity to review the problems and opportunities for the diocese into the next millennium. The cardinal asked for the full participation of the parish councils. We were present when he addressed one of them. One got the feeling that he genuinely wanted participation, rather than asking for it as a matter of good public relations.

One last thing I'd recommend to a parish such as you are – look forward to making a good contribution to the Synod discussions which we have already begun. Be very open in your responses, say what you feel, with freedom, giving the whole spectrum of possible reactions. Don't feel that you have to limit yourselves to saying this or that. Say what the Holy Spirit suggests in the richness of your experience.

The next Pope

When the cardinals gather in the Sistine chapel to chose a Pope, they always begin by discussing the particular problems facing the church of their time, and the kind of person who might be needed to meet them.

If the Pope were to be chosen by the people of Italy, there is little doubt that the vote would go to Martini. So people are interested in

Martini, and the press tries to satisfy this interest. When we first made the approach to do a story on the diocese of Milan, we were warned that we would be lucky to get access to the archbishop – at any one time he has about fifty requests for media interviews on his desk.

In fact we were allowed full access to his public activities (visiting parishes, talking on the radio, addressing young people), but only one rather brief interview, which however eventually became two. As inevitable with a man under such pressure, Martini has to have handlers who see that he arrives at each function as scheduled, spends the correct amount of time, and leaves in time for the next appointment.

It was clear to me that his handlers worry about what he says, or is led into saying. The media are always asking difficult questions where an honest answer can seem to pit Martini against a higher authority. We heard in Milan that his chancery staff were upset by a an interview – a very good interview – by John Cornwell which was published in the *Sunday Times* (April 1993). They felt that some of the sentiments attributed to Martini could get him into trouble with the Vatican. In that situation I felt we could not do a hard interview, even if we wanted to. However that didn't worry me – we had come to do a television portrait, to get the feel of the man rather than conduct an issue-led interview We wanted to see the man in his environment, at his work, at his prayer, with different kinds of people, his body language, not just his answers to tricky questions.

Inevitably his co-workers in the diocese, who admire Martini's leadership, hope someday he will be Pope. Becoming Pope, like becoming prime minister or president becomes harder, the more one is forced to put answers to thorny problems on the record. It seems that in the modern world, those who conceal their views are more likely to get elected to office. Three of the kinds of answers which would clearly rally the Curia to determined opposition are the following:

Contraception

'I am sure that the Holy Spirit will guide the church to overcome the question of contraception as the church has overcome other moral problems in the past. Usury was an almost insurmountable impediment in the fourteenth century, but little by little we began to see the problem in a different light, although it took centuries to resolve it.'

Women priests

As for the issue itself, I think we should come to it little by little, to gradual solutions that will satisfy not only the most progressive but the majority, while remaining true to tradition and within the bounds of common sense. That's my opinion. But I can foresee that we'll have some decades of struggle ahead. When people ask me, and it's usually Americans, 'Will we have women priests?'I answer, 'Not in this millennium'. (The implication of course is that it could be in the next!)

Division in the church between left and right

'My own opinion is that these differences may be unavoidable, as we are not all contemporaries in a biological or a biographical sense. This is 1993, but some Catholics are still mentally in 1963, some in 1940, and some even in the last century. It's inevitable that there will be a clash of mentalities.'

Promoting collegiality among the bishops (and getting into trouble for it)

The Council of European Bishops' Conferences (CCEE) normally meets once a year. Cardinal Martini was elected president in 1987. Martini had plans for the European bishops. He told them that they should meet frequently and become friends – without friendship he said there could be no disposition towards collegiality. Personal contact can help build the unity of the wider Europe. The late Peter Hebblethwaite summed up his hopes for the CCEE in December 1991:

> The Vatican having painted itself into a corner of irrelevance, it is high time the Eurobishops took their responsibility seriously. From the Vatican we can expect control, from Martini leadership … There is one flaw in the optimistic scenario sketched here about the Eurobishops – John Paul II could sack Martini.

Fourteen months later, in a roundabout way, John Paul did just that. He announced that the Council of European Bishops' Conferences (CCEE) would be restructured (without consulting them about the need or otherwise for this restructuring). Furthermore he decided that the members would no longer be elected, but consist solely of the presidents of Episcopal Conferences. This excluded Martini, since the president of the Italian Conference was Cardinal Ruini, who incidentally was appointed by John Paul II, in a break with tradition – previous presidents were elected. The CCEE's headquarters had been in Switzerland. They were moved to Cardinal Ruini's offices in Rome where everything could be under the boss's eye.

Why Pope John Paul distrusts Martini

Some people won't like me saying that the Pope distrusts Cardinal Martini. I don't think the Pope has any good reason to do so. But I think he does, and that one cannot study some of his moves, like the so-called re-structuring of the European Bishops, without coming to that conclusion. And why does he distrust him? Because he shows the independence of a good man who tries his utmost to be loyal, yet refuses to do violence to his own honesty, integrity and intelligence. The following are some more examples of the words and actions of a free spirit.

Preferring affirmation to condemnation

In December 1991, the Vatican held a special Synod for Europe, subtitled 'So that we may be witnesses of Christ who set us free' The synod was largely dominated by the East Europeans, which it seems is what the Pope intended. Not surprisingly, communism was roundly condemned by one and all – Cardinal Alexandru Tondea of Romania for one said that Pius XI was divinely inspired when he declared that 'atheistic communism is intrinsically evil and contrary to Christianity'.

Martini was the only exception among the bishops present to suggest that there were positive aspects to communism, and the church should not reject Marxism in its totality. (Echoing of course Pope John XXIII who said there can be good and commendable elements in Marxism.) The *Irish Times* Rome correspondent, Paddy Agnew, compared Martini's intervention with that of a senior Jewish rabbi suggesting to a gathering of Jews at a commemoration ceremony for victims of the Holocaust, that Hitler was not all that bad. He did good things too, like building the autobahns!

Promoting true ecumenism

Martini has shown a flair for developing good personal relationships with leaders of other churches. He seems to have a close personal relationship with Dr Carey, Archbishop of Canterbury, with whom he has exchanged visits, and with the leaders of the Orthodox Churches. Both Canterbury and the Orthodox feel a cold wind blowing from Rome itself where ecumenism – like collegiality – is much talked about and little practised.

Free speech in the church

According to a report in the *Tablet* of 2 November 1993 about a meeting of the International Association of German-speaking Moral

Theologians in Salzburg, Martini said that too often a clear expression of opinion was misunderstood as dissent, yet canon law obliged the faithful to express their opinions to the best of their knowledge and competence, to their bishops and the rest of the faithful. He regarded it as particularly important that there should be an atmosphere of trust and mutual acceptance between bishops and theologians.

Celibacy

While in England in March 1995, Martini was interviewed by the BBC and his remarks interpreted by an Italian newspaper as evidence that Martini, if he became Pope, would change the law on celibacy. Which forced the cardinal to issue a statement defending the unquestioned evangelical value of celibacy for the sake of the kingdom of God. But he noted that the church already made 'reasonable exceptions' to the rule 'for the good of souls or in special circumstances'.

The candidate

There is a well known saying that those who enter the Conclave as *papabile*, emerge as cardinals. After the experience of a Polish Pope, the cardinal electors may feel a need to return to an Italian once again. However, even if the move is towards an Italian Pope, Martini would not be an automatic choice. His independent line, his Jesuit background and his, however muted but implied, criticism of right wing tendencies in the church, must mean that the Curia will use it's considerable power to oppose his nomination. In fact some believe that the regular tipping of Martini as the next Pope is part of a clever campaign to ensure that he never will be. Cardinal electors don't like being told by the media who they should vote for!

19

SECRET PRIESTS

The underground church in Czechoslovakia,
where bishops and priests were married,
and women ordained to the priesthood

I often feel that to make a memorable television documentary one needs good luck as well as good preparation.

We were on safari through Austria, Germany and Czechoslovakia gathering material for a series on Christianity in Europe approaching the second millennium of the Christian era. We had arranged to do a programme about the church in Czechoslovakia after the collapse of communism. However I was clear that the most interesting and dramatic story in Czechoslovakia was the story of the so called 'underground church' with its married priests and bishops. Our problem was that we had no contact with them. Given that their tradition as an underground church was to shun publicity, it seemed very unlikely that they would open their souls to us, especially when we didn't speak one word of their language.

Our German film was about the generosity of German Christians to the less fortunate in the Third World, which brought us one day to a convent outside Munich where refugees from the Yugoslav conflict were being housed and fed. Having finished the shooting a little earlier than usual and checking the route back to Munich, we noticed on the map that the monastery of Gars was reasonably close by. Gars is the big Redemptorist monastery where Fr Bernard Häring, the famous theologian, lives, with whom we had made a programme two years earlier. We hadn't met him since, so we thought we'd see if he was home, and ask him how he liked the programme.

Häring was at home and seemed genuinely pleased to see us and interested in what we were doing. I mentioned the matter of the underground church. He told us that he had been recently in Czechoslovakia and had met a number of the priests and bishops involved and would be happy to put us in touch with them. He gave us telephone numbers and a letter of introduction. Now the group in Prague trusted Häring, who had tried to help them, and because they trusted Häring, they trusted us. And so a chance trip to Gars smoothed over the difficulties, and made a programme possible which it seems to me in retrospect, might otherwise have been impossible.

A house Mass in Prague

Eva Sharp, our guide and friend in Czechoslovakia, made the explanations and phone calls. We were asked to be at a certain address at nine o'clock on Pentecost Sunday morning. Our meeting place proved to be a terraced house in an elegant square where the trees were fresh with the leaves of a new spring. The houses looked run down – like much of the housing in Prague at the time. We were ten minutes early, and waited round the corner by the car. We tried the bell on the stroke of nine, but there was no reply. Thirty minutes later the locked door still stared at us, and I was beginning to think that we had been led a dance, or worse, made a mistake about the address. At last a man in his early fifties arrived, and apologised – he had to come some distance and the tram had broken down.

We were led to a room on the first floor, looking out on the square, with a very large mahogany table. There were several people already there and more arrived, including a husband, wife and three children. We were introduced to an elderly man, presumably a priest, in a dark brown suit, to whom the others deferred. Another of the men opened a case and set out the chalice, candles, bread and wine for Mass. An elderly lady hovered in the background, but we were not introduced to her. I asked timidly could we film the Mass, and got the impression that this was what they expected. So we set up the camera. The elderly man looked for a nod from us, and then began Mass which he offered with devotion and reverence.

It was only after Mass that I was made aware that the celebrant, Karel Chytil, was in fact a bishop.

We had already briefed our Czech friend, interviewer, and interpreter as to what we wanted to learn about the underground church and the part these men played in it. Being an experienced broadcaster who had worked for the BBC overseas service, I felt confident in letting her proceed and not waste time translating anything more than the very salient points for us. Which meant of course that I did not know at the time exactly what was being said. In fact it was only a month or two later, when all the material had been translated and typed, that I could appreciate the nuances of the interviews.

Before going further, however, perhaps I should set out the history of the underground church as we understood it at the time, before coming to what these former leaders had to add.

The beginnings of an underground church

The story began in 1948 with the communist take-over of Czechoslovakia. Soon after the putsch all the bishops and many of the priests were put into prison, and all religious houses and convents closed and their property confiscated by the state. Before being expelled from Czechoslovakia in 1949, the papal nuncio, Archbishop Gennaro Verolino, went around the country carrying permission from Pius XII for each bishop to choose and secretly consecrate a successor, so that if and when he was arrested or eliminated, there would be someone left to continue his work. This procedure wasn't novel – it had been followed during the persecution in Mexico in the 1920s.

Two Jesuits in their late twenties, Jan Korec and Pavel Hnilica, were ordained bishops in 1951 according to this mandate. Korec became a bishop less than a year after his priestly ordination. Hnilica soon left Czechoslovakia, and spent the rest of his life promoting devotion to Our Lady of Fatima in Rome. (His story, by the way, reminds one of what became a problem in Ireland during the penal days. Some bishops ordained for Irish dioceses preferred the comforts of France, Spain, or Italy to the perilous life of a bishop in Ireland, and there are many letters in the Roman archives written to try to persuade or pressurise bishops to give up the soft option.) Bishop Jan Korec chose to remain throughout the difficult times and, after the collapse of communism, was appointed Bishop of Nitra in Slovakia in 1990, and one year later Cardinal.

Korec received instructions from Rome to follow the practice of having one active and one hidden bishop. In 1956 he secretly consecrated a fellow Jesuit, Dominic Kalata. Later on, secret ordinations to the episcopacy began to increase. Kalata consecrated Peter Dubovsky in 1961. Dubovsky consecrated Jan Blaha in 1967 in Augsburg, and Blaha consecrated Felix Maria Davidek , who is the pivotal figure in the present story. Blaha remained celibate, and his ordination to the episcopacy was declared valid by the Vatican. So there would seem no question of the validity of Davidek's ordination.

Vaclav Vasko is a former director of the Catholic publishing house Zvon, in Prague. He gave us his personal impressions of Felix Davidek whom he knew well in prison:

I spent about four years in the prison at Mírov with Felix
Davidek. He was one of the people who organised university
studies in the prison. In fact one of the reasons he was put in
prison was because he tried to organise a Catholic university in
Moravia. When students were not allowed to complete their bac-
calaureate studies for relgous or political reasons, Davidek
developed and directed a sort of underground school, offering
courses at university level with the help of professors thrown out
of universities. I considered him a man of genius, a graduate of
three or four faculties. He was an excellent musician and also a
poet. He was in very poor health. He was an extremely ill-discip-
lined prisoner and forever in trouble. He was a deeply spiritual
man – I had several conversations with him during our walks,
and he meditated with me on the Way of the Cross and it was one
of the most beautiful meditations I have ever known.

In 1960, when preparations for a general amnesty got under way,
we were individually called to interrogations. Each of us had to
write down a sort of curriculum vitae and our attitude to the
regime. Felix Davidek typically, wrote down: *'My name is Felix
Davidek. I was born on such and such a day, was ordained priest on such
and such a day. The communist state security arested me on such and
such a day. These facts, that I am a priest, that I was arrested and held in
prison by the communist regime, have given me sufficient insight into
present day reality. I therefore expect nothing of you and am ready to die
any time. Signed, Felix Davidek.'* So of course he was not amnestied
and stayed on in prison – God knows how long.

Later I met him once more in Brno. I ran into him and asked him
whether it was true that he had been consecrated bishop. 'Yes it
is.' 'And is it true that you ordain women?' 'Nonsense, that's slander, not true!' Felix was rather undisciplined. I think he was a
neurotic and I wonder whether that genius of his may not have
contained an element of mental disorder. For instance, he totally
disregarded canon law – he did not give a damn. He himself was
totally convinced that what he was doing was absolutely correct –
of course none of us could have foreseen that communism would
collapse – and he wished the church to be preserved and able to
function even in the worst situations of persecution.

The underground church came to be under such men as Felix
Davidek who were tortured and persecuted for their faith, and who
believed that under communism, the church might have to face
even worse in the future.

The officially tolerated, or 'overground' church

Having put the bishops and the active priests under lock and key, and closed most of the seminaries, the communists decided to pay salaries to co-operative clergy, provided they were prepared to toe the party line in public, and keep their ministry to the sacristy. They were forbidden, however, to engage in social work or teach the young about religion. Now many of these priests were genuinely convinced that co-operation with the government was right and necessary in order to provide Mass and the sacraments for believers. Some others probably found the life easy and comfortable – apart from their sacramental duties there was little work to do, while the state paid them a salary. Others could see no viable alternative to going on the run, or to prison. But Bishop Davidek for one, deeply distrusted any priest who took the shilling from a communist government.

The Vatican seeks accommodation with the state

Rome doesn't like underground churches because by definition they cannot be supervised properly, or controlled. So when it became quite clear after the Russian invasion of Czechoslovakia in 1968 that communism wasn't going to go away soon, the Vatican changed its policy and sought an accommodation with the government in Prague. Cardinal Casaroli was the brains and active agent in this 'Ostpolitik,' which led up to the public ordination of three bishops in Nitra in March 1973, and a fourth at Olomuc in Moravia the following day. The government also permitted the re-opening of two seminaries. Archbishop, later Cardinal Tomasek was the recognised leader of this overground church. Continuing discussions between the Vatican and the government meant that Vatican officials had oportunities to travel back and forth to Czechoslovakia, and keep in contact with Tomasek.

The two underground churches

After 1968 one really has to talk of two underground churches. As well as the group which formed around Bishop Davidek, there was another entirely celibate and perhaps less obsessively secretive underground church. This consisted of older priests who returned from prison and were never given licence to minister, as well as younger men who were ordained in East Germany or Poland but had no permission from the state to carry out their priestly duties, and still other priests who for one reason or another had fallen foul of the government, or who did not wish to work in a state sponsored church. Like all underground priests, these men worked at secular occupations and ministered secretly in houses, apartments and holiday camps, but, unlike the Davidek group, they always tried to keep in touch with the Vatican through Archbishop Tomasek.

Mission in the underground church

Fr Vaclav Maly, a celibate priest, described his work as a secret priest:

> I was very involved in the work of the so-called underground church. I lectured, I organised biblical lessons, I instructed people in their religion. I prepared couples for weddings, I said holy Masses. All the things that were impossible to do in churches I did in somebody's apartment. At the same time I had a manual job, and it helped me to live the normal life of an ordinary citizen. I had to get up in the morning to take the tram to work. Living like this helped me to understand better the thinking and behaviour of ordinary citizens. And it forced me to express my faith in a very civil way.

Fr Miloslav Fiala, now spokesman for the Czech Bishops' Conference, remembers the difficult times with some nostalgia:

> It was a very interesting and adventurous life. One had to be very cautious and on one's guard against the police and the authorities while, on the other hand, meeting people whom one could instruct in the faith and who accepted it gratefully. This I considered a great school of life and we remember those times fondly. We had fun even at work. We were, of course, constantly followed. Police interrogations were, especially at certain periods, fairly frequent. I underwent about fifteen of varying degrees of intensity, but thank God I have never been subjected to physical violence except when I was in prison in Prague in 1949...

Bishop Davidek's underground church

The other part of the underground church of which Bishop Davidek was the leader, generally distrusted the clergy of the officially tolerated church, who, they feared, had made a pact with the devil for which the church as a whole must ultimately suffer. Davidek seems to have believed that some day the Kremlin would move in and carry off all the clergy to Siberia, as had happened in Russia in the 1920s. The Soviet invasion in 1968 confirmed these premonitions. Davidek felt that security had been too lax in the early days of the underground church, with the result that the state knew too much about what was going on. So after 1968, Davidek set about ordaining bishops and priests in total secrecy, not even retaining documentary evidence of ordination. It is thought that he ordained about 600 priests and maybe a dozen, or even perhaps as many as twenty, bishops. Some of the latter were married men.

In retrospect, one can see some logic in Davidek's distrust of a church which could merit communist acquiescence. The Stasi files show that he was right in thinking that the seminary was infiltrated by the secret police. And records show that some official priests collaborated with the government to the extent of denouncing fellow clergy.

A married clergy

Davidek ordained perhaps 200 or more married men to the priesthood. This was done legally through a loophole he made, or perhaps we should say found, in canon law. Slovakia had a Greek Uniate church, that is a Greek-rite church united with Rome. The Greeks of course permit married men to be ordained, so Davidek ordained men under the Uniate Greek rite as bi-ritual, that is able to say Mass in either the Greek or the Roman rite. There was an ancient tradition in parts of Slovakia for priests to say Mass if necessary in another rite so that Uniates and Romans could help each other. But as there were no Uniates in Davidek's diocese the priests were in practice working only in the Roman rite. Whatever the theological and canonical niceties, ordaining married men made a lot of common sense. The secret police expected priests to be celibate, so married men were much less likely to arouse attention However, ordaining married men as bishops was a different matter. This would appear to be against both the Greek and the Roman tradition, both of whom require all bishops to be celibate.

Women priests

Two of the married men ordained bishops by Davidek were Jan Krett and Fridolin Zahradnik. Zahradnik said publicly at a press conference that Krett, then deceased, had ordained at least two women. We were told off the record that Davidek himself had ordained women, and that one of these was Ludmila Javorová, who is also said to have been Davidek's wife! She denied both of these statements at the time we made the programme. What she did not deny, but rather found a source of pride, is that she was for many years Davidek's Vicar General, and played a big part herself in recruiting priests for the underground church. Having a young woman as Vicar General was perhaps a typical Davidek move to throw the secret police off the scent. Establishing the facts about the alleged ordination of women was complicated by the fact that the enemies of this underground church, which includes strange bed-fellows, would like to use the issue of women's ordination to dis-credit it. Some of the underground priests believe that the secret police, for instance, encouraged talk about the ordination of women to damage the underground church in the eyes of Rome. Others believe that elements in Rome itself also use this allegation to weaken the credibility of the underground church. However, the issue came into clearer focus in November 1995 when the *Tablet* reported that Ms Javorová changed her story. Bishop Davidek, she now said, had held a Synod in 1970 which discussed the issue of women's ordina-tion, decided in favour, and shortly after he ordained the first women, including Ms Javorová herself. She also claimed to know the names and addresses of other women who were ordained.

A summary of Davidek's policies

Davidek died in a Brno hospital in August 1988 aged 67. When he first set up his underground church, there were no bishops in circul-ation that he felt he could trust, and contact with the Vatican was at least difficult. The church faced a very determined regime whose clear intention was to wipe out religion in a generation or two. His plan for survival had much merit in the early days of the persecu-tion. But then things changed and he did not take the changes into account. After 1968, for instance, communications with Rome became much easier, yet Davidek continued to run his affairs as if contact with Rome was still impossible.

The problems that remained after the Velvet Revolution in 1989

There are many aspects of Bishop Davidek's underground church which the authorities in Rome found difficult to accept.

Distaste in Rome for married clergy

Rome doesn't like married priests in a Catholic community. They tend to weaken the case against a married clergy, and Rome is very anxious for a number of different reasons to hold the line firmly on celibacy. Converted Protestant ministers are a special case and merit exceptional treatment, and don't therefore pose a threat. Neither Rome nor Constantinople tolerate married bishops.

Secret ordinations

Bishop Davidek was undoubtedly what is sometimes called 'a loose canon'. Even at a time when he could have opened channels with Rome, he neglected to do so, and went on ordaining priests and even bishops in the 1970s without reference to Roman authorities. Some too have questioned his balance or even his sanity – and therefore by implication the validity of his ordinations. His defenders however get very angry when any doubts are raised in this area.

Absence of paperwork

Officialdom likes paperwork to establish happenings and facts. Davidek ordained bishops and priests without drawing up papers to enshrine his actions because he deeply distrusted the communist state, and knew that papers could all too easily fall into the hands of the Stasi, and lead to harassment and imprisonment. The absence of records means that there are more priests and possibly bishops in the community who have not yet come forward, but have decided to wait and see what Rome is going to do – if anything – before declaring their hand. If Rome does not offer them what they consider an honourable and satisfactory future within the structure, they may well intend to remain in their jobs and keep hidden the fact that they were ever ordained. One professional married man with a good job and a comfortable income, whom we met, admitted to being a priest in the former underground church. Off the record others told us he was in fact a bishop, although I have never seen this mentioned in print.

Working outside the parish structure

Priests in the underground church were not integrated into a structure like a parish. They were worker priests, doing a normal job, and in the course of that job – as also in their leisure time – they pursued a pastoral ministry. In practice this made them very similar to the worker priests in France – who were condemned by Rome in 1954. This suppression was reaffirmed in 1959, but revoked by Paul VI in 1965, moved perhaps by the spirit of the Vatican Council. But the more conservative elements in the Vatican Curia, and, I believe, within the Czech hierarchy, are unsympathetic, to say the least, to the concept of worker priests. Some of these former underground priests would like to continue their ministry today outside any formal parish structure – partly because that is the way they are used to working, and partly because they genuinely believe that much re-evangelisation is necessary in their post-communist society, and re-evangelisation is less likely to happen within the normal parish.

Conditional re-ordination

When it comes to ordination, church authorities rightly want to exclude any doubts about validity. So once any doubt is introduced, Rome tends to look for conditional re-ordination, the condition being that ordination is only now intended if it wasn't valid the first time. Men, however, who feel they know as a fact they were correctly ordained, and who for many years have practised as priest or bishop, get very resentful when the validity of their ministry is anyway challenged.

Poor information in Rome

When the church is persecuted in a country, some clergy stay with their flocks and some leave. Some of those who left Czechoslovakia ended up in Rome, in the Holy Office for instance, which has been taking the decisions, or not taking the decisions, about the position of those who stayed. People like Bishop Chytil feel very strongly that 'shepherds who left the flock when the wolf came' – to use his own words – should not be making decisions about those who remained.

The biological solution

The unsatisfactory limbo situation in which many of the former underground priests find themselves appears to continue. According to the *Tablet* of 5 August 1995, Josef Rabas, a Czech, and former professor of Pastoral Theology in Wurzburg, Germany, suggested publicly that the best solution for the problem of the clandestine clergy was to let them die out. One of the clandestine bishops, Jan Blaha, who now works as a secondary school teacher in Brno and as a priest at weekends, spoke out publicly for the first time, saying that although he knew Rabas's views were shared by many, such a 'biological solution' was both unacceptable and defamatory, reminiscent of former communist thinking and terminology, and took no account of what the clergy in the underground church had suffered. The *Tablet* incidentally notes that, for whatever reason, Jan Blaha is the one and only clandestine bishop who has never been asked to sign a declaration renouncing his rights as a bishop – for instance the right to ordain, or use the title and insignia of a bishop.

The views of the underground clergy we interviewed

Dr Karel Chytil, the celebrant of the Mass we filmed, fled from Czechoslovakia to Italy when the Nazis came, and there he studied philosophy and theology. Later he made his way to England where he served for two years in the RAF. After the war he returned to study in Prague. Then came the communist coup which, with his history, ended any chance of a professional career in Czechoslovakia. He told us that he did all the most menial jobs imaginable under communism, but the one job which was forbidden to him was intellectual work. Chytil was consecrated as a bishop by Bishop Davidek in 1977. He began to weep when he spoke to us after Mass about his family.

> I have a wife and two sons – but here again, an important point. True to the apostolic tradition, when I was consecrated I subsequently made the promise of celibacy (weeping). You understand. I came to an understanding with my wife that we should discontinue our married life. We would continue to live together, but not in marriage. And that is a great problem for the official church. When I tell them they smile a little, they cannot understand it, and yet it was quite common in apostolic times. Many bishops were married – take Gregory of Nazianzus. The bishop had a wife, had children. In Erfurt there is the tomb of a bishop, Saint Joachim. Next to him rests a holy woman, his wife, and next to them is buried their holy daughter. That was normal in the church and they simply won't understand it.

Bishop Chytil finds it hard to accept that there should be a shortage of priests to undertake the ministry, and at the same time there are several hundred priests from the underground church wishing to re-assume their ministry and for one reason or another, find it impossible.

> It is utterly incomprehensible to me – and here again I speak as a pastor – if I were faced with the dilemma of there being many believers with no priests to minister to them, and also of having at my disposal a group of priests, I would call them, even if they do not fulfil all the official requirements of the contemporary church – I would send them, even press them into service ...

He also argues that celibacy is a charism needing a special calling, different from priesthood. Whether or not one agrees with him, one senses that he is being unwise in propounding such arguments. This is what Rome fears most of all – that allowing married clergy operate as if it were normal would be the thin end of the wedge which would weaken the hold on celibacy.

> Frequently, celibacy is considered a precondition for priesthood. This is in contradiction to the gospels. The apostles once asked

Jesus whether it was admissible to repudiate a wife, and he said 'No'. On this subject he also says that if a man takes another wife, a divorced woman, or even if he looks at a woman with lust, he is guilty of adultery. And the apostles tell him, if such is the relationship between man and woman it is better not to get married. And Jesus replies, 'Not everybody understands this. Only those to whom it has been given'. So Christ is saying that a special calling is needed even for celibacy which is understood only by those to whom it has been given. And that's why I believe that there is a great misunderstanding between the church at present and Christ, in so far as the church requires celibacy as an absolute precondition of priesthood. That contradicts Christ. I must have a calling for celibacy, and if it has not been given me, then these are things I do not understand …

Sometimes it is suggested to us that the church could adopt the so called Anglican solution. Like those married Anglican priests who have joined the Catholic church and receive a dispensation which allows them to serve as Catholic priests. This is not a good solution. We are not asking for a dispensation. We wish the church to accept the validity of the two ways to God – the way of marriage and the celibate way. They are two ways to God, both willed by God, both requiring a special divine calling.

Bishop Chytil was consecrated by Bishop Davidek. He gets angry when he thinks of all the attempts to malign Davidek. He himself took pains to investigate Davidek's credentials.

I am the only one who has known Bishop Davídek such as he really was before God. I was an intimate friend of his at a time when all the others had scorned him. Suddenly in 1982 we received a circular letter from the official church casting doubt on Bishop Davidek, saying that he was a dubious priest illegitimately passing himself off as bishop. I was appointed by our community to find out whether he was competent to ordain priests. I visited him in 1982 and established that he was a properly consecrated bishop with the apostolic succession. And I recommended to my superior to contact Archbishop Meisner of Berlin who already, even in those days of communism, paid regular visits to the Vatican as a close friend of the present Pope. I suggested that he should make enquiries in Rome. We have nothing – all that I have is God's calling but no piece of paper. To keep a documentary proof of my being a priest or a bishop was very dangerous. For me it would have meant prison, and prison for the whole family because in my case they would not only have jailed me, they would have jailed my wife and destroyed my children. So everything was done on the basis of trust. But to get back to Bishop Davidek: Archbishop Meisner happened to be going to Rome and he came back with the information that Bishop Davidek was listed as a bishop in the Vatican yearbook. There could not have been a more conclusive proof – from the Vatican itself! There were other proofs, but at the time this one was decisive for us. It was not all the same to us whether we were ordained by an illegitimate bishop, we wanted to know. I used to say, 'I don't care about the permission for my ordination, but I do care about its validity'. Because here, practically nothing was permitted. But I wanted to be a valid priest before God. And we were told that he figures as bishop in the papal yearbook. And by the way, this is typical of the Vatican diplomacy. They would print in the Vatican yearbook a piece of information that for us was a matter of life and death and yet everybody knew that the first people to read it would be the secret police!

Fr Vaclav Ventura

One of the priests at the Mass, Fr Vaclav Ventura, was of the opinion that the problems of the underground church began when the Vatican and the Czech communist government began talking in the early 70s:

Suddenly problems started when the Vatican, represented by Archbishop Casaroli began co-operating with our communist government. And we have to ask why? Much information must be contained in the archives of the Communist Party's Central Committee. The then boss of their Department for Religious Affairs, a man by the name of Cinódr, laid down a precondition for the negotiations with the Vatican which was mainly about the appointment of bishops. This precondition was the banning and suppression of the underground church. And of course, it was difficult for the state security and for the communists to define what that underground church was. So they concentrated on the group around Bishop Davidek. And from that moment in the negotiations between the communists and the Vatican, the prob-lems for the underground church began.

Of course they then invented the worst slander about the person of Bishop Davidek and his activities, typical state security slander – that he is a fraud, that he is mentally unbalanced, that he is an agent of state security – none of which was true.

Fr Jiri Kvapil, forbidden to work as a priest

The poignant situation of the undergound priests who now find themselves out of a job is perhaps best illustrated by one of the married priests, Fr Jiri Kvapil:

> I worked a lot with children and young people, teenagers, and with a community of married people. The bishop has now forbidden me to undertake these activities without giving me any reason – and the new generations of young children are not being given all the spiritual attention they require. And as for the community of married people, I am not allowed to help them either. I would not mind if the bishops here would allow me to soldier on as I did before – not very much in the open. Nobody needs to know. One meets in daily life so many people who are unhappy, needy, looking for something – which offers priests a special opportunity to serve.

Fr Stejkozová, unemployed, married with seven children

Fr Stejkozová was a married man when he was encouraged to become a priest by the present Cardinal Archbishop of Prague, Miloslav Vlk, then parish priest in Rozmitál. He seems to believe finance is a critical problem.

> In the meantime, while I was preparing myself for priesthood, five children were born to me and my wife, and Bishop Davidek ordained me according to the Eastern Rite. I was active as a secret priest for ten years. In 1989 I reported to Archbishop Vlk with a petition to be integrated into the work of the church, according to whatever was possible. But the Archdiocese of Prague has no conception, no scheme for using ordained and married men and I would sum it up in one word – the reasons are financial. 'We are unable to secure the livelihood of a family, of a priest who has children, so as to enable him to carry on as a priest.' That is the root of the problem.

Mrs Stejkozová was present at the Mass with three of their children. She helped to bring home to us the fact that when a man accepted ordination under communism, the whole family risked their future in the same way as he did.

> I had to agree to my husband's ordination and I was aware all along what it meant. The whole family was involved in that service, risking even physical liquidation. He had a job, and had many pupils, people he taught, formed spiritually and all that,

which meant involving the whole family – we have seven children altogether.

Now, after long years, I myself have taken up a job and the situation in the family has been reversed in a way – my husband is at home, unemployed, and I go out to work. But I am grateful to the Lord – even now I view my work as service. I am a social worker in a prison for violent juvenile delinquents, age fifteen to eighteen. But it pains me to see that there are people who need spiritual guidance and that others are being shamefully prevented from giving them that guidance.

Dr Jan Konzal, married priest, engineer, vehemently opposes conditional re-ordination

Dr Jan Konzal is a telecommunications engineer with a degree in cybernetics. He has a good job, with international travel involved. He talked about his time as a secret priest.

We defined our task as private pastoral care for people who for one reason or another cannot publicly go to church. Either because they were afraid for their jobs, or because the public church is not their cup of tea. There's no point in arguing with them whether this is right or wrong, they simply won't enter a church. They thirsted for the gospel, they longed to live among Christians, so we tried to mediate the possibility for them to get there unofficially, somehow.

I think that our form of pastoral care is still needed in the church, as one of many. Not as the only one, but one of many. And I think that it would be a pity to throw away the experience we have gained, often at a considerable cost to ourselves, and by trial and error. That is our main argument why we should be taken seriously. I think that the church, for its own good, should be able to reach people who are unconventional, and whose numbers are ever growing. For instance in my place of work, among the several hundred of my colleagues only perhaps two find it acceptable to go to church. And yet these are first rate people.

As a married man, Konzal was ordained according to the Eastern Rite, but expected to be transfered to the Roman Rite.

The transfer to the Roman Rite was done merely verbally and with the promise that the then bishop, Jan Hirko, would arrange for us to be given the appropriate documents should circumstances ever permit it. After 1989, we asked him to do this. He

received the lists of names and took them to Rome. He sub-
sequently told us he wanted to prepare the documents for this
transfer, but it was forbidden him in Rome, so he returned home
and has had no more dealings with us.

Dr Konzal spoke of the conditions put to him for resumption of his
priesthood.

Formally the conditions are two – to undergo a theological examination, which presents no problem for us, speaking in all mod-
esty. And they have no doubts in this respect, which is why they
entrusted us with running various theological courses. The second condition, which presents an insurmountable obstacle to me
and my friends, is re-ordination. Because we have not been
released from the bond of the diocese. It is unfair. And so I cannot
accept this condition. Can *not*!

Some others did accept this condition – how many it is difficult to
say. Our Ordinarius, who is celibate and recognised as bishop
although not allowed to function as such, has a list of about 160
priests secretly ordained. Of these about one third seek service in
the public church. A good third would like to be active in the
non-public pastoral care, incognito, till the moment when the person concerned feels the need to receive a sacrament – this may
take six months, a year or may never happen. Such people need
friends rather than a service. And the final third have taken up a
wait-and-see position and I do not know what they think.

According to Dr Konzal, the Vatican offered two options:

The Vatican offered two alternatives to the Czech Bishops'
Conference. One was a Secular Institute – this we would have
preferred because we believe that this form of pastoral care
should not become extinct, and we need fresh blood. But the
Conference accepted the second alternative which requires
priests to become integrated in the parish structure, the structure
of the public church. At the same time I have heard many a bishop
say, 'But we want you precisely as you are!' So that is the big
dilemma of the Bishops' Conference - some of the bishops are
adamant in insisting on the classical form of pastoral care and will
not permit any exceptions.

Fr Jaroslav Duka, OP

Fr Jaroslav Duka is Provincial of the Dominican order, and became
friendly with President Havel when they were both in Pilsen prison

together. He is highly respected, and influential in affairs of both church and state, and anxious to help resolve the problems of the former undergound bishops and priests, but even he did not seem to be able to make much progress.

> We must not forget that we have not always been sufficiently strict with those who, as collaborators with the communist regime, had discredited the church. And now those other people who had really suffered for the church sometimes tend to be viewed as if they had done her harm. That is not a good solution. I have personally discussed it more than once with Archbishop Vlk and once with Cardinal Ratzinger – they have promised that a solution acceptable to both sides will be found. But it is a fact that the question has been complicated not only by the excessive caution of the Vatican negotiators but also by the excessive zeal or lack of caution of some members of the Bishop Davidek group.

The present situation

And so the talk goes on and on. But even now, in the spring of 1996, my information is that little has changed. It is the kind of problem that a Pope with humanity and flexibility like Paul VI would sort out in no time – just like he sorted out the French Worker Priests. But the present powers-that-be in Rome are not of that ilk. However if blame is to be attached for this sad situation, some of it must rest with the local hierarchy and it's leadership. As Dr Konzal mentioned, Cardinal Ratzinger did propose the option of forming a Secular Institute to the Bishops' Conference. Such an institute would have a certain independence which would permit it to incorporate different kinds of ministry and would have been acceptable to many of the former underground priests. Unfortunately the Bishops' Conference – especially, it is said, the Slovak bishops – showed no enthusiasm for this solution. For them it is integration in the parish structure of the public church or nothing. So, if I had to guess what will happen, I would say on the evidence so far, very little, and that many of the bishops and priests of the former underground church – and particularly the married men – will be let die off in a terrestrial limbo, their offer of service spurned and rejected. But nothing would make me happier than to be proved wrong!

20
PERSECUTION AND RESTITUTION
*The cycle of imprisonment and freedom, robbery
and restitution – forty years in the history of the
Czechoslovakian church*

Over the years we attempted many programmes about human rights issues around the world, in places like Argentina, Brazil, Chile, Indonesia. We generally had no permission to make documentaries in these countries, because to ask permission is to alert the right-wing government who may prevent entry, or harass one while one is trying to take pictures, or seize the film on the way out. (We were indebted on one occasion to the US Air Force who flew out our material, although I don't think anyone knew about it in the Pentagon!) At times we took some risks, but by and large it was not difficult to avoid being noticed or bluff one's way out of trouble under most right-wing governments. They weren't that well organised.

However, the story was quite different when one came to Marxist governments. Abuses of human rights by governments in Russia and Czechoslovakia were happening a lot closer to home than South America, but we found ourselves powerless to do anything about them in terms of television. Surveillance in communist countries was at such a high level that one could not hope to expose a foot of film without being observed.

I often felt qualms of conscience, not only on our own account, but for the whole television industry. Important programmes on human rights issues were being made, but only in countries with right-wing governments. So the picture on TV with regard to human rights in the world was totally unbalanced, because in practice only part of the problem could be reported.

I visited Russia in 1978 with a view to deciding whether it might be possible to do a programme there, but came to the conclusion in the end that we could not be sufficiently free. I described some of my experiences in a previous book, *No Tigers in Africa*. I didn't mention others then, because that might compromise the diplomatic service – *No Tigers* was written before the big political changes in Russia. One ambassador, for instance, told me that he was only a short time in Moscow when he went to an embassy reception. Forgetting his glasses he went back to the car and found the chauffeur changing recording tapes in the boot of the car! We were instructed beforehand that we were to say nothing in any embassy building that we would prefer the secret police not to know. At a diplomatic dinner at which I was a guest, the Pakistani ambassador, who was rejoicing in the fact that he was shortly to leave Moscow, addressed some rude parting remarks during the dinner to the microphone in the ceiling! Nobody, neither Russians nor foreign diplomats, would talk to us about anything remotely political – except possibly in a low voice in a public park without anybody in sight. And so on.

At a later stage, we tried to get visas to Czechoslovakia, but were refused. After the so-called 'Velvet Revolution ' in 1989, of course, everything changed and entry became easy. So we decided to do a programme dealing with the contemporary problem of restitution, which at the same time would give an opportunity to document some of the sufferings of the church under communism.

Listening to personal stories in Czechoslovakia made me conscious of parallels to the situation in Ireland in penal times. Clergy were forced into prison or exile, religious education forbidden, religious houses, convents, churches put to other uses, or let decay, their lands seized and held by the state, or distributed among the party faithful. Particularly strenuous efforts were made to eliminate all bishops. Submissive priests were licensed to say Mass as a means of pacification, but with the firm expectation that without religious education or seminaries, the clergy would die out in a generation or two.

Persecution began soon after the communist coup in February 1948. There is something special about a first-hand account, so the following is a careful translation of two interviews with men who suffered in communist prisons. Vaclav Vasco is a layman, former director of a Catholic publishing house, called Zvon – we met him in their offices in Prague. Bishop Karel Otcenasek was ordained a bishop in 1950 shortly after his thirtieth birthday. When we met him prior to a bishops' meeting in Prague, he was Bishop of Hradec Králové. Now, having passed his seventy-fifth year he may have retired.

Vaclav Vasco tells how the persecution began

The persecution of the church started with the sporadic arrests of certain priests, some, for instance, because they read a pastoral letter in defiance of a ban by the state authorities. In 1949 and 1950 terror escalated, and in the fifties till almost the spring of Prague

(1968) it was very intensive indeed. The persecution took various forms. Firstly, the internment of members of the religious orders, of priests, and of all the bishops. Moreover, priests, students of theology and religious were sent, often under the guise of military conscription, to labour camps without any time limit. They had to do forced labour and were under guard, as in prison. Then there were the trials. All of these were staged trials. These involved some bishops, hundreds of priests, some three to four hundred laymen. They were convicted of high treason and espionage – but in fact they had been put on trial as Catholic religious activists.

Interrogation

Interrogation was often conducted during the night. They would wait for you to fall asleep, then they would wake you up and interrogate you till the morning. In day time, you were not allowed to lie down. You were able to sit down, but only so that they could see that you were not asleep. For instance, I would sit down with my head in my hands and start falling asleep. Immediately, they would burst in and make me walk or stand and I was tired to death. And when you are so tired you are capable of signing even a lie. The worst part of it is that you do not know when it will end, and that you never see anybody. When they led me to interrogations, they would take me out of the cell and blindfold me so that I did not see even the corridor. A warder would come along, take me by the hand and lead me along the corridor to the lift and to the interrogator's office. There the interrogator would stand me in a corner, tell me to take off the towel, which I did, then he would talk at me. They would present you with lie after lie. One did not know how long it would take. The fear was terrible – I repeat, they did not beat me but still the psychological pressure was so terrifying that one often could not resist thinking, 'Anything so it may come to an end,' because it (the custody) could last a year, two years. A friend of mine spent over two years in pre-trial custody refusing to sign anything.

The trial

So people would decide to sign even if it was not true, thinking they would say it was not true in the court. And when it did come to the trial you would say nothing because your lawyer, in practice, did not defend you. The prosecution held sway. The prisoner had to learn by heart the statements obtained from him during that one year of interrogations. The interrogator would examine him to see whether he had learned his lesson. When it came to trial, the prosecutor and the judge would consult their papers to see whether the accused was sticking to his memorised part, and if he did not they would interrupt, and adjourn the proceedings. And that's why people would sign statements that they had committed high treason or engaged in espionage, just to escape further interrogation.

The sentence

The trial was a pack of lies from beginning to end, and I was sentenced to thirteen years, of which I served seven. I was first put in Jáchymov to work in the uranium mines, then they sent me to the prisons of Leopoldov and Mírov. The work in the uranium mines of Jáchymov was hard labour. We were not miners, so we had to learn. For a time food was insufficient. But the worst things were the humiliations. When we were marched from the camp to the mine we were tied together with a rope like slaves. We were accompanied by guards with their guns pointed at us and with barking dogs – that's how we would be led to work.

Harassment: The correction cell

Often during the night (the prison authorities) would organise raids. They would take you out of the cells, strip you naked. You were not allowed to learn a foreign language – if they found a vocabulary of foreign words, a prayer, anything in writing on you, they would send you to the correction cells. Correction meant ten, twelve days of starvation – they only gave you something to eat every third day. In the two days in between you were just given a bit of coffee and a small piece of bread in the morning. That was it.

The trials of a bishop

Karel Otcenasek, being a young bishop was given special attention. If he could be broken he could serve the government's purpose well. He told us of his experiences:

The first move against the church

All the bishops, vicars general or bishops' secretaries, as well as heads of religious orders, were either interned together at various gathering points or in their homes. Religious orders were dissolved and their members, who included many thousand sisters, were taken away during one night to so-called concentration monasteries. They could bring with them only what they could carry, and they had to live under a sort of prison regime. What did hurt us then was that the rest of Europe turned a blind eye and did not take up our cause.

How Bishop Otcenasek himself was arrested

Six months after my consecration in 1950 the State Security (STB, the Czech equivalent of the KGB) became interested in me. Several times they tried to entice me to collaborate with the government, because I was very young then, only thirty. I had just returned from Rome. Archbishop Beran was already in internment, so they had plans for me, to win me over. They offered me work in the Prague archdiocese. Thank God, I always rejected them because we already knew from experience that if you give them an inch they'll take a mile. Then, when the press published the fact that I had been secretly consecrated and that I secretly ran the diocese, they took me away, interned me in the monastery of Zeliv where I was kept with religious and diocesan clergy. A month later they isolated me together with Bishop, later Cardinal Tomasek and with Monsignor Suránek – whom they believed to be a secretly consecrated archbishop. They put us into a special cell where we were kept in strict isolation from other priests for two and a half years.

Methods of interrogation

They used physical and psychological pressure, drugs – our treatment was very rough. They beat us, me too, and kept us in solitary confinement. Our interrogators were often utterly uneducated people. There was no talking to them. They were so fanatical that they saw high treason in everything. There was no point in explaining anything to them, especially in the first years. Later, after the death of Stalin and even Gotwald – the first Czech communist president – the methods of interrogation became somewhat less crude.

Serving the sentence

I was eventually sentenced to thirteen years imprisonment for high treason and spying for the Vatican. I can't remember all the prisons I was in, but I have certainly known all the most notorious ones from inside: Pardubice Hradec, Mírov, Leopoldov, Kartouzy, Ilava, Pankrác, Chrudim and others. I started serving my sentence in Mírov where I met some other priests. Conditions were hard there in so far as the slightest failure in accomplishing the set tasks was severely punished by solitary confinement in the so-called underground holes. We were denied visits, letters, and there were constant threats. From there I was transferred to the notorious prison of Leopoldov and finally to the prison of Kartouzy where, some years earlier, Josef Toufar, a parish priest in my diocese, had been tortured to death. They tortured him in a really bestial fashion and finally tore him to pieces. You can say that. We are trying to have him canonised.

Prison work

We had to work in prison, but our work was not as heavy as that of others because we weren't allowed any contact with other prisoners. There was very heavy work, for instance, in the uranium mines of Jáchymov but they never allowed any bishop there, nor did they let us out into the potato fields or help with hay making – in fact we were never allowed outside the prison walls. But for endless months, the present Cardinal Tomasek and Monsignor Suránek and I were employed in sorting out bobbins for the textile industry, and our task was to put like with like and eliminate the faulty ones. And so we went about it very conscientiously and praying at the same time, so as to make life easier for the workers who would have to work with these bobbins some day. And imagine! When we had finished the task, after long months, they burned the lot in the yard, before our eyes. I personally was not all that worried but the spiritual Monsignor Suránek was terribly upset by this disrespect for human work, even if it was only the work of mere prisoners.

Religion in prison

We did not have the bible, the breviary, nothing of the sort, for that was very strictly forbidden. They would extend your prison sentence just for finding one or two grape berries on you, they knew we needed them to make wine for the Mass. Still, from time to time we had the good luck and the grace to say the holy Mass, totally in secret of course. Everybody in the cells, where several of us were kept together, had to pretend that nothing was happening, that some were asleep, others moving about slowly, so as not to arouse the slightest suspicion of the guards because all that was a punishable offence. It was strictly forbidden even to hear a confession, to baptise somebody, or to pray together. It was not so severe even in the Nazi concentration camps.

Freedom

I was released in 1962, under the general amnesty of 9 May. I was so starved of freedom, so hungry for freedom, that upon my release, I had my head out of the window all the time during the train journey home, breathing in the fresh air, so that I completely lost my voice! I had then to find a manual job, though this was difficult because as a former traitor nobody wanted me anywhere. Finally I did find work in a dairy in the town of Opocno, close to the place where I lived. It was badly paid. We worked three shifts, and because I was not married, being a priest, I had to serve on all the feast days, Christmas, the New Year and so on. And there we produced powdered milk for babies called 'Sunar,' and I blessed each packet so that the babies might prosper and put on weight. So now whenever I do Confirmations I ask the age of the candidates, and tell them that they may have grown up not on mother's but on father's milk!

Stories of heroism and suffering like these from Eastern Europe help one to understand Pope John Paul's unwillingness to see any good in communism.

Locking the archbishop out of his cathedral

Bishop Jaroslav Skarvada told us a story about a later period which helps to explain the impossible position of the church during the communist period. When the Vatican Secretary of State was visiting Prague, he asked to visit the cathedral of St Vitus with the nuncio. The archbishop brought them there, but forgot that it was a Monday, and on Mondays all museums in Prague close for the day. So they arrived at the cathedral but couldn't get in. The Secretary of State remarked with a mixture of amusement and annoyance, 'You are the Archbishop of Prague and you have no key to enter your own cathedral!'

The Archbishop of Prague had no key because when the communist government took over in 1948 they confiscated private property, including all property belonging to the church. They didn't even bother to make it legal, believing they would be around for the next thousand years. So unless the post-communist government were to have brought in a new nationalisation law, they had no option but to return property to its pre-communist ownership, where this could be established – or so one would have thought. But nothing in life is as simple as that. Even as late as February 1996, church ownership of the cathedral is still under discussion.

The restitution of Brevnov monastery

The monastery of Brevnov on the outskirts of Prague was founded in 993, and has remained a Benedictine priory, almost without interruption, ever since. During communist times the monastery housed the state archives administered by the Ministry of the Interior, as well as the headquarters of the local Stasi or secret police. The beautiful refectory, with its ornate wall and ceiling, was used as a gymnasium by the Stasi where they used to kick football. We could see the marks of the ball on some of the priceless paintings. The buildings were given back to the monks in 1990, many in ruined condition. About a quarter of a million pounds had been spent on restoration when we visited in 1993 – some from the government, but mostly from foreign donations. The prior, Petr Siostrzonek, estimated that the full job would cost about a million Irish pounds, which he expected to have to find without further state subsidy.

> We would like this monastery to serve again its true purpose – the spiritual peace of all those who live in it, or wish to visit it, or spend some part of their life here. And since we were handed back a ruin, plain and simple, we would like to be given the means of creating, financing, and maintaining such a spiritual oasis. It is indispensable to find resources if this place is to become what we would like it to be, what it has always been, and what it should be again.

What the monks hoped for was to get back the 7,000 hectares of forest and 1,000 hectares of agricultural land which they formerly owned, and which used to provide them with the income to support the monastery. Brevnov has a healthy religious community of monks to justify church ownership and involvement in physical restoration. However, the longer such questions remain unresolved the more local councils and private individuals become less inclined to release their hold on former church property. The monks haven't got their lands back, and as time goes on it becomes doubtful that they ever will.

Two views on the restitution problem

Some see the problem in simple terms: whatever can be established as having been church property should be returned. Anything else is unjust. What the church does afterwards with it's property, whether it decides to return it to the state for civic use is its own business and shouldn't be dictated by the state. The church may well decide to give some of it back, to loan it, to sell it, or make some arrangement with the state to take care of it together. But that is for the church to decide.

Others argue for a more sensitive approach. Fr Valcav Maly, who became the first spokesman of the Civic Forum and played his part in the Velvet Revolution, would not share the view that everything must be returned:

> Basically the church must be poor. When the church is rich, it is bad, it isn't a good witness to the gospel, and the atheists in our society are aware of that. However, when the church looks for total separation of church and state, then it must have certain property as a source of finance – though there should also be other sources. I would like to see believers feel responsible not only for the spiritual life but also for the financial life of the church. The issue is full of problems. Society in general is against full restitution and the politicians are against it. The bishops must be very careful not to ask too much. They must respect above all the spiritual consequences of their decisions

Shadows of the past

According to a census of the Czech people taken in 1900, 92% of the population were Catholic. Yet the contrast with neighbouring Poland, and indeed Ireland, where the church was on the side of nationalism, could not be more striking. The spirit which inspired the founders of the Czechoslovak Republic in 1918 was as much anti-Catholic as anti-Austrian and anti-German. According to the nationalist ideology, the Catholic church had been on the side of the enemies of the Czech nation. Catholicism had been re-imposed on Protestant Bohemia by the Austrian emperors, and the Czech language and culture oppressed in favour of German. So it is understandable that when the first Republic came to be as an independent state after the break up of the Austro-Hungarian empire, there was a considerable anti-Catholic bias among its leaders and intellectuals.

During the Nazi occupation, and especially during the struggle against communism, however, the moral authority of the Catholic church increased enormously, so that in the last years of communist rule, every Mass and every pilgrimage was also a manifestation of a political will against the communist oppressors. Indeed for a brief time Archbishop Tomasek became a symbol for the nation as well as of the church. But all that is now history and things could change rapidly again. Karl Peter Schwarz, and Austrian journalist living in Prague, said he feels that the church should tread very warily in claiming it's rights because of the historical context.

Everytime when the church talks about restitution, the old shadows are coming our from history. And that is something that should be avoided. They should seek, I think, a compromise with the government which would enable the church to be independent without giving the impression that the church wants all its property back.

Conclusion

The church wants to be more than a sacristy church, which is what it became under communism. After forty years, people have forgotten that in the past the church ran many homes for old people, hospitals and social institutions that benefited society. Under communism little in the way of resources were devoted to helping the old, the poor or the weak, so there is plenty of work that needs to be done, and the church would like to be involved in it. To meet social needs like these requires buildings and income. The Czech bishops are understandably wary of depending too much on the voluntary offerings of the faithful when there is no tradition of such giving. There is also a feeling in Catholic circles, not always publicly expressed, that those who would benefit most from privatisation of church property are not the community at large but members of the old communist party nomenklatura transformed into capitalists.

Cardinal Vlk, the leader of the Czech church, summed up the church's position for us, as he saw it:

> Precisely because we have proven that we are able to survive even without property, and have learned not to depend on it, we are well qualified to have the correct attitude to property, and to use it well.

> At a time when society is being given so much space for creative work, the appropriate tools are needed. And with this attitude of the poor in the spirit, with our readiness to serve learned in the past, I think we are well equipped to use this property.

> The restitution of church property is so important because in the past the church has learned how dangerous it is to depend on the state, on the political power. And I think at present church and state are at one in the belief in the need for independence. The state has no intention of financially maintaining the church, as the communist state had done to keep the church under control. This state does not want it, nor do we want it. We want to be free. So we have to find our own finance. One of the sources would be this

property being restored to us, though we are far from thinking that restitution will make us rich.

Fr Jaroslav Duka, Provincial of the Czech Dominicans, also held views on the controversy:

> I partly accept the government view that this problem has to be approached in the context of a new tax law which would give the church access to certain financial resources. (He was referring to a proposal whereby people should be able to earmark part of their taxes for church purposes.) It may also be connected with the proposed new 'Protection of Monuments law' envisaging a new form of co-operation of government, town halls and church in salvaging the national cultural heritage. These laws could, in certain respects, be more important for the church than the restitution of her property. You see, the question of church property is not a question of a rich or a poor church. It also involves an old feudal conception of a church economy supported by ownership of land, in the absence of an adequate vision of, and expertise in, securing new modern sources of church finance.
>
> It seems to me quite realistic to restore to the church that part of her property which is now held by the state, and for the church to renounce that part of her (former) property which is in the hands of physical persons. There is also an interesting proposition, legally and economically speaking, concerning agricultural land. The idea is to set up a land fund to finance the restoration of the cultural heritage including religious and also other monuments, and to help fund non-Catholic churches which never owned much property.

The problem of restitution in all its aspects, secular and religious, is complex. It can't be a simple matter to undo the communist take-over of all private property after a lapse of forty years. Rapid progress was made in the beginning, but as time went on decisions with regard to church property were postponed, and progress came to a halt. In a television interview in January 1996, Cardinal Vlk said he believed that the cause of restitution of church property had fallen hostage to party politics, with the result that another proposal for settling the issue – the eighth such – had just been swept from the table. Elections are coming up in June 1996, which has given the government an excuse to postpone further negotiations until after the election. So the question of restitution of church property remains unresolved.

21
HATCH END

The National Catholic Office for Mass Media in the UK.
And how the Catholic Religious Adviser was appointed to RTÉ

Fr Agnellus Andrew, OFM

In Roman Catholic circles, easily the most important formative influence on religious broadcasting both in Ireland and England was a Scotsman, Fr Agnellus Andrew, Deputy Head of Religious Broadcasting at the BBC. Agnellus was influential because he was an experienced broadcaster with great personal prestige in the most prestigious broadcasting group in the world.

I first met him when I was sent to take a short course for clergy on television organised by ABC Television in Manchester. I was profoundly impressed with his knowledge of broadcasting, his wisdom, good humour, and spirituality. He was also a charmer, so that the great and good in broadcasting beat a path to his door at St Gabriel's, in a suburb of London called Hatch End.

St Gabriel's, Hatch End

St Gabriel's was a very large house, built, I would guess, in the nineteen twenties, with oak panelled rooms and bay windows opening onto a quiet mature garden. I often stayed there – anybody involved in broadcasting was always welcome. His table was open to all, and one could find oneself sitting down to dinner beside a clerical student from Sierra Leone, or an American media executive, or the Director General of the BBC. The food was plain and the English beer flat to my taste, but the conversation, led by Agnellus, was often superb. After a visit to the chapel – which Agnellus made to seem so natural that even the agnostic or atheist was able to be included without embarrassment – all repaired to a large drawing room with a cheery fire, plenty of chairs, and a tray of scotch whisky on the piano. Sometimes there was an evening of pure entertainment, with stories and singing, but most of the time there was informal discussion: broadcasters, when they gather together, tend to talk about their trade.

Some of the English bishops too would enjoy an occasional night or two at Hatch End. It was a chance to get away from the chancery office, and also an opportunity to meet people in the broadcasting profession, which they wouldn't have found otherwise. John Carmel Heenan, late Archbishop of Westminster, and Agnellus were good friends, and he was a frequent visitor. One summer's day Heenan was walking up and down outside the bay window saying his breviary, when he noticed Agnellus, and looked up in the middle of a psalm to say to him, 'Agnellus, your lavatory seat is cracked. It's time you got a new one.' 'So it's not just your head is swelled, Your Grace,' Agnellus replied with a mischievous grin.

Agnellus was kind and charitable, while at the same time he was a shrewd observer of others – which is a delicate enough combination. I remember one story he told about his earlier life as a young Franciscan, with great glee. He started off as a retreat master and occasional preacher. One day one of his older confrères said to him at dinner, 'Agnellus, I notice that you are getting many invitations to preach at important functions and occasions'. Agnellus demurred modestly. The confrère continued, 'But the day will come when you will have an important invitation, and you wake up that morning to find you have lost your voice. You can't possibly preach, you must find a substitute. So you think, "Who can I choose?" Do you choose the best preacher you can find? No. You choose somebody just adequate. And then you will be certain to be asked the next time!'

Radharc makes a film about Hatch End

In 1966 Agnellus asked Radharc to make a promotional TV film programme about his operation in Hatch End. St Gabriel's embodied many of Agnellus's ideas about the role the Catholic church should play in broadcasting. He talked about his Hatch End Centre in the course of this programme:

> I didn't choose Hatch End. It was Cardinal Griffin who chose it and, mind you, I sometimes think when I'm driving up to town that it is a bit far away! But his point was, as he said himself, 'I want you to have a place where you've quiet. I want study and research. If people want to come, well it's a short journey, but you won't be swamped by show business people all the time.'

> The Centre is both the headquarters and the backroom of all our work in Catholic Radio and TV in this country, whether it's for abroad or at home. We've got endless planning sessions, discussions, a lot of people, thank goodness, come – not only Catholics but every kind of person who is connected with the industry. And

then we publish our magazine, we run our *Look, listen groups* – we try to deal with anything affecting broadcasting.

A model for religious broadcasting

Hatch End became the ashram, and Agnellus the guru of Catholic broadcasting in the English-speaking world, while the relationship between the churches and the BBC became the model which the Irish hierarchy were anxious to see established here.

1. At the very top there was CRAC, the Central Religious Advisory Committee, representative of all the mainline Christian churches, which was both adviser and watchdog in relation to religious broadcasting in the United Kingdom.

2. The head of religious broadcasting at the BBC was by tradition a clergyman from the majority Anglican church, although that tradition changed later. Fr Agnellus's appointment as deputy head was objected to in principle by the Archbishop of Canterbury because he was a Roman Catholic, but the BBC went ahead and appointed him all the same. This appointment was made in the 1950s, before the ecumenical progress which followed the papacy of John XXIII. Presbyterian and Methodist clergymen also worked within the religious department. Many clergymen around the country were also appointed part-time religious advisers to the newer independent television companies. So it was generally accepted in England at the time that clerics from the main Christian groups should work on religious programmes within the broadcasting community and be employed and paid by them.

3. Agnellus himself organised *ad hoc* advisory committees outside the structure of the broadcasting organisations to help with ideas and planning of religious programmes

4. Agnellus believed passionately in the need for a well-equipped church-sponsored centre where people interested and involved in religious broadcasting could meet, and where substantive training courses in radio and television could be organised.

5. He also believed in the need to develop a critical approach to broadcasting among the wider public. His vehicle here was an organisation called *Look, listen groups*, which consisted of groups of listeners and viewers, organised from the Centre, who met in their own homes, where they discussed and reported on programmes. He employed a secretary at Hatch End who liaised with the different groups, and who explained their function to us.

It's a group of Christians who gather together and watch a TV programme or listen to a radio programme at least once a month, or more often if they want. They discuss the programme afterwards and they summarise their views and send them to the Centre. We collate these programme views and we send them to the TV programme companies concerned and also to the BBC. We circulate them to other groups too. I think its important the group should know what other people think about programmes and many of them have said to me that they find this the most valuable part of the exercise, to argue about other people's reports rather than their own.

The training centre

Training, however, was Agnellus's major interest at this time. The purpose of our film was to help him raise £250,000 to develop training and production studios at Hatch End. In his own words:

> I remember a bishop in Hong Kong writing to us to say that he had a huge population, among whom radio was having a greater and greater influence. He said he had hundreds of priests and nuns and teachers but not a single one trained in radio and television. He had applied to a number of organisations but they just couldn't fit his priests into their schemes. So he begged me in pathetic terms to accept this man and give him what training I could. I had to write back at that stage and say, 'Well look, I just can't do a thing about it. As soon as we are able I'll give him some kind of meagre training but until we get our studios that will still not be adequate for your particular needs.'

Agnellus was influential in Ireland through his friendships, on the one hand, with Canon Cathal McCarthy, who represented the Archbishop of Dublin on matters relating to broadcasting and, on the other hand, with the broadcaster and businessman, Eamonn Andrews, who had been given the task by the government to chair the television authority and set up an Irish television service.

Canon McCarthy

Canon McCarthy was Dean and later President of Holy Cross College, the diocesan seminary. His speciality was liturgy, so it was natural for him to get involved in radio broadcasting, which at that time largely consisted of broadcast Mass.

Canon McCarthy was, I believe, responsible for my involvement in television. As I understand it, Fr Tom Fehily, Director of the Dublin

Institute of Adult Education, suggested to Archbishop John Charles that, since television was around the corner, he might like to have somebody trained in the new medium. He knew John Charles liked to have at least one member of the diocesan clergy trained in new disciplines – Fr Conor Ward, for instance, had been sent to study Social Science when this discipline first became fashionable. Canon McCarthy happened to know that I used filmstrips and tape recorders to help teach religion classes in the vocational school in Clogher Road, because I attempted a simulated radio programme on the Passion of Christ with the children and approached him to enquire whether it might be good enough to broadcast. I feel sure he arranged the first course I attended in England, calling on the good offices of Agnellus. Later, when it came to sending a priest for training to America, I suggested Fr Des Forristal as a more suitable candidate, not in any mock humility, but because I knew he was more suitable, and I didn't want to get involved in areas where I didn't feel particularly talented, and would therefore be likely to fail. In the event, both of us were sent to spend three months at a television school in New York. I told the details of that story and the foundation of Radharc which followed in a previous volume, *No Tigers in Africa*.

But to return to Canon McCarthy. When radio began, it began in Dublin, so liaison with respect to religious broadcasting naturally became the responsibility of the local archbishop, John Charles McQuaid, who anyway liked being responsible for things, or per-haps better, didn't like others to be responsible! The other bishops were willing to wear this arrangement in the case of radio, but when television began to appear on the horizon, they moved to make the church interest in broadcasting a national rather than a local affair. And so a compromise was reached. The Conference of Bishops appointed Archbishop Thomas Morris of Cashel as their representative for media affairs, and he chose an advisory commit-tee which was broadly representative, and which he called the Catholic Television Interim Committee – interim, because it was hoped that some permanent committee like the English CRAC might later emerge. The niceties were observed with regard to the Archbishop of Dublin by making Archbishop Morris the president, and Canon McCarthy the chairman. The first members included Dr J. G. McGarry, editor of *The Furrow*, Monsignor John McCarthy, a moral theologian from Maynooth, Dr C. B. Daly and Dr Jeremiah Newman, both of whom later became bishops. Lay members joined the committee later.

The Catholic Television Interim Committee (CTIC)

Since this committee had been set up by the hierarchy without the involvement of the Broadcasting Authority, the broadcasters were at first a little wary of it, but soon, however, a working relationship developed. The basic work of the committee in the early days was to come up with religious programme ideas, and suggest and approve persons who might be invited to appear in them. Although I was not a member, I was sometimes asked to attend, and later was appointed chairman of a sub-committee called the programme planning group. The committee in the early days felt it had to screen panel members and keep out anyone who might be too critical of the institutional church. I remember a discussion as to what would happen if someone promoted heretical views in a programme – would it be necessary to correct the heresy the following week? One way suggested was to pre-record the show and edit out the offending piece. However, it was explained that editing a programme in those early days was difficult and expensive and not a normal option. One of the first programmes was called 'The Enquiring Mind', hosted by Maxwell Sweeney. Experts sat in a semicircle with Maxwell in the middle, and discussed some religious topic. Russell Murphy the accountant – who became better known to certain broadcasters in later years – was on the approved panel, and appeared several times on this programme. I remember him lying back in the chair, smoking a cigarette in a very long holder, looking wise, and saying little or nothing.

Some of these activities of the committee – when viewed thirty-five years later – may arouse a smile. However the world was different then, and their actions seemed reasonable and normal at the time. Remember it was then little more than five years since Anthony Eden refused to be interviewed on television about the Suez crisis! He made a statement instead, and answered two pre-arranged questions, without follow up. While earlier in the century the Dean of Westminster had refused permission for the broadcasting of the Duke of York's marriage service on radio on the grounds that 'the service would be received by a considerable number of people in an irreverent manner, and might even be received by persons in public houses with their hats on!'

There were also, I think, inherent problems which church people had to work through with broadcasters to find a *modus vivendi*. One simple division of programmes in the religion field is into programmes *about* religion which are really religious public affairs programmes, where broadcasters are rightly concerned about their freedom to comment, and *purely* religious programmes which include worship, preaching, teaching. Now anything to do with worship or preaching was always considered the responsibility of bishops in canon law, and still is.

This committee, eyeing the British model, then set about another task – to persuade RTÉ to accept a religious adviser who would be full-time with an office and a salary. A sort of Irish equivalent of Fr Agnellus. A policy decision like this inevitably involved the Chairman of the RTE Authority, Eamonn Andrews.

Eamonn Andrews

Eamonn Andrews was a good religious man, and in his early days he had been a prominent member of the Catholic Stage Guild, whose chaplain was a Franciscan, Fr Cormac Daly. Members of the Stage Guild admired Cormac Daly. He had a bit of the stage thing about him, which inevitably meant that not all his actions or pronouncements appealed to the presiding archbishop in Dublin, the territory in which the Stage Guild mostly operated.

One day John Charles decided he had enough of Fr Cormac, and told his superiors to remove him, which they did. The members of the Stage Guild were upset by what they considered this high-handed treatment. One of those who never forgot nor forgave the way Cormac was treated was Cormac's friend, Eamonn Andrews. So when Eamonn became *gauleiter* of the new Irish TV channel, he resolved that Archbishop John Charles McQuaid would be allowed interfere with it as little as possible. And how do I know all that? Well, largely from Agnellus, who was of course another Franciscan, and good friend of both Cormac and Eamonn.

But to return to Eamonn Andrews. Sometime in 1960 the secretary of the Dept of Posts and Telegraphs, Leon O'Broin, who was friendly with John Charles, arranged a meeting for Des Forristal and me with Eamonn. At the time we presumed it was at John Charles' suggestion. We met him in one of those small antiseptic offices at the top of the GPO with linoleum floor and green walls over varnished wainscoting. It was a most uncomfortable meeting. Eamonn was polite, but seemed very reserved, even suspicious, and said very little. He asked us about what we had learnt on our television course in America and what our plans were. There wasn't a lot to say because we didn't have much in the way of plans. We did say that we were trying out some ideas in experimental programmes, and perhaps we might in the future be able to make a contribution. But any comments he made were few and hardly encouraging. It seemed to me afterwards that he was meeting us because somebody had asked him to do so. So he met us. And that was that.

Negotiations for the appointment of a priest adviser to RTÉ/TÉ

Later, when the Catholic TV Committee was negotiating to have a priest appointed in some capacity to Telefís Éireann, as it was then called, I was asked to draw up a memorandum advocating an appointment and giving the reasons. I did some research into the practice elsewhere – the BBC employed a number of clerics full-time, while every ITV company seemed to have a paid part-time adviser. Similarly a priest worked full-time in RAI in Italy and KRO in Holland. It wasn't a problem for me to produce a persuasive document because I believed, and still believe, that in the Irish context at least, a priest should fittingly work in the religious programmes department – though I recommended that he be an adviser rather than a director or producer. Meetings were held between the committee and the Director General, Kevin McCourt, where this issue was discussed. John Charles, the archbishop, also spoke to his old friend Eamonn de Valera about his desire to have a priest appointed, who mentioned it to Sean Lemass, who passed the message on to Eamonn Andrews. This was probably a counterproductive move since it would only have reinforced Chairman Eamonn in his fear and distrust of the archbishop.

I wasn't personally involved in the negotiations about a priest adviser, but J. G. McGarry let me know at one stage that the committee were happy that there would be an appointment soon and that the appointed person would be me, and I'd better get ready for it. I didn't show a lot of enthusiasm and pointed out that I would be happier to make a freelance contribution to broadcasting via the Radharc film unit, which was now up and running. But he dismissed my objections. My lack of enthusiasm had three grounds. There is inevitably a lot of politicking and fighting for resources in a broadcasting organisation which I understood was part of the job, but it didn't attract me. Secondly, I had genuine doubts about my own intellectual and imaginative ability, and one tries not to take up posts one does not feel able for. Lastly, I felt the adviser might have difficulties at times liaising between a strong archbishop like John Charles and the Broadcasting Authority – although this was less of a problem now that there was the buffer in the CTIC.

Sometime during this period of negotiation about the job, I was in London staying with Agnellus Andrew. Agnellus made an appointment for me to meet Eamonn Andrews. I can't remember how he explained the purpose of the meeting, but I know I didn't ask for it. I met Eamonn in the dressing room of 'This is Your Life' when he was being made up for the show. Eamonn was much nicer to me this time. He talked encouragingly about the Radharc Film Unit and said he wanted to see it supported. I was pleased to hear that, but at the time didn't see this as adequate reason why he should ask to see me at the time. I presumed however I was being vetted.

The appointment of Fr Dodd

When Dr McGarry warned me that the appointment was imminent I took time to prepare plans – and prepare myself psychologically for the new responsibilities. Then one day in Montrose – in the sound dubbing department I think – a technician asked me what I thought of Fr Romuald Dodd's appointment as religious advisor to TÉ. First there was a feeling of shock – then the beginning of mixed emotions which I tried to hide.

It was embarrassing, to say the least, to be told to prepare for a job and then find oneself the rejected candidate. I was also in a slightly dangerous position. Because of my interest in Radharc and the opportunities for freelance production, I had never shown much enthusiasm for working in TÉ. Dr McGarry at least knew that. I would have said as much to Agnellus Andrew, who in retrospect I felt almost certainly knew what was going to happen, being close to Eamonn. Could it be that the mysterious appointment with Eamonn in his dressing room was not so much to vet me as to assure me that there was nothing personal in the decision? Might John Charles, or the committee, feel that somehow I had connived with others to make fools of them and give the job to somebody else?

Fr Romuald Dodd OP

The man appointed as religious adviser to TÉ had spent much of his career abroad working in the Vatican Archives and in the Middle East. The only time I had ever met him was sometime in the previous year when a Fr Pichard OP, doyen of the clergy involved in television in France, came over to Dublin, and Des Forristal and I were entertaining him to supper in the Glencormac Hotel near Kilmacanogue. Another priest whom I had never met turned up, and as dinner approached showed no sign of leaving. I felt obliged to ask him to stay, which he did. He talked mostly in French to the Dominican, so I did not get to know much more than his name, which was Romuald Dodd OP.

How his appointment came about was as follows – this of course I only learned at a later date. Whereas the Catholic TV Committee themselves felt assured that I would be appointed, and that this had been agreed verbally with RTÉ, they felt that as a formality they should submit more than one name. Des Forristal's name was given as a second name. What about a third? Fr Jeremiah Newman, later Bishop of Limerick, volunteered the information at the meeting that he had met a Dominican called Fr Dodd OP who was supposed to be interested in communications. So that became a third name. (Jeremiah told me this some years later – adding ruefully that he felt two names would have been enough.) When the list came in to Eamonn Andrew's hands he saw his chance. Romuald Dodd's name was submitted by the CTIC, so no bishop could validly complain if he were appointed. RTÉ could have a priest, but one from a religious order who was not directly subject to the Archbishop of Dublin. And so Fr Dodd was appointed. The CTIC felt it had been tricked but could do nothing about it. John Charles was, needless to say, not at all pleased. I was instructed by him to have nothing to do with Fr Dodd.

Keeping my distance from Dodd

I had now three reasons to stay aloof from Romuald, who made gestures of friendship which I am afraid I largely ignored. There was the order to have nothing to do with him from my archbishop, which he might check up on. There was the danger of anyone thinking I had colluded in thwarting the CTIC's wishes. And anyway, I felt that Radharc needed to preserve its independence, because if we ever came under a religious department we might have to share the same budget. And whatever good intentions might be in the beginning, in the long run (and for both of us it did become a long run), heads of departments don't like handing over large amounts of their slim resources to freelance producers over whom they have little control, and who do their own thing. RTÉ put me under great pressure to knuckle under, including some arm-twisting by the Director General himself. But I held out, even to the point where I said that if it had to be that way, then I was no longer interested in continuing to produce programmes.

The last word on Fr Dodd

As for Fr Dodd, who was so unexpectedly (for himself) appointed to RTÉ, and who worked in various capacities there for twenty-seven years, what can I say? We were friends, but never very close. I felt somehow that he was never comfortable with me, and perhaps because of that he talked too much, which I sometimes found tiresome. But I think he was a good choice, even if not appointed in a conventional manner. He was generally admired and liked in RTÉ. His academic qualifications and precise general knowledge of church affairs gave him authority. He was a good linguist. And though he may not have been a great programme maker, people whose judgement I trust said his programme judgement was very good. In his position that was more important. When it came to liturgical commentaries, and particularly on big Roman occasions he was invaluable, having a good mellow voice, and more important, a good memory for names and faces and a thorough knowledge of the Roman scene. He also fulfilled a priestly pastoral role within RTÉ, and helped many people in their difficulties. I had few of these abilities. Besides, apart from the initial shock, I may well have been saved personally from a no-win situation, sandwiched between Telefís Éireann and the hierarchy, dominated at the time by John Charles McQuaid, both of whom would have had very different expectations of what religious broadcasting should accomplish. At the same time I think something was lost. The possible opportunity to form a bridge early on between the two worlds, the Catholic hierarchy and the Broadcasting Authority. Agnellus Andrew provided such a bridge in the BBC. I am not saying I or anyone else could have provided that bridge. I don't know. Nobody knows. But Romuald Dodd never really did. He died unexpectedly at an international television week in Bolzano, Italy, which we both attended. I was with him when he died, and spoke the few words at the Requiem Mass in Bolzano which most of the delegates attended. It wasn't hard to find nice things to say about a man who was so respected and loved thoughout the broadcasting fraternity.

And a last word on Fr Agnellus

Agnellus left Hatch End to go to Rome as vice president of the Vatican's Communications Commission. He was not very happy there, nor was he very effective. The president, Archbishop (later Cardinal) Deskur, who was a Pole and a close friend of John Paul II, had been incapacitated by a stroke. The Pope hadn't the heart to remove him, so he asked Agnellus to take over the work, but left Deskur in nominal authority. And while Deskur was incapacitated, it wasn't to such an extent as to prevent him from interfering. In his absence from Hatch End, people began perhaps to realise how much the Centre depended on Agnellus's presence and charism. Agnellus retired there from Rome but died not long after. The

Centre was wound down and what remained of its operations were transferred to an office in central London. The studios at Hatch End that Agnellus had planned so lovingly were demolished and the land sold for apartments.

22

THE COMMUNICATIONS CENTRE

Ireland's response to
the Vatican Council's Decree on Commmunications

The Communications Centre was a purpose-built building with offices, a classroom, a library, and a radio/TV studio, situated at the corner of Booterstown Avenue and the Stillorgan Road, in Co Dublin. It housed what was called the National Catholic Office for Mass Media.

In 1970 the hierarchy arranged for a national collection in every church around the country in aid of the church's work in media at home and abroad, and particularly in aid of this Centre. RTÉ was co-operative and screened two programmes made by Radharc, one called *The Mountains don't Matter* and the other simply, *The Communications Centre*. The Centre programme opened with what at the time was prophecy, and now is old hat!

> One day within the next twenty years a TV aerial will be raised in the most isolated village in Africa, and there will no longer be any remote places. The world will be a village where every man and every nation is involved with all the people of the earth as with their neighbours.

An in-house production

In retrospect this programme was an in-house production, because I was Director of the Communications Centre, as well as being a founder member, and at that time part owner, of the Radharc film production unit. And to some extent I am surprised in retrospect that RTÉ ever allowed us to produce a programme on the Centre for showing on television. However I always made sure to keep the Centre and Radharc distinct. The Centre was an initiative of the hierarchy. Radharc was then a partnership between two priests, Des Forristal and myself, which we ran as a business – not to make money because neither of us took a salary from it – but to pay for itself. And if it suited us to have some working space at the Communications Centre for a number of years, we always paid a commerical rent for it.

Because a programme on the Centre was, if you like, incestuous, we decided to make a simple film which showed what went on within the classrooms and studio, and which gave impressions of a wide range of activities, without pretending to be independent and critical. Most of those activities no longer continue. The central building remains, but nowadays it is rented out to secular production agencies.

Little has been written about the Communications Centre that I know of. And yet in terms of resources and effort it was a significant attempt to carry out directives of the Second Vatican Council in the field of communications. So I think it is reasonable to set out here some of it's history, and the thinking that went into its operation.

The Vatican Council Decree on Media 'Inter Mirifica'

Having succeeded in persuading RTÉ to accept a priest as a religious adviser (see Chapter 21), the Catholic Television Interim Committee set up by the bishops (known as the CTIC) set about implementing the Vatican Council Decree on the Media. the Archbishop of Cashel, Dr Morris, was particularly interested and enthusiastic, having been on the commission which drew up the relevant Council decree. As is traditional for Council decrees, this document was in Latin, and known by its first words 'Inter Mirifica' To understand what the CTIC was about, one must take note of this decree which the CTIC, (and its successor, the Communications Centre Committee), tried faithfully to implement. Paragraph 21 of the decree reads as follows:

A National Office for Press, Radio and TV

As this Apostolate, to be effective, requires pooling of ideas and resources on the national level, this Sacred Synod decrees and orders that National Offices for press, cinema, radio and television be organised everywhere and assisted in every way. The chief role of these Offices will be to guide the consciences of the faithful in the right use of media and to encourage and co-ordinate all Catholic activities in this field. In each country the direction of such Offices will be entrusted to a special committee of bishops or to a bishop who has been delegated. Lay persons with a competent knowledge of Catholic directives and of media are to be given a share of responsibility in the work of these offices.

In 1964 the CTIC set about appointing a director of the then non-existent National Office, with the task of drawing up goals and plans under the direction of the committee, bearing in mind the ground plan laid down by 'Inter Mirifica'. I was appointed.

Heady talk in 'Inter Mirifica'

Inter Mirifica was in some ways a naïve document, and the bishops at the Council were made aware of that by the professional journalists when the draft first appeared. However it was agreed to accept it as it was, and put together a team of experts to draw up a 'Pastoral Instruction' after the Council which would supplement the decree, yet have more finesse in its expression. But whatever *Inter Mirifica* lacked in subtlety of expression, it made up for with enthusiasm.

> As it is utterly disgraceful that sons of the church stand idly by while the world of salvation is stifled or impeded by lack of the (admittedly vast) technical and financial means required to operate media, this Sacred Council calls on them to remember they are in duty bound to support and promote Catholic newspapers, periodicals, film enterprises as well as radio and television stations that exist to uphold and defend truth and make Christian values prevail in society. (Par 17.)

It was this sort of heady talk that lay behind the plans drawn up for the Irish national media office which, it was decided, should be called 'The Communications Centre'. As to what this centre was supposed to do, the decree was particularly specific about the need for training.

> Immediate steps must be taken to provide training for the Apostolate in the field of communications to priests, members of religious communities and lay people with the right aptitudes. (Par 15.)

> Methods of media education – especially when designed for the young – are to be encouraged, developed and oriented according to Christian moral principles. They are to be applied in all grades of Catholic schools, in seminaries and in apostolic associations for lay people. (Par 16.)

Finding a site for the National Office

My first task as director was to find a site for this national centre. With RTÉ in Donnybrook, there was obvious merit in finding a site on the south side of the city. The Christian Brothers in St Helen's had land at the extremity of their property bordering the Stillorgan Road and Booterstown Avenue which I felt they might be willing to sell for a good cause. I was anxious to get a good look at it, so one day I decided to climb up the wall at the corner of Booterstown Avenue when the road was quiet in the early morning. I had begun to look for a good grip with my feet when I heard a car coming and quickly dropped off. Unfortunately it was Jack White, assistant programme controller RTÉ, going in early to work. He stopped and asked me could he give me a lift anywhere, which I declined with embarrassment, not feeling able to explain that I was sniffing out a piece of property without the owner's knowledge or permission! I don't think the Brothers were that anxious at the time to sell, but fortunately for the committee they owed the Archbishop of Cashel a good turn, so we got something over three acres at a modest cost.

Finding the money

When the Centre was first mooted in 1963, the Conference of Bishops had no common funds to pay for anything much beyond the paper they used at their meetings. However some bishops knew that the Catholic Truth Society had an old investment in the Bank of Ireland which had much improved in value in recent years, leaving a current nest-egg of over £60,000. The hierarchy had a certain lien on the CTS and they determined to raid this nest – by persuasion of course. I was not party to this arrangement which solved an immediate problem of how to pay for the new Centre, but which left some loose ends. In particular, when the Communications Centre came into operation in 1967 it had a fresh, independent committee – the successor to the CTIC – whereas the Catholic Truth Society, with its own structure of committees, was the legal owner of the land, buildings, and equipment. (This anomaly had to be eventually straightened out by a merger of the two organisations into the Catholic Communications Institute of Ireland – more about that later.)

Planning the Centre

In due course the committee directed me to draw up a plan for a training centre. Before going back to the committee I felt the need of an architect to estimate what a purpose-built building might cost. I drove around Dublin looking at some of the recent architecture, and decided that what seemed to me the most pleasing body of work was designed by Andrew Devane, of Robinson Keefe and Devane. Andy put a price on my sketch – about £12,000.

I brought my plans with trepidation to the CTIC, wondering how they would react to such large scale expenditure. The reaction was the opposite to what I expected. Dr J. G. McGarry was the only professional media man on the committee, and therefore a major influence. I remember him saying to me across the table, 'You are thinking far too small considering the importance of this venture'. The committee also decided to ask the Director General, Kevin McCourt, to help me with expert advice on the planning and construction of the Centre. At his request, two engineers agreed to help with the design, George Waters on technical services and Tom Hardiman on operational questions. And so the size of the studio was doubled, and the specifications upped to professional standards. My original £12,000 eventually became £44,000.

A studio built to professional specifications

In later years I often regretted this decision to build a relatively large professional studio, and that we didn't stay with something simpler. The following are some of the reasons:

1. It gave unsympathetic elements in the media a stick to beat us. Why was the church building a professional television studio? Was it intending to take over television programmes, or start its own service or what?

2. It aroused expectations which we couldn't meet. 'There you have a fine studio. Why aren't you using it to produce programmes?' But unfortunately a studio is only one element in programme production. Apart from producers, scriptwriters, designers, set makers, and talent, one needs an experienced studio crew, any of whom if incompetent or inexperienced can wreck a programme. A production studio also requires broadcast standard equipment. At the time the Communications Centre was built, a broadcast standard videotape recorder would have cost as much as the Centre site, building and equipment put altogether!

3. In the beginning it was the only training studio in the country, and it was nice to have a studio which had a professional feel about it. However what was not perhaps adequately foreseen at the time was that equipment would quickly become miniaturised and portable, so that one could set up a training studio pretty well anywhere there was a large room. Rather than bring clerical students from Maynooth to a short course in Dublin, for instance, it became more sensible to send a small team to Maynooth with portable television equipment.

The opening of the Communications Centre

Courses in broadcast production began in February 1967 while the formal opening was delayed to the following 3 April. This was quite an occasion, with President de Valera and the four archbishops and the nuncio attending Mass in the Centre, surrounded by a healthily representative gathering from the media themselves. It fell to me to preach the sermon. At this stage I am glad to say I can't find the text.

Broadcast training courses

In my personal view, the Centre did its best work in the early years when it ran eight-week courses in broadcasting. Many of the people who made their mark in religious broadcasting in the 70s and 80s came out of those courses. James Skelly in the BBC, Gerry McConville in UTV, Dermod McCarthy, Pat Ahearne, Billy Fitzgerald in RTÉ and a number of others who made a substantial contribution abroad: people like John O'Mahony, Ruth Kidson, Pat Casserly, Colm Murphy, David Owen and many others.

However I never felt that the ultimate success of the broadcasting courses was measured just by the numbers that went to work in broadcasting. I was convinced by Marshall McLuhan and others early in my career that the great turning points in history were not occasioned by philosophers or even generals, but by significant changes in the pattern of human communication. In 1969 I spoke to a group of clerical students, and if I now quote a substantial piece of that speech, it is because it sums up my thinking as to why I felt it was important that clergy try to understand the broadcast media – an understanding which is best achieved by exposure to the whole production process in radio and television:

> The last great turning point in the history of communications, the invention of printing, was also a turning point in the history of religion. This was hardly a coincidence. The invention of printing not only made it possible for the ideas of the Reformation to become widespread, but also provided the stimulus for these ideas in the first place.

> The printing press broadcast the writings of the reformers in the vernacular languages. Moreover it made the Bible widely available – for the first time the man in the street could encounter the word of God in a setting that was separate both physically and morally from the church. It was printing that made private reading possible, and hence also private interpretation and private judgement. It is clear now that the official church had no understanding of what was happening. The learned men of the church considered the printing press a toy and the vernacular booklet as irrelevant. They refuted the heretics, in a lot of learned debates conducted in Latin, unaware that the real battles were being

fought and lost elsewhere. It was half a century before men like St Peter Canisius appeared, a child of print who understood the new world, and by that time the unity of the faith had been irretrievably lost.

There's a parallel here for our day. Once again we have a significant change in the communications patterns sweeping the world. Once again we have the educated establishment, in the church, the professions and the universities, finding it difficult to adapt to the new media or even to take it seriously.

This is a new situation, and something that it is difficult for you and I to grapple with, because we are children of a pre-television age, but it is urgent for us, as supposedly professional communicators, to try and understand it. If we can better understand the changes brought about in society, in the church, and in the human race through the coming of television, then we must be in a better position to communicate with contemporary man. There are some who feel that electronic man will be more receptive to the Christian message than print man. Print man is logical, compartmented, individualistic. Electronic man is open, committed, community minded. 'One of the consequences of electronic environment is the total involvement of people in people,' says Marshall McLuhan, adding that 'the Christian concept of the mystical body – all men as members of the Body of Christ – becomes technologically a fact under electronic conditions'. Sometimes there seems to be a wide gap between technological fact and spiritual reality. Nonetheless the television age may well prove a very fertile field for receiving the Word of God. Provided we, as the husbandmen, know how to cultivate it.

There's no question in my mind that the advent of television makes it necessary for the church to make some reappraisal of policies with regard to appropriation of men and resources. One Protestant theologian, Albert Van der Heuval, put it rather strongly when he said: *'The media have taken the place the pulpit may once have had, and the churches would do well to recognise it. I am not one who says that numbers grow more important when they are larger; but what we are often doing is ignoring the crowds. It seems to be ridiculous that theological scholarships outnumber scholarships for the study of media'.*

What I am suggesting to you is that the advent of television is much more significant than most people realise. I think the clergy must do a lot of hard thinking if the theological implications of a television age don't pass them by. But I don't see how they can be in a position to do any thinking, unless they have some opportunity to think and study about television as well as about theology. As Van der Heuval puts it; *'At this juncture scholarships in media may be as important as scholarships in theology'.*

Fundamental to my philosophy of broadcasting is that understanding radio and television is impossible from the outside. No amount of reading or lectures make up for lack of praxis. One needs to immerse oneself in all stages of the broadcast production process to be qualified to think and talk about it. And that is what a course at the Communications Centre provided. And it was of value for anybody in a leadership position, independently of whether or not they had any opportunity afterwards to get involved in broadcasting.

Media training courses for young people

That philosophy also spilled over into the media courses the Centre organised for schools, which were unique and innovative in their day. In the practical course at the Centre, a class of up to twenty schoolchildren were involved in the preparation of a TV news bulletin which was recorded and played back to the group before the end of a long day. The Centre also organised month-long training courses for teachers during the summer to help them offer media education courses in their own schools. Material promoting these courses in the late sixties gives a flavour of what was intended.

If, as it is said, education is a preparation for life, then education must change when life changes. The average person spends eight hours sleeping, eight hours working and eight hours doing everything else. In countries which have a well developed television system, many people spend half that eight hours watching television. Some surveys in America have shown that children are spending more time watching television every day than they spend in school. A survey of the leisure habits of the Japanese shows that the average man in Japan reads for half an hour every day and watches television for nearly three hours. Yet despite the fact that in developed societies today people spend nearly six times as much time watching television as reading, educational systems all over the world still emphasise a literary culture to the almost total exclusion of the visual. If it is important to educate the critical faculties with respect to literature, surely it is even more important to develop critical faculties with respect to this leisure-consuming monster, television. If this is not to be done in school, where is it to be done? And how can teachers teach about television when they know less about it than their pupils? This is, after all, the first generation of schoolchildren brought up on television from infancy. Can teachers ignore the fact that some children have seen thousands of hours of television, and processed more information in their own minds about the world around them than their grandparents were presented with in a lifetime, before they even start school?

Educators must stop being snobbish about television. The study of television, and indeed the study of the mass media, must be accepted as an essential part of the school curriculum. But before teachers can do this, they must know something about television, something more than the kids they teach. The Communications Centre is anxious to provide this kind of training for teachers to help them bring about this essential media education

Training in journalism

From the beginning, the Centre also provided courses in journalism with a full-time director, Douglas Grainger. In fact the Centre was the first institution to run courses in journalism for either clergy or laity. Places like the Rathmines School of Journalism were a later development. The rationale for providing training in journalism for clergy was outlined at the time in promotional material.

1. The contribution of clergy to the national and provincial press is small when one takes into account their numbers, and the fact of their vocation as ministers of the word.

2. The influence of the Irish church in theological circles is diminished by the small written output from Irish theologians.

3. Catechesis in the past has suffered from the absence of suitable home-produced texts for use in schools.

4. Irish missionary endeavours have been hampered by an absence of suitable textbooks in the local language. Other missionaries seem better prepared to provide their own textbooks.

5. A facility in putting thoughts on paper is often a necessary link between good ideas on the one hand, and effective action on the other.

6. Religious magazines especially need help. Their output, while considerable in quantity, is sometimes lacking in quality.

Intercom - a magazine for all the clergy

Once the training element got going, the Centre began to get involved in other areas. One of our better iniatives was to start a magazine called *Intercom* which went free to every secular priest and religious house in the country. The hope was that it would become an organ providing ideas and stimulating discussion among clergy. The difference between it and other magazines was that whereas some people took out a subscription to *The Furrow*, some to *Doctrine and Life*, some to the *Tablet*, everyone got *Intercom*. A priest could therefore refer to a current article, knowing that all his clerical friends also received it – even if they hadn't so far read it. *Intercom* was produced in the journalism department of the Centre at an economic cost, and while I was in command took no advertisements, but depended for its income on a letter on the back page every Christmas, reminding priests that it cost money to produce, and if they thought it a good idea they might send us a contribution. Many never paid, but enough did to keep it going, and those who didn't still received their copy – unless of course they asked not to, which very very few ever did.

Whereas I claim the basic idea, the format and contents of *Intercom* were evolved from the group who revolved around the Centre. One crucial suggestion which I feel helped acceptance of the magazine came from Fr Des Forristal. This was to provide some feature which priests might feel filled a practical need. So we prepared suggestions for homilies and the parish liturgy. The other vital factor was the first editor, Gerry Reynolds CSsR, who brought a special charism to the job. *Intercom* is still a force on the clerical scene, although some aspects of the organisation of it have changed, and different editors have made their different marks.

Free newspapers

Another idea I proposed was to distribute countrywide a free national Catholic newspaper. This was before the freebies appeared in Ireland. I think I picked up the idea in America. This would have been a very large undertaking, although viable I felt at the time. Cardinal Conway seemed intrigued by the idea, but scared of the resources that might be needed. I can't remember what the committee felt, but I never pushed the idea, presumably because I was not convinced of it's value.

Press and Information Services

A position paper prepared for the committtee of the Institute in

1969 set out the need for a Press and Information Office. It pointed out that the church in a number of other countries already provided this service and other hierarchies who had been hesitant, like the Scottish and English hierarchies, had recently taken the plunge.

In setting out the changed situation which made press and information services advisable, the document pointed out that whereas the church might have been a strong voice in essentially rural communities in the past, today there were many other voices seeking the attention of the human eye and ear. The absence of a press office seemed to imply a lack of awareness of the way things are said and policies shaped in a modern community. It also might seem to imply that the church wished to avoid formal dealing with the media, the presumption being that the church had something to hide.

The document also pointed out that a church Information Office is never a one-way service. It provides a two-way flow of information between church authorities and the press, not only interpreting one to the other, but keeping church authorities informed about the preoccupations of the press and public on specific topics. The argument concluded by suggesting that a press office was a necessary adjunct to leadership in the contemporary world:

> Being led in a democratic community means choosing from conviction to follow. The media are important factors in the formation of this conviction. In our day and age there is little point in offering wise leadership unless it is seen to be wise, because if it is not seen to be wise then there may be nobody following.

The Communications Centre set up an information service with a qualified archivist assisted by Fr Tom Stack. A cutting and abstracts service from the press and religious magazines was made available for bishops and subscribers, but I am not sure that it was as valuable in practice as it seemed in theory. From the beginning, however, it was intended that this information office would form a basis for the more important press office. That needed the appointment of a press officer, which the committee rightly felt must be chosen by the hierarchy or their delegates. In the end it was decided by the hierarchy to make the Press and Information Office directly responsible to the Conference of Bishops. This was reasonable and had the further advantage that it assured independent funding. However, I did not think it reasonable that whereas I was supposedly director of the National Office for Press, Radio and Television, and had prepared much of the arguments and research leading up to this appointment, the only part I was asked to play in choosing a candidate was to act as doorkeeper for the interviewees in a Dublin hotel!

A Research and Development Unit

We had several people on the Communications Centre committee from backgrounds of management and the public service, so it is not perhaps surprising that pressure was put on me to work towards setting up a Research and Development Unit. There was not any problem in selling the idea to Cardinal Conway – it was the kind of thing he understood, having a well-organised mind. Other bishops were not so sure. I remember calling on Bishop Lucy in Cork, who had taught Sociology in Maynooth, expecting that the idea of sociological research would interest him. I pointed out that there was little or no statistical information available about the church in Ireland – people said that vocations were falling, but nobody had reliable statistics, so nobody really knew. 'Maybe it would be better not to know,' the bishop rejoined!

Despite Bishop Lucey's lack of enthusiasm, an R and D unit did start in 1970. It's first director was to be Fr Eamonn Casey, but he was appointed Bishop of Kerry before he could take up the position. I went to the cardinal looking for a replacement. After some hesitation he released Fr James Lennon who laid the goundwork for all further research with the first Religious Attitudes and Practice Survey in 1974. In later years the R and D unit moved to Maynooth College.

The media training centre in the 70s

The Communications Centre continued training programmes with a succession of directors. Peter Lemass took over from me and he was followed by Bunny Carr, Pat O'Brien, Colm Kilcoyne and Tom O'Hare. But towards the end of the seventies and into the eighties, the Centre slowly died a natural death. Its only function today and for the past number of years is to provide a source of income to subsidise other activities of the Catholic Communications Institute – a larger body into which the Communications Centre had been absorbed in 1969. In the first stage of its demise, the Centre was rented to RTÉ as a training centre, retaining the right to a certain minimal use, and then later to other television production agencies. It now provides more income in a year than the building originally cost – though not of course in real terms. But the concept of training in broadcasting and journalism was not maintained, and that I surmise for a variety of causes, some, but not all, related to money.

1. Escalating labour costs

One of the trying facts of life is that, as time goes on, organisations seem to always need more cash each year to do even the same things that they did before. More people are needed to do the same work, people are paid more. Courses are made more complicated and require more facilities.

The Communications Centre began to function in the era where priests and nuns were relatively plentiful. There was no reason to predict the substantial fall in vocations which began in the late 60s and early 70s. There was also a different attitude to priests and religious working for church operations. In the old days the practice was that clergy and sisters received basic support from their institutions and worked for free after that. I had a chaplaincy which provided my basic support, and I worked for the Communications Centre (and later for the CCII which evolved from it), for thirteen years without ever taking a salary. The salary from my convent and Mass stipends, bed and sometimes board from the CCII, was sufficient to meet all my needs. But towards the end of the 1960s the climate changed and the feeling was that priests and religious should be paid the going rate for the job. If he or she wanted to donate the surplus to charity, or if the sum was given to his or her superiors, that was the worker's privilege. What was now called the exploitation of cheap clerical labour began to be frowned upon. Fr Jack Kelly SJ, who worked at the Centre for some period, was a strong advocate of this point of view. I lost the argument.

2. Schools don't pay their way

The work of the Centre was a form of education, and there are very few educational institutions that pay their way, especially when the clerical clients don't have any monetary or career improvement prospects as a result of taking the courses. The one activity that was lucrative in the early days was doing television appearence courses for businessmen. But soon others got into the same game to earn a living, while it seemed to some – including members of our executive committee – that training businessmen or politicians was not what a church agency should be about, even for part of the time.

3. The hierarchy's inability or unwillingness to provide running expenses for the Centre from either a national collection or their common fund

The Vatican Council document is unequivocal about the need for an anual national collection to support church initiatives in the communications field.

To strengthen more effectively the various forms of the church's apostolate in the field of communications, let a day be allotted each year by bishops in all dioceses of the world on which the faithful will be apprised of their duties in this matter. They will be asked to join in prayer for this cause and to make an offering. (Par 18.)

The members of the committee of the Communications Centre shared the belief in the initial planning stages of the Centre – a belief which turned out to be very mistaken – that the local church was somehow bound to implement the decree of the Vatican Council on mass media, and the ensuing Pastoral Instruction, which seemed to make an annual collection for media work obligatory. Lay committees in particular didn't realise that Vatican decrees were open to different interpretations, especially when there was any question of raising finance! Bishops don't like national collections taking money out of their dioceses, which they badly need for projects closer to their own heart. They feel they have enough things to pay for within the diocese itself. So decree or no decree, there was only one national collection ever and only some of that went to the Communication Centre.

4. An opening out and closing in

The Vatican Council had been possible because Pope John had been willing to share decision making with the bishops. This sharing of authority was to be institutionalised in collegial synods, national pastoral councils and so on. In all this the laity were expected to have an important role. This was the kind of church that fitted with a society rapidly changing under the influence of the audio-visual broadcast media. People needed to understand broadcasting to see how it was changing everybody's lives, and how the church should adapt to this new world. So the Communication Centre was relevant and in the thick of a developing church. However the Council wasn't many years over before a sharp frost came to cut short this early spring. The notion of collegiality died quickly and centralised control came back in. Maybe the church has to say 'No' to the world and be in it, but not of it. And maybe it had to re-establish a tight control by Pope and Curia. But if that is so, then the institution does better to avoid radio and television. And there is not much point in providing a centre to teach about broadcasting when the prevailing ethos suggests that the wiser policy would be to keep away from it.

5. Others began to do the same thing

In one way, what might have seemed a successful outcome to it's activities reduced the need for the Centre itself. People who attended courses became enthused by the idea of media training and were anxious to provide it more efficiently and economically for their own people. This became easier as equipment improved and became cheaper – as happened very rapidly in the early 70s. Thus the Missionaries of the Divine Word built a studio at Maynooth, the Redemptorists built one at Marianella, the Church of Ireland at Braemor Park. My own instinct was to advise against this rash of studios on the ground that it was easier to set up a facility than find the right people to make use of it. And if there were resources to spend on broadcast training, they should not be spread out too thinly. However, I never did argue that way publicly. It was more important to see people enthused and doing something about training, than to pour cold water on their initiatives. Dog-in-the-manger attitudes should have no place among Christian broadcasters.

6. Different conceptions as to what the Centre could accomplish

Many senior clergy, including a significant number of the bishops, had a certain conception as to what a national office for mass media might accomplish. Some elements in this conception were never obtainable, or if they were, we didn't obtain them. For instance, one of the frequently expressed hopes was that a group of lay people and clerics would be trained and then form panels from which individuals would be drawn to appear in programmes and speak for the church. The idea didn't work because the nature of media producers is to flee from such panels and to seek their own independent experts. And because people who feel they are where they are to defend an institutional point of view consistently give that impression, which damages their credibility. And because it's in the nature of the media to want to reach and question the policy makers rather than somebody the policy makers hope will let them off the hook.

7. Mixing goals and priorities

The importance of broadcasting, the way it was changing our world, and the importance of understanding these changes never caught the imagination of many rural bishops, more concerned about paying off the debt on refurbishing the cathedral in accordance with the latest liturgical thinking from Vatican II. However there was some unease about how well priests were adapting to the new liturgy in English, and of course, the perennial unease about the standard of preaching, and what might be done to improve it. So the Centre came under pressure to do something it hadn't been particularly designed to do, which was to help clergy to say Mass and preach better. Courses were devised to use the then relatively new medium of videotape as a means for evaluation of sermons and liturgy. For a period there was a great demand for these short courses. But they were very demanding on staff energy, with the result that the broadcast training at times did not get enough attention. And in time every seminary purchased its own video recorder, so the whole novelty of seeing oneself as others see one disappeared, and the demand for such courses died off.

8. Mergers and other distractions

Towards the end of the 1960s, the anomalies arising from the fact that the Catholic Truth Society owned the Communications Centre while an independent communications committee ran it, suggested the idea of a merger between the two. The merger, I am afraid, turned into a take-over, and there was some acrimony, especially as the CTS were employing management consultants at the time, who for their own reasons were unsympathetic to the merger. So this marriage of the Communications Centre and the CTS – which consisted at the time of one shop in Dublin and a publishing unit which between them were losing money at the rate of £30,000 and more a year – was a traumatic affair. It took up a lot of committee time, and a lot of my time as director. The new unit was called – by a compromise decision which I was reluctant to agree with – 'The Catholic Communications Institute of Ireland' (or CCII for short).

Presuming it had been properly funded on its own, the Communications Centre would I believe have been better to stay on its own, because the power in any organisation goes to where the money is being made. In the CCII that in later years proved to be publishing. Education and service, which is what the Communications Centre was about, costs money rather than makes it.

9. Putting the emphasis on publishing

In 1970 therefore I found myself planning a facelift for an old shop in Lr Abbey Street – again with Andy Devane – and looking for somebody to direct the publications department, and hoping the expertise on the committee could find ways of stemming the substantial losses. By this time it was clear to me that the hierarchy would not grant an annual collection, or ever provide substantial funds for the Institute. So money would have to be earned, and the only way that could be done was through substantial publishing. Now the hierarchy were planning catechetical courses for the schools. Previously they had given this plum job to other publishers. We decided to go hard after it and managed to convince the hierarchy that we could and should do it. The Dundalk Programme for secondary schools and the Children of God series for the primary were publishing successes and made substantial money for the Institute.

Resignation

Then just when the payoff was in sight, and the money was beginning to roll in from the catechetics programmes, I told Dr Morris, Archbishop of Cashel, that I would like to resign as Director of the Institute. In one way I was sorry not to have enjoyed the position which I had looked forward to and never experienced – having enough cash to do things properly and pay for them, instead of having to scrimp and save and add things to the overdraft. But a number of factors suggested resignation, only some of which might have been enough.

1. Stale directors and fresh committees

I had had fourteen years working with committees, and I was tired of it, and I felt this might begin to show. People came on committes for three years: some were asked to stay for another three, others left sooner rather than later. So there was a continuous and healthy turnover of people, some with new ideas, many with ideas which had been proposed and either implemented or rejected years before – though possibly for the wrong reasons.

Now I am not for a moment denigrating committees. The committee system is necessary for the good of an institution like the CCII and the protection of its director, while a good committee is more than that – it is a great blessing. Many of the best ideas in the CCII and the know-how to carry them out came through committees. But committees keep changing, and if the director remains too long he finds that new people bring up ideas which he feels are not feasible, or which have already been tried and failed, or would fail because of reasons that the newcomer to the committee is not aware of. Having made up one's mind once about a problem or opportunity, one tends to marshall the same arguments for or against the next time around. But maybe it *would* work this time – if there were a new director to look at it afresh!

2. A shift in the power base

The CCII had now become a viable organisation through the substantial profits generated by catechetical publishing. We had a talented Director of Publications, Fr Oliver Crilly, backed up by a very competent colleague and friend, Seán O Boyle – later the founder of the Columba Press. Power in the CCII now lay in their department because that is where the revenue was. The publishing division had a history of acting independently, a tradition to some extent resulting from Fr Dermot Ryan's chairmanship of the advisory publications committee, a post which he held up to his appointment as Archbishop of Dublin. As director I therefore had two alternatives: the first was to establish more control over publications and make myself, in reality if not in name, Director of Publications. I hadn't really the stomach for that. The other was to recognise that power had now moved to publications, and suggest that the Director of Publications become Director of the Institute.

3. The culture of change and moving on

Part of the management culture which I breathed in from the committees was one of doing a job and then getting out. Never staying too long in the one place and so on. Being a proud person, I never wanted to reach the stage where people wanted me to go, or have people feeling that I was clinging on to control for longer than I should.

Then there were other kinds of work that attracted me. With Fr Jim Lennon going back to his diocese, the post of Director of Research and Development was vacant, and that appealed to me. Then there was the Radharc Film Unit, in which I had a founder member's interest. I liked film making, and I liked the intensive form of travel that at times it involved. I felt too that there were opportunites to produce more programmes.

My position in CCII was also somewhat compromised by the executive committee's Special Report to the hierarchy in 1976 which was critical of the way the hierarchy, and in particular its finance committee had dealt with the Institute. (This report is considered more fully in Chapter 23, *The House Hunters*.)

But I enjoyed my time at CCII. I enjoyed working with clever and dedicated people in the committees. I enjoyed an excellent relationship with my immediate boss in the hierarchy, the Archbishop of Cashel. He is a gentleman who always sees good in others, and tends to trust them. He certainly placed a lot of trust in me, more perhaps than I deserved. He is naturally conservative in outlook, but open to be persuaded of other points of view. In fact he was always open to new ideas, and full of ideas himself. He was much respected by other bishops – with one exception – and by committee members of CCII. Of some who became close to him through long association with the executive commitee, one could say that they came to love him.

23

THE HOUSE HUNTERS

Bishop Eamonn Casey, in some earlier incarnations

Peter Lemass: 'Has Fr Casey's coming to the Housing Aid Society made much difference to you'?

Masie Ward: 'Oh terrific, he is an absolute ball of fire. And of course he combines very unusual qualities in that he is both eloquent and a good organiser.'

In 1963 Masie Ward was one of the best known Catholic English-women. Her grandfather was involved in the Oxford movement with Newman (later cardinal), and others. She had kept up the family literary tradition with several works, including biographies of Chesterton, Newman and her father Wilfrid Ward. She married Frank Sheed and together they founded Sheed and Ward, perhaps the most important Catholic publisher in English in its day.

In her capacity as chairperson of The Catholic Housing Aid Society she came across Eamonn Casey and was quite captivated by his ideas, energy and enthusiasm. She used her considerable influence in clerical society to ensure that Eamonn was released to work for her.

Eamonn's father was a creamery manager from North Kerry who settled in Adare in south Limerick. So Eamonn was of rural stock with a strong southern accent and ebullient manner. Masie Ward was petite, English upper class. They were an unlikely pair. But she was quite bowled over by her 'ball of fire'.

Eamonn's almost frenetic energy affected people in different ways. J. G. McGarry, editor of the Maynooth pastoral magazine, *The Furrow,* said to me one day back in the early sixties, 'You know, after speaking to that man you would have to wring out your shirt'.

Fr Casey CC: An ideas man

It was through *The Furrow* that I first came in contact with Eamonn, who was then curate in St John's Cathedral parish in Limerick. He used religious filmstrips in his teaching work in the parish schools –

having reviewed and evaluated them first with a teacher friend. I also began to use filmstrips when I was put teaching in the Dublin vocational schools, and came to hear of his reviews. I visited him in Limerick, and before I knew what hit me, we were jointly reviewing filmstrips for a wider audience in *The Furrow*.

I learnt quickly that Eamonn was an ideas man – which meant he had the ideas and you did the work! That annoyed me at the time, and it is something about Eamonn that has annoyed many other people since. However, I understood it better later in life. Eamonn's great talent lay in analysing problems and finding solutions. But if he himself were to have to carry through all his own good ideas, only a small number of them could come to fruition. And he himself wouldn't have time to hatch any more!

The emigrant chaplain

There wasn't much happening in Limerick in the late fifties and early sixties, and many of Eamonn's parishioners were going to find work in England. So Eamonn volunteered as an emigrant chaplain, and went to Slough, near London, in the autumn of 1960.

> When I arrived in Slough I conceived my job to be to find out what were the particular problems and needs of the migrant population – obviously problems and needs which they wouldn't share with the settled population of the area, and therefore which would not necessarily be served by the traditional parish institutions. And having teased out what they were, to see what could be done on a community level to solve them.

Eamonn surprised some people by refusing to take up parish duties immediately.

> I moved out among the people for quite a number of months because I didn't want to put my preconceived ideas on the situation. The first need I became very conscious of was for some kind of a social framework within which the newly arrived emigrant would build up his or her own personal life and thereby become more content and happy. Secondly I found the problem of lodgings – both their low standard, particularly for girls, and the difficulty of getting them. Thirdly I found the need among them for some kind of social welfare scheme. I met so many genuine cases who for one reason or another needed some financial aid now, and the proof of the fact it was genuine was that over the period 85% of what was given out by the social welfare fund has been

repaid. And finally I found this housing problem which was the basis of many of the other difficulties and moral problems that I found in the area.

Eamonn developed successful initiatives in all these four areas. Our programme stuck to the one for which he became best known – housing. His first initiative in housing was a bank loan scheme where he placed some money in the bank as collateral against loans which he authorised. It came about, he told us, as a response to an immediate problem.

> It was a family of five children where one child had just had an operation for a hole in the heart and they were living in a basement flat from which they were evicted. These people came to me and said that if they could get £200 they could purchase a house in Bristol and the husband get a job there. I felt it was extraordinary that £200 could make the difference between people living in appalling conditions and people living in normal conditions, so I got them the money and they bought the house in Bristol. It was then that the idea struck me that there must be many other people like this. I didn't quite understand how anybody could purchase a house for £200 but I decided to find out, and to see if there were other people in such a situation.

> Then there is a certain kind of person and the possibility of purchasing a house never enters their mind. I remember one occasion I said to a man – his four children had been put into council homes while husband and wife were in lodgings – and I said to the husband, 'Peter you have got to buy a house'. And Peter looked at me in consternation and said, 'My God! Father, how could I buy a house?' You see they didn't know the machinery, they didn't know it was possible.

Of all his many initiatives, the halfway house was perhaps the most imaginative. In this scheme his organisation purchased houses in poor repair and refurbished them.

> The first house we bought, we were able to make five two-roomed flats. Now into these two-roomed flats we took in five young couples, two of them having their babies, the other three expecting their first baby. Three of them were about to be evicted and two of them were paying an exorbitant rent. Now this flat unit would have been worth on the open market – it sounds appalling – but it would have been worth about £5.10s or £6 a week. In actual fact we found that from the Society's point of view

£3 was the economic rent. But instead of charging them £3 we charged them £4.10s, which is still a reasonable rent, explaining to them that thirty shillings of this was what we call compulsory saving, which, provided they were good tenants, and provided they eventually purchased a house, we were prepared to give back to them at the end of their tenancy for each week they were in this particular flat.

Partly because the Catholic Church in England is small, and not part of the establishment, and partly because of Eamonn's persuasive personality, the Housing Aid Society could call on a whole team of house agents, lawyers, solicitors, and builders who gave their time and expertise for free. So Eamonn had a very professional organisation to support his work and solve his problems without ever having to worry about fees. And this was an important part of the success story.

I remember two things about being with Eamonn in London that were not part of the film.

The smart driver and the pious priest

One day we were driving together in the car, and he said casually, 'It's going to take us about twenty minutes to get where we're going, so there will be time to say the Rosary'. It is the kind of thing most people might expect one priest to say to another in those circumstances. But they usually don't.

From his earliest days he was a fast driver. I commented on his swift weaving through the traffic near Hyde Park corner.

'It's OK,' he replied, 'just keep your eye on the rear mirror.'
'Why?' said I, innocently.

There are many stories related to his driving, and he used tell some of them with glee himself.

I can remember hearing him tell more than once of a dash up a small country road to get to a Confirmation on time. Near the end he went over a bridge and the car left the road, landed with an almighty thump, but proceeded apparently none the worse for wear to its destination. After the ceremony the bishop threw the case in the car, got into the driving seat and turned the key. The car wouldn't start. Eventually a local mechanic was summoned. After a brief examination he reported.

'You have no battery, My Lord.'

'Of course I have a battery.'

'No, My Lord. You have a hole where the battery once was!'

Eamonn had a Rover at the time, and the battery was in the boot. It seems that going over the bump it shot in the air and then came down with such force that it went through the floor. The car carried on its own generator – but only of course as long as the engine kept running.

He told another story against himself. When he was living in Inch, he used drive to Killarney every day through the parish of Annascaul. Eamonn met the parish priest of Annascaul one day and said to him a little mischievously:

'Father X, I drive through your parish every day, and I have never yet seen you walking the road.'

The answer came back quick as a shot:

'And perhaps to that, My Lord, do I owe the fact that I am alive and well and here talking to you.'

Priest to bishop

Eamonn's work in England impressed the Irish hierarchy. He didn't fulfil all of the usual requirements in candidates for the episcopacy, but after the Vatican Council the Conference of Bishops had become involved in setting up commissions and committees, which in turn wanted to do work. These included the Commissions for Justice and Peace, Social Welfare, the Laity, Communications, and later on, after Eamonn was a bishop, the Third World agency, Trócaire. So there was a felt need for somebody within the hierarchy with experience of managing affairs, looking after finance and so on. In light of the glowing reports coming from across the water, Eamonn seemed to be the man.

The problems of the Communications Commission

As Director of the Communications Commission, or Catholic Communications Institute of Ireland (CCII) to use its full and unfortunate title, I welcomed the idea of a bishop who would look after finance.

The Communications Institute had a highly motivated committee of qualified and experienced people from media, the arts, business and administration. Over the nineteen-sixties a whole programme was worked out and implemented to provide the Irish church with information, research and development, and media training facilities. This programme was supported by Thomas Morris, the Archbishop of Cashel, who was the member of the hierarchy in charge of communications, and just as importantly, by the President of the Conference of Bishops, Cardinal Conway.

Research, information and training services require substantial resources. In the early days after Vatican II this did not seem a problem, because one of the Council decrees laid down that there should be a national collection for communications every year. There was one collection in 1970 but the hierarchy could not agree to hold another. The alternative proposed was to levy each diocese for a contribution to a common fund which would support the various national commissions – which included Social Welfare and Justice and Peace as well as Communications.

Unfortunately John Charles McQuaid, Archbishop of Dublin would not agree to pay his full share, and the other bishops were not willing to accept the principle that he shouldn't. So nobody paid, and the CCII got into a situation where key members of the hierarchy wanted certain activities to be continued, but the hierarchy as a whole couldn't agree to pay for them. The result was that the CCII began to get deeper and deeper into debt to the banks, who around this time were charging interest rates of between 8 and 14%.

After Eamonn became a bishop in 1969, he was made chairman of an Episcopal Finance Committee. Now at last we felt something would be done to remedy the impossible situation the Communications Institute found itself in.

Alas, however, his appointment didn't make any difference. The Archbishop of Dublin was to blame. So there was change in Dublin. Archbishop John Charles McQuaid retired at 75 and Dermot Ryan became archbishop in 1972. Again it was hoped that Dermot would support national commissions like CCII where, indeed, he had served on the executive committee. In the end he not only did not support them, but he set up parallel committees, commissions and even a diocesan press and information office before there was a national one. These new diocesan structures had to be paid for, so again we had a Dublin archbishop who would not support a national effort, and Eamonn's finance committee didn't seem to be doing much about it.

Archbishop Dermot Ryan 'solves' the problem
So the CCII still continued to drift further into debt. Its Council

asked for permission to close down the research unit, but were told not to do so. They asked permission to rationalise their assets but were refused permission. Eventually Archbishop Dermot pushed through his own plan at a bishops' meeting, which involved selling Veritas House – a valuable property in the centre of Dublin belonging to the CCII – to pay off the overdraft. He invited me up to St Rita's, his home on the Stillorgan Road, and suggested we walk in the grounds of Belfield, UCD. There he told me the news. This decision came totally out of the blue. Knowing that neither I nor the Council of the Institute could be expected to approve such a move, he had acted first. Both of us knew that the hierarchy were not accustomed to going back on such decisions. I listened, and said little. When I got home I phoned the chairman of the Council.

The decision by the bishops may have been within their powers, but it made rather a laughing stock of the whole idea of lay participation in decision making, and left the impression that the Council was responsible for a mess which the hierarchy had to take drastic action to control.

With the support of the chairman and executive committee, I prepared a tough report which set out the history of the Council's dealing with the hierarchy, quoting letters and documents. It was a report to the Council members of the Institute, but a copy was also sent to each bishop. That set the inter-palatial phones buzzing. Bishops are busy people who tend to see their first responsibility to their own diocese. Most of them regret the time they have to give to national questions. So when some strong character like Archbishop Dermot comes pushing a point of view and supposedly solving a problem, few others can summon up the energy to oppose him. Nevertheless when the bishops read the report we sent them they got distinctly nervous. Apart from the rights and wrongs of the situation, if a copy of the report had got to the press – it never did but who was to know that it mightn't – the bishops as a whole might have appeared guilty of shoddy treatment of one of their own largely lay commissions. Needless to say, the decision was reversed.

Even if I was tempted to knuckle under myself and accept a *fait accompli*, I was clear that my responsibility as the officer serving the Council of the Institute made it necessary to defend their record in management – quite apart from my own. But I was quite well aware at the same time that, by the nature of the case, I was closing off any possibility of a further career in service of the bishops. One thing no executive can ever expect to get away with is to threaten the authority of, let's call it, the group management – in this case the bench of bishops. A civil servant may go any distance in persuasion, but if a decision is made by a minister, the servant cannot expect to force a change in that decision and maintain a position of trust. Even if they agreed, as I know many of the bishops did, that what I had done in the end was for the best, it set a dangerous precedent.

I blamed Eamonn Casey and his finance committee for the debacle which made it necessary to prepare and circulate this report. The clear understanding in setting up the Hierarchy Finance Committee was that they would sort out the problem of funding for the commissions, including the CCII. Or if funding could not be arranged, to abandon the costly non-revenue earning activities like research. (Not abandon one of the revenue earning areas which was what Dermot proposed.) If finding a solution meant that Eamonn and his finance committee had to take on Dermot Ryan, so be it. It was bishop to bishop. I was a priest. It was quite different for me to take on a bishop, to say nothing of my own archbishop to whom I was subject by definition. I know that Dermot bullied Eamonn, and Eamonn was afraid of him, or at least never seemed willing to take him on. For in the end, Eamonn, despite his great abilities, seemed to lack self-confidence, particularly when faced with someone of supposed intellectual superiority.

I think Eamonn should have stood up to Dermot and resolved the question of financing the national offices, or else have resigned as chairman of the finance committee and made his resignation and reasons public, or if not public at least widely know in ecclesiastical circles. The mere threat, I believe, would have probably been sufficient to solve the problem.

In the end I believe the CCII could have sorted out its own problems much more efficiently if there was no finance committee and it had been left control of its own assets.

Working for bishops

I sometimes feel that clerics give out about their frustrations as if somehow frustration was peculiar to the clerical state instead of part of the human condition. Some frustrations come from Murphy's Law, some come from the fact that other people may have a different point of view as to the best thing to be done. My guess is that there is very much more frustration in business or the civil service than in the church. It is just that lay people haven't as much freedom to give out about it. They need the job!

I had frustrations working for fourteen years for the Irish hierarchy, and I have just indulged myself giving out about some of them. But by and large I have the happiest memories of working for the bishops. I was trusted, and given great encouragement and great freedom and great support – as were the mainly lay committees who monitored and advanced the work. It was a most enjoyable and fulfilling time in my life, for which I owe a debt of gratitude – especially to Archbishop Thomas Morris, former Archbishop of Cashel, to whom I was principally responsible, but also to the dedicated men and women who worked on the committees.

Working in and out of the institution

When I used work for the hierarchy as Director of their Mass Media Office, I avoided all remotely radical organisations. There was, for instance, the Association of Irish Priests, which priest friends of mine like Peter Lemass and Billy Fitzgerald joined and took an active part in. This latter organisation was in essence a body to challenge the authoritarian excesses of Archbishop McQuaid, and to help protect those that he might unfairly discipline. I never joined. I defended myself by pointing out that there were two ways to work for change, directly within the organisation, indirectly by criticism and protest from outside the organisation. Both are valid, both are needed. But one can only engage in one of them at a time. Civil servants can't sign public protests criticising their minister. They may, however, without anybody else knowing of it, try to change his mind.

There is another aspect of working within or without the institution which is interesting, if less clearly acknowledged. I perceived a change of outlook in myself and in others when we were working within and without the institution. In fact, Peter Lemass and I passed each other out in different directions twice! When one is working for bishops, meeting bishops, trying to please bishops, one begins to think like them and so did I. When one was working for the Association of Priests as Peter was, things looked different. One of the only times Peter got really mad with me was when, as director of a film for Radharc on the changing face of religious life in the US, I refused to film an interview with what I considered to be an off-the-wall nun in Dubuque, Iowa. (This was in 1966 and the beginning of the exodus from the convents.) He was the radical then, and I the conservative. Then later in the seventies Peter Lemass was working closely with Archbishop Dermot Ryan, and I was now working outside the institution for Radharc. I remember feeling he was going right-wing – quite different from the man I had previously known. I have found it helpful and humbling to note that environment affects one's point of view, and have tried to take account of it, both in judging myself and others. We all like to think we are independent in our attitudes and judgements. But the truth is that we are very influenced by the last person we were talking to, and the second last …

Eamonn and Annie

I spent a day and a night once with the chairman and deputy chairman of my Council in the by now famous house in Inch, Co Kerry. In fact I am almost sure there was an American cousin in the background. When the story of his amorous involvement broke, it was my first thought. Was it she?

I was saddened by the revelations of this affair with Annie Murphy. We are all sinners in different ways, and none of us can afford to be casting stones. But not all of us have to do such a public penance for our sins as Eamonn has. Despite the crititicisms I have made with regard to his handling of the Episcopal Finance Committee in its relationship to the Communications Institute, I always admired him and considered him a friend, and do to this day. But I also understand some things about him better.

I had always felt the really great potential there in the young Bishop Casey was never fully realised. Living under this sword of Damocles for seventeen years now seems to me sufficient explanation. He had many many fine initiatives to his credit, but I feel he could have been even better. This amorous involvement early in his episcopal career, and the knowledge that it might/must become public someday, and the internal debate as to the best course to choose – resign or try to keep it hidden – must have done much to take the edge off his drive and enthusiasm.

The loneliness of a bishop

In retrospect, being a bishop was not perhaps the best thing for Eamonn. He was and is naturally a gregarious type – one of the lads. Loneliness was bad for him. Bishops tend to become very lonely people because, outside their own family, they find it very difficult to relate to other people.

Part of this is due to the titles and paraphernalia that surrounds their office. If you are a bishop, how can you have a normal relationship with other people who start by kissing your ring, and con-

tinue calling you 'My Lord' or 'Your Grace'? One might rejoin that a
bishop could refuse to use such titles, but that doesn't solve much
because the laity still feel obliged to respect them – unless and until
the church as a whole abolishes the rings and titles system.

Relating to the laity is still easier than trying to relate to one's own
diocesan priests. If you are a bishop, how can you expect priests to
act normally towards you when you have the right to claim almost
total obedience from them, which they have promised to you at
their ordination? How can there be normal fellowship with them
when you and they know that you can change the manner and loca-
tion of their work and of their abode tomorrow, without consultation and with minimal notice? Where you can post them to a good
and happy parish, or to a remote and miserable one with a tyrant
for a parish priest? How can a priest react sincerely and normally
with you when if he acts one way, you will likely think him ingrati-
ating, seeking favours, ambitious? And if he acts in a different way,
he seems to you unfriendly, distant, cold? The priest himself is conscious too of his fellow priests, and how they will think of his relationship with the bishop. Will they think he is trying to curry
favour, hoping to be rewarded more handsomely than his peers
with a comfortable trouble-free parish? These are the kind of problems that arise when the system concentrates so much power in the
bishop's hands. One is reminded of the words of the centurion to
Our Lord, which I like to remember in the sonorous phrases of old
Douay version: 'I say to one, go and he goeth, and to another, come
and he cometh: and to my servant, do this, and he doth it'.

Reporting 'the affair'

I don't have the stomach myself to go into all the rights and wrongs
of the Annie and Eamonn saga. Besides I think most people were
satiated with the acres of newsprint comment published at the time,
much of which inevitably saddened me because I was his friend.

However there is one clear point which I think can be made and
should be made.

At the time the story broke, many journalists and letter writers
made it an occasion for questioning celibacy, and every married
priest in the country seemed to be asked for comment. Now there
are grounds for questioning celibacy, but I don't think the Eamonn
and Annie affair is a good one. As I understand it, the institution of
celibacy was never an issue – no more than the institution of marriage is an issue when someone has an extra-marital affair. The fact

that someone fails as a celibate is no better an argument for abolishing celibacy than the argument that the institution of marriage should be abolished because some are unfaithful to their marriage vows.

It seems to me that Eamonn never wanted to be a natural father, never wanted to marry Annie, whereas Annie, perhaps, might like to have married Eamonn. If Eamonn had wanted a stable relationship and children, he could have resigned from the clerical state. I think he wanted to be a celibate priest and bishop, and failed at times through human weakness to live up to his principles, and deeply regretted his failures. Many seemed to feel that he should have resigned earlier from high office, but that is a different matter. He did in the end resign, but did not seek to marry. And he did what he had always said he would do when he finished his time in Galway, which was spend some years in a Third World country as a simple missionary.

24
NEW DRUMS FOR OLD
Arguing for a wider community involvement
in Radio and TV

I remember Cotabato City in the Philippines for a number of reasons. One was the occasion of our arrival at the airport where we were greeted with a large banner across the entrance which read, 'Cockfights every night of the week in honour of the Immaculate Conception (by courtesy of Pepsi Cola)'. Another was the occasion of our leaving. We arrived at the airport in good time to find our twin-engined Japanese YS-11 waiting on the runway. The time came to board the plane and the time came to take off. But nothing happened – we were left standing in the open-air waiting room of palm leaves and bamboo. An hour passed and still nothing happened. Nobody seemed to be around to explain. We had been warned at the time that PAL (Philippine Airlines) stood for 'Plane Always Late' – though I am sure that is no longer true. After about an hour and a half another aeroplane of similar type arrived. As soon as it came to a standstill, men got up a little ladder and took off the rear cowling of one of the engines. They then removed what looked like a heavy lead battery from the new arrival and fitted it into the rear of one of the engines on our plane. When it was in place the mechanic waved, and our pilot started first one, and then the other engine. The battery was then removed carefully and returned to the first plane. Clearly somebody decided we didn't need a battery to fly – and we hoped he was right. A young hostess appeared for the first time to announce to the passengers – all of whom had been watching this starting procedure with great interest and some trepidation – that our flight was now ready to depart for Cebu.

In 1967 Mindanao was the new frontier in the Philippines – their very own wild west. The government was advertising Mindanao as 'land of promise', and people were being encouraged to move from the crowded northern island of Luzon and settle there where the population was small and land was plentiful. Cotabato city had a thriving riverfront with a jumble of wooden building – banks, trading posts, commercial agencies, timber walkways and balconies overhead. It looked like an etching of an American town in the 1870s.

We went from the city with some Philippine nuns to visit a typical fishing village on the seashore called Parang, about thirty or forty miles to the north. The beach was its main street, and no ordinary wheeled vehicle could move on the soft sand. Yet even in this remote place in 1966, the people had their transistor radios and were in touch with the main centres of population in Mindanao, if not with the whole world.

The extent of the revolution brought about by the transistor radio is difficult to appreciate some forty years later. When I was a child my grandfather's house in Sandymount was lit by gas, not electricity, so he had to have a battery-operated valve radio. It required two batteries, one a wet battery, which we children used bring down to the village to get charged in the radio shop – keeping it upright so the acid didn't spill. The second was a high tension dry battery made up of, I would guess, sixty cells, which cost a lot of money and was fun to break up when it ran out of juice. In 1960, less than twenty years later, I bought my first pocket transistor radio in a shop on Broadway, New York. By 1966 radios had become so cheap to buy and to run that even the poorest of families in remote places like Parang seemed not too poor to afford one. With the coming of the transistor radio, no village could ever be completely isolated again. And in the Third World, where many couldn't read, and few could afford to distribute or buy newspapers, radio suddenly became the crucial means of communication.

To somebody used to monopoly radio, as radio was at the time both in Ireland and the UK, it was a revelation to me to find that Cotabato, with its population measured in thousands, had several radio stations, and that the most popular, with the call sign DXMS, consisted of one room and a transmitter mast! As I remember it, the one room was about eight, or at most ten feet square. It housed a large second-hand RCA sound mixing unit, a microphone, and record turntables. One person sat in the middle, with room for two or three others to stand behind. When we were filming, the station was putting out a drama with three characters. The three characters – which included one woman – were played by the male presenter/technician, who changed his voice to fit the different parts in the soap opera. When this apparently obviously tense and emotional episode came to an end, the actor(s!) went out for a smoke during the closing music, while another presenter slipped into the chair.

DXMS had a part-time director and a small part-time staff. What really amazed me was that broadcasting went on for 17 hours a day. At the time, Radio Éireann was broadcasting less than 13 hours a day on a single channel – with a staff of about 300.

DXMS was a commercial radio station owned by the Catholic diocese of Cotabato which not only paid for its own operation, but earned enough to pay the expenses of the diocesan seminary as well. The island of Mindanao at the time had a population of about a million, but roads were poor and transport difficult, and there were only thirty priests in total to serve their religious needs. So a radio station owned by the diocese became a useful tool in catechesis, and for keeping in contact with the faithful in remote areas.

Now one wouldn't wish to compare the quality and complexity of Radio Éireann programming with what emanated from that little boxroom in Cotabato city. But it set me thinking about the small resources needed for a local station which could command an audience, and be quite adequate to meet most community needs, and which seemed to permit involvement and participation of a kind not permitted by the Rolls Royce operations of Radio Éireann and the BBC.

After that I had opportunity to visit other local radio stations in America, and became convinced that local radio had a big future. I felt I wanted to say something about this, and the opportunity came when I was invited to respond to a paper by Stuart Hall on 'Broadcasting in a Free Society' to be delivered to the Irish Humanist Society in a Dublin Hotel. (Why a priest should be asked to address the Irish Humanist Society may possibly be explained by the fact that the lady organising the event was the spouse of my dentist!)

I hate public speaking, and when I have to do it my pulse doubles its speed and blood pressure hits about 200. This occasion was a little more intimidating than usual for several reasons. As soon as it became my turn to speak, Eoghan Harris, the well-known writer and broadcaster, stood up and made an unscheduled speech about how I, as Director of the Catholic Communications Institute, was trying to take religious broadcasting out of the hands of RTÉ, and Eoghan felt that was a bad thing, and therefore presumably I was a bad thing. As far as I can recall, he left after his protest without instigating a debate. I began my presentation. The next thing I remember was that Conor Cruise O'Brien stood up in the centre of the audience and made to leave. People made way and chairs moved to let him out of his seat. Conor's face and figure are well enough known to ensure that nobody much was watching or listening to me until his exit had been accomplished. Whether he was going to the toilet or rushing to another appointment or making a protest I was never sure, but I don't remember him returning.

Re-reading what I wrote and said then, I was pleased to find some of it ahead of its time, and some of it still relevant. So I am not going to apologise for giving it another airing. The meeting was on a Friday evening, 9 June 1972.

> Ladies and Gentlemen. My favourite broadcasting station is called KQED in San Francisco. I like the station because it is democratic, and because I think most broadcasting systems are oligarchic, if not autocratic. (And that includes our own.)
>
> At any one time, programmes at KQED are produced by thirty or more local groups and organisations representing a cross-section of San Francisco's community interests. The various groups appoint their own producers, employ their own talent and format, and produce their own programmes which are then broadcast by the station to the public at large.
>
> In this system, the broadcasting day is divided among the community groups as fairly as possible by mutual agreement. Programmes may include Black Unity, conversation in Swedish, music from China or from American Indians; sandwiched between animal lovers, adventures in ESP, the case for a united Ireland, and so on and so forth.
>
> Regular training workshops are organised by the station which enable groups to take proper advantage of the broadcasting medium. Training is given both on technical and presentation levels. Groups are taught how to edit effectively, how to integrate and balance different programme components and how to interest an audience.
>
> I like the KQED system, because it fits with my philosophy of broadcasting, which is that broadcasting is simply an extension of man's ability and right to communicate, to speak to and listen to his fellow men. In Irish broadcasting, we are all free to listen, but very few are free to speak .
>
> It seems to me that most of what is usually said about freedom of speech in broadcasting relates to freedom for an elite broadcasting group. If broadcasting has to be made by a small oligarchy of

producers and administrators, then so be it. But I don't think it has to be, I don't think in a democratic community it should be, and with technical developments in the very near future I don't think it can be. So I would like to see responsibility in broadcasting much more widely dispersed, and particularly at production level, because that is where responsibility really matters.

When I was told in 1959 to get interested in broadcasting, I was terrified. Television seemed an extremely demanding, even mysterious profession, where only very special people had anything to offer. And I wasn't special. Since then, experience as director and editor of half a hundred programmes on a part-time basis has taught me several things.

Firstly that broadcast production isn't mysterious. It's like driving a car, or speaking Spanish. Just as many people have to acquire these skills as part of normal living, so many people could acquire skill in broadcasting.

The second thing it taught me was that the real power and responsibility and freedom in broadcasting is exercised at producer level. Suppose for a moment that you were about to direct a programme for television. In most cases you will chose the subject yourself – it may have to be okayed by the programme controller, but he can have very little idea what you really have in mind, and in the end he will have to trust you. Every now and then he will say no, just to keep up the pretence that he is in charge. If so, you present the idea again under a different name.

During the preliminary research, you must decide more or less what you want to say about the subject, and from then on the programme becomes angled, or if you will, slanted or biased in that direction. Next you will have to decide the pictures you want to shoot, the particular person to do the interviewing, the people to be interviewed, and the questions to be asked.

Having seen the resulting material, you decide the order in which the pictures will be shown, the parts of the interviews which will be kept and the parts to be thrown away – one normally shoots anything between three and ten times the amount of film which can be ultimately used. After that you make the final decision about commentary, the order of ideas, choice of music, sound effects – truly in television production the director is king.

That is the way it is, and the way it always will be, unless one is to stifle the responsible creativity which is the *sine-qua-non* of worth-while broadcast production.

When a producer decides, as he must, hour by hour, minute by minute, what is proper to put before an audience, which may include half the population of the country, his judgements must spring from same basic standards. These standards may be partly set by the broadcasting organisation, but mostly they are the product of the producer's own moral, social and family back-ground, his education, his political, cultural and religious beliefs. These are going to be very different in different people. In other words, the bias will be different.

A national newspaper critic once said of a programme I was involved in that it would have been different if it hadn't been made by priests. Exactly. If it wasn't that way there might have been little justification for making the programme in the first place. Every creative decision made by intelligent, responsible human beings must betray their bias, which is to say their person-ality, their total personality – unless one asks them to be totally cynical and hypocritical, which would be much more dangerous. Could you make an unbiased programme about apartheid? I cer-tainly couldn't.

So quite apart from the question of the rights of the community to a greater share in responsibility for broadcasting, there is another question. If it is humanly impossible to produce a worthwhile, impartial, balanced programme, and I believe it is, then the only long-term safeguard against broadcasting as a whole becoming slanted in one direction or another is to share the responsibility for programming through the community as widely as possible and reflect the whole spectrum of points of view.

So far as RTÉ is concerned: I think that a Dublin-based monopoly will become increasingly irrelevant with the growth of home video-cassette equipment, satellite broadcasting, and above all, cable, with its capacity to broadcast forty or more different tele-vision programmes on the one piece of wire.

I think therefore that there should be an immediate division in the functions of our Broadcasting Authority. At present it purports to act as trustee of the Irish people in broadcasting matters, while at the same time acting as Board of Management of RTÉ. RTÉ should get its own Board of Management, and let the Authority become the licenser and controlling agency for all broadcasting in

Ireland, be it Radio Telefís Éireann, Radio Telefís Cork, or Limerick or Galway or Sligo, or perhaps in the future the Belfast Broadcasting Corporation, or BBC.

It is in this context of an expanded broadcasting system that I would like you to consider any seeming threat to jobs arising from anything I have said. There must always be need for full-time professional broadcasters, and in an expanded broadcasting system, an increasing need. All I am saying is that there should also be room for people who are willing to give a year or two or three to broadcasting, but don't wish to make it a permanent career. There should be room also for part-time broadcasters, as I was once privileged to be. It is reasonable to presume that many others would like to have that privilege as well, and once again may I say that in a society where communications are supposed to be free, I don't see why they should be denied it.

So far as government is concerned, the one power I would most like to see given up is the power to decide the licence fee. Broadcasting is being starved of money because the government, for political reasons, are unwilling to raise it. Other countries like Denmark, Sweden, Austria, Norway, pay more than double our licence fee, life still goes on, and they have just about the same number of grumblers as we. Money, by the way, can have quite a lot to do with freedom when you can't afford to do what you believe to be right. Besides, one might have less misgivings about politicians phoning Montrose if the Director General were not dependent on their goodwill to get an extra few bob.

So far as advertising is concerned, I know people who have strong feelings about advertisers who interfere with programme content. I wish that was all we could blame advertising for. The real villain in the history of communication was the man who introduced advertising as a means of paying for media.

The curse of advertising, and where it imposes severe strictures on freedom in broadcasting, is that once one commits oneself to fund communications from advertising, one has to maximise the audience. To a great extent one moves thereby from the information business into the world of entertainment. When information gets confused with entertainment then a frightening credibility gap can build up over quite a short period.

In our little country, many of the people I meet seem to think this has already happened.

Today, twenty-four years later, I still feel that if broadcasting had been organised from the beginning on the basis of what was good rather than what was expedient, radio and television would never have been handed over to commercial interests.

When commercial criteria control information

The USA is the prime example of commercial TV – it has never known anything else. The sole criterion – even of news programmes – is the ratings; the weekly, even daily measurements of how many viewers are watching out there. If you edit or present the news on one of the big networks, and the ratings go up, you get paid more (lest you be tempted by a higher offer from another channel); if the ratings go down you get fired. The result is a range of similar news services which feature star presenters, which deal largely with national rather than international news, which are uncritical of US public policies, and where no picture is allowed to last more than 2.5 seconds – because that is what psychological studies say is the best length to hold people's attention without boring them. The further result is that a nation of 250 million, who own half the riches in the world, and much of its military might, are kept largely ignorant of the subtleties of international affairs, while at the same time being flattered that they are the guardians of freedom and democracy around the world.

The essential difference between commercial TV and TV which is not governed by commercial criteria is that the latter has at least the possibility of being free to tell people the sometimes unpalatable truths, whereas commercial TV has no reason to tell anyone anything except what they want to hear.

Christianity and commercial broadcasting

If the churches had done some thinking about broadcasting, and more importantly, took it as seriously as it warrants, it would have opposed the commercialisation of broadcasting tooth and nail. Why? Because happiness is the natural goal of every human being, and Christ told people that happiness does not lie in acquiring possessions. Commercial television preaches the contrary message, day in and day out. It is therefore fundamentally un-Christian. It promotes acquisitiveness and selfishness, and its art is to do that very effectively. For seven to ten minutes every hour – and more in some countries – the whole community is being indoctrinated to believe that one can't be truly happy without body sprays, hair washes, a holiday in Bermuda, a white rum on a tropical isle, a BMW, 'the ultimate driving machine', a television with Nicad stereo, or an aftershave to entice all those tall beautiful women whom one is never fortunate enough to meet in ordinary life.

This negative aspect is quite separate from the harm done to programme quality and value by the commercial pressures to maximise the audience.

The state and commercial broadcasting

There is plenty of sociological evidence of the problems generated for society by this artificially stimulated pressure to acquire goods. When television was gradually introduced across the US in the 1950s, studies revealed that the thieving rate jumped sharply in each town or city immediately television was introduced. If I need the 'ultimate driving machine', and can't afford to buy one, then perhaps I can 'borrow' one down the street to satisfy this new need.

The economics of commercial broadcasting

The delusion seems common that commercial television somehow costs the community less than broadcasting supported by tax or licence fee. A moment's thought however makes it clear that it really costs the community more. For in addition to the cost of making programmes, there are two extra substantial costs in commercial broadcasting. One is the cost of producing the advertisements themselves, which can be of the order of a quarter million each. The other is the cost of profits paid into the pockets of the shareholders and out of the industry. Who was it said that a television licence was a licence to print money? Now the people who advertise have to earn the money – not only to pay for the programmes and the advertising commercials, but also to pay out large dividends to the shareholders. This can only be done by adding these costs to their products. So in the end, the community pays more for commercial television.

The concentration of power without responsibility

Spiro Agnew, Richard Nixon's hit man where the media were concerned (who got hit himself when the media went after him), is often quoted on the question of control in television:

> ... this little group of men who through TV wield a free hand in selecting, presenting and interpreting the great issues in our nation. They decide what forty or fifty million Americans will learn of today's event in the nation and world. We cannot measure their power and influence by traditional standards. The American people would rightly not tolerate this concentration of power in government. Is it not fair and relevant to question its

concentration in the hands of a tiny and close fraternity of privileged man, elected by no one, and enjoying a monopoly licensed
and sanctioned by government?

It is a question that has to be continuously asked, even if one is only
to be reminded of the awesome media power wielded by individuals like Rupert Murdoch – power which is responsible to nothing
more than a gigantic bank account.

If commercial control of the international media by a small number
of wealthy businessmen, responsible only to commercial criteria, is
a danger in print media, as many seem to believe, then it is very
much more so in broadcasting, and particularly television. One is
free to buy or not to buy a newspaper or magazine and bring it into
one's own home. One is less free to exclude a television programme.
One may choose to turn it off, but that is a lesser option. It is like
having a range of violent, sadistic, pornographic magazines permanently in one's living room. One can choose not to read them. One
can tell one's children not to read them. Most people would prefer
not to have them there at all.

Political motivation for introducing commercial broadcasting

No one should ever be in doubt that the motivation for establishing
ITV in England, and for setting up a Third TV channel in Ireland,
has little to do with extending the range of broadcasting available to
viewers. Commercial considerations always reduce the range of
programmes, since the overall commercial aim is to go for the
majority audience, while broadening the range means making programmes for a range of smaller audiences with different interests –
which unfortunately doesn't make commercial sense. Ten commercial stations all chasing the majority audience are governed by the
same commercial criteria, and are therefore all likely to be doing the
same thing. The range and quality of non-commercial broadcasting
agencies is also reduced, because no matter how high-principled
the board of governors tries to be, in the end the ratings matter to
the self-esteem of the programme producers, and they get caught
up in the race for the larger audiences as well.

Politicians always claim that by promoting commercial television
they are promoting competition, which everyone will agree is a
good thing. They seem to overlook the fact that competition in
broadcasting is perfectly possible without commercialism. Furthermore, competition in programme quality is more important than
competition in audience quantity.

The real reason, I suggest, for introducing commercial television in these islands has had little to do with promoting choice and much to do with the irritation of British and Irish governments of the time with their national broadcasting systems. Politicians, trade unionists, businessmen, churches all perceive an independent media to be biased against their particular interests. Most have to suffer without being able to do anything about it, but politicians are the one exception. In the name of the people they claim power over broadcasting, and rightly so. But they can abuse that power, as arguably they have in the past by such actions as dismissing the Broadcasting Authority without adequate reason, by unfairly limiting the national broadcasting's access to revenue, and by setting up commercial stations in competition so they can play one station against another and give their favours to whichever is kinder to their point of view.

Fighting lost battles?

The battle against commercialism in radio and TV was lost so long ago that it may seem idle to discuss it now. On the other hand, the industry has changed and is changing in such a way as to perhaps permit a rethink.

Television is dividing up into special interest areas. There is the movie channel, the sports channel, the discovery channel, the pornographic channel. The increasing tendency is to require separate subscriptions for each service.

What is important about national services is primarily news and current affairs, education and the arts – popular and unpopular. This kind of programming could be moved away from political and commercial concerns, and paid for by licence fee, collected as part of the tax-collecting process. Hollywood movies and sports are more and more being cornered by specialist channels with megabucks behind them. Why bother competing?

The television licence fee in Ireland could be trebled tomorrow without hurting most television viewers, while special arrangements can be made for the pensioners and unemployed. There may be a process to be gone through in educating the community first, but that is not beyond the wit of government. In fact it would be a very valid way to use the power of advertising!

25
THE MOUNTAINS DON'T MATTER
*Some thoughts on the mission of the church
in the media age*

By 1970 there were a number of former students of the Communications Centre working in media around the world, so we pushed them into making a report on their work on film and sending it to us. A programme called *The Mountains Don't Matter* was assembled from these reports, and included material from Ciaran Kane working in Hong Kong, Tom Devitt in the Philippines, Adrian Smith in Zambia and a talented young nun from India who had made her mark on the *Late Late Show* some months earlier – Sr Candida. We described the finished programme as 'the first attempt at a worldwide view of the church's use of radio, film and television in the developing countries'. And maybe it was!

The early 1970s was a time when people still talked with great optimism about the church's involvement in media. World Communications Day was marked with a Mass at the Communications Centre, to which the media were invited. I spoke during Mass in May 1974 about the Pastoral Instruction issued from Rome in 1971, called by its first words in Latin, *Communio et Progressio*.

> *Communio et Progressio* is an optimistic document – very optimistic, and strong. It sees the media as 'gifts of God, which in accordance with his providential design, unite men in brotherhood'. The document points out that Christ commanded the apostles and their successors to teach all nations, to be the light of the world, and to announce the good news in all places and at all times, and continues,

> *It would be difficult to suggest that Christ's command was being obeyed unless all the opportunities offered by the modern media to extend to vast numbers of people the announcement of his Good News were being used. (126). Since the Media are often the only channels of information that exist between the church and the world, a failure to use them amounts to burying the talent given by God. (123)*

There were many aspects to Christ's own mission – healing, liberating, witnessing, proclaiming – but only the last can properly be called evangelism. The church continues this mission of Christ, teaching, praying, feeding the hungry, working for peace and justice, reconciling men with God, but above all, proclaiming the good news about a person who was God, and an event which was his coming among us. Evangelisation then is the process of proclaiming that good news, particularly to those who have not heard it, or who have not understood it, or who have not responded to it, or who have forgotten it.

The importance of the mass media for the church is that they offer perhaps the only access to millions of people who have not heard the gospel, or who have not understood it, who have not responded to it, or who have forgotten it. Five million people attend religious services in Britain on Sunday. Twenty-five million watch or hear a religious programme.

I am aware that evangelisation is not so respectable a word as it used to be. To some it suggests paternalism, cultural imperialism, and lack of respect for the freedom and belief of others. Maybe. But without evangelisation Christianity wouldn't exist, and without continuing evangelisation, Christianity would die in a generation.

Time perhaps has tempered, though by no means killed, some of that optimism manifested in *Communio et Progressio*. I think this is partly because the broadcast media have changed dramatically in the subsequent twenty-five years, and partly because the church has changed – though not in the way that many of us had hoped – and partly because of the increasing shortage of full-time personnel. With regard to the latter, when personnel are diminished in any organisation, the tendency is to devote those that are left to carrying on the traditional functions, rather than develop new fields like communications. This may be poor policy but it is very human and understandable.

With regard to the dramatic changes in the media and the various problems relating to the effective presence of the church in media, I append a series of thoughts for reflection – some of my own and some borrowed. In the tradition and spirit of broadcasting, I try to show two sides to each issue – where I can see them!

The church and the media – problems and opportunities
The gospel seeks commitment
The churches aim to persuade people of the truth of the gospel mes-

sage. Broadcasting however does not, and cannot, assess the claims of any church or religion, and therefore prefers religious presentations which are soft and acceptable to people of any or no beliefs. Being a Christian is about being committed to a body of teaching. The church feels bound to preach this gospel, and seek commitment from its followers. This is not possible in the secular media.

On the other hand, there are usually some categories of programmes, such as liturgical programmes, where one can speak as church. And one should recognise that the media have done much good in promoting an ecumenical approach to many issues.

Complex issues can't be expressed in soundbites

Church teachings are often complex, the result of centuries of thought and experience, and therefore difficult to do justice to in the hectic world of broadcasting. Where attention has to be grabbed and held amidst a multitude of other distractions – including the urge to see what programmes are on the other channels – the subtlety of church teaching may well be impossible to convey.

On the other hand, Christ's teaching was such that the simple peasants of Judaea had little trouble in understanding it. The truth can sometimes be hidden in scholarly hairsplitting. If media put pressure on the church to clarify its teaching and make it accessible to all, that may be a blessing.

Determining one's beliefs by referenda

The media are accustomed to deal with issues in a democratic society, and tend to apply the same criteria to the church which is by nature hierarchical. The teaching of the church is not decided by referenda or elections or surveys. Attempts to hold to traditional positions are usually looked on very critically by the media.

On the other hand, when one looks at church teaching in a historical context, one finds a number of once authoritative teachings which the church eventually reconsidered in response to arguments put forward by the People of God, who are also illumined by the Holy Spirit.

Lionising the dissidents

Dissident theologians are lionised and given much media coverage. Theologians supportive of church teaching are of less interest to the media. Media put a high value on personal freedom. Those who criticise authoritative teaching are seen as being on the side of freedom, and the media cultivate them.

On the other hand the media have a duty in a democratic society to present a balanced picture, and this is especially true of broadcasting where there are statutory requirements to be fulfilled. If this is not done and voices are drowned out, then there should be vigorous community protest. At the same time, the history of the church even in this century warns us to be careful – so many of the great theologians were initially considered dissidents, and only later in life were accepted as prophetic figures.

The church's essential message is unchanging – the media want novelty

This is a serious problem. Broadcasters are very much attracted to exploring new moralities and challenging traditional values. The gospel message is no longer new in the same way as it was in the first century. It is exciting to challenge traditional beliefs and break barriers – to be the first programme to talk about some new exotic system of meditation on the cosmos, or deviant sexual activity – if there are any left that haven't been fully explored! Breaking barriers attracts attention from other media, which is a very important part of the satisfaction quotient of a radio or TV producer.

On the other hand, bringing out the new in the old is the perpetual challenge the church faces in every aspect of its preaching. The same problem had to be faced for many centuries before radio and TV.

The gospel means 'good news'. In the media good news is no news

News is typically negative – disasters, deaths, wars, earthquakes. Lord Northcliffe is supposed to have said that 'News is what someone somewhere wishes to suppress. Everything else is advertising.' News of the church tends to be about such things as priests leaving the ministry, or rows between theologians and the Vatican, or lately, the sexual sins of the fathers, with the end result that the church – as seen in the media – always seems to be in turmoil.

On the other hand, this problem of news being negative is not a problem confined to the church. Every organisation, including the state, faces the same problem. It is a challenge that must be faced intelligently. Part of the answer is to use the news, however negative it may seem, as an opportunity to be positive.

Having one hand tied behind your back

The church, because of claiming the high moral ground, has to be scrupulous about charity, about not infringing the rights of others, about not offering scandal, about telling the truth in all things. Sometimes these requirements seem mutually exclusive.

On the other hand, if church leaders believe that 'the church is the pillar and ground of truth', and that 'the truth will make you free', then they should normally have confidence that they will be able to find a way to tell the truth in charity – with help from the Holy Spirit. Or am I being naïve?

Religion in the media has so many competitors

In the early days of broadcasting, when people only had one or two channels, they would watch religious programmes and enjoy them. Now when there are so many alternatives, the average viewer tends to choose the least demanding among options – sport, comedy, and soap opera. Serious programmes have suffered in this way across the board – there is a diminishing audience for all public affairs programmes.

On the other hand, the church's voice faces competition in every facet of life. Withdrawing to the desert can't be the answer.

Media marginalise religion

Bryan Wilson, writing in *Religion in a Secular Society*, said:

> As long as the church connives in using the media, the media controllers can use this fact in their own defence as an evidence of their social responsibility. But given the religionist's necessary assumption that religious truth is pre-eminent, and the claim it makes to a dominant place in the minds of men, the relegation of religious material to a marginal place in the programmes of mass communications is itself a derogation of the religious message.

This might well be true in other cultures, but I don't think it can be said of Ireland – certainly not yet. And where or when it does become true, the challenge should be to fight it, rather than give in and withdraw.

The image and the word

A story repeated in the *Irish Times* of 3 November 1990 is recorded as 'known by heart by everyone involved in the business of image making'. It concerned Lesley Stahl, a high powered reporter with the American CBS TV Network, who during the 1984 campaign in which Reagan was re-elected, put together what she thought was a damning report on Reagan's manipulation of the media. The report showed footage of carefully staged Reagan photo opportunities: the president visiting old folk, tossing a football, mingling with black children, and so on. Over the images her report described Reagan's use of such images to distract from the actual effect of his policies which were inimical to the old, the poor and the black. As soon as the news bulletin was over, she got a call from the White House to say, 'Great Piece. We loved it.' 'Did you,' she asked, 'listen to what I said?' 'Lesley,' said the official, 'When you show 4 minutes of great pictures of President Ronald Reagan, no one listens to what you say.'

I think any churchman has reason to be depressed by that story. We Christians are people of the word. We can put the Christian message into words with comparative ease. But we seem to have very few worthwhile images, and lack confidence in the use of whatever there is. It seems to me therefore that, in terms of television, the important way that Christian belief will be passed on may be through the example of Christian people, who express their goodness in the image they project, and whose goodness communicates the love of God to others.

I think of Pope John XXIII. I wrote of him elsewhere that while I never met him, I once saw a documentary about him: 'The commentary was in Italian, of which I didn't know enough to keep up with. Yet I was deeply moved just looking at the images, and am moved even now when I remember them. For John seemed to have all the qualities that bring out love and respect and trust in human beings. You could read it in his face and his movements and his gestures, and the faces and body language of everyone who met him.'

In the past, churchmen were honoured and respected because of their position. They had the authority of office and that authority was respected – whether or not the holders were in fact very Christian in their actions or their being. That no longer happens in the broadcasting age. In broadcasting, authority in matters Christian comes from manifest goodness flowing from a genuine Christian belief. The more a Christian leader can think and act like Christ might think and act, then the better he or she will perform in media. It's a simple formula – sanctity wins!

Television – a rival religion

The word 'religion' comes from a Latin word meaning to bind together. Religion binds people together about the fundamentals in human existence. It has to do with life and death, love and hate, birth and death, sowing and reaping, playing and praying – the very themes that supply the pap of television. The central point in every home, the new *lares* and *penates* of the modern household are not the statues on the mantelpiece or the flickering light before the picture of the Sacred Heart, but the flickering image on the coloured screen. Television too partakes of the universal quality that Christianity once had. Francis Xavier used the ritual of the Latin Mass in India, which was identical to that used in Ireland or Iceland. Nowadays one can travel the world and watch CNN or Baywatch in Durban, Dum-Dum, Dublin or Duluth. Within television too their are cults. Sport for instance. Perhaps twenty times as many people watch sport on television as actually go to the contests. Sport is about achieving the goals through struggle, controlled by strictly applied rules. It has its moments of ecstasy and its coloured vestments. A metaphor for religion?

Harvey Cox had a provocative comment on media religion:

> The media preachers tell us what our transgression is: our armpits are damp, our breath is foul, our wash is grey, our car is inadequate. They hold up models of saintly excellence before our eyes: happy robust sexually appreciated people who are free, adventurous, competitive and attractive. These blessed ones have been saved, or are on the way. And the sacramental means of grace that have lifted them from perdition are available to you and me – soaps, deodorants, clothes, tills, cars. Mass media culture is a religion, and we rarely get out of its temple.

The problem of clerical dress

The egalitarian ambience of TV is what makes it unkind to people in uniform. Guards on the beat wear uniform to be recognised as guards, not as people, and to be able to be clinical about doing nasty things, such as arresting people. Soldiers also wear uniforms and special caps to divide themselves off from the rest of the human race, so they can shoot them as needed. People who appear in uniform on TV say predictable things, like 'We're here to get on with the job,' and 'I proceeded to the scene of the crime'.

Many years ago when Peter Lemass and I tried to teach something about broadcasting to clerics, he used make the point by talking to them on videotape in an open shirt, and then in the course of his talk seemingly absent mindedly putting on a collar. It was like a blind coming down, and most of the watching clerics sensed the fact and commented on it afterwards.

The unfortunate fact is that television isn't very interested in people in uniforms, which is one of the reasons why religion doesn't always sit comfortably with TV. Clerics are much better, and much more demonstrably successful, as communicators on radio. In the beginning of Radharc, Peter Lemass, Billy Fitzgerald, Des Forristal and I appeared on television in clerical collars. I knew it was wrong then, but the times didn't seem to permit an alternative. To this day there seems to be no way a secular priest can appear in public in Ireland without a clerical collar and not seem to be somehow denying his priesthood. We need a recognisable clerical dress which includes a conventional collar and tie, and some acceptable emblem – for Catholic priests possibly a cross on lapel or tie. In my view it is not a small problem. And even more so when one finds the Pope again in November 1995 telling priests and nuns to get back into clerical dress.

Broadcasting makes authoritarian leadership unworkable

One thing they always tell you on a broadcasting course is that a radio or television programme is a private conversation between two people. There may be a few million eavesdropping, but it is only in the context of a private conversation that broadcasting works. A conversation can only take place in what I might call for want of a better term, an ambience of equality. Its uniqueness and worth comes from the inherent dignity of all human beings, and the universal interest in human experience.

Before broadcasting, society was naturally authoritarian. Leaders spoke from on high and were never subject to questioning by the masses. Inhabiting a different world, it was possible and indeed practical for the leader to generate an aura of mystery and higher wisdom, since his or her actions or decisions were never open to be examined or tested by anyone but their peers. When broadcasting began, politicians refused to be questioned – they read statements. Deferential and previously vetted questions only began to be asked in the middle nineteen fifties.

For some years now, politicians have been at the beck and call of media, and are expected to grin and bear a grilling that only practice and determination (and lessons from Carr Communications) could fit a human being to bear with equanimity, not to mention politeness. The furore about child abuse has brought senior clerics into virtually the same arena as the politicians – without either the training, or perhaps the personality to bear such pressure. Media compatibility is not something the Vatican seems to take much heed of when making episcopal appointments!

And while we all rejoice in the success of broadcasting in putting pressure on leaders to justify their actions and show how they are being responsible, we should also recognise that it can be harder to lead when everyone is looking for the feet of clay.

Index